Bodies in Motion

LIANA BROOKS

OTHER WORKS

Find other works by the author at
http://www.lianabrooks.com

NEWTON'S LAWS

Bodies In Motion
Laws of Attraction (forthcoming)
Newton's Cradle (forthcoming)

Bodies in Motion

LIANA BROOKS

ISBN: 978-0-9945238-3-9

www.inkprintpress.com

National Library of Australia Cataloguing-in-Publication Data
Brooks, Liana 1982—
Bodies In Motion
376 p.
ISBN: 978-0-9945238-3-9
Inkprint Press, Canberra, Australia
  1.   Science fiction 2. Space colonies—Fiction 3. Romance
      fiction 4. Science fiction—Women authors

Summary: A civil war tore them apart. Can a cold war bring them
back together?

First Edition: September 2017
Printed in the United States of America.
Cover design © IndigoChick Designs.

DEDICATION

To Mrs. Lauren Wilhoite-Willis,

who struggled through having me as a student for three long years, but never yelled at me for writing books in class. I will always remember the question game, the French in English, and the violets on your window sill.

NEWTON'S FIRST LAW OF MOTION:

A body in motion will stay in
motion until acted upon by an
external force.

A BRIEF HISTORY OF THE MALIK STAR SYSTEM

1300 Before Landing (BL)—Malik System discovered by the Explorer-class vessel *Imperial Pearl*.

1100BL—Malik III and Malik IV planets terraformed to support human life.

1000BL—First wave of colonization begins.

900BL—Wormhole connecting Malik System to the Empire collapses, leaving both colonists and fleet ships stranded.

600BL—Tensions between fleet and colonists reach breaking point and isolation is declared. Several crews land their ships and give up space flight.

36-18BL—The first civil war between the Warmongers, led by the Baulars, and the Allied Crews, led by the Carvers. The war was declared over the orin crystals used for fuel by the fleet.

18BL—The Carver shuttle *Leto* crashes near Tarrin and 6-year-old Perrin Carver is rescued from the wreckage.

5BL—Perrin Carver and Hermione Marshall are accepted into the Academy.

2BL—The second civil war begins with Old Baular and his grandson Mal leading the Warmongers, and Perrin Carver leading the Allied Crews in defense of the colonists.

LANDING

3 years post landing—BODIES IN MOTION begins.

1

SELENA

THE PROBLEM WITH VACATIONS, Selena reflected as she adjusted her sweater outside Cargo Blue, was that reality was always waiting at the end. A quick search of the local security cameras found one that showed the peeling sunburn on her right shoulder blade.

Such was the curse of pale-skinned, ship-born Fleet personnel. Anytime she left the foggy belts covering the city of Tarrin, she barbecued like a shrimp, no matter how much sunscreen she applied. Otherwise, she'd flee even further from the Fleet Enclave and make her home on the equatorial beaches of the planet they were trapped on.

She panned the camera and checked her left shoulder. Black ink made a starscape that disguised three silver scars as shooting stars. The painting covered her shoulder blade and part of her upper arm. As the artist had promised, the skin-paint had kept her from burning as much, though it still had the over-stretched feel of a burn. With a few adjustments, her uniform covered most of the temporary art; it would keep her from having to explain to her colleagues.

Her forearm warmed, a warning that someone was about to contact her through the tech implant tucked between her radius and ulna.

She hesitated too long and the call came through, a persistent ping against her skull as the phantom image of her best friend floated on the edge of her vision.

Selena turned off the visual receiver and answered. "Genevieve," she said with a smile as the image of her vivacious, red-headed friend appeared floating against the backdrop of landing gear that supported the grounded fleet.

A grounder would have thought she was talking to herself, but grounders wouldn't set foot near the neo-city-state of Enclave. The rocky beach served as a city and tomb for the survivors of the last war.

"Selena!" Gen gushed. "Starcom to Selena. Where are you? I'm covering for now."

"Delayed, but almost there." Selena hoped Gen wouldn't hear the lie. She'd been standing in the shadows of the Enclave pub for nearly a quarter hour.

"The *Lorenza* could get here faster," Gen said, referencing a long-dead ship whose crew were found skeletonized at their stations. Gen blew hair off her face. "Stars above, you're an hour late. The whole fleet is flying faster than you."

Selena turned on her visual long enough to roll her eyes at her friend. "Ha, ha, funny. That joke needs to be forcibly retired." Sooner rather than later. The fleet couldn't fly without fuel, and the Malik system they were stranded in held precious few deposits of the orun crystals needed to power the ships.

"If you don't come," Gen said threateningly, "I will teleport to your apartment and drag you out in your pajamas."

"I'm not at home," Selena admitted. And she wouldn't have let her best friend come to her new house if she was.

Gen was smart enough to realize that the small palace Selena had bought in downtown Tarrin wasn't paid for by her official OIA salary. The paygrades for the Office of Imperial Affairs had last been updated when the Malik system was still in contact with the empire, making them 900 years out of date.

Technically, taking a second job wasn't treason, but there were enough people in the fleet who'd see it as a betrayal that keeping it secret felt right. Especially since Gen's captain was one who would scream the loudest.

Gen clapped. "Selena! Stop stalling yer engines and get in here. This isn't some Fleet Tribunal, just our friends. You, me, Carver. I left a message for Marshall. You know. People we like."

The light of understanding dawned. "Carver? This is so you can snuggle up to Perrin Carver without your parents watching?"

"Yes," Gen admitted, not looking the least bit contrite.

"You're only dragging me along so I can cover for you while you make out in a corner, aren't you?" She masked the relief with mock anger. At least Gen wasn't trying to set Selena up with one of her cousins. Or, ancestors forbid, Gen's handsy older brother.

Again.

Gen opened her eyes wide with an innocent smile. "Maybe."

"Gen!" Selena rolled her eyes. "Doesn't he have his own place?"

"Just the bachelor's dorm. The Carvers didn't have any ships except the shuttle his parents crashed in. Making out next door to

Mom and Dad? No. And the BOQ? It's so tacky. You can hear everything through those walls."

Selena hid a smile. "I'll be there soon enough."

If Gen ever caught wind of how panicky the thought of a relationship made her, Gen would make it her life's goal to see Selena paired off. And there wasn't a man alive who she could imagine getting close to now.

Her implant helpfully pulled up an image of a tall, broad-shouldered, lean-muscled fighter with skin black as the night between stars and emerald-green eyes.

She pushed the memory away.

Lieutenant Commander Titan Sciarra was striking, intelligent, and had a body she'd cross battle lines for, but he was also out of reach. There was no point in chasing a man who wouldn't give her the time of day.

Another crew shuffled past her into the bar, black patches with silver fists on their shoulders.

It was getting harder to pretend she belonged in Enclave, with the fleet. Once upon a time, she'd known every crew's patch without thinking. She could name captains, their ships and their seconds by rote. Now she would need to tap into the fleet's information nexus if she wanted to know who they were.

She stopped at the edge of the door to tug her lightest shields into place. A few minor adjustments would keep bugs away, keep beer off her clothes, and prevent anyone from hacking into her implant. They could still send messages, because disallowing that would have raised eyebrows. And they could still hit her. But she could always hit back.

Selena rolled her shoulders and strutted into Cargo Blue. It was a battlefield, but she was the last captain of the Caryll family, and she wasn't going down without a fight.

Whatever crew owned Cargo Blue probably hadn't had much of a decorating budget, but at least they'd stuck with a theme: oversized cargo boxes were piled up to make walls, seating, and tables. Olive-green safety webbing draped from the ceiling between blue lights. Fog used for fire drills on the ships pumped across the floor to hide the concrete beneath.

There was no bouncer at the door, but people were still hanging around the entrance.

As a rule, the fleet was cautious, and the young faces she saw belonged to fleet members who had never ventured outside their own crew more than a few times, even though the fleet had been grounded for nearly three years.

Tables to the left, bar ahead, dance floor to the right... and that meant the back half of the cargo hanger had been partitioned and karaoke would be in the back right corner. After a few minutes of weaving through the human crush, she found Gen, already sitting in Perrin Carver's lap and giggling.

"Selena!" Gen jumped up and hugged her. "I was beginning to worry!"

"How many people are in here?" Selena shouted over the music.

"Everyone under forty?" Gen laughed. With a small hand wave Gen put up a minor sound shield, muting the music. "People are going to stir crazy. Combine that with the anniversary—"

The anniversary.

Today.

The day the war had begun, the day the united fleet had died.

They'd been dying for four hundred years, well aware that the reserve of orun crystals was depleted and there was no way to move forward with the ships they had.

Old Captain Baular had seen the deposit of orun on the fifth planet as their saving grace. He'd get it even if it meant killing the grounders. And, coward that he was, he'd ordered his grandson to lead the first attack instead of leading it himself.

That opening skirmish began and ended in the dark, with Titan Sciarra in the infirmary, and five Academy fighters missing or damaged. But by lunch of the next day, every officer belonging to crews allied with the Baulars withdrew.

Seven months later, heated words turned to live rounds.

"Selena?" Gen asked quietly, placing a hand on her arm. "You didn't know the date, did you?"

"I was trying not to think about." If she had, she'd have cut her vacation to the islands early. Maybe even made her pilgrimage to the small cay where she'd ditched her stolen fighter after driving off the attack.

She rolled her shoulder, stretching the deep scars. "It snuck up on me."

"First round, we drink to the Lost Fleet, and all who've gone on to crew it. I'm buying," Gen said with a touch of forced joviality. "Carver's been making friends. Tell her, babe." She pushed Carver's shoulder.

Perrin Carver was tall, broad-shouldered man with shy, hazel eyes that hid a wicked sense of humor.

Selena's heart fluttered just a little at the memory of a time when she'd fancied herself in love with him. He'd been the ideal starsider: intelligent, good-looking, and charismatic. They'd been friends of a sort, but even that relationship had soured when she'd realized he'd been getting close to her so he could learn more about Genevieve Silar.

Carver nodded and held out his hand. "Hi, Selena. How are you?"

She tapped the back of his hand with hers, letting him test her shields. "Good. How's the Starguard?"

"Booming." The commander of the Starguard smiled, white teeth flashing, but there was a tightness around his eyes. "Everyone hears about guardians being allowed outside the Enclave, or working with the Jhandarmi, and I'm drowning in recruiting requests. Captains of larger crews invite me to Captain's Mess so they can introduce me to their best and brightest. Half the time I can't tell if they want me to marry into the crew or take the fleetlings into the guard." His shield was still attached to hers, scanning her as he talked.

All he would get from her was polite interest. Her heartrate didn't spike or dip at the mention of the Jhandarmi. Her smile never flickered.

"Maybe you should lock down Gen," Selena said. "If you had a spouse, no one would try to get you to marry into the crew."

Carver and Gen shared a look, and Gen sent a ping of information that Selena's implant translated as an ongoing debate over crew name and a place to live.

Carver sent something similar; a picture of his bachelor's quarters and his one ship.

There was no room for them to marry and have a family.

"Enclave is a temporary solution," Selena said out loud. She'd lost the taste for communicating by implant years ago. "If we—"

A heavy hand wrapped around her waist as someone wearing too much cologne stepped far too close to her. "Hello, Selena."

Hollis Silar, one of Gen's many siblings, kissed her temple.

Simultaneously, Selena sighed, sent a shock through her shield to Hollis's hand, and elbowed him in the gut. "Hi, Hollis. I see you're still bathing in cologne rather than water."

He stepped away from her, an easy smile still in place.

It wasn't that Hollis was bad looking; plenty of women found him handsome. It was that he was equally affectionate with every woman he saw and he couldn't keep a secret to save his life. Or anyone else's. He'd chase anyone with a pretty smile and fell in and out of love a couple of times a day.

"Nice to see you too, Selena. Now, everyone, you're all going to look at me, smile, and laugh like I'm my normal, dashing self," he said, his smile never changing. "You haven't been paying attention, but I'm not a member of the Starguard for nothing. We're being watched. Now take your nice drinks from the waitress and keep your eyes on me."

Hollis nodded to the waitress and handed out four cups with bright purple liquid. "Bruised Stars all around. Guaranteed to make you giggle, or so the guy at the bar told me. Although he's a Seutaai, so take it with a shield in place." He handed Selena her drink with a smile, but turned immediately to glance over his shoulder.

"Big brother, who are we looking for?" Gen asked with a slow drawl. "Is it a friend who you might have forgotten to call back after a night out?"

Hollis shook his head. "No, I thought I saw some of the Lee crew. Make that, I'm certain of it."

Selena grimaced. "As long as Rowena isn't here."

"Did you call me?"

Startled, Selena looked up to the face of her least favorite woman: Rowena Lee. "Hello," Selena said politely. "I see you're still alive. That's…" *Unfortunate.* She nodded and took a slug of her Bruised Star.

Rowena held up a tray of electric blue shots. "My crew thinks I can't out-drink anyone in this bar. I probably can't go toe-to-toe with alcoholics like the Silars here. But No-Shot Selena?" Rowena set the drinks on the table. "I can out-shoot you in the stars or on the ground."

Gen sucked in air between her teeth and sent Selena several urgent pings telling her to ignore the Lees.

Selena muted Gen. "I took plenty of shots in the war. As I recall, I disabled three of your big birds. *Bassi, Aryton, Theoano…* Bang, bang, bang." Selena mimed firing with her finger. "Three shots. Three silent ships."

"Not kills," Rowena said. "A whole war and you never blooded yourself."

That was it, the memory she didn't want to face; the time she'd almost taken Death's claim and risked killing someone outside of war.

"That's uncalled for," Hollis said, trying to step between them. "Selena, why don't we— "

Selena pushed Hollis aside and grabbed the first shot. She tossed back the potent drink and shattered the glass on the table. "Go suck vacuum, Rowena. You're a pissant yeoman with no hope of command."

"I went to the Academy, same as you, Selena. I fought for the fleet." Rowena slammed a shot back. "You fought for the mudlickers."

Selena took another shot as the first started to fuzz her judgement. "I prevented the Baulars from committing mass genocide and destroying the civilians along with the fleet."

Rowena took her second shot. A crowd was gathering and that seemed to feed her cruelty. "The Lees survived the war. We're still here. How many Caryll captains are there? Oh, right, one. Can you count that high, No-Shot? You have any idea how easy it would be for me to end you right now?"

Selena took the last two glasses and slammed them both back.

Gen pinged her, giving locations, counts, and identities of the Lee allies in the crowd.

Hollis stepped to her flank, ready to defend her.

She stood, anger burning through her veins. "Sure, your crew outnumbers mine. I guess on paper, it's not really a fair fight, is it, Rowena? But you were trained as a flight leader, and what do Carylls do? Hand-to-hand combat. Maybe I should thin your ranks, starting with one mouthy yeoman."

2

TITAN

THERE WAS NOTHING WORSE than being called by the commander to handle a disturbance ten minutes before the end of shift.

Titan checked the time as he left his desk. Cargo Blue had officially opened less than three hours and already there was a fight that would close it down permanently if someone lodged a complaint with the Captains' Council. He pulled up his shields and a Guardian Veil that allowed his implant to produce a visual representation of the shields everyone was wearing.

Then he sent Rowena a ping telling her to stay on the *Danielle Nicole* until he sorted this out. They'd have to celebrate her birthday elsewhere.

Rowena sent a memory of bright blue drinks tinged with anger and humiliation. She was already at the bar.

Already fighting.

Titan ran, skidding on the loose gravel outside of Cargo Blue. It was a tangle of blue lights and yellow-green shields. He could see the information eddying there, everything someone might think a potential lover would want to know: name, rank, age, crew information, battle record... The information swirled a few inches above their skin, data slowly snaking along their shields.

He pinged Rowena again and got a location lock. He tried to send her a message, to warn her he was coming in uniform and couldn't help in a brawl, but she was either too focused or intentionally blocking his contact.

It was easier for his nerves if he pretended it was focus. But he'd been friends with Rowena since forever. She only blocked him when she was planning to get into the kind of trouble that started wars.

Pushing through the crowd, he caught sight of Rowena's black hair, stepped in, and pulled her away from the person she was arguing with.

An angry fist backed by telekyn collided with his jaw and rattled his brains.

He brought his shields up as he held Rowena back.

His attacker wasn't someone he instantly recognized. Their shields were opaque, hiding their body; there was no data stream, and the shield was spiking. They were in full battle mode.

Desperate for a better resolution, Titan pulled on the Starguard files, trying to force more information. His opponent's shield turned slightly blue... A captain.

Titan looked around. Noted the commander trying very hard to avoid becoming a target. And there, in the streams being traded back and forth, Rowena's challenge. Was she that eager to enlist in the Lost Fleet?

People were milling, and even with the Guardian Veil making him think faster so time seemed to slow, there wasn't enough time to make this right.

"Captain," he said to the angry figure. "I'm on duty for another seven minutes. I'd rather not be here all night doing paperwork." It was a gamble, but it paid off.

The shields powered down to a quiet glow. Still no data, but now he could see his opponent clearly, a pale, elfin woman, with moonlight for hair and deep oceans for eyes. Her wispy skirt matched her eyes, and the thin, white sweater that fell off one shoulder was little more than a curl of cloud.

She was beautiful. But then, she always had been.

Captain Selena Caryll.

Rowena was feeding him the memory of their drinking contest and insult war that led to his bruised jaw. If he'd known that he would have gone in shields maxed. Angry fleet captains didn't pull their punches.

Commander Carver stood up, his red-headed lover hiding behind him. "I think we should go home. Silars, Lees, and Carvers are banned from the premises for the rest of the night. Sciarra, make sure they all get home all right."

Titan nodded. "Yes, sir." The joys of being one of Carver's top lieutenants. He turned to Rowena.

"Sorry," she mouthed as she provided a flood of information. A bad day on the ship, the need to burn some energy, and seeing Selena Caryll had pushed her over the edge.

Not that she was ever far from it.

He shook his head. He pointed at her cousins, Jion and Alexi. "Get back to your ships. I'll come by as soon as I get off duty."

Mars, his younger cousin, appeared at the edge of the crowd, waiting for orders.

"Help them," Titan told him. Mars was technically still a cadet, a fleet officer in training, but he was on track to be one of the Sciarras' most lethal assets. If the Lees ran into trouble between the dead ships, Mars would keep them safe.

"But…" Rowena looked miserable

"We'll have your party in the hangar bay."

"My captain won't allow it."

"Mine will," Titan said as Mars stepped closer. "Did you hear that?" he said to Mars. It would mean calling in favors and taking an extra duty rotation to repay his crew, but it would be worth it. Rowena deserved a celebration and he knew for a fact he was the only person in the fleet willing to wish her happy at the moment.

Mars nodded. "Party at our place. Got it." He smiled at Rowena, leaving Titan to clean up the mess.

He turned, looking for Captain Caryll, and saw her slinking out the side exit. He was there in time to catch the door as it closed.

Caryll glared up at him. "Is there something else you needed, *Guardian*?"

"I was ordered to escort you home." It was close enough to the truth, but she saw through it.

"Carver wouldn't have ordered you to do any such thing." Her smirk was cruel.

"If something happens to you between here and your quarters, he won't remember that. I'll walk you home."

She turned with a stomp and moved forward rapidly, shields on max protection. Less than fifty yards from the door, she stopped. "This is ridiculous. I'll be sober in a few minutes, and I can take care of myself."

"That's what I'm worried about. Row—the woman in the bar issued you a direct challenge."

That stopped her. "I won't go off seeking revenge in the dead of night. Review the transcript. I never accepted her challenge, only said maybe I should. Now, can you please stop stalking me?"

"I could walk with you," Titan offered.

"How about in front, so I don't feel like I'm going to get a knife in my back?"

"I could do that." Titan walked a few paces in front of her.

He couldn't ping her. Attempts to get a data hit off her shield failed. Every tracking measure he used slid off like oil on water. He was stuck glancing over his shoulder every few steps.

Caryll followed along, surly, but moving toward the BOQ attached to the OIA building.

They'd made it halfway home before she stopped. Titan turned and watched her wobble on one foot as she rubbed her other ankle. "Did you hurt yourself?"

"I broke my heel."

His heartrate jumped in alarm. He'd almost had her safe and now he'd broken a captain.

Caryll must have sensed something because she held up a strappy shoe that was, indeed, missing a heel. "My shoe. Not my talus. I'm fine, but I'm going to cut myself on these rocks. Why don't we have grass here?"

"It's a fire hazard when ships take off." He rattled off the rote answer, though none of the fleet ships would reach the stars again. "We could walk on the path. It's not soft, but it's not as bad as the rocks."

"Oh?" She looked to the right. "When did they finish that?"

Titan frowned in confusion. The path had been completed over a year ago. Maybe she'd seen someone sweeping it or repairing it. With a tight smile, he offered her a hand and helped her hobble to the sidewalk, where she kicked off her other sandal.

It was the coldest contact he'd ever had with another human being. No information at all. She was furious and locking him out of every normal interaction.

He tried smiling.

She scowled.

"I'm sorry about ruining your evening," he said, his mind turning over all the ways this could go horribly wrong. He was just doing his job, she'd see that. His recording of her contact would protect Rowena's life, but Captain Caryll could still sanction the Lees. He winced. "This is probably not how you wanted to spend tonight."

"Ya' think?" She rolled her eyes and started walking, keeping pace with him.

"Cargo Blue set a record tonight."

"Really?" One word with a ship's weight of contempt.

"It's the shortest-lived venue ever in Enclave. The previous record was held by Star Shooter, a bar funded by the Alun crew. It burned to the plastic shell in a brawl seventy-one hours after it opened."

"Who thought booze and grudges were a good combination?" Caryll asked. "Is someone expecting for us to kill each other off? Is this the Starguard's idea of population control?"

"Oh, no, our idea of population control is hiring Silars."

She slowed and turned to stare at him in wide-eyed horror.

A misstep. A serious, possibly fatal, misstep.

Titan laughed weakly. "Sorry. I know you and Hollis are…"

A pale eyebrow rose over her dangerously dark blue eyes. "Hollis? And I? I don't think there's a way to end that sentence well."

"He tried to come back for you when I broke up the fight," Titan said, almost babbling in panic. Although, now that he ran

20

through the memory, Hollis had reached for Caryll, but she hadn't reached for him. She hadn't so much as glanced at him on her way out. "Maybe it's a bit one-sided?"

Caryll shook her head. "As far as I know, the only thing Hollis and I share is wanting to spend time with Gen." She continued walking, but slowed a little when he wouldn't keep her burning pace. "Shouldn't you, I don't know, be checking the perimeter or something?"

"I did that," Titan said. "We actually had some activity tonight." That seemed like a safe topic. She was a captain after all. It would be in the reports in the morning. "Someone broke into the old terminal."

"The what now?"

He pointed across the way to the squat building. "That one."

"Oh, the museum. Probably someone just wanted to look at the pictures and artifacts."

"There's pictures? I didn't know anyone went in there."

"Did they break anything?" Caryll asked.

Titan shook his head. "No, it was weird, someone teleported in, but I think they came from outside Enclave. Which is bizarre. The sign-out sheet doesn't show anyone leaving and whoever did it didn't use their authorization codes."

"We have authorization codes for going through the Enclave Shield now?"

"We've had them for two years. Ever since we put up a new shield."

Caryll looked upward with a slightly surprised look on her face. "Huh. I hadn't noticed."

"It's there every day. I guess, if you don't leave Enclave you wouldn't need to notice?"

She nodded. "It's a good shield."

Titan checked it under the Guardian's Veil and nodded. "One of my best. I didn't think anyone could slip through it without triggering an alarm, but this person slid along it. It was like they anticipated the code I'd use and wrote themselves a door."

She nodded again. "Your shield, you say? You were good at them in Academy."

"One of the best." His implant pulled up the old rankings. Vanessa Baular—ancestors grant her rest—had been the best. Her son, and his former best friend, Mal—ancestors grant him rest—had tied with Hermione Marshall for second. Titan had held the third spot until just weeks before the war broke out when he'd been bumped by... "Selena Caryll."

"Yes?" She turned with a look of confusion and surprise.

"You beat me in the shield test at Academy."

"Yes." The word was divorced from any emotion, her face blank and uncaring.

"So, you would have the skill level to open a door in the Enclave Shield."

"I suppose." She shrugged and her sweater slipped an inch, exposing raw, red skin that was peeling from an energy burn.

His breath caught in fear. "Is that from tonight? Did Rowena do that?"

Caryll looked at her shoulder and tugged her sweater back up. "It's a sun burn. I'm fair skinned."

Titan tried to picture how anyone could get a sun burn in uniform. Even if she'd stripped down to a tank top for sparring outside, Enclave in the spring was a cloudy, rainy, dreary place. And a tank top would cover more skin. "How?"

His mind slipped to ways that a body could be fully exposed to the sunlight, like on the top of a ship, lying naked on a blanket with a lover.

He squashed that thought, and the sliver of jealousy that came with it, as fast as he could.

Selena tugged her sweater closed. "I was visiting somewhere warm."

He pulled up the Starguard log, as much to distract himself from his lascivious thoughts as anything else. "There's no travel itinerary for you."

"I didn't file one," she said as they approached the building.

"You traveled out of the Enclave without a guardian and without letting us know where you were?" That was not going in his report. Captains were way above his pay grade. But... she should have let someone know.

The door opened at her silent command. "I handle land deals for the OIA and the Captains' Council. If my contact says they have an opening in three hours, I don't have time to file an itinerary and get Carver's permission. Besides, what's a guardian going to do that I can't?"

"Protect you."

Her smile was cold. "I'm a captain. If I can't handle it, a guardian won't be able to either."

"We're trained in unarmed combat. Non-lethal techniques."

She stomped to a halt, furious and threatening even with tousled hair and a thin skirt. "I'm a Caryll. I know in your shriveled Sciarra brain that probably only means Traitor and Idiot, but I was training in non-lethal combatives when you were learning how to pee standing up. The Starguard training manual was written by a Caryll, and all it has is the basic moves. Trust me, I'm fine." She stormed towards the Enclave's outer doors.

"The doors to the bachelor's dorms are to the left."

She came to a stop, barefooted under the empty dome of the OIA lobby.

"You didn't know that, did you?" Titan asked as he put the pieces together. "You don't have a ship to sleep in. You don't have a lover, or you'd have called for them by now." Her back stiffened. "You teleported in because you don't live in Enclave."

When she pivoted, the look on her face could have peeled paint. "Bravo, Sciarra. You're a genius. If you check the fleet registrar, what's my residence listed as?"

He pulled up the file. "An apartment."

"Across the street and outside Enclave."

In the wastelands between the Enclave and the main part of Tarrin. Filled with vagrants, people running from the law, drug dealers...

It was a security nightmare, but technically it was her crew's security nightmare, not his. Which meant he couldn't justify walking her home.

"I never sign in or out because it's a bother. Carver knows where to find me if there's an emergency. So do the captains on my contact list. Is there anything else you need from me before I retire for the evening? I'm tired. I'm sober. I want to go home, soak in the tub, and get some sleep. Maybe order some take out. I haven't decided yet."

Titan hesitated. Every instinct told him to do his job, protect the fleet, keep the captain safe, even if she hated his presence. But he couldn't.

He sighed. "If you'd like to press charges for the evening, I'll need your signature on some paperwork." He hated himself for saying it, but the fleet had rules. Rowena had lost rank after the war, and with it she'd lost the right to start a fight with Selena Caryll.

Caryll wrinkled her nose in disgust. She looked away at the wall with a sour expression. Then she shook her head, the distaste vanishing behind a captain's placid gaze. "Rowena was having a bad day. We all were." Her angry scowl softened slightly. "How's your jaw?"

He touched the cheek she'd punched. "Sore. I've got a split lip, but I'll live." With some of the officers he could have teased them, asked them to kiss it better. Trying that with Caryll would probably get him a black eye. Or worse. That didn't mean he didn't imagine soft lips and a smile of apology.

"Are you going to file a complaint?" There was a guarded look in her eyes. She was expecting the worst. There was no reason not to; their crews had never been friendly.

Titan silently measured the power differential between them. A captain with no crew, from one of the youngest crews, against the Sciarra name and traditions.

The wrong move with her could start another war. So he shook his head. "As you said, we were all having a bad day."

There was a ping, finally, the image of a purple-pink cloud used in the Academy as code for gratitude.

He smiled in understanding. "Have a good night, captain."

"Good night, guardian." She stepped out of the Enclave, passing through the shield like it didn't exist and then winking out of sight. She'd teleported without sound or light.

It wasn't meant to be erotic, but evolutionary fleet genetics were in play: power was alluring. The combination of power, brains, and beauty were practically hardwired into his brain to trigger all sorts of chemical cascades. He could pick it apart, even halt the progress of the nascent emotions, but he didn't particularly see a reason why he should. Besides, there were bigger problems than a minor, momentary attraction.

Titan went to his desk and pulled up Carver's contact information.

Ten seconds later a projection of Commander Carver appeared, floating over Titan's desk.

The commander ran a hand through his hair and sighed with annoyance. "Another problem?"

"Maybe a small one. Captain Caryll opted to leave Enclave for another housing option."

Carver shook his head. "Not a problem. She has an apartment. It's well shielded."

Titan hesitated. "Sir... was..." He sighed in frustration, not sure how to explain his concerns.

Carver looked tired, and his attention kept shifting from the monitor to something else in the room. Probably Genevieve Silar.

"Sir, if she'd been one of my crew, I wouldn't leave Caryll alone tonight. She wasn't just angry. Her defensive shields were up, she was taking things hard. And I know Yeoman Lee was out of line. I'm fully aware of that. But..." He shrugged.

The commander motioned for someone to join him, and sure enough the young Silar lieutenant slid onto his lap wearing little more than a pink night slip.

"Lieutenant," Titan said politely, keeping his gaze pointedly on his commander's face.

Carver had a steady lover who'd probably be his wife by the time the year was out; he didn't need to rub it in. Besides, pale pink was an atrocious color on Silar. She needed a steel gray or copper red, something martial.

That could be filed under the list of things he would never, ever tell anyone.

"Gen, do you think Selena was acting abnormal tonight?" Carver asked.

"She was cranky, but she wanted to go somewhere in Tarrin proper, not Cargo Blue. That's it," Silar said.

"You don't think she was upset by what Rowena said?" Carver asked.

Silar shook her head, tossing bright red curls that caught on the commander's bristles.

Titan squelched a surge of jealousy. It had been a long time since he'd had someone to hold that close.

"Selena's heard all that before. From everyone," Silar said. "She'll be fine. But, if the guardian is worried, I'll contact her. Would that make you happy?"

"I was doing my due diligence," Titan said. "If you believe Captain Caryll is in a good mental state, I won't worry about her."

"Selena's never in a good head space," Silar said. "She doesn't have a crew and she spends more time at work than with her friends. That's not healthy. But it's not new either. You'll see, she'll be dancing at Cargo Blue next weekend. Unless it's shut down by then."

"Captain Caryll mentioned that too, sir. We may need to consider allowing more passes for people to leave Enclave."

Carver held up his hand. "We'll worry about that later. Are you going to check on the Lees?"

"As soon as I'm done here, sir," Titan confirmed.

"May I make a suggestion?"

"Yes, sir."

"Find a reason to spend the night with the Lees or at the office. If your crew sees your face right now, we're going to be filing incident reports and reprimands for the next month. Not that you can't request a reprimand for Captain Caryll, she was out of line, but once we go down that road it won't end."

Silar looked offended. "She had every right to punch Rowena! It's not Selena's fault Sciarra got in the way of her fist."

Titan pressed his lips into a thin line. "I don't want a fight with the Carylls, sir. Even if there is only one of them."

"Thank you," Carver said. "Have a good night. Tell Rowena happy birthday from us."

"Yes, sir." That was a lie, but a polite one that would keep the peace. He closed the transmission and stared into the darkness after the vanished Selena Caryll. In another world, in another fleet...

It was a silly thought. They'd all made their choices years ago and now he had to live with his.

Seven hours later, Titan rested his head on his desk with the overhead light dimmed and remembered why he never went partying with Rowena if he didn't have the next day off. Even with his nanites working overtime, he had a hangover.

There was a soft tap at his door. "That brutal?" Carver asked.

"Good morning, Commander." Titan tried to stand and gave up as the room spun.

Carver snickered. "I went drinking with Rowena once. My first year at the Academy when I'd made the flight team, she invited me over. Were you there? Baular was. A couple of Lee officers."

"I remember three days of drunken blur," Titan said. "Mal—ancestors keep him—brought something over from his dad's private collection. I don't remember what it was."

"Golden fire? Gilded sun? Something like that?"

"Gilded Sun Whiskey from the first continent." Titan sighed fondly at the memory. "Now I remember. Mal had welts on his back for a month when his parents found out. It was a museum piece. One of the last bottles from the first wave of colonization."

"Ancestors keep him." Carver sighed. "He wasn't always a bad man."

"Best of a bad lot," Titan said. "The Baulars were cruel to everyone, even their own crew. But a lot of the old guard were. It's hard to know, in the thick of it, that what your captains and elders are doing is wrong. Until you have a good captain, you don't realize what a bad one is. Mal—may the ancestors welcome him to the Lost Fleet—would have been a good captain."

"Maybe," Carver said. "He had problems."

Titan shrugged. "We all had problems. We were barely adults. Nineteen, twenty years old and making choices that got hundreds killed. It's a bit ridiculous when you think about it. Things needed to change and we thought it was the only way to go."

"And now we change again," Carver said. "That's why I'm here."

Titan raised an eyebrow.

"I saw your report about last night. And I wanted to say thank you, personally, and not as the commander. Selena's a good person once you get to know her. So, thank you for letting things slide."

He shrugged again. "If she'd accepted Rowena's challenge, I might not have."

"The hardest part of battle is having ammunition and a target, and not taking the kill shot," Carver said. It sounded like he was quoting someone. "This was one of th—"

He stopped and his eyes glowed silver. "Can I use your wall screen?"

"Sure." Titan pinged his commander with the code to use the wall's teleconference screen.

An old, round-faced man with bright red cheeks appeared, leaning far too close to the monitor on the other end. "Commander Carver."

"That's me," Carver said.

Titan turned on the lights and shut his office door with a thought.

The round-faced man frowned at him. "And that is?"

"One of my men," Carver said. "Who are you?"

"Commandant Tyrling of the Jhandarmi's Third Corp. I'm the sector commander for this area. Did you receive our message last night?"

Carver shook his head. "I haven't sorted through the paperwork you sent yet."

And Titan knew he never did. Anything sent over by a grounder was dropped in a file unopened.

"When you didn't respond immediately, I feared you'd ignored the memo. Hence the call. Our intelligence operatives believe someone has paid for an attack on one of your Starguardians."

Titan winced at the fumbled name. The guardians were in the Starguard, but there were no *Starguardians*.

"Starguard, excuse me," Tyrling corrected as if he was being prompted by someone off screen.

"Do you have any more information?" Carver asked. "The name of the target or the assailant?"

"Not at this time."

"May we speak with your intelligence operative?" It was a fair request. Even the phrasing of the assignment could give them clues as to who the threat was coming from.

Tyrling shook his head. "Out of the question, I'm afraid. Our man is on a deep-cover assignment. He only slipped us this information because it could destabilize the current truce."

"Thank you for letting us know," Carver said. "I'll put Enclave on lockdown immediately and make sure we reinforce the perimeter."

Titan smirked. No one was getting through his shield. Not unless someone had hired Selena Caryll as a hitman, and somehow he couldn't see No-Shot Selena taking up murder-for-hire as a hobby.

"We'll update you if we learn more," Tyrling said with a nod, before closing out his monitor.

Carver grimaced. "This is not going to make Gen happy."

"Was she going somewhere today?"

"No, but there's a flyer race scheduled for this weekend and she was planning on entering."

So was Rowena, now that he checked his schedule.

Grumbling, Carver dropped into the chair by the door. His eyes were unfocused.

Titan waited.

Finally Carver came back from wherever he'd mentally wandered off to. "This is not good."

"I know, sir. Especially since it means we'll be denying requests to leave Enclave. And after last night, we need a distraction."

Carver nodded and licked his lips. "Okay..." He nodded again. "How much do I need to pay you to streak naked through Enclave?"

Titan raised his eyebrows.

"It'd be a distraction," Carver said with his signature smile.

"Maybe you should ask Silar," Titan said.

"Everyone's seen Hollis naked. There's no novelty value." Carver stood and paced. "Do we have any other distractions?"

Titan mentally listed everything he'd used to keep junior officers from causing trouble out of boredom. "Mock battles aren't a good thing right now. Sports won't work. We could try a shielding contest?"

"No competitions," Carver said. "We need something to defuse the tension, not start another war."

"Options fail me." Titan shook his head.

Carver glared.

"I'll go… find something. Rowena has better intel than anyone in the fleet, maybe she knows who would want an officer killed."

"Fine." Carver nodded as he stood up. "Contact me as soon as you have something. But make sure it's something good."

"Aye, sir."

3

ROWENA

THE COM CRACKLED WITH static. It didn't have to—Rowena had kept the part for repairs on hand for years now—but it was one of the little warnings that told her someone was trespassing into her domain.

Technically, the crew, ship, and even her engineering section belonged to her captain—and Hoshi never let her forget it. But, since they'd held the same rank until the end of war, she couldn't really find it in her heart to forgive him.

Now his round face appeared on the screen, thin-lipped and angry. "You have a visitor."

Crack in the hull! Her favorite curse tumbled through her head. She pressed her lips together and surveyed the partially-dissected environmental array she'd been cleaning. With a shield over it, it'd be protected from debris until she could finish up. "I can be up in the conference room in ten minutes, sir." As long as they didn't mind her looking like she'd gone straight from cleaning fryers in the kitchens to engineering and hadn't showered since yesterday.

"Don't bother. I'm sending them down."

Which meant they were either Lees, or…

Titan Sciarra materialized at the edge of the engineering safety doors, wearing his all-black Starguard uniform with the tiny gold leaf for his rank.

"Commander," she said politely, not bothering to get up off the floor.

"Permission to enter?"

Rowena nodded and dropped the personal shield that kept the *Danielle Nicole's* engines safe from junior crew, and her safe from everyone.

"Spring cleaning already?"

"If I can't get these filter coils cleaned, we'll have to replace them, and Hoshi doesn't know who to trade for them." She did, just like she knew almost everything else going on in Enclave, but Hoshi wasn't going to ask and she never volunteered anything.

Titan sighed as he looked around. "I'm surprised your captain let me in if you're this busy."

The engineering look understaffed, but it was by choice, not necessity. No one was allowed in the engine room unless Rowena wanted them there, and she never wanted anyone in her space. "Hoshi thinks you might be trying to court me. The Sciarras have better ships and political leverage. He's willing to trade unwanted kin for that."

"Um…" Titan looked nervous.

"It's an assumption they run on, not me." She put extra emphasis on 'they' to differentiate the rest of the fleet from their little dangerous duo. "Don't worry. Your bachelorhood is safe for another day."

"Ro, if…"

She shot him a quelling glare. "We've been over this. I'm not using a marriage contract as an escape hatch from a bad situation. I don't want to be Sciarra. You don't want to be Lee. And, no offense, but I tried kissing you once, and licking a wall is more exciting."

Titan laughed.

Rowena went back to scrubbing coils. "What are you doing here in your all-blacks? Is this a formal reprimand for last night at Cargo Blue?"

"Nah, it's a recruiting drive," Titan said as he leaned against the bulkheads. "I want you to join the Starguard."

"Ha ha. Funny." She stuck her tongue out in distaste. Three years since they'd made landfall on this vicious mudball of a planet, nearly 300 executions and banishments, and still the Warmonger crews weren't welcomed into the fleet's political system.

The Allied crews who'd protected the planet from Baular's Warmongers had offered the survivors seats on the Captains' Council, which was nice. And she appreciated that they'd spared her life—most days—but she'd find the Lees' missing space station before the Starguard offered her a job. She'd killed too many people in war, destroyed too many rival ships, been too good at being a Warmonger officer to ever be forgiven.

"What's this really about?"

"Really? I need your help with something."

If it had been anyone but Titan, she would have kicked them out. But he was her friend. Her only friend, after last night. "Parts and repairs I can handle, but I don't solve people problems. Unless we're moving a body."

"That's close to my problem."

She looked up in surprise.

"Do you know of any feuds going on in Enclave?"

"Besides the usual ones?" She pulled up a list on her implant. "I mean, the general Allied verse Warmonger tension is there. A couple of the smaller crews are scrapping over salvage rights. The Silars are baiting as many high-level officers as they can, and giving Carver blue balls in the process. Sciarras. Lees. Crack, I'd start a war if I thought you'd forgive me. Anything is better than this." She gestured to the parts that should have been replaced a century ago. "It's not natural, fleet holding still. We're explorers caught in this prison."

"It's for—" Titan started the standard lecture and she shut him down with an electric shock from across the room.

Ancestors bless telekyen and implants.

Rowena glared. "It *was* about safety. Three years ago. Now, it's about fear. Cultures that stagnate die. That's what we're doing here. We're clinging so hard to the old ways that we're going to strangle ourselves."

Two civil wars in under forty years, three years of being stuck down a gravity well on this mud ball of a planet… Every night she dreamed of breaking free of the atmosphere.

Every night she dreamed of her hull cracking around her, leaving her to die in vacuum.

"You saying you're going to go marry a grounder?" Titan asked her.

"Not if my ancestors came to me in a dream and told me to!" She spat on the floor. "A grounder couldn't keep up with us. Not this generation. But, with training? Maybe my nieces and nephews could marry in."

Titan nodded agreement. "How is Nia anyway?"

"Nine months pregnant, acting like she's eighteen months along, and likely to kill you if you don't use her proper name. Aronia is married now."

They both chuckled at her tart delivery. Nia was a year older than she was and had spent most of their childhood reminding Rowena of it. Her rushed marriage at the start of the war had been fueled by love, but also in large part by Nia's wish to be older.

"Ro," Titan said as he took a seat and his smile fell away. "If you wanted to attack the fleet, destabilize us, who would you kill?"

She raised her eyebrows. "What's my goal?"

He shrugged. "I don't know."

"What do you know?"

"The Jhandarmi in Tarrin think there's a credible threat to the fleet and that a hitter has been hired to kill an officer. By officer I assume they mean someone augmented, but..." He shrugged. "That's it. So, who would you kill?"

Rowena stood up. "For pure chaos, Perrin Carver. His crew was allied with the Baulars at one point. He has firepower and respect on both sides. He's charismatic and well-known by the grounders. Kill the figurehead and we'd have chaos."

"No, we'd have Marshall or a Silar in charge," Titan said.

"Killing Marshall is always a tempting thought, but it's not a smart play. She's nearly as powerful as Carver, held her own against the Baulars, and her family has political connections on all three continents. That's not an anthill you want to kick."

Titan nodded in agreement. "One of the Silars?"

"But which one?" Rowena asked. "There's a few thousand of them. I'd murder Hollis myself if I were ever alone with him without witnesses, for no other reason than I want to wipe that smirk off his face. But, there's the problem."

Titan raised an eyebrow. "Too many witnesses?"

"No, too much skill. If you or I wanted to kill someone, how hard would it be? Warmonger or not, we're still among the elite. Who could take you down?"

He grimaced. "Carver and I are evenly matched. He has more brute force, I'm better at shielding. Hollis Silar..." Titan's lip curled into a sneer. "He's wicked fast with a knife. Lots of brute power, but low focus. It'd be anyone's fight. Marshall is better than me with a shield, but doesn't have finesse."

"Marshall doesn't need finesse. I've seen her kill with augmented force and her bare hands. Even if you won the fight, her ghost would kill you."

"Which leaves you," Titan said. "Maybe my cousin Mars. My captain." He paused. "Caryll?" It was a question, not an addition to their list of elites.

Rowena rolled her eyes at the name. "No-shot Selena? Perfect aim, decent shields, and no kills to her name. She's too nice. And that's beside the point. What I'm saying is, if we wanted someone dead, it wouldn't be a matter of 'if', but 'when'."

"Right."

"Fleet doesn't hire hitters. Especially not mud-loving grounders. Not for a personal vendetta."

Titan crossed his arms. "So it isn't personal."

"Or the person is very weak."

"It could be someone from outside the fleet hiring. Anyone around here would just find a Warmonger officer."

"Rowena," Titan's voice held a note of warning.

She held her hands up in apology. "I'm just saying! If you wanted someone discretely vanished, all the fleet knows to ask a Lee. Unless they wanted you dead, of course," she said as a bit of a joke. It hadn't been that many generations ago that the Sciarras had been the assassins of the fleet. Two of her uncles had done it before the first civil war, trying to thin the enemy ranks before chaos broke out. It hadn't worked.

Titan sneered at her. "You wouldn't take work from a Silar anyway."

"True." She rubbed a hand over tired eyes. "This isn't helping, is it?"

"We have six people who probably didn't hire the killer," Titan said.

"Out of how many billion on the planet?"

"Keep it simple. Let's assume the client and target are both local. A grounder hitter means outside Enclave, because they can't get past my shield without help."

"So, your victim is someone who might leave Enclave," Rowena said. "That narrows it down a bit."

Titan nodded. "A bit, but not enough." His eyes glowed for a moment. "I've got an incoming transmission."

Rowena nodded to her board. "It's secure."

The board turned on, showing Perrin Carver, lips pressed in a thin, tight line and eyes narrowed. He nodded. "Rowena."

"Commander." She looked up at Titan, trying to guess how serious he'd been about the recruiting drive joke.

"Sir?" Titan looked wary, which was actually promising in some ways.

Carver eyed her and grimaced. "You need to get back here, Sciarra. We have a situation with the delivery."

Rowena raised her eyebrows.

"Sir, you sent me here to get information," Titan said. "It's Rowena. She'll know in five minutes even if we don't tell her, and there's a decent chance we'll have to come back and ask her to use her connections to gather intel for us anyway."

Carver frowned then turned his green-eyed glare to her. "Why don't you work for us?"

Rowena looked up at the catwalks running over the engine. "Mmmm... Almost everyone in the Starguard has tried to kill me at least once," she said, counting it out on her fingers. "I've killed some of their family. Hoshi would have a temper tantrum if you recruited me before one of his nephews. Oh, and I hate you all." Her smile was sharp enough to cut bone. "That's four good reasons."

"War's over," Carver said as Titan said, "She's joking."

:Am not.: She sent the thought to Titan on a tight beam. :None of them were there when I needed help. No one defended me.:

:This is me defending you. No more wars.: Titan's voice stayed impassive but there was a rush of emotions attached.

She rolled her eyes. "Sorry, hangovers make me grumpy." It was a weak excuse, but Carver looked ready to forgive.

"There's a problem with the supply delivery in Tarrin," he said.

"I'll take a squad to pick it up instead of sending two people," Titan said. "It won't be an issue."

Carver shook his head. "It was dropped off last night and the alarm went off ten minutes ago. The Tarrin police called me and the Jhandarmi. You need to get to the main office and handle things here while I go figure out the situation."

Crack in the hull. The fleet had managed to get along with the city-state of Tarrin without calling in the cross-border negotiators in the Jhandarmi for three years. The local grounders shouldn't have called in the Jhandarmi unless there was body going cold.

"Yes, sir. I'll be there immediately," Titan said.

"Are you out of your star-crazed mind?" Rowena demanded as she held out a hand to keep Titan in place.

40

:Rowena Eden Lee!:

:Titan Sa'ïr Sciarra!: Rowena gave him a mental push. "Perrin, we're on lockdown. Did you slam your head against a hull this morning?"

Carver looked confused.

"You can't go, sir," Titan said, catching on finally. "If you die, there's going to be chaos."

"I can't send a pair of rookies out there either!" There was an edge of desperation in his voice. Carver had always had that weakness, an unwillingness to risk his people. "I'm not getting anyone else in the fleet killed today."

The need to volunteer choked Rowena. She'd trained for this. Worked her butt off for years to prepare for this. But she couldn't break the inertia of defeat.

"I'll go," Titan said. "Captain Sciarra won't mind. I'm a neutral party, so none of the other captains will feel insulted, and my crew is stable enough that if something happens to me, they'll survive."

"No!" Rowena protested in unison with Carver.

Agreeing with him left the taste of bile in her mouth.

On screen, Carver leaned back in his chair. "I know the streets of Tarrin. I grew up here."

"I make a better defensive shield," Titan argued.

Carver shook his head. "You don't look like a grounder. You don't move like one."

"I've taken the training to leave Enclave," Titan said. "I know all the distribution routes. If you'd let me go out to guard a minister from the OIA, why not to do this? All I need to do is go to a building and check the records. It'll take less than an hour."

"A little bit more," Carver said. "Teleporting in is going to attract the kind of attention you can't afford." He shook his head.

41

"I'll go. The grounder family that adopted me after the crash still sends me clothes on my birthday every year."

"I'm serious, Carver," Titan said, standing up. "Sir. If someone's going to get shot at, let it be me. I can take the hit. Even if I get killed, it won't endanger anyone else. I'll let my captain know I volunteered. Rowena is my witness."

:This screams trap in big, blood-red letters.:

:Let someone try,: Titan said silently. :I'm a commander in the guard, I have the right to this fight. If someone wants to attack, let them see a Sciarra.: For a moment a flame-blue knife flickered into existence in his hand away from the screen, then burned out.

Carver looked unhappy.

"You know it's the best choice," Titan said aloud.

"Doesn't mean I like it," Carver said. "Fine. Go. Report back as quick as you can. Lee?"

Rowena raised her eyebrows in question.

"If you hear anything on the back channels about this, tell me immediately," Carver ordered. When she didn't respond quickly enough, he snapped, "I mean it!"

"Yes! Fine! Good grief, Carver. You're commander of the Starguard, not the hull-cracking Marshal of the Fleet!" She rolled her eyes at him. And to think they'd almost been friends once.

Titan slapped the com console, turning it off and making it wobble.

"Gentle with my tech. I don't have the replacement parts for that."

"You should have been polite."

"I should also be a ranked officer who isn't treated either like a pariah or a child," Rowena said, trying to check her annoyance.

He winced. "I'm sorry. It's not..." He closed his eyes and dropped his shield enough for her to catch the terror he was

42

carrying. The fear that one wrong move would plunge them all into unending darkness.

Carefully, she wrapped an inner layer of her own shield around her sympathetic thoughts and then sneered. "All doom and gloom, Sciarra? Living in this gravity well is making your brain melt. This isn't a problem. It's a temporary setback."

His laugh was weak, unbelieving. "And last night?"

"Bruised egos," Rowena said. "I was mad Silar was paying more attention to No-Shot than me."

A guffaw of laughter burst from Titan's mouth and he gripped his abdomen. "Oh, ancestors! No! I have this image in my mind." He covered his mouth and shook his head.

Rowena smiled. "See? It's not all bad."

"Remember when we did those training flights on the old fighters and the environmental system malfunctioned on mine?"

She nodded.

"It feels like that. I'm frantically trying to reset the system, telling myself not to panic, praying to my ancestors that the light will flip back on. Every breath is getting harder. And... the lights are not coming on." He bit his lip, catching his words. Admitting that would have meant death before landing, socially if not literally. With the old Sciarra captain it could have been literal.

"You survived."

"I keep thinking my luck's run out."

She picked up the coils—working with her hands helped her think. "Mal and I thought you were dead, that night you crashed. But you got home. Ancestors, or guardian spirits, or random chance... whatever. You teleported from the planet's surface to the medical ward on your own power. You don't need luck."

Titan ran a hand over his damaged left arm. "I don't know if I was entirely alone. It never felt that way."

"And you aren't alone now. I've got your back. If you get in trouble out there, holler. I'll break your shield and come get you."

He smiled. "Thanks."

"Go on." She waved him out of her engine room. "Go be a good little guardian and save civilization."

"See what you can find out about all this? Please? Names of anyone who might be outside the shield, and anyone who might be nursing a serious grudge."

Rowena nodded. "I will, but only because it's you asking."

"You're the best, Ro." Titan stepped into the hallway to teleport out.

"Stay safe, Sciarra."

She watched him wink out and then reset her shields.

An assassination and a theft. She hadn't seen those coming.

Some days she missed the clean order of battle. It had been awful. People had died by the dozens every day. But people hadn't lied about how they felt.

If they were angry, they shot at you.

If they were happy, they told you.

If they loved you, they kissed you.

Not that anyone had loved her, and it wasn't like she'd ever trusted the rest of her crew to have her back, but it had been uncomplicated. She followed orders, shot at her targets, and waited for death to enlist her in the Lost Fleet with her ancestors.

Now... She looked around the poorly-lit engine room, silent as a tomb.

Now she had to make other plans. Death wasn't coming for her, and neither were the living.

Titan better come back safe.

The only reason she didn't punch a hole through the Enclave shield and fly one of her ships off into the black was because she knew Titan would be upset. He'd already lost too many friends, suffered through being injured and helpless while people he loved died around him.

She couldn't bring Mal back, or Titan's parents, but she could make sure he had a friend no matter what.

4

SELENA

SELENA PUSHED HER HAIR out of her face and gritted her teeth as she read through the Tarrin police reports again. The city-states were loath to share information with each other, and only slightly better at sharing information with the global defense force known as the Jhandarmi. Sometimes she thought the local police went out of their way to make their reports a nightmare slog of disjointed sentences and poor spelling just to make the Jhandarmi swear.

This report was about suspected questionable activity between citizens of Tarrin and the city-state of Grise Harbor to the north. Of course, the Grise Harbor police hadn't followed up on a known fugitive boarding the hypertram, and none of them had thought to tell the Tarrin police so they could pick Emery Kaffton up on arrival.

And now the report was over ten hours old and Kaffton's tram had arrived over eight hours ago. If he'd stayed in Tarrin, he'd already gone to ground.

Pulling up the files on her implant, she sorted through the mess of data always available to her. Everything was there with a thought, from the locations of the wrecks in orbit, to the maps of the solar system to an analysis of the composition of the dirt she'd stepped on walking to work. She mentally pushed that aside and opened up the Jhandarmi files on smuggler Emery Kaffton.

Thirty-one, light-brown hair, dark-brown eyes, favored women as lovers but had no long-term relationships. Wanted for questioning as an accessory to the crimes of theft and extortion in the city-states of Bellis, Quintiin, Harstad, Sandur, and Rodebay. Convicted of crimes of smuggling, forgery, and theft in Tarrin, Bellis, Clyde River, and Kivalina.

Kivalina Constabulary also wanted him in connection with an unsolved questionable death.

He was a busy man, Emery. With a fondness for art and dead drops.

She opened her eyes and a map of the art district of Tarrin. Her implant provided an overlay of blueprints and highlighted possible spaces accessible to an unaugmented grounder.

"Caryll?"

Selena looked up at the sound of her name, saving the data and maps to her implant for later use. "Yes?"

Her boss, bald and sweating even in the cold of the office, stepped into the doorway. "You have plans for today?"

She held up the report from Grise Harbor. "Kaffton might be in town. I thought I'd wander the art district, see if I could lay eyes on him or one of his known associates. Why?"

"One of the fleet members is leaving Enclave," Tyrling said.

Her eyebrows went up. "You told them it was dangerous? That there's a legitimate threat?"

"I talked to Carver himself. Or someone who introduced himself as Carver. Our files are slim." He let the unasked question dangle in the silence.

She closed her files. "Your files are going to stay slim." She'd stubbornly refused to budge on data sharing. The Jhandarmi didn't get fleet personnel files, and she didn't talk about Jhandarmi cases with the OIA or Captains' Council. It was safer for everyone that way.

Tyrling frowned. "The fleet warehouse downtown had an alarm go off. The Tarrin police sent someone and they're reporting that it's empty, but we told them we'd look into the matter."

Selena swore under her breath. "That was the medical shipment." Moving from the low gravity of space to the full weight of sea level on the planet was hard on frail bones. The medicines combated the lack of bone density and the trouble with the new bacteria and allergens they'd encountered since landing. "On the black market..." She shook her head. "A few thousand dollars at best."

"Here," Tyrling said, agreeing. "Smuggled out to one of the islands it's worth a bit more. But we don't have enough island trade that I'd worry about it. A thief is most likely to try to ransom the goods, same as they did with the hospital shipment two years ago."

"Mud-lickin' bastards." She blinked. "No offense meant, sir."

"None taken."

She pressed her lips together in thought. "What are the odds of a known thief and hitman being in town when we have word about a possible assassination and a major theft of fleet property being unrelated?"

"Not good," Tyrling said.

"That's what I was thinking. Did you try to wave the Starguard off the case?"

"We tried," he said. "They sent someone all the same. Probably curious to see the extent of the damage."

"Do you know who?"

Tyrling shook his head. "Carver said he'd send his best officer. I assume his second."

"That would be Hollis Silar." Selena closed her eyes as a million scenarios streamed past, none of them good. "I'll go. I can either divert or defend. Hollis has an ego the size of a planet but he's amiable and malleable. Getting him back to Enclave won't take much more than convincing him I'll meet him for dinner sometime."

Tyrling chuckled. "Sounds like a terrible trial."

"Fleet hasn't figured out fine dining yet, but it'll be a nutritionally ideal meal with a conversation about training programs and the quest for a new flight simulator that feels like the real thing." Even to her it sounded like a terribly boring evening. Another sign she didn't belong to the fleet.

Maybe she never had.

"Keep your comm on," Tyrling ordered. "We'll try to get a better lock on what's going on while you're out there. And keep your head down, Caryll. Don't become someone's target of opportunity."

She grabbed her purse and gave him a grim look. "No one's managed to kill me yet."

"Keep it that way."

It took twenty minutes on public transport to cross town and reach Row Lane, the thin transit strip that divided the warehouse district from the art district of Tarrin. Selena had dressed to fit in, with a swinging blue-green skirt and knotted sweater that looked flirty while keeping the spring chill away.

The cloud cover over Tarrin had finally broken and it was actually a sunny day. If she looked up into the clear, blue sky, she could see pinpoints of light, like stars in the daytime—the remnants of ships lost in the battle for Malik V. The ruin of the *Persephone* was up there somewhere, a dull ache against her skull.

A bright-green sky shuttle zipped past, ruffling the pale spring leaves on the trees and reminding Selena where she was.

With a sigh, she refocused. The *Persephone* was dead, she wasn't, and there was work enough to do just now. She turned down Row Lane, a peaceful haven on the eastern edge of the city, and looked around for Hollis Silar.

Neither her tech scan or a visual scan spotted him.

That was one small miracle; if she hadn't beat him to the site it would be harder to explain her presence. She muted her shield so the guardian wouldn't run off, and put her work scroll up. Name, rank, position at the OIA, and a tag that said she was on business.

There was a warning pressure against her shield that signaled Hollis's arrival. She stepped into a bodega and bought a bribe she knew he couldn't refuse: peppermint candies.

Smiling, she stepped out into the street—and straight into Titan Sciarra.

Her plan shattered. Hollis liked candy and wouldn't question anything. Sciarra hated her, probably even more now than he had the night before.

"Captain." His voice was low, empty, condemning.

"Guardian."

They stared at each other for an uncomfortably long moment.

"Didn't you receive a notification about the lockdown?" His green eyes narrowed in suspicion.

This would have been so much easier with Hollis. "I check my messages at set times so nothing disturbs my workflow. I must have missed it."

"You need to return to Enclave immediately and either bunk at the BOQ or with a friendly crew tonight," he said in a voice too calm for her peace of mind.

It would have been better if he'd yelled. But there was no emotion coming from Sciarra, nothing to work with, no buttons to push. She'd have to lie until she found a way to maneuver him back to Enclave. "That won't be possible for a few hours. The Tarrin police contacted me about the break-in because I handle land deals for the OIA. I need to inspect the premises and file a formal complaint." It was a flimsy excuse that was easily checked on.

"I wasn't informed of that protocol."

Her heartrate ticked up in panic. "It was done along informal channels. A peace offering."

Sciarra nodded, probably calculating the advantages of taking a friendly overture from Enclave's nearest neighbor against the possible fallout of letting an OIA official wander Tarrin alone.

"If the Starguard would like a copy of the report, I'll be happy to forward it to you," Selena offered. "Mint?" She held the bag out for him.

Sciarra recoiled as if she'd offered him spiced beetles from a market on Descent.

"No? More for me, then." She walked toward the warehouse, used for ordering from grounder companies who wouldn't deliver to Enclave.

Sciarra followed. "It's not safe for you to be here right now. Carver wants one of the guardians down here. How about I check this out, and I'll send you a report?"

"Hmmm." Selena paused, pretending to consider it for a hot second. "Let's see... The advantages of you going are, what? You've had some basic forensic training and practice hand-to-hand combat at the gym every day?"

He shrugged in agreement. "More or less."

"While the advantage of sending me is that I know this city, work with the locals, have contacts on the police force and in the Jhandarmi offices, and can blend in with a crowd. I've also had basic forensic training because I was command track and am a captain, I have as much combat training as you, and more actual combat time. Of the two of us, who is actually prepared to be here? Me. Besides, there's a wonderful little cafe a few blocks away that makes an amazing salad sandwich."

The footsteps following her halted abruptly. "The what now?"

"A medley of raw vegetables with seasonings on bread. Sometimes with cheese. It's really very good despite the name." She smiled, acting as if nothing had happened the night before. The bruise on his jaw was eating at her conscience as much as his presence was eating at her calm. She had to deactivate a warning subroutine on her implant just to quiet the notification that a Warmonger was close enough to attack.

He needed to leave.

But he was staring at her. Watching her. Studying her.

Selena took a deep breath and forced herself to hold his gaze. This was not a fight she could afford to lose.

"A salad sandwich?" he asked, seemingly oblivious to inner turmoil. "That does sound slightly more appetizing than the lentils and ration bars at Enclave," he admitted with a tentative smile.

Tension unwound from her shoulders. They were getting along. Ish. Tolerating each other. Not killing each other.

It was a big step.

"I'm staying," Sciarra said. "Even if you are too."

She wrinkled her nose in distaste. Tyrling was not going to like this development.

"I can't leave an OIA officer outside Enclave alone." Sciarra tried to ping her, but it bounced off her outer shield.

When she looked at the options, there wasn't much choice. Sciarra wasn't going to leave, and she couldn't leave, so she'd have to deal with his presence.

Having another shield nearby hurt, on some fundamental level. Like being touched after years of sensory deprivation, it was a reminder of how much she'd lost. And a stark reminder of the pain waiting for her every time she returned to Enclave.

Sciarra stood beside her, waiting in stony silence.

"This is ridiculous," she muttered. "Let's get this done with and move on." She swept down the street, tension coiling in her back as she saw the damage to the warehouse.

The door stood ajar, hanging off the hinges like a drunk on a three-day binge. The cracked doorframe was stained with explosives soot. Inside, the shelves were bare. Some had fallen to the ground, and even her quiet breathing echoed in the emptiness.

She pushed the door aside with a frown. "Who does guard duty down here?"

Sciarra's eyes flickered with light as he tapped his implant for the information. "Two grounders hired from local security firms. They come in and accept shipments, and wait until a guardian arrives to collect the shipment. The truck arrived early and the pick-up wasn't scheduled until later this week. They aren't required to stand guard."

"Hmm." Selena looked around. It wasn't a big warehouse. Just enough room for a medium truck, a pair of desks by the front door, and a locked room where shipments would wait. "Is it me, or does it seem like someone went to a lot of effort to break all the doors here? The loading bay door's bent. The front door is askew. The safe room door is broken. That's just sloppy." And her implant couldn't match the damage to any known gang in the city.

This was a childish display of temper. Which ruled out Kaffton, much to her disappointment.

Sciarra was watching her with narrowed eyes.

Selena lifted her chin. "Is there something you'd like to say, guardian?"

"For an OIA official, you seem to have a very definite idea of how a break-in should run. I'm wondering how you would do it."

"With lock picks?" Selena shrugged. "It's a starsider warehouse with our locks. They aren't easy to break, but a grounder would try to pick them first. I suppose a Starsider could, but no one has the kind of control needed to pick a lock through telekinesis and none of us would know where to find lock picks."

Privately, she amended that thought. Carver and Marshall probably could, and she had a set issued by the Jhandarmi, but that was information Sciarra didn't need. Ever.

He frowned in confusion. "Knowing how to pick a lock with an implant would be priority information. The crews wouldn't let that sort of rumor get out."

"They wouldn't talk about locks, but locks aren't the only delicate, hard-to-find things that need expert manipulation to unlock." She gave him a suggestive smile. If she was going to feel uncomfortable, then so could he.

Understanding slowly dawned on his face. A frown turned to a one-eyebrow-raised look of speculation, to both eyebrows lifting as his lips puckered, fighting a laugh—and finally a wicked, delightful smile. "Oh."

Selena winked at him. "Uh-huh."

He looked at the ground chuckling. Curious green eyes looked up to meet hers, and then Sciarra looked away again, shaking his head.

"We had free time at the Academy," she said with a shrug. "Thoughts on the mode of entry?"

Walking to the center of the warehouse, Sciarra looked around. "The doors look like an aggressive hull breach. The inside looks like they were rushing, unsure of the Tarrin response time. Maybe they weren't locals."

"Maybe they weren't grounders," Selena said. "A groundsider wouldn't have used charges, they would've used a lock pick or a crow bar. Or they would have talked their way inside. The damage suggests someone using telekyen-plastique to blow the locks."

"Is this something that came up at the Academy too?"

She bit the inside of her cheek and tried to remind herself that, as an OIA minister, she wouldn't have any training that addressed crime prevention or techniques. "Crew training?"

"That sounds like a question, not a statement," Sciarra said.

She shrugged. "I learned how to breach ships. It's not that unusual."

"Starsiders involved in a theft in Tarrin proper?" Sciarra shook his head as he lifted a shelf and pushed it against the wall.

"Plastique isn't that hard to come by. Anyone from a demolition team or a construction site could steal some."

There was no way to articulate her gut instinct. Grounders had all but forgotten about the fleet. The war had only touched the uninhabited outer islands of the second continent, and barely. What most people had seen were distant flashes of light, some unseasonal meteorites, and nothing more.

"I don't see a motive," she said.

"Ransom."

"For the theft, yes. For this destruction?" She shook her head.

He sighed. "An inside job means hassling the captains and having everyone search their ships for contraband." Hands on hips, he leaned his head back and looked at the ceiling. "We are going to be so unpopular this week. First a lockdown. Then a shakedown."

"Or you could contact a few people who know the black market on Enclave, arrange a buy, and not bother anyone."

Sciarra gave her a look of suspicion that was going to be permanently etched on his face if he spent any more time with her. "Again..."

"I meet with grounders. It wasn't possible to have clandestine meetings when we were in the stars, but we can here. It saves trouble all around."

"Do you know Carver has a vein on the side of his head that pops out when he's angry? When I file my report, with this conversation, his whole face will turn red."

"So summarize," Selena said. Her phone rang. "Hold on."

"What's that?"

"Grounder communication. I have other errands to run today." She put up a heavy sound shield so Sciarra couldn't eavesdrop. "This is Caryll."

"Good news and bad news," Tryling said without preamble. "One, you can ditch Silar. The attack on the Starsiders won't be a mass attack. It's a hit on a man named Titan Sciarra. As long as they stay on lockdown, he's fine."

Selena looked over her shoulder at Sciarra. "Um… when you talked to Carver, what did the man in the background look like?"

"Charred?" Tryling said. "Darker than an islander, light-colored eyes, black hair. Looked like he would fit in on Descent. They get too much sun up there. Turns 'em all crispy."

"Right…" She rolled her eyes skyward in a prayer to her ancestors. "There's a problem. Carver's best agent for this job, the one he sent downtown? He's Titan Sciarra."

Tyrling swore creatively.

Sciarra was watching her with a cold, appraising look. Probably trying to read her lips. Wincing, Selena pulled the phone away for a moment. At this rate, Sciarra would break her cover by the end of the day. Then her life would look as good as the *Persephone's* shattered hull. She dropped the sound shield and smiled at Sciarra. "Almost done."

He nodded.

"I need a Jhandarmi presence down here now," Selena said.

"Paperwork and red tape," Tyrling responded, and she could practically hear the bitter rant in his head. "Tarrin police are dragging their feet."

"So, let them show up."

There was a stunned silence from the other end of the line.

"Tyrling?" She looked at her phone to make sure she hadn't lost the connection.

"Are you serious? You think fleet would allow it?"

Probably not, but if she didn't ask, they wouldn't know. Except Sciarra was here… She dropped the phone to her side and lowered the sound shield again. "Would we object to an assist from the local constabulary?"

Sciarra's eyebrows went up in surprise. "Are they offering?"

Her implant loaded a list of concessions the Tarrins wanted that she could use to bargain with. Tech was out. So was most of the fleet's medical supply, unless she wanted to give up something only the Carylls had.

Near the bottom of the list she saw something that might work. "The Tarrin police want a joint station at the crossroads shopping plaza outside Enclave. If we agreed to allow it, we'd get help and goodwill for nothing."

She could practically hear Sciarra's thought process.

The crossroads plaza had been a mistake, a big land rush in the first days of Landing when Tarrin businesses thought the fleet would bring in a wealth of new customers. They hadn't counted on the fleet having no real concept of money. Everything was barter, trade, or homemade.

Within a few months, the buildings had been abandoned and new group of black market entrepreneurs moved in. It was the kind of place where you could find any drug on the planet, and get a complimentary knife in the back on the way home.

"I can swing a few votes in the Captains' Council," Sciarra said.

Selena nodded. "Tyrling, tell the Tarrin police we'll allow them on site, and they'll have access to a real live Star Guardian." Her hand trembled slightly. There were about to be a lot of people here. She put the sound shield up again. "Everyone needs to be vetted. Keeping Sciarra here is a risk."

"A calculated one," Tyrling said in a soothing tone. "Keep him in the building, get the work done, and then you can send him back to Enclave."

"I still want to check out the art district," she said. "That's Kaffton's stomping ground."

"He's probably not involved," Tyrling said. "The timing is off."

She stared at the bare warehouse wall. "When you see the scavengers circling, you know a crew's dead," she said.

"What?"

"Kaffton is in town for fun. He's here because something big is going down."

"That's why I have my best agent on the case. See you soon." Tyrling hung up on her.

Closing her eyes, Selena used her implant to calculate the odds of survival. Sciarra was the only guardian from a warmonger crew; getting him killed would burn any bridges to peace they'd built.

Getting any guardian killed would bring the Starguard into her mess, and they'd want explanations.

Going back to Enclave left her with more questions than answers...

Sciarra raised an eyebrow. "Problems?"

Only if you considered death a problem.

She slammed the phone shut and dropped the sound shield.

"Captain?" Sciarra looked at her questioningly. "You look like you've bitten into a lemon." His eyes narrowed. "What are you doing that you don't want a guardian to see?"

Bullets flying at your head.

"Trust me, a lemon would be preferred. In about five minutes this place is going to be swarming with Tarrin police, their forensic teams, and a load of Jhandarmi agents all wanting to gawk at you."

His eyebrows bounced up again. "Me?"

"You're the guardian. The rare, mystical, magical Starsider they've never seen before."

"What does that make you?"

She scoffed. "Average. A few of them know who I work for but I'm not..." There was no way to sum up the difference. Titan Sciarra was a striking man in any company. The way he held himself, the darkness of his black skin and the sharp green of his eyes... Even the way he watched people was intimidating. His family claimed Imperial ancestry and it was easy to see. People looked at men like Sciarra and wanted to follow them, to bask in their glow and taste of their glory.

When people looked at her, they saw a washed-out figure who passed from memory as soon as she was out of sight. She was forgettable. It was an asset when working for the Jhandarmi, but it wasn't something Sciarra could understand. She doubted anyone had ever forgotten him.

"You're not what?" he pressed, sending a querying ping to her implant.

"I'm short," she said. "Easily overlooked."

He snorted in amusement.

Ha, ha. Selena Caryll, the butt of every joke. Her jaw clenched. "You'll need to modify your shield before anyone arrives. The grounders have different weapons than us. Carver has the shield modifications back at Enclave. You can teleport out, pick them up from him, and come back if you feel the need to."

Sciarra smirked, mocking her. "Are you really suggesting that the two of us couldn't handle any problems that might arise? Two Academy-trained officers? Sciarra and Caryll? There aren't many better fighters than us."

"We're not exactly battle compatible. And I want to spare you. Everyone knows Sciarras aren't particularly interested in spending time with—what did you call them in the Academy?—mud-licking, soft-bellied toads? Something like that."

"Now you're just making excuses." Sciarra's shield bumped hers. Not a rough pressure or an attack, but a focused touch, almost a caress.

"What?"

"We both know there's really one choice here. We're either going to Enclave together, or staying here. Either way, we're staying together. And, if it helps, I'd enjoy the opportunity to meet my counterparts from the Tarrin police force."

For a moment she thought she'd heard him wrong.

The Warmongers' dislike of grounders was the entire reason they'd had six hundred years of isolation. And, as for working together, the idea didn't have engines. Sciarras and Carylls had been, if not bitter enemies, then uneasy rivals for power within the fleet since the first days of isolation.

She shook her head. "Maybe I should go back to Enclave. I think there's an audio glitch in my shield. It sounded like you were making a friendly overture."

"Well, my plan was to start friendly." He took a step forward.

"And then stab me in the back?"

His eyes glanced up and left. "Mmm, noooo." Sciarra looked at her. Really looked, eyes roving up and down her body as he smiled with masculine delight. Then he looked her in the eye. "Last night, I was going to ask you to kiss my bruised jaw, but I thought that might be too much. Too fast. Seeing you again today, I've realized I need to set a different course if I want to reach my target. So, friendly overtures first, then... we'll see."

Fight.

Flight.

Freeze.

Those were the three things humans had evolved to do in disasters, and although she'd been trained to fight, she froze.

There was a disconnect between her established reality and what she was hearing, and Selena couldn't find a way to reconcile the two. She didn't have friends left, aside from Gen. People didn't want her. She wasn't loveable.

All she could do was shake her head and wait for the REM cycle to end.

Sciarra took advantage of her inaction and closed the gap. A flight of green sparks flew off their colliding shields and then he was there, a hand's-width from her body.

Smiling.

She tensed in terror and his smile faltered.

"Selena?" He stepped backward, giving her space to breath.

Her heart raced and she shivered from the ice cold of memories. She shook her head, not quite understanding. Still not processing. She wanted to put her shield on max; she was ready to fight now. But Sciarra wasn't fighting and it didn't make sense.

"Captain Caryll?"

Slowly, her implant cycled through the reset program. Hormone levels dropped, her implant took control of her heart-rate, forcing it to slow, and her diaphragm spasmed, drawing in a deep breath of the dusty warehouse air.

"Can I help you?"

"Help?" Her voice was flat, her shields pulsing as she fought to suppress the battle memories. The smell of burning flesh and the screams of the dying as the infiltration team moved forward...

The sight of Hermione Marshall, broken and bloodied and near blind, but holding the head of Baular sergeant who'd been between her and escape from the interrogation pit aboard the *Rong*...

The empty nights when she reached out for her crew from the darkness in the BOQ and found no answering ping, no reassurance that anyone was alive but her...

Sciarra took a tentative step forward, testing the edge of her shield.

It took all her control not to slice him in half.

Logically, she knew he didn't deserve it, but a part of her could only see him as an enemy. It was the only way to stay alive.

He took another step toward her. "This isn't a battle, captain."

The memories flowed across her field of vision and she knew her eyes were glowing white-blue. She blocked out everything, cutting off the relays from her optic and auditory nerves until there was a blissful cocoon of blackness all around her.

Nothingness surrounded her.

Complete sensory deprivation.

A real, human touch, gentle against the sleeve of her arm jerked her back to reality.

Gasping, she came back, staring at the bright green of Titan Sciarra's panicked eyes.

"Selena?" He sounded wary. Concerned?

She brushed her hand across her face and calculated how long she'd been out. *Seconds.* "That was... unexpected."

He opened his mouth to say something, then shut it.

Information pinged against her shield, images of the Sciarra crew with a counselor of some sort. Feelings of survivor's guilt and fear. Questions unspoken.

For the first time in a long time, she acknowledged a ping, answering with a quick negative. "I had an OIA debriefing. Nothing more."

"I'm sure there are other crews who would be willing to share a therapist."

"Not one I would trust." Her breathing fell into a regular rhythm again. The war was over. Reality was her, standing in a looted warehouse, with Titan Sciarra holding her arm. Alarming, but certainly not a battle.

She brushed his hand off, trying to regain the isolating space that had become so familiar over the years. "Are you going back to Enclave?"

"I think it would be better if I stayed here."

Part of her had expected him to run. Everyone else had.

Sciarra tilted his head, trying to gauge her reaction. "Was it something I said? Is there a way I can avoid hurting you?"

Subtlety was not a known Sciarra trait. "If you could avoid trying to alter my reality, that would be wonderful. I've been crewless long enough that contact like..." The words faltered and she waved a hand. "Like *that*, is suspect."

"If I promise never to lie to you, would you believe me?"

Selena arched an eyebrow. "Are you still a Sciarra?"

Titan shook his head. "No. At the moment I'm a guardian."

That was not the answer she'd expected. Her legs tensed, ready to step back. But she couldn't. Captains didn't retreat. It didn't matter how raw her soul felt, how uncomfortable she was standing this close to someone from fleet; her only option was to push forward.

She lifted her chin in defiance. "Your shield isn't adapted to handle grounder weapons." A final push back, to see how long he would hold on.

He smiled. "You can fix it." It wasn't a question, but a statement of trust.

There was a certainty to his words that soothed the ache. With a quick nod, she brought up the schematics for a shield, preparing to overlay them across Sciarra's existing network.

"Ready?" Lines of light appeared over his arm, weaving a bright net of green and gold. It was a genuine peace offering, like an animal rolling over to expose its vulnerable belly.

If she wanted, she could kill him right now.

Selena watched the pattern for a moment. It was a much deeper connection than she'd planned, one that would involve connecting their implants and sharing information freely. An intimate moment of technosynchrity.

Taking a deep breath, she reached out and placed her hands over Sciarra's. She closed her eyes and tapped her implant, watching the internal display as she built Sciarra a better shield. There was a feather-light touch on her shield that she felt on her mind.

"May I return the favor?" His voice was low, warm, and controlled.

What he wanted was a level of trust she'd never consider showing a Warmonger, or even a friend. But a guardian was owed that level of respect.

With a thought, she made her shields visible, rippling layers of energy that swirled and changed with mercurial grace.

The colors blended, the muted, silvery tones of her shield filtering in between the bright green lines of his.

Sciarra twisted his shield to incorporate the new energy.

It was statistically impossible to create a perfect blend of shields with two people working. It required their coding styles to be perfectly balanced, but there it was.

Something else was there too, memories that weren't all hers. Snapshots of things on Sciarra's mind: her in Gi pants practicing in the Academy gym, Rowena laughing, a hospital room filled with painful sorrow.

Selena opened one eye and glared. "You're projecting." Like finding fresh water in a desert, the sudden rush of joy made her stomach swirl unpleasantly. And she couldn't handle his emotions right now.

Couldn't reconcile the memory of her smile from Sciarra's mind with the memories of war.

She'd died on the *Persephone*. Her body hadn't quit moving, but whatever spark made her uniquely Selena Caryll had been destroyed along with her dreams and her future.

"Sorry." The images vanished with an almost audible click, but emotions remained. Curiosity, contentment, doubt.

There was a safe place here if she wanted it.

"Shield complete." His voice became a physical sensation, his words reinforced by thoughts, emotions, and a quick push against the physical shield.

Outside she heard the police car pull up.

Selena muted the shields, making them once again invisible to the naked eye. "Time to play nice. Guardian."

Sciarra smiled at her. "Yes, captain."

5

TITAN

SELENA CARYLL PULLED HER hands away, shields on high, and he felt only skin. There should have been a tug, the warmth of friction as their shields fought to separate, but there was none. Their shields were identical.

The corner of his lip twitched up in a smile.

He hadn't been the only one projecting. Fear and anxiety were high on Caryll's mind, which was normal all things considered, but he'd also caught a memory of her watching him with a sense of appreciation.

She didn't hate him.

It was a slender reed to build a house of dreams with, but what had Fleet Marshall Tandroi said during the third wave of colonization? 'All great achievements begin with a single thread of hope.'

Caryll froze halfway to the door, almost making him collide with her. She shook her head and he felt rather than saw her run a diagnostic. There was an accusing glare on her face when she turned. "Did you say something?"

Titan shook his head.

"You're certain?"

He nodded.

"It's just... My implant pulled up famous quotes by Fleet Marshall Tandroi and highlighted one. It's a subroutine left over from Academy..."

"I was thinking about one of his quotes," Titan admitted. "I probably had famous quotes set to add to my shield scroll..."

"...and since you just worked on my shield, the information uploaded automatically," she finished. "Let me shut that down real quick." Her eyes turned a brighter blue for a moment but he saw no other change. "Try adding something to your scroll."

He put the symbol for Allied Crew on his scroll.

"Stop setting a bad example. Lying is a crime, you know," Caryll chided.

"Things change," Titan said. "Allegiances change. If you knew my captain, maybe you'd get along with her. Maybe our crews would be allied."

Her laugh was sharp and bitter. "Poisoned honey, Sciarra. The rose's sweet scent conceals the biting thorn."

"What's that mean?"

"It means any good offer from fleet is a trap. Allied crews?" she scoffed. "At what price? My blood? My genes? My tech? My crew?"

"We're not like that—"

"You're fleet," Caryll said, cutting him off. "You're all like that. Crew first, the rest of humanity can breathe vacuum." Her skirt snapped and swirled as she turned angrily away. "You're all the same."

Titan watched her walk to the door in confusion. It was obvious there was a crucial piece of data missing in his analysis of Selena Caryll, but he didn't know where to go looking for it. If she'd accused him of being like the other Warmongers, he would have understood, even if he disagreed. But the same as the Silars? As Carver? As Marshall? Those were her friends and allies.

Unless… they weren't.

He watched Caryll greeting the arriving police officers. Her shoulders lost some of the tension they'd been holding, and she smiled at the officers as if welcoming familiar faces. She shook their hands in the grounder style. And the dark cloud of fury didn't return until she turned to face him.

:Is everything all right?: he asked over a tight beam.

Across the dark warehouse, Caryll stared at him. Motes of dust danced in a lancing sunbeam and the silence seemed to stretch to the ends of the universe.

:Caryll?:

She turned to a dark-skinned man with a bright magenta streak in his coarse, black hair. :Everything is fine.: A smile flashed across her face, dangerous as a shark's fin cutting through the waves. "Detective Jamar Hastings," she said as she pushed the dark-skinned man forward, "this is Guardian Titan Sciarra."

Hastings held out his hand.

For a brief second Titan considered refusing the gesture of equality, but he caught himself and reached out to shake the man's hand.

No shield. No augmentation. No protection.

In the fleet, Hastings would be no more than a low-level enlisted sailor.

"Here I thought everyone in fleet was as pale as you, Lena." Hastings smiled and nudged Caryll's shoulder.

Titan's smile grew tight.

:Your shield just went to battle mode,: Caryll said.

:That's not the correct diminutive of your name.:

:I get to decide what I take as an insult.:

:I'm the guardian here.:

:And I'm the captain.: Cold, blue eyes met his. :Behave.:

:Yes, ma'am.:

Hastings coughed. "I feel I'm missing something."

"Only a silent debate over protocol for this particular situation," Caryll lied. "I think I'll work with the crime scene techs and leave you two to argue with the Jhandarmi officers over who gets to canvas the neighborhood for information."

"I hate knocking on doors asking for info," Hastings complained.

Caryll shrugged. "Not my jurisdiction, I'm afraid. My hands are tied."

Hastings sighed as Caryll walked away, pulled out an electronic tablet, and turned to Titan with an apologetic half-smile. "Guardian, my apologies, I suppose we are more informal than you're used to."

The scent of Caryll's soap was still clinging to him. Minutes ago he'd been a thought away from public indecency. He cleared his throat. "I can manage with informal."

"Wonderful." Hastings smiled. "Perhaps you could tell me how the Starguard would normally conduct this type of investigation and I can find where our procedures match."

Titan raised an eyebrow as his implant scanned for the relevant data.

Hastings took a step back, wary.

"Were my eyes glowing?" Titan guessed.

"Yes, is that normal?"

"Only for an augmented officer accessing information on their implant." He lifted his left arm to signal where his was, buried in the muscles between his radius and ulna. "As for the procedure for theft, we don't have one. The last theft on record was over seven-hundred years ago."

"A crime-free society?" Hastings chuckled as he shook his head. "Must be nice."

"Not crime free, but ships are easy to patrol. Everyone is in charge of something, there's constant surveillance." Memories of the fleet before Landing turned his mouth sour.

:Sciarra?: Caryll sent feelings of concern and worry.

He responded with a placating thought as he grimaced. "The crimes that are committed in full view of everyone are often more vile than theft, because you've convinced everyone that an atrocity is acceptable."

Hastings stared at him.

Realizing he was probably scaring the grounder more than necessary, Titan moved on. "Crime is very limited in the fleet. A senior officer knows where everyone in their crew is at any given moment, either by pinging their implant or their call sign."

"Call sign?"

Titan touched his shoulder. "A, um, insignia almost?"

:What is the grounder equivalent of call sign?: he asked Caryll.

:Communications patch.:

"A communications device worn on the shoulder. It keeps the children out of restricted areas, opens doors, allows you to find anyone on your ship."

"That makes finding out if one of your people raided the warehouse easy," Hastings said.

"If I know the time of the attack, I can check the shield log," Titan said. "Everyone leaving Enclave is supposed to register with the Starguard and it would be posted on the log." He altered his shield enough so his voice carried to Caryll.

Hastings drew his head back quickly and muttered a word under his breath that Titan was fairly certain Carver had said was not to be used in public.

"Problems?"

"There." Hastings nodded to the doorway where a bullish man with reddened skin and a bald head was climbing out of a black car. "Tyrling. This is not good."

It was the same man who'd called Carver earlier in the day. "Why is he bad?"

"He's the Jhandarmi regional director," Hastings said as Caryll moved to intercept Tyrling. "If he's shown up, this isn't a routine case." The police officer covered his mouth and muttered another curse.

Caryll caught Director Tyrling and steered him away from the crime-scene techs.

"Detective Hastings." Tyrling nodded as he approached.

Hastings gave a tight-lipped nod in return. "Director."

Tyrling studied Titan. "And you are?"

"Guardian Sciarra, sir. You spoke with my commander this morning."

Tyrling glanced at Caryll before nodding. "Of course."

"To what do we owe the honor of your arrival, director?" Hastings asked, every sign indicating he wanted the Jhandarmi officer gone as soon as humanly possible.

:What am I missing?: Titan asked Caryll.

Her face remained perfectly blank. :Politics. We invited the Tarrin police, having the director of the Jhandarmi arrive too is...

unexpected.: There were other thoughts there, a typhoon of emotions and memories, but all of them too well shielded for Titan to catch.

"The timing of the crime caught my attention," Tyrling said as he looked around. "There's, what, two dozen shelves? How full was the warehouse?"

"There were six-hundred, seventy-three boxes of supplies in twenty-nine large containers," Titan said with a frown. "Why?"

Tyrling pursed his lips. "The alarm went off less than thirty minutes ago and the place is empty."

A tight beam of information came from Caryll, approximate weight of the boxes, average loading times. Titan lifted a shoulder in a casual shrug. "With the right people you could clear this place in under six minutes."

"An Starsider could," Caryll said. "A grounder couldn't."

Hastings raised his eyebrows. "And a person from Enclave would leave a trace in your shield, wouldn't they?"

Caryll's mouth pinched into a frown. "There are a few ways around it. And the stolen goods wouldn't need to go back to Enclave—"

"But it wouldn't make sense to move it in the city either," Titan said. "And there'd be a trace smell, at least of the explosives. The air smells fresh, not burnt."

"That's a problem," Hastings said. "If we don't have a timeline, you can't check your logs, can you?"

The Jhandarmi director nodded as if he'd been expecting this news. "There was a similar case two months ago in Wellden. A warehouse was robbed overnight of a large shipment of weapons headed for the militia armory. The alarm went off the following morning, tampered with and preset. Neither the Wellden police nor the Jhandarmi have had any luck tracking down the culprits."

"It's a jump from weapons to medicine," Caryll said. "Two different resale markets. Very different set of laws."

"Perhaps the intention isn't resale," the Jhandarmi director mused. "With the current population crisis in some of the city-states, it's not hard to imagine one of the vocal separatist groups looking to stockpile supplies for a new colony on the second continent. Or for a war."

Titan shook his head. "Our medicine was for pregnant women and the elderly. A few vitamins for the children. None of it would be useful in war."

"It would be useful in a siege," Hastings said.

The warehouse fell silent for a moment.

Hastings shrugged. "If someone want to de-seat a ruling authority, having medicines of any kind could win people over."

"Or it could be as simple as a ransom demand," Caryll said. "This isn't helping. We need the security footage from the street and we need to talk to the guards. For a heist like this, the thieves had to know how much there was to steal and what equipment they'd need to lift it. These boxes aren't light or small."

"Where were they ordered from?" Tyrling asked.

"The shipment came into port in Clyde River and came by tram."

"The Jhandarmi will talk with the dock workers and the tram operators, since neither belong to a city-state's jurisdiction. Detective, I trust you'll be able to secure the security feeds?"

Hastings nodded. "I have people collecting the independent feeds from shop owners now, along with witness statements."

"That leaves the guards," Caryll said, and her eyes glowed a soft white-blue. "Martin Larangi has already arrived at the police station voluntarily. That leaves Eton Prow." She frowned. "I don't have an address on record for him."

Hastings pulled out his tablet and began a search at the same time Titan checked his implant.

"Nothing on record," Hastings said. "His last known address was condemned last month. He's listed as migrant." He grimaced apologetically. "Technically, it isn't illegal. He has another six weeks to register a home of address."

"Guardian records only have the old address," Titan reported. "He didn't inform anyone in fleet that he was moving."

"I'll put the word out," Tyrling said. "The Jhandarmi might be able to uncover something."

Caryll shook her head. "Prow favors the art district."

Titan turned to her. "How would you know that?"

"I've talked to him before. He took this job so he could spend more time working on his glasswork. He was, at least in his own opinion, becoming very talented. And he was given a standard fleet com, an old JK-37."

He had to check his implant to find something similar. "That's an antique."

More than an antique—the last working one in the Sciarra holds had fallen into disrepair before the fleet had separated from the colonists. "It worked for him?"

"Once we modified it with some current grounder tech, yes." Caryll looked to Tyrling. "I might be able to trace that, but not from here. There's too many tech baffles downtown. I'll actually need to walk the grid."

"Fine," Tyrling said.

"Unacceptable." Titan shook his head. "The fleet is on lockdown. We can modify something the police have to search for whatever element Caryll thinks is out there."

"Um..." Hastings looked confused. "What would we use? How would we do this?"

Caryll pinged him with the sign for annoyance. "They don't have the tech, Sciarra."

"We can provide Caryll with a bodyguard," Hastings said.

"Or the Jhandarmi can," Tryling said.

"Or," Caryll said, "you boys can stop making this an ego contest and remember that I'm fully capable of walking down a city street all on my lonesome."

:There's been a threat against fleet,: Titan told her. :You shouldn't be alone.:

:I don't look fleet,: she replied as she smiled at Tyrling. "Sir, detective, I'll contact you as soon as I find Prow."

"We," Titan corrected. He nodded to the two men. "A pleasure to meet you both." A quick teleport and he was standing outside the door, waiting for Caryll. :You shouldn't have done that. It makes the fleet look weak. Divided.:

She did something then that cut him off. No ping. No information streaming. Her shields almost vanished.

Titan frowned, trying to figure out what had happened.

Caryll kept going, weaving past the forensic team with her skirt snapping in the early spring wind.

He fell in behind her and sent her a questioning ping. :Shields?:

"My shield is there, but the art district has a lot of very sensitive pieces of tech meant to detect anyone trying to take illegal photos or make recordings of musicians. A shield on full guard will set it off," she explained. "And I didn't divide the fleet any more than it was already fractured. I'm doing my job."

"Technically, you're doing my job."

"OIA handbook section one-thirty-nine, subsection G." Caryll led him across the street and into a park where a screen of trees hid the view of the warehouses.

The relevant data hit his implant hard. "The OIA land officer shall handle the hiring and firing of civilian employees? I'm not sure that applies."

"It does." Caryll stopped in the shade of a large tree out of sight of the police and Jhandarmi. "Your shield is still too loud. Give me your hand."

Titan held his hand out so they almost touched. His shield shimmered and even with the Guardian Veil it seemed to vanish, though he knew it was still there. "That's a nice trick."

"Don't try to replicate it, you might explode. And don't use the glowing eyes outside of here. The grounders will notice." Her words were tense, agitated, her body language dismissive.

Somewhere, he felt he'd missed a segue. They'd been getting along amiably before the police arrived. Caryll had been almost flirtatious, for Caryll. But now, he was apparently an inconvenience.

He let his patience slip a little. "I'm going to pretend you said that because you care enough not to want me hurt, and not just because you don't want to clean up the mess."

Titan let her enjoy the silence while he sent an update to Carver. "The guardians in Enclave will start making inquiries with the people who have done pick-ups before. And Carver wants to debrief us, the sooner the better. When can I tell him to expect us back?"

Caryll looked unsure for a moment, then shrugged. "Two hours, maybe three?"

"I'll tell him we have a romantic luncheon planned." Titan winked at her, just to see what her reaction would be.

It was the same startled silence as before.

He sent her a memory of laughter and the bright blue-green that was the Academy color-code for good fun.

There was the tiniest crinkle at the edge of her eyes. A hint of a smile as she pursed her lips that didn't reach her eyes. "What would your crew say if they could see you now, Sciarra?" Caryll shook her head as if disappointed, but her smile was genuine.

"That I'm being a perfect gentleman."

"That has so many meanings in fleet."

It did, and for a moment he allowed the thought of Caryll naked under him. Or on top, sunlight spilling over her pale skin as her head rolled back in pleasure…

"Titan Sciarra!" Caryll punched his shoulder, not his face, which was an improvement.

But the bright pink blush on her cheeks was not putting his libido in check.

"I'm sorry." He was, sincerely sorry… at least that she'd caught the spillover of his thoughts.

There was a moment where they were too close; her emotions grazed his mind, touching and leaping off again, leaving cascades of thought in their wake. She'd been stressed in warehouse with so many people around, worried about something going wrong, worried about safety.

"Caryll, you know I wouldn't let anyone hurt you."

She stopped walking and stared at him in confusion.

"You were… worried? At the warehouse." He shook his head as he realized he hadn't understood her correctly. "You weren't worried?"

"Not about myself, no."

None of the thoughts he'd caught from her had expressed concern for the grounders. Which left only him. "You were worried about me?"

Her eyes widened in exasperation. "A little. You're a high-profile target, easily recognizable, and I don't know what would happen if you were injured in Tarrin. I can't even imagine what your crew would say if they saw us keeping company. There are too many variables and too many ways this ends badly."

"Let me worry about my crew's gossip." He took a few long strides to catch up to her. "For now I'll keep you company, keep my shields up, and make sure your report to Carver won't include a corpse. Okay? Let me do the worrying. It's my job. I'm charged with finding ways to make life better for everyone in the fleet. Improve morale."

Caryll sighed and he could feel her relax just a little. Her tired look became sardonic. "Morale? Does imagining me naked help with that?"

Titan titled his head to the side in an apologetic shrug. "It improved my morale."

"While crossing the border of decency. What if it made me uncomfortable?"

"Then I'd apologize profusely and scrub those images from my implant's data bank. But..." He leaned down to whisper in her ear, "it didn't make you uncomfortable."

She met his gaze, vivid atmosphere-blue eyes filled with a myriad of emotions. "Anything between us would lead to a fallout of cataclysmic proportions. Your crew would have a fit."

"I'm not worried about my crew. Only you." He felt her shields tighten. "Because I'm your guardian today, and my job is to take care of you."

"Nice recovery, Sciarra." She tossed her hair over her shoulder and continued toward downtown Tarrin.

He fell in step. "Captain, how much trouble am I in and how much groveling do I need to do to get back in your good graces?"

"None," she said with another cryptic smile. "You were never in my good graces so you, logically, can never fall out."

"And you'll forgive the Sciarras as soon as the seas turn red?"

She shrugged, her shields sharing nothing with him. "What's to forgive? We've been at odds since the Empire was still around, and on the opposite sides of two wars. At this point, the matter is settled. We don't see eye to eye."

"Our crews didn't," Titan corrected. "You and I might." It was more of an afterthought, a suggestion to himself rather than an attempt at flirtation.

"As individuals." She said it with the tiniest frown, as if she wasn't sure what she thought of removing them from the safe definitions or crew stereotypes.

Titan was certain how he felt: like he was in free fall. There was a sense of freedom being out of uniform, away from his crew and cohort, alone with Selena Caryll. Or as alone as anyone could get in a city.

If there wasn't a robbery to deal with, he'd be almost giddy. Although, without the robbery, he wouldn't have had this chance. He'd have to thank the thieves when he found them.

He'd told Rowena he felt like he was choking to death in Enclave, and he was. This was the cure. Being away from everything for just a moment. Shrugging off history...

Sunlight shot through the branches again, filtering through Caryll's skirt.

... taking risks.

He looked away because it was his job to scan for danger, not because he didn't enjoy the view. There were a fair number of people walking under the trees and eating lunch at the benches that lined the divide between the warehouse district and the art district.

Gazes followed them, but they weren't threats, they were looks of admiration.

"Do you have an actual plan for finding Prow, or are you just hoping to catch him out picnicking?" Titan asked.

"The com has telekyen and several other rare minerals. We walk. We scan. We hope we get lucky. Unless you think Kafftan is going to run out into the street in front of us, which seems unlikely."

"The thief? What are our chances of finding him?"

Caryll's face settled into a sour frown as she passed him the relevant information. "Low."

He chuckled as he adjusted his shields to passively scan for telekyen, a useless practice in Enclave where everything had it, but not here.

The brightly-colored shops had nothing made from the one substance the fleet couldn't live without. It was a little mind-altering to realize that no one out here but Caryll and himself could manipulate an object with a thought, or teleport, or shield, or share a thought.

Caryll's focus shifted suddenly to something across road. Grabbing his hand, she pulled him across the cobblestone street to a small art gallery that seemed to specialize in paintings of fountains. "I've been meaning to see this showing."

Titan looked at six rows of nearly identical paintings of a three-tiered fountain surrounded by roses in shades of pink.

"It's supposed to be a metaphor for women." She stopped in front of one and tilted her head to the side. "Although, the red roses look a bit unhealthy if these all represent vaginas."

His eyebrows went up. "Why did you say that? All I saw was a fountain."

"But"—she smiled wickedly—"if you look long enough, a familiar, yonic shape forms. Surrounded by rosy buds, gushing forth. The fountain has a nice domed shape, almost like a…"

"Oh. Don't. No. Gushing?"

"Would you prefer moist, or pulsing?" She was laughing at his discomfort.

Titan shook his head. "You're a horrible person." But she was smiling now. Her emotions were melting into her shield again, and it felt wonderful.

"You said you wanted to make me happy." A pink blush tinted her cheeks as she realized she was emoting again. "Who else was I going to share this with? Genevieve is the only one who would dare come downtown with me and if she knew what this was supposed to represent, she'd buy every canvas and plaster the walls with them."

A brief vision of Starguard offices covered with vaginal metaphors made him shake his head. "I accept you not buying Silar one of these as a peace offering."

She lifted a price tag casually. "You know, at these prices, I might want to shock the Starguard more than I want to have peace with you."

He looked over her shoulder. It was more than he wanted to pay for anything, but Caryll probably had crew funds invested in more ventures than his salary allowed. Although a quick check of his implant didn't show an official record. If she was living off only the OIA salary, she couldn't afford a single rose bud, let alone the whole garden.

It was another fact to file away. Caryll was an intriguing puzzle of a person. She'd always seemed comfortable in her own skin. Uninhibited. It was one of the first things he'd ever noticed about her.

The first time he'd seen her in the Academy he'd been struck by the dichotomy she presented, moonlight-blonde hair against the black of her martial arts uniform. She'd always looked so gentle, and yet her skills had marked her as one of the most dangerous people in their cohort.

And now, dressed to blend with the groundsiders, looking sweet and flirtatious, the dichotomy was still there, because in her eyes he saw hardness and deception.

His files on Selena Caryll defined her as a quiet individual with a gift for shield coding and an outstanding shooting record in the Academy. She was supposed to be bland, another face in the fleet, but Titan was beginning to suspect Caryll was hiding more secrets than the Starguard intelligence officers had guessed.

Titan wanted to uncover them all.

Without warning, his implant override engaged, bringing up tracking data. Someone carrying small amounts of telekyen was moving down the road one block over.

"That looks promising," Caryll said. "Ready to go meet Prow?"

"Lead on, captain." He pulled the Guardian Veil on, letting the world slow around him as he prepared for battle. The background colors became muted except for one bright spot, the glow of Selena Caryll in battle mode, steady and bright as the moon.

For the first time in years everything felt right.

6

SELENA

THE ART DISTRICT WAS a colorful beehive of hexagonal plazas, with statuary of various kinds on the display in the center. Once upon a time there was probably a theme behind the displayed art and the shops. But whatever the original plan had been, the art district was now a microcosm of civilization, an eclectic mix of legal businesses, illegal enterprises, food shops, and housing that moved against the background of a musician playing a haunting melody on a dulcimer.

The spring wind knocked pale pink blossoms to the ground and Sciarra sent her a flash image of her framed by the falling petals.

Selena shot him a quelling glare, but stored the image in her implant. It had been a long time since she'd felt beautiful, and even longer since someone she trusted told her she was. Sciarra undoubtedly wanted something—the fleet economy was built on barter—but for the moment she didn't let it bother her. Their quarry was up ahead, winding through the narrower streets lined with makeshift apartments, and her way was clear.

Prow's signal vanished.

"What happened?" Sciarra asked.

"He probably crossed into the boundary of another tech baffle. They're woven throughout the area so no one can teleport in and out with ease. It was the one thing the Tarrins insisted we do before Landing."

Sciarra followed her out of a plaza with the statue of a winged lizard and into an alley. "Were they that concerned we'd steal something?"

"Invade their homes, rob their banks, desecrate their holy places. The grounders have a long history of seeing the fleet as savages. In most of their literature, we're slavers and pirates."

"That's awful."

"It's why Tarrin let us land. Their city was built by colonists who mutinied en route and landed without permission. It's a point of pride for them." She walked slowly, dragging her hand across the daub and stone walls of the older buildings. Beneath the surface, she could feel the metal bones of a ship that had been stripped for parts to build this place.

By bouncing a signal through the building, she could get an impression of how many people were moving inside. Not many right now. It was midday and even the most reclusive introvert in Tarrin would venture out to find a quick meal from a street vendor. Half the apartments didn't have running water, let alone electricity to preserve food.

Selena's scan caught the presence of telekyen. She looked over at Sciarra. "Do you read that? Upper southwest corner?"

Sciarra closed his eyes. "One level from the top, a minute amount of telekyen. Small enough to be a comm or a weapon."

"Do we want to call him, or just drop in?" There wasn't movement in the apartment that she could sense, but there was a heat signature.

"I prefer the element of surprise." Sciarra stepped in front of her, opening the door and heading for the stairs.

Selena was about to object, but that would lead to an argument. Trained guardian versus trained undercover Jhandarmi. Life would be so much easier if she knew the fleet would accept the joint operation. Or even entertain the slim possibility of a joint operation.

The inner walls of Prow's building were constructed of weathered Cyprus wood, aged but still smelling faintly of the brackish waters found east and west of Tarrin. Other smells were there too: sweat, garlic, the sharp scent of cheap cleaning products.

"If this were a ship, I'd give them a new environmental system," Selena muttered. "I wouldn't even trade for it, just gift it."

"If you have one lying around, I know a ship that could use one," Sciarra said as he walked up the warped and creaking stairs.

"I don't have one in port, but two of my ships have undamaged environmental systems in orbit. I could teleport up and get one if I need it." Her poor *Pomona* and *Anhur* wouldn't be able to handle the stress of flying through Malik V's dense atmosphere, but the ships were there, still hers, even if they were only good for salvage.

Sciarra's shield bumped against hers, fusing into it again. His emotions and surface thoughts became like a second line of her own thoughts. He was worried about her, and feeling more protective than he had a right to. Even as a guardian.

Gently, she pushed his thoughts away, mentally imagining them like translucent bubbles that she could blow into the wind.

"I'm fine."

"You already had one flashback today."

"I was finding my balance," she grumbled, refusing to think of where her misstep had led. She'd fallen into Sciarra, literally, and it was as confusing as it was revelatory. She'd forgotten how wonderful it felt to be cared about, to have the constant mental touch of a crew member.

Borrowed crew member.

Warmonger, she told herself sternly, trying to push Sciarra back under his assigned label. Sciarras and Carylls weren't meant to be allies.

She bumped into him, not realizing he'd stopped.

His green eyes were bright, even in the shadows of the poorly lit hallway. "If Prow turns violent—"

"I can handle myself," Selena promised. "I don't like killing, and I hope I never have to kill. I know it changes people. But, if it comes to that, I can. Shields are prepped, and I think I could punch a hole in the baffle if we need to teleport. Hopefully, Prow will remember we represent his employers and remember how much he likes the generous salary we offer him."

"That would be nice," Sciarra said. "But if he doesn't, your top priority is teleporting back to Enclave."

That wasn't going to happen, but she buried that thought deep. Tyrling's informants were very good at their jobs. If they said that one of the guardians was being targeted, she was willing to believe it.

Sciarra held out his hand, scanning the building, and nodded to the second door on the right. The weathered green paint was peeling and if there had been a number before, it was gone now.

Selena leaned past Sciarra and knocked.

The door fell open with a squeak.

"No lock?" Sciarra touched the doorframe, inspecting it. "It's not damaged."

"I thought I picked up a body when I scanned earlier, but maybe he's out? Or he forgot to lock it before he fell asleep?" Crime in the art district was usually limited to theft from the shops or an occasional pickpocket; no one in these buildings had anything worth stealing.

With a sigh, she knocked on the open door. "Prow?" she called into the dark room. "It's Selena. I've brought a friend. I wanted to check on you. Prow?"

There was silence ahead.

She stepped into the apartment, little more than a square with thin, lacquered walls subdividing the small space even further. Sunlight peeked through a dirty window covered by a heavy, black curtain, and fell out around the edges. "The com is here. Look in the back room."

Sciarra nodded and turned left.

The smell of the apartment was off. A sour, bilious smell that turned her stomach. She pulled the curtain open and looked at the worn furnishings in the light: an oblong cloth sack overstuffed and only vaguely couch-like, a turned-over metal crate for a table.

"Captain," Sciarra's voice from the back room was tense, and his shield was blocking his emotions.

"What's wrong?" :Are you all right?: she asked on a tight beam.

:You need to stay out there.:

She teleported across the apartment to stand behind Sciarra.

Prow lay on the floor, a seeping pool of blood under his head, a shocked expression on his haggard face.

Her breath caught in unexpected terror.

Sciarra stepped in front of her and flooded her with a sense of peace, his versions of happy memories bombarding her. Faces, snippets of music, pictures of roses…

"Please stop." She gave him a mental shove. "Step out while I scan the body."

"Why? He's very obviously dead."

A pale blue light fell from her fingertips. "For explosives. Someone must have sanitized the reports you saw."

She didn't want to.

The memory of her mother's lifeless body returned. Her fighter had been attacked and the Baulars agreed to return the prisoners in life pods if the Carylls agreed to pull back. Selena wasn't sure if her mother had been alive when her fighter was captured, but the Baulars put her in the life pod dead, and booby trapped.

Sciarra's hand wrapped around her forearm. "Stop."

"I need to do a secondary scan."

"You need to stop and ground yourself." He stepped between her and the body again. "Look at me. You're shaking. Your heart is racing."

It was. The sense of panic never seemed to go away, no matter what she did to distance herself from the war.

Sciarra stepped closer, trying to physically block out the light and sounds of the building. "Look at me. Listen to me. Name five things you see right now."

"Green eyes. Black hair. White shirt. Yellow wall." She looked up. "Yellow-ish ceiling? That's a terrible color."

Sciarra ran a soothing hand over her back. "There. Do you feel more in the here-and-now now?"

His hand was warm and heavy against her body, dangerously intimate. "Yes."

But another thought invaded. :Stay here. I need to find the comm.:

Her scans put it somewhere in the kitchen area, although calling it a kitchen was generous. The room that shared a half wall with the entry had a shallow sink, a shelf, a small washing unit for clothes, and drawers. She checked them all until she found the black, palm-sized com unit issued to Prow.

Laying the com unit on the ground, she made a fist. She focused and connected to the com unit, then opened her hand wide.

The pieces of the com unit flew apart, every individual piece hanging in the air as if caught in time. One piece didn't belong. Selena plucked it from the air and shielded it, then let the com until fall back together.

"Impressive control," Sciarra said. "What did you find?"

"A listening device." Selena held about the round, red piece for him to view. "It's not a style I recognize, but the Jhandarmi might. Prow is freshly dead. I scanned him walking not ten minutes ago."

Sciarra frowned. "I scanned telekyen, and enough to be a com unit, but we don't know that was Prow."

"Who else would it be?"

"I don't know, but Prow is already cooling. I think he's been dead more than ten minutes, and we didn't pass anyone on the stairs coming in."

She frowned. "We need to call Hastings. Poor man. I'm going to need to buy him flowers to apologize for all the extra work the fleet is asking him to do."

"Maybe you could buy him some roses." Sciarra winked.

Despite the stress, she giggled. "I don't think he'd appreciate that much."

"There's no accounting for taste," Sciarra said with mock condescension. "Give him a call, I'll start looking over the body." He was just a little closer than he needed to be, close enough that when he reached out to touch her cheek, she didn't have time to pull away. "Do I need to take you back to Enclave first? I can call Lieutenant Silar and have her meet us at the OIA building if you need someone. Two triggering events in a day isn't healthy."

She let his hand linger on her for a moment longer before touching his wrist and pulling him away. "I'll be fine. This is an unusual series of events on an emotional anniversary. But I want to be here. I knew Prow. I want to help catch his killer. If I leave now... If I leave now then I really am the coward everyone thinks I am."

"It isn't cowardice to let other competent people do the job when you feel emotionally compromised. It isn't dereliction of duty to take care of your mental health." He reinforced his words with a sense of acceptance, a silent way of saying he would support her either way.

It was unprofessional to let someone support her this much, but she allowed the connection between their shields and their thoughts to grow.

:It isn't unprofessional,: Sciarra said. :A guardian is meant to protect a captain when they're away from their crew. This is exactly what I'm meant to do. And it's what friends do.:

Regret twisted like a knife. *Friend.* What a bloody, dishonest word. She closed her eyes, hiding her pain from Sciarra. Hiding the hurt of a thousand betrayals and the terrible regrets she'd built her life on.

Turning him away was the easy way out. It was what she'd done with everyone, a stalling tactic that gave her room to heal. Or for wounds to fester.

She gave his wrist a squeeze and let go. "Thank you, guardian."

"You're welcome, captain."

She couldn't stand outside both the fleet and the grounders forever, but reentry was going to suck.

7

ROWENA

ROWENA SLUMPED IN THE back corner seat of Cargo Blue with a heavy shield turning the rest of the bar into blue shadows and faint music. All it took was a day and a lockdown to turn a throbbing mess into a quiet chapel of despair and broken dreams.

Titan pushed a plate of fajitas in her direction. "Eat something. You look like you haven't taken a break all day.

"Look who's talking." She hadn't stopped since 0400, when she'd been called to fix a seal on the environmental system of the Tenshi crew's *Wángzuò*. Things had gotten worse from there. It was 2200 and she was nursing her first glass of water for the day like it was her last. And Titan looked worse.

He sat across from her, slouched over, arms folded on the table and his chin on top. Half his meal was eaten and the rest was slowly congealing.

"What happened to you?"

"First we have the Jhandarmi with their psych campaign telling us someone is hunting a guardian." He rolled his eyes. "Then the warehouse was cleared out. I wound up stuck between a local detective and a Jhandarmi regional director, and then our main suspect was found freshly murdered." With a heavy sigh, he closed his eyes. "Murder should be outlawed just for the paperwork it causes."

She dipped a chip in the accompanying sauce and eyed it dubiously. The chef was trying to cook grounder-style food, but she wasn't sure they'd picked the right combination. Orange sauce and corn chips sounded like a bad combination. "Could have been worse."

"Not by much."

"I had a broken environmental system, fleetlings to train, and one of the engineers on the *Aryton* had a nervous breakdown. Top that."

"Grounders. More grounders. Dead grounders. And two nervous breakdowns from the fleet officer with me. Both panic attacks triggered, at least in part, by me being there." He sat up with a scowl. "Am I that bad?"

"Bad?" Rowena scowled back at him. "At what?"

He crossed his arms. "I've made enemies before. But I've never run into a situation where I couldn't get someone to like me. She didn't even want to be near me."

Normally she'd applaud rattling someone's cage, but Titan looked sincerely worried. Reluctantly, she opened her accumulated files on Selena No-Shot Caryll. It was a slight misnomer. Caryll shot at people, but she never killed anyone—just destroyed ships with reckless abandon. Rowena's files on her, beyond the damage done, were sparse.

She closed her mental file and sighed. "She has no crew. She has no lovers. Of course she freaked out. It wasn't you. She pulls away from everyone."

"I'm not a threat to her."

"Everyone's a threat to Caryll," Rowena said. "Stars above, even the Silars are pushing for her to join their crew. They've been trying to get her to give up her rank and name for over a year now. An isolated fleet officer with their back against the wall isn't someone you approach without caution. Any one of us might attack in that situation."

Titan frowned and looked away. "She panicked."

"Really?" Rowena asked skeptically. "Because we're talking about someone I've been face-to-face with during a hull breach and she didn't bat an eye. We were both shielding and teleporting wounded out, but if I'd made a move, she probably would have had her first kill. I can't picture her panicking."

"I triggered a flashback. So did finding the body. Why can't I fix this?" A jumble of images came with the words. Titan was in a near panic himself, just because Caryll had been moody.

She laughed at him. "You can't fix anything. It's not your problem."

He shook his head in frustration. "I'm Titan Sciarra. I'm supposed to be one of the most influential people in Enclave and I can't even make an OIA officer believe my offer of friendship is real. What's that say about me?"

"That they have poor taste in friends." She pushed the half-eaten meal away.

Titan locked down his shield and looked away.

She nudged his shield and he withdrew even further. "Seriously? Why do you even care what Caryll thinks about you? Why would you—" She stopped herself. Her fists curled under the table. "Titan," she said, warning him. It wasn't easy to beat sense into a Sciarra, but she was willing to try. "You can't get involved with her. Not emotionally."

"Rule 6."

"When at all possible officers should attempt to make allies of all crews in the fleet to promote harmony of thought and unity of action?" She raised an eyebrow. "You're talking about allying with the Carylls? The Sciarra crew?"

He leaned across the table. "What would happen if the fleet stopped thinking about allied or unallied? If we stopped being Warmonger versus Carver's Allies?"

She mimicked his body language. "Complete. And. Utter. Chaos."

"The only things that don't change are dead," Titan said. "The fleet is stagnant. We're dying. This could be our way out."

Rowena stood up. "Go get some sleep, Ty. You've lost your mind. There are some choices we can't come back from. Lines were crossed, and there's no way to repair them. Even if by some miracle we erased the grudges, we don't have enough ships to support everyone. We don't have the orun to fly the ships. The fleet's been dead for years. The next step is all of us leaving Enclave and becoming grounders. That's it. That's the only option, other than mass suicide."

"I refuse to believe that."

She spread her hands in surrender. "Believe what you want. The writing's on the hull. If Caryll is half as smart as everyone thinks she is, she's already found a wealthy grounder to cuddle up to."

Titan looked shocked. "You wouldn't do that."

As if she and Caryll had anything in common. "I don't cuddle," Rowena said, tossing a credit on the table for her meal.

Titan looked up. "Are you leaving me alone to wallow?"

"I am leaving because I have to be awake in six hours, and you need time to come to your senses."

He muttered something under his breath.

"What was that?"

Titan shook his head. "Would you back me? If I tried to make us a third choice, would you back me?"

"Of course. Always. For anything. Even the bad ideas."

He grinned wickedly, pure Sciarra daring. "Even if I pursue Selena Caryll?"

"Watching you stumble into disaster is one of my favorite activities. Right up there with plotting ways to kill Silars and erase Hoshi from existence. You want to chase her, I'll be right here laughing at you. But it'll be with love."

"What happens when I bring her home?"

A few of her spare brain cells fused in panic at the thought. She didn't have a contingency plan for that. Yet. It was something to add to her to-do list for the morning. "I guess I'd make my peace, if she did. I'm sure there are worse things. The heat death of the universe. The sun going nova."

"I could bring home a Silar," Titan said perfectly deadpan.

She shuddered and gagged. "See? We already found a worse option for you."

Their eyes met and they both laughed.

"Can I walk you home?" Titan asked as he stood up.

"I can get there on my own."

"Yeah, but I know Hollis Silar has the night off and might wind up here. And I was not joking about the paperwork for a homicide being awful."

She tilted her head in a shrug. "I could make it look like an accident."

"How about we let him live. Just one more day?"

Rowena rolled her eyes, dropped the shield, and walked out of Cargo Blue with Titan. Even their jokes about killing the Silars were getting stale. Not that she hated them any less, but it was no longer a fiery rage, but a stony hate. A well-worn path of animosity. A hatred as familiar as the frayed blanket on her bunk and equally comforting.

Gravel skittered in front of them as Titan kicked at the rocks. "What would it take to rebuild the fleet? To get rid of all the hate?"

"Mass amnesia?" she said, only half joking. "We did things..." She let the weight of the memories filter in. Overhead, one of the dead ships sparkled in the moonlight. "Even under orders, I knew some of those things were wrong. But, in the moment, under orders, with everyone watching?" She shook her head as the fear and fury drained from her again. "If I can barely stomach what I did, how can I expect anyone to forgive me?"

"Carver and his side aren't innocents."

"But they weren't the aggressors. We were." Her gaze fell to Titan's left arm where the long sleeves covered the damage he'd taken in their first, foolish attack. "For a lot of us—for me— hating them is the only thing that justifies what happened. As long as I can see them as villains, I don't hate myself so much for what I did. You're lucky you don't have to carry that weight."

A breeze off the ocean brought the smell of brine.

They followed it, winding their way between the forest of landing gear, and the scent of ozone and rust.

Titan stopped at the edge of the Lee shield and looked up at the stars.

Up above, Rowena could identify three easily-visible wrecks, and beyond that a stretch of stars that had once been the Lee homeworld. "See how far we have fallen, the forgotten generation, the children of distant stars," she quoted the old poem.

"See how far we will travel, the rising generation, the ancestors of a million tomorrows," Titan said.

"That's not in the original poem."

"I don't care. It's time to write a new line, reclaim the stars, create a new future for ourselves. I'm going to. Tomorrow, I'm going to broker peace between the Sciarras and Carylls."

Rowena smiled sadly. "What would you do for an encore?"

"I have no idea. But I'll think of something." He leaned over and bumped his forehead against hers, something he'd learned from Mal as a kid. "Good night."

"Night." She watched him walk into the darkness before she teleported to the ramp for the *Danielle Nicole*. There was no night watch posted; Hoshi said the shield would hold.

Hoshi didn't know what a real attack looked like.

Until the Landing, Hoshi had been commander of the *Alessandra Giliani*, a cargo vessel that sat docked in the *Danielle Nicole's* smallest hold. His only job had been keeping critical components out of the hands of their enemies, something he'd done by selling to minor neutral crews in exchange for luxury items.

In a fair universe, Hoshi would have been spaced years ago. Instead, Rowena was sneaking into her ship trying to avoid questions about why she was coming in so close to curfew.

She ran a hand along the inner plate of the ramp, a scarred section broken by energy lance fire and repaired in a rush. Back then, she'd run on pure terror. Slowing down meant watching her ship dissolve around her under the barrage. Running too fast got her reprimanded for trying to overshadow her elders, her cousins, everyone who was supposed to get lauds and honor before her.

It had been terrifying, but easy. She'd never had to think too far ahead. Never planned for anything, because they would win or die. Losing, facing life without the engines on, that wasn't supposed to happen.

Quick, light steps running along the metal corridors made her turn.

Her cousin Lotus turned the corner, long black braids whipping behind her. "Rowena! I've been all over the ship looking for you!" Her face was flushed and the pulse in her neck raced.

"Why didn't you ping me?"

"I wanted to keep it quiet. Not disrupt anyone…" Lotus let the sentence drift away. "We need you in the medical ward."

Rowena took a deep breath. "Is it the sterilizer again? I can put it on the top of the list for my morning repairs."

"It's Aronia." Lotus pressed her lips together as if swallowing a sob. "She's… There's problems with the baby. We need to get the neonatal machines running. Now."

Before Lotus finished, Rowena had teleported straight to the medical bay. Aronia was the only immediate family she had left. She'd fought the war to ensure Nia never had another miscarriage, done everything she could to protect her big sister from the tragedies they faced. She wasn't going to let one stupid, faulty machine take away her sister's happiness again.

8

SELENA

SLEEP EVADED SELENA LIKE a fighter jet dodging her kill shot.

Adding pillows, changing the blankets, nothing settled her.

Other discomforts had been a choice. She'd given up the *Persephone*. She'd chosen to live outside Enclave. She had consciously decided to cut herself off from contact with the fleet on an emotional level.

But her implant was now constantly pinging the ether, seeking a connection, searching for her missing crew.

After years of the program running dormant and forgotten, it was awake and seeking. Desperately searching for the connection she'd had earlier.

It hurt.

The absence of Titan Sciarra burned like a phantom limb.

Being near him, shields melding, surface thoughts blending with his... She stared at the ceiling. It had been like finding oxygen again after drowning. Every day since her crew left, she'd spent surviving. Limping along.

Today she'd been alive again. Fully aware and awake in a way she hadn't been in years.

She turned over on her bed, cheeks burning in the darkness. It wasn't sexual, not entirely. Sciarra was a temptation. If she were a little bolder, if she wasn't certain the fallout would kill her, she'd take the risk.

But it wasn't sexual frustration keeping her awake. It was the full contact that went past the physical. If there were such a thing as souls—and she wasn't sure she wanted to believe there was life after death, to be honest—then being connected to crew was spiritual. Being able to experience another person's thoughts, to know where they were, to beg them for comfort from the nightmares... It was a drug. Before the war she'd never thought of it that way, but once she lost them all, when her crew's implants cut her off as the survivors walked away, then she'd understood what held the fleet together.

It was sheer stubbornness that had kept her alive after she'd been viciously cut off.

The mental anguish had crushed her. She'd lost weeks broken and sobbing, and fought for every millimeter of recovery. And in one day, Titan Sciarra had ripped her scars open, leaving her bare and shaking.

Their shields had synched. For a few glorious hours she'd felt whole.

Now, her implant searched, reaching out for the connection again. And she had to stop it. Had to break down the program and force herself to swallow the pain.

Almost unconsciously, she reached out and tugged at the telekyen handle of her drawer. The knife she wanted floated into the air, the tantalizing promise of relief.

Carver hadn't realized the temptation he'd handed her when he'd gifted her the obsidian knife. One for each of his best fighters: Gen, Marshall, Hollis, and her. The others took them as trophies. She could only picture cutting a long slit in her forearms and watching the blood run out, carrying away her pain.

The sheathed knife spun, the hilt catching the moonlight pouring through the window.

It would be so easy.

With a heavy sigh, she propelled the knife against the far wall with a thought, letting it sink hilt-deep next to the other marks from the other nights death had tempted her.

She wasn't going to sleep. But she could distract herself.

In the room filled with shadows and weak light, she dressed, then teleported to the Jhandarmi offices. There were several days' worth of security footage to watch and the sooner she closed this case, the better.

Tyrling found her there as the sun crept into the sky. "Is this an early morning or a late night?"

"Yes?" Selena guessed as she loaded the footage of the street taken by a bodega four buildings down from the warehouse.

"Find anything?"

"Lots of questionable clothing choices, two cases of indecent exposure, and one person who looked out of place but it turned out to be me." She couldn't even force a smile. "I'm not sure how they got in, but this one should have better angles."

Tyrling grunted in encouragement. "I know you're riveted to the street-style show here, but I'd like to tear you away for a few minutes."

Selena looked up, and then glanced over her shoulder where a woman with intricate braids and dark brown fauxhawk was watching with an expression of disdain. Her implant measured the curve of the stranger's jacket, her shoes, the hue of the dye... It matched an outfit sold exclusively on the continent of Descent, which meant the woman was either well-traveled in grounder terms, or from the Jhandarmi home office in Chakari.

Tyrling stepped aside, giving her room to stand.

"Of course. I have all the time in the world."

"Agent Caryll, allow me to introduce Miss Elsa Hartley from the information division."

"Miss Hartley." Selena nodded politely to the frosty woman and felt the keen absence of augmentation.

Grounder customs were so clunky. They'd spend a whole conversation dancing around introductions and social niceties, when all they needed was an info packet of relevant data bounced off someone's shield in picoseconds.

Hartley returned the nod but held fast to her briefcase, not offering her hand. "Is there somewhere quiet we could discuss this matter, director?" The way she said *quiet* suggested *secure*.

Tyrling led the way to a soundproof room at the center of the building. Windowless, with thick walls and a security screen, it was the most secure location in the building, aside from the lockdown rooms in the sub-basement.

Even having grown up on a spaceship, the room made Selena feel claustrophobic. There was something about the silence, the way the room absorbed sound so every voice became thin and reedy, that made her shiver.

"We found the cause of the break-in," Tyrling told Selena.

Hartley's eyes narrowed a fraction of a millimeter, a tiny crack in her cold visage.

He shrugged. "The motivation for the break-in and the delayed report," Tyrling corrected. "All three major task forces were mobilized yesterday. It was the first time we had to do inter-agency checks and someone took advantage of that."

"An unknown individual called the Jhandarmi home office at 1751 local time," he continued, "requesting a full list of operatives who'd graduated from the training house at the global complex in Royan. The individual presented the credentials of a Tarrin police sergeant, and the information was released. The sergeant was reported missing this morning. He'd been attacked and unconscious since yesterday morning."

Selena sucked air in through her teeth. "That's bold. How much information did they get?"

"The names and faces of every graduate from the training house in a four year period," Tyrling said, frustration in his voice. "Which means they have the majority of our undercover operatives unmasked."

Hartley placed her briefcase on the table. "The information we sent out was sanitized, but there are several ways it could be used."

"Sold to the highest bidder?" Selena guessed. "If someone staged this for profit, that would be the best way to make money. Unless they're targeting a single individual."

From the briefcase, Hartley pulled several pages of photos and basic ident: initials, assigned continent, major skill set. "These are the agents we believe are the high risk targets. All assigned to Icedell and embedded with major crime syndicates. We're doing our best to pull them in. The ones in Tarrin were rounded up and arrested with other criminals on false charges in the early hours of the morning. Until we know their covers are intact, we're keeping them in isolation cells."

"The problem is we don't know where the information is," Tyrling said. "Or who has it. Or why. And we can't send the Jhandarmi in."

"There's the Tarrin police," Selena said. "Are they offering any assistance?"

Tyrling and Hartley exchanged a look.

"We're not ready to discuss all of our undercover operations with the police at this time," Hartley said. "Not if we can handle the matter internally."

Selena raised an eyebrow.

Tyrling grimaced as he acknowledged her silent assumption. "You aren't on any of the lists. You know the city. You could move through the underground with the identity you've already established."

"We'd like someone to move around the art district today," Hartley said. "Stir up some dust. Look for Kafftan. See if he's collecting a crew."

"Look for trouble," Selena said. "I can do that."

Hartley nodded. A slim smile spread across her lips. "Excellent. Director Tyrling will brief you. Director, I'll wait for you in your office." She repacked her briefcase and stepped outside.

The door clicked shut ominously behind her.

Selena took a deep breath. "This isn't the same as luring an art thief out. I've never worked with violent criminals, only white collar crime."

"You fought in a war."

"I survived, almost. There's a difference."

"Can you do it?" Tyrling asked. "I wouldn't ask if I had other options. The longer the information is out there, the more likely it becomes that one of my agents will die out there. We still have two we can't bring in. Jalisa Tam and Kristoff Sands."

Jalisa had been the one who helped her establish her undercover identity. Selena bit her lip and looked away. Leaving Jalisa and Sands out there… "Okay. What do you need?"

"Remember the business you were trying to create when we recruited you?"

She nodded.

"You legitimized it, didn't you?"

"It's legal, but I never did anything with it."

"Today you're going to go to Tarrin and shop for territory."

Selena raised her eyebrows. The grounders didn't use that term lightly. It meant actively declaring she was in the area, with a business, ready to compete with the established businesses. "That's going to draw attention."

"And fire." Tyrling pulled up a map of the city-states. "The hypertram from Bellis leaves in ninety minutes to arrive here midmorning. I need you on it, with a ticket and a background that people can check. Dressed like you have money and weapons."

"I suppose just letting me shop is out of the question? I can do surveillance while shopping."

He smiled sympathetically and shook his head. "Shopping for art won't stir up trouble. Shopping for a troubleshooter will." He pulled up a map of the district. "See the yellow zones?"

"Yes." Small blotches between buildings. "Dead zones?"

"Exactly," Tyrling said. "There's no security feed covering those areas because of art, or signs, or sometimes just poor planning. The security system hasn't been updated in decades and everyone knows it. We let it stay that way because, usually, we can have someone down there monitoring the blind spots if we think something might happen. Today we can't. But we know Kaffton likes his dead drops. My bet is he'll use one of these."

"If he's the one reaching out to sell the data."

Tyrling shrugged in acknowledgment. "Even identifying who is crawling out of the shadows with the Jhandarmi locked down will help."

"Anything else, sir?"

"Yes." His semi-permanent frown returned. "We need to manage the fleet." His expression was conflicted. "It's likely that there is no direct threat to the fleet or the Starguard."

It was Selena's turn to frown. "We know hitters were hired."

"If Enclave hadn't been on lockdown, how would they have handled the break-in?"

"By sending the guardians." And not allowing the Jhandarmi or police to help. If the thief's goal had been the Jhandarmi data, they couldn't allow the guardians to handle everything alone.

Tyrling nodded. "Exactly. The only way to get everyone down there and get political posturing so the list could be accessed was to keep the fleet out of it. But, if we tell them…"

"…Then they change their behavior and everyone realizes we're on to them," Selena finished for him with a sigh. Lockdown made everyone antsy, but better to have them feeling claustrophobic than have two Jhandarmi officers brutally killed. "Carver can keep a secret, and he needs to know."

"How many layers do I need to go through to get to Carver?" Her boss's voice was loaded with cynicism.

"None. I'll handle him." She gave him a casual, Jhandarmi salute, two fingers touching her temple. "I'll contact you as soon as I have something."

He held up a hand. "Teleport outside, please. If people walk in and never walk out of this room, other people ask questions."

"Of course. I won't scare the locals." She left the office, taking the stairs to the ground floor and stepping outside. A small bird bath marked the one area out of sight of the cameras, and she teleported from there directly to the OIA building.

In a perfect world, she'd have time to change into a uniform, but there wasn't time to get dressed, find Carver and Hollis Silar, change back into clothes for the mission, and reach the hypertram station on time.

The guardians would have to deal with being scandalized.

She crossed through the empty offices where she was supposed to work, brushed the dust off the lift's buttons, and stepped inside.

The lift smelled of lime soap and disuse.

From the speakers, an off-key song played, but even her implant couldn't name the singer. From the accent and lyrics, she couldn't tell which crew it was, or if the singer was fleet at all. It was entirely possible the sound system was playing a song from when the space port was still an active port.

The lift dinged, and she stepped out from the calming blue glow of transit to the false-daylight and low ceilings of the subterranean lair the Starguard had claimed as their own after Landing. She tugged at the edge of her jacket, made sure her knife was well-hidden, and put up her shield banner.

CPT SELENA CARYLL – OIA – ON DUTY

:Selena?: Hollis Silar's familiar code connected with her implant almost instantaneously. :What's up?:

She focused on his location and teleported several halls over. "Hi, Hollis," she said as she fell into step.

He was leaving the main atrium, taking the wide stairs two at a time without noticing, and looking more than a little tired.

"Late night?"

Hollis chuckled sourly. "The worst. Tonight it was nightmares about a hull breach."

"You?" He'd never once mentioned having trouble sleeping. At least not to her. And despite her disinterest in his romantic overtures, it felt like something he would have shared.

"Amira's," he said, sending her a picture of an angelic little girl with strawberry-blonde hair and the familiar golden-brown Silar eyes. "She's my second-cousin-twice-removed's third aunt's godchild's great-niece, and I pulled family duty two nights in a row."

Family duty. On a working ship, someone had to take care of the kids, and losing good people to fulltime child rearing hadn't always been an option. So the crew took turns being the caregiver. The closer a person was related to the child, the more hours they worked. The more distant relatives wound up with other chores, like sitting up once a year with a colicky baby, or tutoring a slow learner.

"It's been a long time since I did that." Years. Maybe she could find a crew who needed an extra adult to play with kids for an hour or two.

"I have it once a year, at least until Perrin and Gen finally do something official and give me a proper nibling. But somehow I managed to get the five-month old twins who were teething one night, and Amira's night terrors the next. And now I'm on my way to go train eager little fleetlings in hand-to-hand combat." He yawned.

That blew her plan right out of orbit. There weren't many guardians who were trained for the kind of work she was doing, and the thought of another day in close company with Sciarra made her heart race in terror.

She slowed to a stop, pulling on Hollis's arm. "Could you find someone else to do the training? I need a guardian for something this morning."

Hollis's smile was sleepy and somehow still wickedly suggestive. "Selena, beautiful, you know I'd love nothing more to let you whisk me away for anything you want to do."

"It would be work," she clarified, crossing her arms.

He shrugged, still smiling. "Still. You're one of my top…"—he paused to count—"… top six favorite women in the fleet. You know I'd do anything for you if I could."

"Ouch, I'm only number six?"

"Well, my mom, Gen is my sister, my cousin Terza, Marshall of course because one day I can pretend she'll fall in love with me, my Auntie Lottie, and you."

"I thought you hated your Aunt Lottie."

"I'm a complex person," Hollis said with a look of complete innocence that meant he was avoiding the conversation.

Selena widened her eyes and tried to look sympathetic. "Please? For me? Couldn't someone else do the training today? Like… Sciarra?"

"Nice try. He had them for the last unit. It's my turn."

"Carver?"

"In meetings all morning, starting in about twenty minutes."

"Brendan Earies?"

"Handling crew issues."

She tried to think of another guardian who was good at hand-to-hand. It wasn't really a well-developed skill for most of the fleet. There were too many variables—from the shields to the maneuvers—and most of the fleet preferred simply shooting their enemies. "Marta Kriswolden?"

"Sprained wrist from training. She's on limited duty for another week."

"A non-guardian? There are some decent fighters out there. Gen could do it, even."

"She took over Amira when I left."

"Mars Sciarra?" Titan's younger cousin was growing up to be quite gifted, and she'd heard rumors about him already.

Hollis winced. "He's a year younger than some of the students. He'd be fine, but it would be politically awkward."

"Aronia Lee."

"Eight months pregnant!"

She'd forgotten that. Which left… "Rowena Lee?"

Hollis tilted his head in speculation.

"She can throw a punch," Selena said. "And block. I'll vouch for that. Please, Hollis? I'm on a tight deadline here and I need someone who can leave now. I will sign whatever paperwork you need to get her here."

He sighed. "You have no idea how much I'd love to take you up on that."

"I hear a 'but' coming."

Hollis grimaced as he nodded. "Even if we thought Hoshi Lee would let Rowena come work with us, which I don't think is likely, and even if Rowena agreed to help the guardians, which is also unlikely, it takes at least two weeks to process everything and get all the signatures."

She groaned.

"I love your enthusiasm for having me all to yourself." Hollis winked at her with a teasing smile.

The urge to punch him was really overwhelming, and she hoped her glare made that clear.

He sighed and shrugged away the rejection. "If you need a guardian, you can have Sciarra."

"I don't *want* Sciarra."

Hollis started walking again. "Come on, give him a chance, Selena. He's a cute guy. Nice muscles. Pretty eyes."

"Do you want Sciarra?"

He shrugged. "I'm game as long as there's a pretty smile, but I'm not his type."

"Neither am I. We had to spend time together yesterday and it was... tense." Terrifying. Soul-crushing. All-consuming. Addictive.

Titan Sciarra was so many things and all of them spelled trouble for her. He made her crave all the familiar comforts and closeness of fleet she'd never have again. It was like begging depression to come and destroy her.

Hollis's expression darkened, taking on a lean, dangerous look. "Did he threaten you?" His voice was calm, but promised certain death if she gave the nod.

"He was an exemplary guardian and his behavior was beyond reproach." Aside from the out-of-character flirting. "But I didn't enjoy being with him."

"Your other options are Trimo, Geer, and or one of the Wens," Hollis said.

None of them could keep up. Most of them couldn't even teleport to Bellis without needing an hour's nap and some fluids. "Fine," she said through gritted teeth. "I'll take Sciarra. But I won't like it."

"I'll go grab him."

"I need to talk to Carver too!" she said as Hollis sped up.

"Got it." He winked and teleported out of view.

The jury was out on whether Hollis would wind up being a freelance lover for the rest of his life or if someone would lock him down. It would have to be someone very intense, Selena decided. Someone who could see past the flirtatious smiles to the tactical mind he hid so well.

And someone with a lot more patience than her.

Ancestors help them.

As she walked to the conference room, she checked the time: fifty-two minutes until the tram left. Carver better not dawdle, or she'd be spending the rest of the day on the battlefield with no backup.

9

TITAN

FOG CURLED OVER THE hypertram tracks as the rain beat a
dreary tattoo on the roof. A feeling of alien otherness consumed
the station. The walls were stretched too high, the passageways
felt too narrow, the people who scurried past with their eyes
averted were thin, short, and silent. Titan looked around with a
frown. These were the coordinates Caryll had given them in their
brief conversation. He was dressed for the mission. But she was
missing and he felt like an over-sized idiot.

The timepiece on his wrist was heavy, cold, and useless. The
black sweater he was wearing clung in the damp air and left him
chilled, not warmed. Caryll didn't seem like the type to play mind
games with him, but if she didn't appear in the next five minutes,
he was tossing the tickets in the nearest recycling bin and
teleporting back to Enclave.

He turned again, watching the crowds streaming through the main checkpoint and lobby, and his heart stuttered as his other senses flew onto high alert.

Selena cut through the throng like a shark in the shoals, wearing tight black pants and a silvery-blue shirt that riveted his attention. Her pale, moon-blonde hair was swept up in a sleek ponytail, and even at a distance he saw the dark makeup lining her eyes. She looked up at the platform, and pinged him, trying to find his location.

:Selena.:

Their eyes met across the crowd.

:Guardian.: She sliced through the mob of passengers, sleek and lethal, and took the stairs up to the boarding platform as the hypertram pulled in behind him.

Titan held her ticket out. "First-class passenger car, like you asked." He pinged her with a question mark.

"Thank you." She watched the slowing tram. :It makes us visible and trackable.:

:I never thought those would be good things.: The face of his watch caught the tram light and he noticed it perfectly matched the blue of her shirt. A small smile tugged at the corner of his lip.

Selena turned to him, the bare hint of an answering smile on her lips. "Did you have time to review the data I sent you?"

"I did." He nodded as the proximity between them allowed their shields to meld. His heart rate dropped to beat time with hers. "Did you bring the identification?"

A whistle sounded and the station loudspeaker announced the boarding.

Titan took the lead, and noticed a new weight in his pants pocket as he approached the gate. Sliding his hand into the pocket, he felt a heavy wallet. :That was a neatly done teleport.:

Selena's answering thoughts were fuzzy, distracted and tense.

They found their seats near the front of the tram, a comfortable, semi-private booth perfumed by the bright coral flowers in the built-in vase and a lingering scent of rain. Titan let Selena pick her side—back to the front of the train—and sat across from her. "Is everything all right?" Her emotions were swirling just out of reach and he couldn't gauge her mood.

She pulled on a black jacket, cut to emphasize her slender build, and shrugged. "I expected things to resolve faster than this. Being used..." Her lips curled in an angry grimace. "I don't like being played the fool."

"No one does."

Another whistle sounded, lower this time, and the doors to the hypertram slammed shut with authoritative finality.

"This should be interesting," Titan murmured.

Selena's nose wrinkled in disagreement. "An inefficient waste of time."

"But remarkably advanced considering what the colonies started with."

"I suppose."

The hypertram slid out of the station, the outside scenery blurring as they raced past.

Titan put a minor sound shield up, not enough to block out everything, but enough that no one passing by would hear their conversation. "Have you been on one of these before?"

"A few times," Caryll said, still holding her emotions tight. "We landed in the port outside Tarrin, but for a few weeks we were looking at housing some of the crews here in Bellis. The OIA job gave me the right to travel and purchase land and houses, but there was too much push-back. The grounders were scared of us, and the fleet was scared of losing its identity." She shrugged.

"Did you consider taking your crew here?"

The look she gave him was icy. "Briefly. Before they left."

A memory spilled out over her shield: her fears and her hopes as she bought apartments for the nearly 600 Carylls who had survived, of seeing a bright future, and then learning they'd betrayed her.

Titan sent thoughts of sympathy mixed with affection. Losing his parents in the war had been hard enough, even though they'd been distant in the final years. He couldn't imagine losing his entire crew.

She scowled at him. "I don't need your pity."

"I'm not offering any. I was trying to let you know I understood a bit about betrayal. My last captain tried to kill me, you know." Neit had been his mother's little brother, his uncle, and an unholy terror that Titan was happy he helped Elea kill.

"That's not quite the same."

"No. Not quite," he agreed.

A woman wearing a red vest over a pale gold shirt and black slacks stepped beside their seats.

Titan dropped the sound shield. "Yes?"

"Would you care for a complimentary snack? This tram offers a selection of the finest Bellis food products to all our first-class guests."

Caryll sent an affirmative signal but didn't turn away from the window.

"Yes, thank you," Titan said.

The woman smiled brightly and brought over a basket with the red, black and gold Bellis flag on it. "Enjoy your morning."

After putting the sound shield back, Titan picked through the food. "Five Winds bramble jam. Five Winds sausage. Five Winds bread. I feel like I'm missing a joke."

"The *Five Winds* was the first colonial ship to land on this continent," Selena said.

"I thought it landed in Tarrin?"

She shrugged and looked over at the food. "Both Tarrin and Bellis claim the ship landed in their borders. Tarrin even has part of it on the north end; they use it as a concert hall. But realistically the ground here is too swampy ten months of the year and it either landed on the beach near Enclave or further north near Kivalina."

Her shields stayed tight.

"I don't think anyone appreciates how much you gave up when the *Persephone* was lost."

"Not lost," Selena corrected. "Lost would be forgivable. I gave up the *Persephone*. Intentionally let her crash. All for strangers. If I'd lost her in battle, it would have been a tragedy. But giving up? The fleet will never accept that." She turned her attention back to the window.

He leaned back in his seat. "Do you know what my penance was after the war?"

"I didn't really expect your captain to make you do anything. She took the command with your help, and you weren't in the war. Officially."

"True." Officially he hadn't been much of anything. Unofficially, he'd been in the first attack on the planet—a fact he hoped he'd never need to share with her.

He weighed what to say to her. *See how far we have fallen, the forgotten generation, the children of distant stars.*

Rowena's words echoed in his mind. 'The fleet's been dead for years. The next step is all of us leaving Enclave and becoming grounders. That's it. That's the only option other than mass suicide.'

Here lies a sailor, enlisted in the Lost Fleet too soon. May their name never be forgotten. Death is their captain now. Death their ever-sure companion. The words to a sailor's dirge older than the fleet.

If he accepted Rowena's prediction, there was no point in saying anything else. But...

Under the table he rolled up his left sleeve and ran his thumb down the thick, silver grooves in his skin. He should have died in that crash. His implant had overload and he'd never found an explanation for why the electrical overload ended at his elbow, instead of following his nervous system to his brain.

Maybe his ancestors had blessed him. Or maybe Death was a coward. Either way, he wouldn't be a Sciarra if he was willing to go down without a fight.

Danger to the left, danger to the right, ahead a certain death, and behind a certain fight.

The fleet needed a third option. They needed someone like Selena Caryll, someone who could navigate the city-states and see ways to integrate traditions. She'd had a plan once, and he had a feeling that it was the same plan he needed now.

Which meant he had to win her trust.

He sent out a small pulse along their shared shield, a polite request for attention.

Selena glanced at him, expression disinterested.

"Elea, my aunt and captain, saw being Mal Baular's second at the Academy as crime enough. My penance was making a projection of what would have happened had the Baular attack succeeded. I wrote a 1100-page treatise on why following bad orders is horrible, using that information and other historical examples. Every year, on the anniversary of the first battle, I address all the under twenties in our crew."

"Sounds horrifying," Selena said without any emotion.

"It made me suicidal," Titan admitted. "I realized that if Baular's attack had gone as planned, the planet would have been uninhabitable and we would have all died within 37 months. Starvation would have killed anyone who didn't commit suicide."

That got her attention. She turned, brow furrowed in confusion as she shook her head. "You don't know that for sure. Baular may not have attacked in the end."

"I saw the battle plans."

Her eyes narrowed. "From the medical ward?"

"Someone I knew had a copy."

"You can say Rowena. Everyone knows she has the best intel."

He smiled in confirmation. "Mal sent her a copy at some point. I think he realized something was off but couldn't pinpoint what. The Baular projections assumed the strike would free the orun deposit in the south sea."

"There's no math to support that."

"The older Baulars were better at intimidating underlings and shouting orders than they were at running figures. But I doubt they did even the basic research. Old Baular ran on pure ego." The rot had run deep in that crew, ancestors forgive them. "If you hadn't given up the *Persephone*, we'd all be dead," Titan said quietly. "And I don't think anyone's ever thanked you."

"No," she admitted. "And I doubt they ever will."

"Thank you." He backed the words with gratitude and hope.

Selena had accented her high cheekbones with a silvery-blue that matched her shirt, and as she blushed the color leaned toward the palest amethyst. She bit her lip, then shook her head. "I wish you wouldn't. There isn't a day that goes by that I don't hate myself for giving up the *Persephone*. It was my duty. The best way to save the maximum number of lives. And I hate myself for it."

"You shouldn't. It was a risk, but you survived."

She looked into his eyes, opened enough of a channel to let him feel the weight of the memories she was hiding. There was nothing there but despair. "I didn't survive. I died with my ship. Lost everything. It took a while for my crew to leave, but they were as good as dead when I went into that battle. I failed them. I failed my parents, my ancestors. There's nothing left."

He reached across the table and took her hand. "You think that. I know, I see that memory. But there's something else there too. The seed of something. From the ashes of defeat come—"

"—the greatest victories." She finished the quote for him and pulled her hand away. "Platitudes won't give me the future I want."

"And what do you want?" This was where faith kicked in. Part of him knew what she would say, because it was what everyone wanted. Part of him was terrified that she'd given up hope—like Rowena.

"My ship. A new ship, I suppose. A crew." She drew in a breath and squared her shoulders. "I want the fleet back. I want to be part of something where I'm respected instead of mocked. I want a fleet that thinks about protecting what we know is left of humanity, rather than trying to destroy it with petty in-fighting and ridiculous wars." She sighed. "It's impossible. Like asking for the sun, and moon, and stars."

The last time he'd felt this happy had been the day he'd learned Rowena and Mal weren't being executed. It felt like the first time he'd flown solo. Or like falling in love. "All right."

"All right?" Her laugh was sharp and bitter. "All right what?"

"You want the fleet back, so we get the fleet back."

Selena looked at him like he'd lost his mind. "Is your hull cracked? Did you spend the night breathing in engine fumes?"

"I'm serious."

"You can't be serious, Sciarra. Ships aren't something you wish into existence. You can't say, 'Let there be purple unicorns!' and have them grazing in the park. The fleet is fundamentally broken. If there were a way to fix it, trust me, I would have found a solution. I've been obsessing over this since the day I lost the *Persephone*."

"No one thought Old Baular could be stopped, but you managed."

She rolled her eyes and looked back out the window. "There were other ways to stop him. Most of them involved a catastrophic loss of life though. So here we are."

"Look up real quick."

Selena looked up into the blue sky where the first few wisps of storm clouds were visible on the horizon. "Am I supposed to be seeing anything?"

"The moon."

"What?" She frowned at Sciarra. "Everyone knows you can't see the moon during the daytime here. It's not reflective enough."

From his data banks he pulled an image of a page from a child's storybook, a woman drawn all in shades of white and blue and silver. She stood against the gray background, between a brown woman and blue man. "Once upon a time, Ground and Sky had a beautiful daughter, pale and fair," he quoted.

"I know the story! What's the relevance?"

He sent her twin images, one of the moon in her pale dress standing next to the golden sun, outshone and ghostly. Then the same image of the moon woman standing with the embodiment of night, dark and handsome.

"When the moon was with the sun," he said, "no one could see her brilliance. She had to move to the night so everyone could appreciate her. The moral of the story always was that one small change can make a big difference."

Selena twitched an eyebrow up. "I thought the moral was 'don't date abusive people who want to overshadow you'."

"That too." He leaned forward. "We could work together. Be allies. The Sciarras are still a warmonger crew. Limited privileges. Limited access to the world outside Enclave, but eventually we all know that will fall apart. Either the trapped crews will rebel, or the allied crews will have to bend. Someone has to forgive first."

Her eyes grew cold. "The other crews are all waiting for me to fold. They're waiting for me to realize I can't survive alone so that I'll come begging for refuge. Take a lower rank. Offer them some priority Caryll tech. Something like that. Pardon me if I'm suspicious that you just happen to be here offering to work with me for free. On anything. No strings attached."

"I have crew and tech. I have respect from most of the fleet. What I don't have is a single person who believes there's a future for the fleet. Except for you."

She laughed in surprise. "Me? You think I'm optimistic about our future?"

"You're still here, despite everything. You still care. The fleet needs that. I need that. Everyone around me is willing to give up without a fight. I won't, but I can't do this alone."

Selena turned to the window, looking more like the Moon in the child's storybook than she could have imagined. "You're asking a lot of a stranger."

"I'm asking a lot of a friend," Titan said. "But I'll make it worthwhile."

A whistle cut through the sound shield and he realized they were approaching the stop at Tarrin.

With a practiced air, Selena erased the conflicted emotions from her face. She turned to him, looking as impassive as stone. "I'll think about. For now, we have a job to do."

It wasn't a no. He pulled out the wallet she'd given him and checked his identity. "Ti Tan of Descent. I work for the Carrilloni Combine?"

She pulled a business card from her breast pocket. "Selena Carrilloni, tech and medical supplies, at your service."

"Carrilloni? A variant of Caryll?"

"The name my non-fleet ancestors used when they settled on Descent. The line was dormant, but I was able to resurrect it for business purposes. All it takes is a little bit of money and a genetic scan. Half the fleet probably has claims to titles and properties on the planet."

"That bit of news does not help me convince everyone that the fleet can stay together."

Selena leaned forward, for the first time finally engaging with him. "If you learned anything at the Academy, it should have been that we need to circulate our people more. Marshall went head to head with the best the fleet had and burnt our engines hard. Some of the people in Enclave need to step out. They were born fleet, but they weren't born to be like us. Maybe they'll be artists, or musicians, or poets, or bankers, but they deserve the choice to not be in the stars. They deserve the chance to choose both, or neither, or some third option we haven't thought of yet. For that, I'm willing to fight."

The tram rolled to a stop.

Titan stood and held out a hand for Selena. "Miss Carilloni."

"Mister Tan." She took his hand and stood. "Shall we go cause trouble?"

He dared a smile. "That would be delightful."

10

SELENA

THE STORM THAT HAD been building over Bellis was on the distant horizon as Selena exited the hypertram at Tarrin's main station. If the familiar scents of linden trees and the sea breeze didn't give away the city-state, the buildings did. The architecture was overtly Tarrin, lots of arches and curved corners that seemed designed to stamp into visitors' heads that they were not in the rival city-state any more. Even the portrait of the Lethe family, owners of hypertrams the world over, was in a nice round frame.

Selena arched an eyebrow at the vacant smile of Sonya Lethe, Tarrin-born Lethe heiress, and wondered what to do next. Tyrling's directions had been vague, and information had been uploading to the Jhandarmi database as she traveled. There were too many possibilities and not enough certainties.

"You're frowning," Sciarra murmured as he stepped up beside her, blocking the spring chill.

"I'm debating the merits of walking into the art district, slamming people's heads together and demanding answers."

He tilted his head as he considered the idea. "Tempting, but not good for the fleet's overall appeal."

"The Combine's brand," she corrected. "Remember who you are."

"A slightly menacing gentleman from Descent who might be here to purchase land, or art, or a little of both." He made a show of looking at his watch. "All the good businesses should be open. Shall we prowl?"

A corner of her mouth twitched up in a smirk. "Indeed." To everyone watching they weren't just outsiders, they were wealthy outsiders dressed in the height of Descent fashion. They'd blend in well on the streets of Royan, but here in Tarrin they stood out. Being the center of attention was fine when everyone was simply sizing up her sexual appeal, but this level of scrutiny made her hair stand on end.

The train station opened out to the grand terrace, a series of long, shallow steps, and then onto one of Tarrin's many formal gardens. It wasn't the right time of year for the grand display, but there were hints of the show to come: pale green buds ripening on frail flower stems, dark dirt turned and nourished by gardeners dressed in the deep ocean-gray of Tarrin's civil service.

:Do you want me to hail a cab?: Sciarra asked via the implant.

:We can walk. Tyrling gave me a map of blind spots and I want to see if we can get between here and the art district without leaving it.: She sent him the map.

Sciarra sent back a sensation of disgruntlement. :The station is wide open, where could he have dropped out of sight?:

:The first blind spot is near a food court in the indoor shopping plaza.: It was redundant to send him the image of the glass and steel building ahead of them, but she did anyway. Terminal Plaza had once been the stopping point for the tram, before the rail had been extended to the port. Now it was part botanical garden, part tourist trap.

Stepping in front of her, Sciarra caught the heavy door and held it open. "After you, miss."

Selena pulled up the map again as they stepped inside to the dry warmth of the shopping center. The lower level had the food court that smelled of grease and intoxication, an indoor river, trees that caused the major security concerns, and a row of knick-knack shops. :Do you see an opening out of here?:

:Maintenance door to the left of the bagel shop,: Sciarra said. :There're trees blocking the view from two angles.:

She checked the schematics. :Passcode protected, so there's no camera on the inside until the hall splits.:

They stopped in front of it and let the other people flooding off the tram flow past.

Sciarra gave the handle a wiggle. "Locked."

:Could you get through it without augmentation? Kaffton has none.:

A security guard came into view, following the crowd and pausing here and there to give directions to tourists.

Sciarra pulled a paper map out of his pocket. "It came in the food basket. You said you wanted to look at the dress shop first?" he asked, a little louder than was necessary.

"Only if they carry Kellington's designs," she said. Her mouth snapped shut with a frown as the guard stepped out of sight.

"What tools would Kaffton have had?"

"Whatever professional tools someone like hi—"

A worker in the bright blue-and-orange stripes of the Dreamy Cream ice cream shop shoved between them and unlocked the door.

Sciarra grabbed the handle before it shut. "The security here—"

"Is abysmal," Selena agreed. "But it's likely how any thief would get in."

They stepped inside the service hall, a small, cramped space overwhelmed by the smell of cooking grease. Ahead of them, the worker's footsteps echoed off the concrete walls.

:The next security array is at the T-intersection ahead. Camera, motion sensor, and a heat sensor,: Selena said.

Sciarra's eyes glowed a bright green as he scanned the area, the information trickling back to her on a slight time delay.

Even during the war she hadn't always appreciated a constant stream of intel from the rest of her squad; it kept her from thinking. Sciarra's information was different though, no commentary or assumptions, just flat data. Facts without chatter. The scan he was using showed the support beams in the wall, a hairline fracture that needed repairs in one of the floor panels, and a hidden door halfway down the hall.

Cautiously, Sciarra pushed on the wall panel. The door fell back with the hydraulic whine of a mechanized hinge. :Are these on the city blueprints?:

:When this was still the main tram terminal, there were tunnels running between the platform and the loading area so that luggage and trade goods weren't unloaded into the torrential rain. They fell out of use after the tremors from the big groundquake on the other side of the bay. The ground settled, the sea level came up a few inches, and the tunnels were prone to flooding.: It took only a second to pull up her implant's codes for lighting and make her hand glow. The slightly-bluer-than-natural light illuminated narrow steps leading to a basement area.

The floor had probably once been concrete like the rest of the tunnel, but repeated flooding had left a thick layer of settled dirt. Heavy boot prints, spaced out for a person with a long stride, were easily visible over fading layers of older tracks.

Sciarra stepped down onto the dirt and put his foot along the tracks. :Twenty-nine centimeters. Tall.: He looked down the length of the tunnel. :Unguarded, nearly forgotten... If I were a smuggler I'd map this out. When was the last rain?:

:Three days ago. There was a mist this morning, but not enough to dampen the tunnel.:

He climbed the steps to stand beside her. :Those footprints are probably fresh then. And the height would match Kaffton. Should we follow it?:

No.

Traipsing down a dark tunnel, following a violent man's tracks without backup sounded like a terrible idea.

That was the problem with being the only line of defense. The guardians weren't trained for this kind of investigation. The Jhandarmi were in danger. The police weren't to be trusted. Which left her.

And, because her ancestors enjoyed playing cruel tricks on their posterity, Sciarra.

Cursing everything, she nodded.

Sciarra turned and shut the door behind them.

The sudden cessation of sound was like being on a dead ship. Her heartrate jumped in alarm. They were alone.

A sensation of comfort and calm flowed through their shared shield. Sciarra touched her shoulder and gave it a gentle squeeze. :Claustrophobia?:

:Something like that.:

Sometimes the man could be so dense. Of course he didn't see himself as a threat. She shouldn't either. That was a vestigial fear left over from her younger years. But, if she stripped away the fear Sciarra inspired, what did that leave? Under the pretense of looking the tunnel over, she watched Sciarra. Again. Tall, dark, intense and built for war, Titan Sciarra had always left her heart fluttering with a potent mixture of attraction, fascination, and trepidation. It was an illogical reaction.

Selena took the lead, shining her hand light ahead of them as she tracked their progress on her mental map. It was a surprisingly quick walk from the terminal to the edge of the art district when there weren't buildings to worry about. Stairs began appearing regularly, most of them leading to dead ends walled off by more concrete.

The walls transitioned from concrete to rougher stone, and finally to brick.

:There's light ahead,: Sciarra said, following up with a mental tug at her clothes as he used his implant to stop her. :More heat signatures too.:

She shared the map with him. :Cafe Alsur is directly above us.: With multiple blind spots leading to the cafe. Deception wasn't a fleet trait, generally speaking, but she'd read enough books on spy craft and smuggling to appreciate the location. Someone could disappear near the tram station and arrive here, then escape into the warren of alleyways between the shops.

:Don't tell the police, but their security is pitiful,: Sciarra said.

:Decades of neglect and a push for privacy will do that,: Selena answered. :They have enough trouble watching the cams they have. Adding more would stretch the budget and they'd lose votes. Tarrins don't like being watched.:

:No one does. It doesn't mean you turn a blind eye.:

Shining the light at the base of the stairs to the café revealed multiple sets of footprints going in and out.

:Do we keep going, or go up here? It looks like Kaffton likes the place, or else there are a lot of tall yaldsons around.:

Before Selena could reply there was a sound up ahead of stone scraping against stone. She froze, shutting off the light and listening.

The sound of heavy breathing echoed in the dank passage, followed by the sound of stone scraping over stone again, and heavy footsteps hurrying away.

Body heat was the only warning that Sciarra had moved closer to her. :What do you make of that?:

:Kaffton loves dead drops, but we couldn't be that lucky.:

There was a ping with a question mark.

:It's a grounder thing. They leave goods or messages in a pre-determined location for someone to pick up later.: If only it could be that easy.

Without really considering, she started walking ahead. Her shield blipped with an incoming data packet and the darkness in front of her transformed into phantasmic green and black.

Her surprise must have registered with Sciarra because the returning emotion was a self-satisfied smugness mixed with the pleasure of impressing her.

:I'm not that impressed,: she lied.

:Not even a little? That was some very dainty recoding. Look, I even worked in a sound shield and a light vision shield. Anyone looking at us will see shadows against a black background.:

Knowing he couldn't see her face in the dark, she sent him the memory of a very annoyed expression. :This is where ghost stories come from.:

He sent her an animated specter from a children's holovid that had been old when her grandparents were young.

:You need to find new material.:

Sciarra moved in front of her, heading towards the sound.

Selena grabbed his arm. :I don't like this idea.:

:Why not?:

:We're trapped here if we're not careful. We can't teleport out without triggering alarms that'll make the whole continent think Armageddon has come. We don't know this place.:

A warm hand covered hers and a calloused finger ran over her knuckles. :They can't see or hear us. I'll keep you safe.:

:I can keep myself safe. You too, if it comes to that. But a stray bullet can do just as much damage as being trapped down here. Even if it bounces off our shield, it'll draw attention.:

:You never did infiltrations during the war?: Skepticism underlay every word.

She drew her hand away. :I was always close enough to teleport out.: Not every crew had implants that allowed for long range teleports, and not everyone could mentally handle a long range jump, but that had never been her problem.

War memories bubbled to the surface and she realized Sciarra was probing, trying to understand. Hiding the truth was a matter of pulling up other memories, like running at the Academy gym, or gardening with her parents before she left home.

"I know what you're doing," he whispered in her ear.

Licking her lip, she smiled in the darkness. "I would hope so."

:I'll figure out your secret.:

"What makes you think I only have one?" She brushed past him, running a hand over his chest. Dealing with Titan Sciarra was like mental gymnastics, or flying through a minefield. It was all fun and games until something went *crash*.

Selena put space between them. She'd trusted people before, been their friend, defended them no matter the risk and she knew where it led. As long as she was useful, Sciarra would play at being handsome and charming. Once he had what he wanted, he'd go.

It was how the fleet ran. Family or not, friend or not, if someone wasn't useful they were forgotten. And she had nothing left to offer them.

Something of what she was thinking must have bled over into the shared channel, because Sciarra stepped in front of her, stopping her progress. :You need to stop thinking like that. Negativity like this is going to get you killed.:

:It hasn't yet.: She crossed her arms.

:Last time you were in a serious fight was over three years ago.: He reached out, finding her shoulder and holding it gently. :You know what depression and battle-brain does. It's a cargo you can't take into this fight. I'll go alone, if it's needed, but you can't go on like this. You'll get someone killed.: It was an order from someone used to command.

And he was right, ancestor's forgive him. She'd been running solo missions for too long.

Taking a deep breath, she shut her eyes and focused on shoving the maudlin thoughts away.

Sciarra followed along the code path, ripping at the memories.

She gasped at the sudden invasion until she saw what he was doing. Not destroying, but recoding. Cutting the code that triggered a physical response and leaving the memories powerless. It was invasive, but not meant to harm.

Still, she stopped him. :You don't have the right.:

A line from the Starguard manual appeared in her message bank, listing the right of a partner to handle panic situations with extreme measures in the field.

:We're not partners, Sciarra.:

There was a low-pitched growl of disagreement, and then he sent her the data packet so she could finish the rip herself. :We're partners. Like it or not.:

:What would your crew say to that?: It was a last, desperate bid for distance.

:They'd say, 'Lucky Titan.':

Selena let it go. Arguing with him was like trying to fly without fuel: it got her nowhere. There was something between them, but when the job was over and everything found its balance again, he'd lose interest.

Maybe.

There was another touch on her arm. :Come on. Before we lose the heat trail.:

The bright red source of heat on the wall ahead was already fading. Sciarra went ahead and pried the brick loose. There was a small pocket of space. :Empty.:

Frustrated, Selena flexed her fingers and turned the light on again. Kaffton's boot prints were clear, but another set ran over them, leading on ahead and to the left. :I knew our luck wasn't that good.:

:He's not far ahead,: Sciarra said. :Let's go find out what he took from here.:

She watched her *partner* walking ahead for a long, silent moment. That was not how this was supposed to go. There were expectations. Traditions. Excuses.

Titan turned to look back at her, sending her a sensation of question and concern.

:I'm coming.: *Partner.* Somehow there was already a mental space for him. With a smile, she moved forward.

11

TITAN

THEY'D GONE BEYOND THE perimeter of the art district and the walls were changing back to the concrete foundations of heavier buildings. Whoever they were following, they were moving fast. Once or twice they'd rounded the corner and seen a light up ahead, but then it turned a corner, leaving them trailing again. Titan was about to turn the latest corner when he heard a low voice, indistinct in the darkness.

Another voice answered, higher in pitch but still low enough to suggest a man.

Selena leaned forward, peering around the edge of the wall. :Kaffton and someone else. Their lights are pointed down.:

He felt her frustration as well as his own. :Do you see anything that looks like a list? Papers? Data chip?:

:Nothing yet. Charging in is no good unless we get the data.:

:Let's get Kaffton and then get the data from him,: Titan argued. :This is not the time and place for Caryll kindness.:

:We can't kidnap grounders.:

He frowned. :Even if we give them to the Jhandarmi? I could tie a bow or something…:

A sound he'd never heard before cracked through the hall. Titan froze, watching the ceiling.

:Gun!: Selena ran away from him towards the sound.

There was no choice but to follow. Heavy shields up, he ran after her, towards the fallen man.

Kaffton didn't see them perhaps, but the dust was enough to warn him. He fired twice, and then ran.

Selena lit up, glowing like the moon as she knelt beside the man. "Dead. He's not in the database. Crack my hull, Tyrling isn't going to like this."

"What's he got on him?" Titan asked, keeping the shields up and watching the path Kaffton had taken.

Selena patted the man down. "Nothing. Nothing." Something crunched audibly when she patted his hip pocket. "Something?" She reached in and pulled out a thin strip of paper. "An address in one of the newer areas. Nouveau Riche, style makers, and heirs… It's a good place to mingle at a party and do some business on the side. Lost Fleet take Kaffton, why did he shoot?"

"Didn't like the terms maybe?" Titan guessed. "Or didn't want to wait to get paid."

She shook her head. "This is the man we followed from the dead drop. Kaffton wouldn't have handed over the list if he hadn't been paid. And he'd have no reason to shoot a potential client." She looked at the man's face. "We need to get above ground and have the Jhandarmi ID him. Where's the last place we saw an exit?"

Titan closed his eyes and visualized the map he'd recorded as they'd followed. "We're near the center of town. Heavy shields above, and the last open entrance we saw was over two klicks back."

With a swipe of her hand, Selena projected the map of the city over the map of the tunnels and the map of the blind spots for Tarrin security. "Here, over by the old hospital and the city's original morgue. They had six sublevels at one point. I bet there's an exit there."

"Why dig so far down?"

She looked up in surprise. "Officially? If you ask the Tarrins it was to keep the bodies cool. Caryll database says that some anti-imperialists were housed there in the early days of colonization. Icedell was meant to be a penal colony. Descent was going to be a vacation spot for Imperial workers; the workforce would come from the penal colony stock."

"I never heard that."

"The Carylls were sent to set it up, originally. But the captain who led our armada didn't think it was feasible. After the wormhole collapsed they saw no reason to pursue it." The soft glow that surrounded her changed to a cold, deep-sea green and fell over the dead body. "That'll keep him until we can get someone down here. I have facial scans and fingerprints."

"I was about to suggest that." Titan crossed his arms. Finger-printing a victim was a rather esoteric practice these days. It had gone out of use when implants became common.

Selena stood and brushed a loose strand of hair back from her eyes. "Let's go. I need a signal."

Their connection filled with schematics of implants as Selena quietly picked apart the design, trying to find a way to send a signal past the layers of rock and shielding above them.

"We could just break the shield," he muttered. It was a very, very good shield. Anomalously good, in fact. There wouldn't be any slipping through without triggering an alarm. But that's why begging for forgiveness had been invented. "Who put this shield up?" he asked as the corridor narrowed.

Complete lockdown. The flow of shared information cut dead. Selena's eyes widened with projected innocence. "I don't know."

:Liar.:

"I can't say?"

The gun sound cracked again. They'd caught up with Kaffton.

Habit made Titan reach out mentally to pin the man down, but Kaffton had no telekyen on him.

Selena ran forward, enhancing her shield as she moved and presenting only a blurred shadow for Kaffton to see.

Kaffton fired again. The bullets ricocheted away, sparking off the walls as they bounced.

Perhaps panicking, Kaffton ran. He turned a corner, moving out of sight, and there was a heavy groan of a metal door closing.

Turning the corner in pursuit, they saw the sliver of daylight vanish with a thud.

"No!" Selena ran up to the door and banged her fist on it. She wedged her shoulder against it and pushed.

Focusing on a brute shield, Titan followed, pushing with all the weight he could concentrate on the door.

It squeaked, caved in at the center, but didn't budge.

"We need to go back the other way," Titan said. "There's not another exit near here."

"I do not have time for that."

Selena's face was suffused with rage, her eyes glowing a bright stellar blue. She reached her hand out and ran it along the door, looking for a weak point.

"We have to—"

She clenched her hand into a fist and the door crumpled in on itself like a wadded linen.

Titan stared in disbelief at the tiny ball of metal hanging suspended in the air. "That's…"

"An opening." Her voice was a dangerously low growl of fury and command.

Scared by Selena Caryll… Even if he replayed the memory for his crew, no one would believe him. "I am so glad you learned that trick after the Landing."

"I didn't."

The crumbled door spun on its axis over her palm and then shot ahead, flying across the empty parking garage on an arching trajectory. It cut a deep groove in the stone floor as it landed.

An attack like that… "Can you do that with all metal?"

"I can do it with anything," Selena said as she stalked toward the entrance.

"Don't crumple the suspect. We need to question him."

Her shield spiked, flipping from defense to full offensive attack.

And then she took a deep breath and seemed to return to normal. "I've lost him anyway." She pulled out her phone. "I'm calling the Jhandarmi in. We need to get this area locked down and searched."

Glaring at her phone, she continued walking toward the exit.

:You're inviting another attack, pacing out there.:

:Let him try.: There was a quick flash-thought of Kaffton attacking and the metal of his bullets stretching and looping to become binders for his legs.

:There's not enough metal.:

Selena shot him an annoyed look. :A girl can dream.:

140

"Tyrling, yes, it's Caryll. I need a team at my location ASAP. We have an unidentified male victim and Kaffton is at large and armed." As she listened to the Jhandarmi's response, she glared at the quiet buildings outside. "Understood, sir. I'll expect you shortly."

:They're on their way. Do you see any movement?:

:None. He could have gone up, or kept running. There aren't many security blindspots here. We'll find him.:

She continued pacing in a way that made it clear that it wasn't just Kaffton's escape bothering her. There was something else, a private goal she wasn't sharing.

Titan crossed his arms and waited. He wasn't quite as good as Rowena at getting secrets out of people, but he could get them eventually. Right now, though, he wasn't feeling patient.

Reaching out with a thought, he tugged at Selena's arm.

Her shoes scuffed the ground as she paused and turned. She tilted her head to the side and he felt rather than saw her confusion.

Words seemed inadequate for what he wanted. It was safety, but something more. If she'd been crew, he would have opened her arms to hold her, check her for physical injuries. If physical touch wasn't allowed, he wanted at least physical proximity.

With an understanding half-smile, she walked over to him. "You're being a little overprotective."

"You're being a little reckless. I'm trying to balance out this partnership we have."

Her shoulder bumped his arm. "If you think this was reckless, it's a good thing you slept through the war."

"War is different."

She shook her head. "No. It's all the same." She sighed and looked off into the distance. "Millions of years of evolution and we're still trying to crack each other's skulls open like a single death could solve all the problems of humanity."

"Funny how it's the opposite," Titan said. "All the problems I see could be solved with a little forgiveness and love."

A wintry smile touched Selena's lips. "Yeah? Even your bruised jaw?"

He touched it, feeling the lingering ache. "Nothing a kiss couldn't fix."

Her smile blossomed into something real. "Maybe later. The Jhandarmi are here." Selena patted his arm and walked away, leaving him with nothing but hope.

12

SELENA

THIS WAS WHY FLEET didn't keep secrets. When your movements could be tracked, your thoughts read, every micro-expression analyzed, there was no way to keep a secret for long.

You can't tell anyone. Marshall had never been soft, or that close to crying. She'd begged Selena to keep the secret.

Three years ago, it had seemed easy enough. Back then, the very idea of someone from fleet coming to the municipal heart of Tarrin was unthinkable.

She'd stumbled onto the city's shield by accident, recognized it because she knew the only people available to create this level of shield were too busy. Shields this intricately coded took weeks to build, sometimes years. It wasn't thrown up overnight between a meeting of the Captains' Council and the delegation from Tarrin.

Now, standing in an abandoned parking garage beside a prying Titan Sciarra, the fear of him realizing—the fear of having to explain—was making her break out in a cold sweat.

"It's all right," Sciarra whispered as he leaned closer.

She shut her eyes. To him, this probably looked like a post-attack adrenaline jag. A simple reaction to being shot at. It would be hard to make him understand that being shot was only a threat if she cared whether she lived or not—at least without letting him see how much of her soul the war had destroyed.

Four black Jhandarmi vehicles pulled up outside the garage.

Titan caught her hand as she walked away. "Do you want me to take the lead?"

"No. Thank you. I'm angry he got away, not hurt."

"You can't win every battle."

"You can if you're Caryll," she said without thinking. It had been not her family motto per se, but rather her parent's response to her childhood insecurities. *Can't* was never accepted.

I can't.

You can if you're Caryll.

They'd probably meant that she could because of who she was. But even as a child, she'd heard, 'You aren't really one of us unless you can do this.' Failure meant becoming an outcast.

Some things never changed.

Tyrling took off his sunglasses as he walked into the shadows. "You two found a dead body or made one? The answer changes who I can send in."

"Kaffton shot a man I can't identify," Selena reported.

"You're sure it was Kaffton?" Tyrling looked skeptical.

"Captain Caryll saw him pull the trigger," Titan said.

Selena zapped him, not hard, but enough to make his mouth snap shut. :He did not need that information!:

144

:Why not?: Sciarra sounded bewildered.

:Kaffton has never had enough evidence against him to bring him to trial. A witness—:

"A witness?" Tyrling's smile was the calm before the storm, the promise of destruction on an epic scale. "Did he see you?"

She shrugged. "I was projecting a visual shield. It's possible, but unlikely."

The Jhandarmi officer laughed out loud. "Oh!" He raised his arms above his head and stepped into the sunshine with a smile. "Do you see how beautiful today is?"

:Is he feeling well?: Titan asked.

:You just handed him the biggest intelligence coup of the decade. I have footage of Kaffton murdering someone. It'll be enough to get him executed in half the city-states on the continent, or make him hand over names of bigger targets.:

If she were Kaffton, she'd be standing nearby with a sniper rifle.

Tyrling walked back to them. "The crew is going down. We'll have the body identified and autopsied by tonight. The medical team needs to know if you're injured."

Selena shook her head. "A little hungry from running, but no injuries. Do you want us to stay?"

"I'd rather you didn't," Tyrling said. "Take my vehicle, leave it downtown, and get back behind your fancy defenses."

"What about the list?" And Jalisa. "We don't have it. I didn't complete the mission."

Tyrling held up a hand. "We're searching the area on a grid. Kaffton won't be able to move freely. If he's smart, and time and again he's proven that he is, he'll hole up and wait for the buy."

"We don't know the address will lead to the buy," she argued.

The director raised his eyebrows. "At that address? We both know it," he said in a softer voice.

She looked away, not quite ready to quit.

"You put him on the run. We have him on camera. We can track him down."

"And if the list gets out?"

"We're putting contingency plans in place right now." Tyrling looked over at Sciarra. "Ah, Commander? Guardian?"

Sciarra took an at-ease position. "Guardian."

"Please inform your commander that we'll have an update for him in a few hours."

"Will you have more information about the threat against the fleet at that time?"

Tyrling and Selena shared a look. It would be better to tell him the truth... but perhaps not here in the open.

"I'll have something," Tyrling said. "The vehicle should recognize your code, Caryll. Leave it somewhere convenient."

Grinding her teeth, she went to the car. The problem was that it made sense. The Jhandarmi had the personnel and infrastructure to hunt for Kaffton. A full crew of people working for them. It stung that she wasn't in charge, and it was strange having the backup when Tyrling so often let her fly solo in the field.

Walking away went against training and instinct.

Her shield buzzed as someone tried to ping her, but no message came through. Frowning, she looked over at Titan to see if he'd noticed the intrusion.

He nodded as he opened the car door. "Incoming call. One of the Sekoo crew is out here doing a monthly pick-up, but she pinged the Starguard to say someone's following her."

Climbing into the driver's seat, she frowned. "Did she get a look at them?" There wasn't a fleet presence at this end of town, but they'd been in the news and anti-fleet sentiment could make the Sekoos a target of opportunity for bigots.

"She didn't say." He stayed outside the vehicle, a worried expression on his face.

"Get in," Selena ordered. "You can't teleport from here."

Sciarra looked conflicted.

"Let me rephrase that: Guardian, I am coming with you. Fleet personnel must travel in groups of two or more during a code red threat." After all this, there was no way she was letting him wander off to get shot at.

He raised an eyebrow. "It's convenient that you remembered that rule just now."

"I knew someone would be along shortly," she said sweetly. "How far away is the Sekoo?"

Titan sat in the car with a smug smile as he pinged her with the coordinates. "I think you should admit there's a reason you kept me around yesterday. Something other than protocol."

"And I think I'll pull rank, remind you I'm a captain, and that I often get to do what I like."

"One day, maybe you'd like to do me."

Selena leaned in closer. "You are very sure of yourself, Guardian."

Oh, he was sure of himself. And on another day, in another place, she would have appreciated that.

"No one has ever accused me of being indecisive."

His implant was pinged, and Selena felt it as a shiver in his shields. They were way too close for comfort or common sense.

If she could have commanded the world to fall away and leave them alone, she would have. Just for the chance of having a moment of happiness. Two people alone. No history. No responsibilities. No judgment from crew or friends.

The possibility sparkled between them for a heartbeat as Sciarra's green eyes fell to her lips and then met her gaze, full of questions.

Pressing her lips into a thin line, Selena pulled away. "We should go, guardian."

"Yes. Captain." He caressed the word as he said it, piling promises into his look.

"We have a poor, lost crewperson to rescue." She gave a stern look. And, because his memory of her smile was so easy to access, she pinged him with that. A wicked smile and a laugh colored by his own pleasure at the memory.

She pulled into traffic and programmed the vehicle for their destination. Once the autodriver engaged, she was able to settle back and pretend to relax. Post-combat protocols engaged and she started archiving the events of the day, letting her codes work through the memories and sort the details for evaluation later.

A restful silence filled the car as it crept through the slow city traffic.

Sciarra's shield pulsed for a moment, nudging hers and delivering a flurry of thought-moments into her database. Smiles, sensations, colors, and tunes of forgotten songs all bundled together in a classic Personality Profile.

She rolled her eyes as she suppressed a smile. "How old are we again?"

"Not too old to flirt like children." He sounded smug, but there were still questions in his eyes.

Selena shook her head in response to the unasked question. "I never put together a profile like that."

"Why not?"

She shrugged. "It was never a priority. There wasn't a break between school and war."

"The war ended."

Her throat tightened. "No, it didn't. It went underground. It went silent. It went cold. But it never ended. I have door shrapnel in my back if anyone needs a reminder."

Sciarra looked like he was about to say something when the car beeped to signal the end of the ride.

Taking control of the steering, Selena found a parking space and turned on the locate button. They were near the edge of the business district, where there were plenty of holes to teleport through.

The street was nearly deserted, except for a woman pacing nervously in front of the opening to an alleyway. The tangle of unruly brown curls didn't make her standout as fleet or grounder, but the arm patch, a field of white with a golden unicorn, marked her well enough.

A quick ping revealed her name and crew affiliation. Lily Sekoo, age 31, crew tech first-class aboard the vessel *Golden Apple.*

As they approached, Lily brushed her curls from her face and beamed up at Sciarra like he'd hung up the moon and stars. "Thank you so much for coming, guardian. I was so worried." She squeezed past Selena to grab his hand.

Their shared outer shield bent around her, creating an unlikely bubble.

Selena raised an eyebrow and let her emotions rise to the surface. :How well do you know her?:

:Not that well." Titan smiled politely. It was easy to picture him using the same smile with a lost child, and that's exactly the impression he sent back to Selena. "I'll be happy to accompany you back to your ship, sergeant."

Lily glanced over at Selena with a cold look. "Captain Caryll?"

"I'll be happy to come along." It wasn't quite a lie. She did enjoy doing her job as a fleet officer.

"I'd rather you didn't," Lily said.

"Article fourteen, under the rules and regulations for handling a fleet emergency, states that personnel must travel in groups of two or more during a code red threat," Sciarra said with a wink over Lily's head. "I need to escort Captain Caryll back to Enclave as well."

Lily sighed and pressed herself against Titan. "I suppose rules are very important to you as a guardian."

"Yes," Sciarra said.

To Selena, he sounded slightly bewildered by the question.

"And tradition?" Lily batted her eyelashes like a teenager.

"Of course."

Lily squeezed his arm as Selena looked away to hide a laugh. "I suppose, in some way, I'm rescuing you, aren't I? It'll be quite the coup at home. Me, saving Titan Sciarra from the boredom of walking with No-Shot Selena."

No-shot doesn't mean I can't punch a snotty tech, Selena thought. She must have still been too closely linked with Sciarra because there was an answering echo, a memory of a laughter and a fleeting smile on his lips.

"Can you teleport from this distance?" Sciarra asked Lily.

She flushed bright red in embarrassment. "Not right now. My ship's tinker realigned my implant last week and it's been having problems with distances.

"But we have a transport pad nearby. We're down here every week picking up scrap metal for repairs. I shouldn't have left the yard, but I wanted to find a present for my sister. There's a short cut down this alley," Lily said, cutting to the right, past the brick façade of a small repair shop.

"Did you get a good look at who was following you?" Sciarra asked.

"I don't know if they were," Lily confessed with another blush. "It was more a feeling, you know? I did see one person. A woman, I think. She was wearing dark clothes."

Sciarra nodded. "Did you see her face?"

Lily shook her head. "I saw her profile, but it was just a mud face, you know? All the grounders look the same."

"Did you log her in your implant?" Selena asked, trying to keep her voice calm.

The Sekoo woman stared for an uncomfortably long moment at Selena before huddling closer to Sciarra. "Who would think to do that?"

"Anyone with combat training," Selena said. Belatedly, she realized she was dividing Lily from the Academy-trained officers like herself and Sciarra. "And some crews have mandatory threat logs. Either would work."

"I'm a tech!" Lily squeaked. "I wouldn't hurt anyone."

"Funny," Sciarra said, "because you made it sound like Captain Caryll should be ashamed of her lack of kill record."

Lily drew away in ire. "I'm not saying I can't kill if my crew needs it. But my hands have better uses. I'm trained to repair delicate ship's instruments. Risking me in combat would be a waste of my training. You," she shot Selena an angry glare, "were taught to kill. It's the only thing you're good for. And you failed at it."

"Carylls specialize in non-lethal takedown tactics and strategy," Selena said, with a practiced calm that only barely edged toward chilly. "But that's really not important."

"Especially since we're no longer at war and we're all looking for new specialties," Sciarra said, playing the peacemaker.

Selena's implant was pinged with a question mark and a note of concern. Titan wanted to know if she was upset. A tech insulting a captain in front of a guardian could be cause for an intercrew rivalry, if not a full request of reprisal in front of the Captains' Council.

She met Sciarra's eye and shook her head. She wasn't interested in starting another war, only in ending this one.

Something scraped the edge of her distance shield and she stopped, holding up her hand. "What's ahead?"

"Only the scrap yard and the Sekoo teleport pad," Lily said, still scowling. "Why?"

Selena ran her tongue along the inside of her teeth trying to explain without giving away how well her shields worked, or how well the Jhandarmi had trained her. "It feels off. Too quiet."

"Everyone's probably at lunch," Lily said as she tugged at Titan's hand again, urging him forward.

"An empty scrap yard is an excellent place for an ambush," Selena said. She looked at Titan, wondering if it was training or lingering paranoia from the war that was making her hair stand on end.

Sciarra stopped walking. "Are you sure?"

"I specialized in tactics, remember? The scrapyard is out of the view of every city security camera and away from the main street." She opened the logic process she was running, letting Titan see the threat matrix she'd run.

"My defense shield isn't picking up anything," he said.

Neither was hers. Not a real threat, at any rate; only an odd, almost percussive electronic pulse on the edge of her range. "Are your shields tuned to pick up grounder weapons?"

"Why would a grounder attack us?" Lily asked. "We've never hurt them."

Both Selena and Sciarra stared at her naïve statement.

"There are people upset we occupied a rocky, unwanted beach," Selena said. "I assure you, those are the friendliest ones. The war didn't end that long ago."

Lily's petulant frown turned to a scowl. "That's fleet business, and none of theirs. Who are they to judge? They abandoned the Empire!"

"They colonized a planet in the name of the Emperor," Selena corrected, wishing she could pull them away from the yard. The hairs on the back of her neck were standing on end and the percussive pulse ticked faster and faster.

"If they'd been loyal," Lily said, "they would have moved to a system with more resources and fewer war ships."

Sciarra cleared his throat. "Captain, sergeant, this conversation is fascinating and I'd love for you to continue you it... in Enclave, away from here."

"That's an excellent idea." Lily marched forward, turning the corner into the scrap yard.

Sciarra went after her.

Cursing her temper and training, Selena followed. She couldn't pull rank now, and she'd lost the chance to persuade Sciarra into taking a safer route. Which meant the best she could do was shield them all, and hope that whatever anomaly she'd detected ahead wasn't life-threatening.

She turned the corner just as the pulse became bone-grating, rising in pitch.

The far side of the scrapyard bloomed into a fire ball and everyone threw up their shields; but as it hit her outer layer, Selena felt the draining pull of a magnetic bomb.

Lily dropped, crumpling to the ground with a scream— injured or scared, it was impossible to tell.

Sciarra ran for the fallen Sekoo girl.

Forcing her way through Lily and Sciarra's shields, Selena grabbed them both. Lily's shield was already too weak. Sciarra's energy reserve was perilously low. It took all she had left, but she pulled them into a teleport, smashed the shield over Enclave, and dropped them outside the OIA building.

Then her knees gave out. She landed in the volcanic gravel with a breathless *umph*.

"You broke the shield again," Titan muttered with a dazed expression. He met her gaze and found the energy to check on Lily.

Selena closed her eyes. "I went through without a code. It's intact and we're alive. Whine less."

"You could have used a code."

"New rule, if someone comes in without a code, it's me. Problem solved."

He rolled his eyes and helped Lily to her feet. "Are you all right, sergeant?"

Lily nodded, then spun and vomited.

Sciarra looked over. "What about you?"

"I'll be fine. I can walk to the OIA infirmary."

"That was a long teleport with extra people."

She lifted a shoulder, too tired to argue. "I've had worse days."

Lily wiped her mouth. "What was that? I'm not... I'm not hurt, only sick. Drained." She ran her hand over the forearm. "My implant is dead."

"Localized EMP blast," Sciarra said. "They're meant to disable electronics or implants. I'm not sure how we got out."

"Layers of shields," Selena said. "Hers. Yours. Mine. With enough strong shields you can buy a few seconds to teleport out of danger." A memory grabbed her: storming the Baular strong-

154

hold to rescue Marshall. An EMP blast had deadened her implant and she'd fallen into the cold blood of her comrades. Rising again, and using her body to shield the weaker fighters…

They'd returned not victorious—because there was no victory in war—but alive.

Titan caught some edge of her nightmare and reached for her.

She jerked away. He wanted to comfort her, and she couldn't handle that right now. Instead, she focused on this disaster. "They meant to disable us, then attack."

He nodded slowly.

There was a flurry of inquiring pings as people noticed their sudden arrival.

Selena ignored them.

Lily spat on the ground. "Dishonorable bastards."

"Do you need help?" Sciarra was still looking at her.

"No." She shook her head. "Get Lily to her crew."

His eyes narrowed. "You're to stay in Enclave, Captain Caryll. That's an order."

"Where else would I go?" Selena asked. "I can't teleport right now and I'm not walking out."

With a reluctant nod, Sciarra turned his full attention to Lily Seko.

Selena stepped away, heading for the OIA building and the bachelor's quarters. But the smell as she opened the door was too familiar. The hint of ozone and lemon cleaning polish turned her stomach and she tensed, waiting for the burn of plasma fire.

Slamming the door shut, Selena stood outside the building, terrified of going back in. Sciarra was almost out of sight, lost in the forest of landing gear and makeshift sheds that littered the Enclave.

There was still a slight charge in her implant.

Enough.

Maybe enough...

Her heart raced at the thought of going back inside and facing her memories again. Better to die in a failed teleport than go back in. At least it would be painless.

Her phone rang. Groaning, she answered. "This is Caryll."

"There was a blast downtown," Tyrling said. "That you?"

"Someone planted a bomb at the Sekoo's junkyard."

"The who now?"

"Minor crew," Selena explained. "Weak tech, poor leadership, junkers of ships." There was a distinct lack of comfortable-looking chairs in the vicinity and the guardian at the front desk was watching her to closely for comfort. "No one died. I think."

Tyrling shouted to someone closer to him, then said, "Can you get down here?"

She looked down at her body. There was blood, but most of it wasn't hers. "Sure. I'll find a way. Teleporting is out for a bit."

"I'll send a car," Tyrling said.

"See you soon." She hung up and headed for the main exit.

The guardian behind the desk stood up. "Um, ma'am? Captain?"

Selena kept walking.

"You're not supposed to leave, captain. Guardian Sciarra's orders."

"Guardian, my apartment is across the street. I'm going to get clean clothes. I'll be back soon," Selena lied. "Would that be acceptable?"

He shrank down in his chair.

For the life of her, she couldn't place his name or crew.

She stopped, trying to place the feeling. He was just another guardian, another piece of the great machine that was the fleet.

They came, they lived, they died, and what happened in between so rarely made a difference. "What's your name?"

He blinked in surprise. "Um, Jandu, ma'am. Jandu Triem off the *Pilgrim*. My grandmother was Caryll, she was a medic on the *Etain*."

The *Etain* had been retired before she was born and the Triem hadn't sent any officer candidates to the Academy while she was there, but she nodded. "Thank you for your diligence, Guardian Triem. I'm sure it's appreciated. If Guardian Sciarra checks in, please assure him I'm in perfect health."

"There's blood on you..."

"It's not mine!"

"Simply verifying, ma'am." The young guardian stared hard at the floor.

Shaking her head, Selena walked out. Maybe she could con Tyrling into buying her a working lunch. The thought of the coming debrief was making her head ache. Tyrling might want Kaffton on trial, but if she found that idiot first, she was cracking his skull on the nearest wall for stirring up this much drama.

Her secrets weren't going to be secrets much longer.

13

TITAN

"NEPHEW!"

His aunt's voice knocked Titan out of the meditation. The pain from the inexpert stitches the *Sabiha's* medtech was putting in his side burned. Inhaling sharply, he stared up at the black ceiling, dotted with green gems in the constellations of the Sciarra home system, to regain his composure. "Hello, auntie," he said with a resigned sigh.

Elea Sciarra stepped out of the shadows, her face an unreadable mask, her shields opaque. His mother's younger sister was made of the same mold as most Sciarra women: ebony skin, shining hair caught in thick, black braids that were pulled away from her face and coiled crown-like on her head, a face of bony angles and focused lines. But, where his mother had an expression of polished stone, Elea had small cracks that made her look human—smile lines around her eyes. The hint of creases around her mouth.

Right now, her lips were creased in a frown.

"Captain?" Titan would have lowered his shields as a show of respect and submissiveness if he were still capable of making one.

The captain held up a tablet. "What is this?"

He frowned in confusion. "A tablet? Ma'am?"

She rolled her eyes. "I'm your oldest surviving relative, Ty, but I'm not senile. I meant: Why did you request information about a declaration of courtship from the database?"

"I couldn't access my implant and I needed a distraction, ma'am."

"Ma'am me one more time and I'll turn this into a formal conversation and plant your butt in the brig."

The medtech froze, ready to run if a fight broke out.

"Sorry, auntie."

Elea nudged the tech. "Finish up, Dumaka. He's already in enough pain." She set the tablet down and held out her hand to do a scan. "Suns of the homeworld, boy. What did you get yourself into? There are reports of a fight with a grounder, a bomb, and you come home looking like you went into a fight wielding a kitten!"

He closed his eyes. "It was unplanned."

A hard hand smacked against his aching head. "You're an officer, Titan! You're supposed to plan!"

"I was supposed to be following up on a lead into the warehouse break-in. Nowhere in the mission brief was murder mentioned."

"You were with someone from an allied crew, alone, and murder didn't cross your mind?"

"No, auntie."

Dumaka finished the stitches in Titan's side and tied a knot. "You'll need to keep it clean until your nanites repopulate," he said in a soft voice. "No extreme activity, no exercise, and no..." He gulped, practically hyper-ventilating. "... no sex. For at least a week. The bandages will need to be changed every twelve hours."

"Thank you, Dumaka," Titan said. "I'll be sure not to rip your fine work."

The younger man smiled gratefully. "I didn't mean to be personal when I said..." He jerked his chin in a lurching nod.

"Sex?" Elea asked. "Dumaka, how many times had I told you this? The chief medic on the ship should know about the sexual activity of the crew. You keep us healthy. You need to know what we are doing with our bodies."

"But Titan doesn't—" Dumaka's bright green eyes went wide with fright. "I mean, I know you could, Commander."

Elea sighed and patted Dumaka's shoulder. "That's... that's probably good enough. Good try, Dumaka. Good try. You're dismissed."

Dumaka fled the medbay with graceless haste.

"I keep trying to build up his confidence, and still." She shook her head and sat down on the bed beside Titan as he sat up. "How bad do you feel?"

"I've definitely had worse. Even with Dumaka's inexpert work." He looked at his aunt. "We need to trade for a new medic. If something serious happened, he couldn't handle this bay alone."

Elea picked up the tablet again. "Is that what this was about? A new medic?" She shook the tablet at him as if the words would spill out onto the deck.

He winced and locked down every thought from the day. His aunt's shield was close enough to his own that she picked up stray thoughts if he wasn't careful. "It wasn't for anything specific. I just had some questions because it came up in conversation."

"Ty, I've known you since you were born. I was your first trainer. I was the one you went to when someone pulled you behind the training mats to steal a kiss, because you were worried Damia would be angry."

"She would have been," Titan said. His mother would have been angry at the interruption and the fact he couldn't defend himself against unwanted advances. But he'd been seven, still using a gauntlet instead of an implant, and worried he'd hurt someone. "You gave better advice anyway."

"So why are you researching courtship and not looping me in on the conversation?"

"There's not really a conversation to have yet," he said as he reached for his shirt. "More of a passing thought."

"A declaration of courtship is not something you spring on your favorite captain."

But you aren't my favorite captain, auntie. He bit his cheek to keep from smiling. "The individual in question has made it clear they aren't ready to consider courtship yet."

"Yet?" The captain pounced on the word. "You keep saying *yet*. When do they plan to be open to the idea?"

"She hasn't told me that. Yet."

Elea raised a quizzical eyebrow. "Is there a rival I need to be aware of? You did walk into a bomb today. I can't stress enough how upsetting I find that."

He shook his head, trying to sort out what he'd seen and felt the day before. "I think she's unsure of my intentions and believes an alliance might be risky, politically."

"Really?" The captain's face fell into a neutral mask, then she blinked. "It isn't Captain Marshall, is it?"

"No!"

Hermione Marshall was as far from his ideal spouse as the sun was from a blackhole.

Plus, there was the lingering sense that Marshall belonged to Mal—ancestors welcome him to the Lost Fleet. Eventually, Marshall would find a lover and he'd have to choke on the bitter gall of letting even that memory of Mal go. But, until that awful and probably eventful day, Marshall was logged in his mind as Mal Baular's problem. Ancestors protect anyone else who tried to get near the ruthless woman.

His captain shrugged. "I'm not fond of all the crews out there, but, politically, the more allies we can gather, the better. And we need new blood in the crew. She'd be welcomed."

"That's going to be a sticking point," Titan said. "If she ever lets me near her, at least. She's very high ranking in her crew."

"Oh." Elea looked at the tablet. "That's why you'd need a declaration? To ensure that there weren't any last minute surprises if you decided to pursue marriage?"

"I think the officer in question would understand that I was serious if I made a formal declaration. Flirting makes her suspicious. Or repels her," he admitted the fear. "It's hard to tell."

"Does she seek out your company, laugh at your jokes when no one else does, and compliment you on regular basis? I've found those are good indicators of interest." She smiled. "Although, you know my relationship history. Damia's little sister. The mousy Sciarra engineer."

"And the captain who killed her captain to take control," Titan said with a grin. "If you weren't my aunt, that kind of personal resume would put you on my radar."

She chuckled. "I imagine the officer you wish to court is equally fierce."

"In many ways. But with fewer kills despite being in the war. She was primarily a shielder, I think."

Or he'd thought. Until he'd caught a glimpse of Selena's memories. She'd had the kill shots so many times and not taken them. "She has good qualities though."

"I should hope." His captain's enthusiasm had cooled enough for him to notice. "I also hope you'll remember that the crew look up to you, Ty. If you bring home someone because she's beautiful, and not an asset to the crew, there'll be talk. We're trying, but we've always been a working crew. There's no room here for you to have a pretty sidepiece."

He nodded. "I know. I'll be careful where I bestow my affections." His implant pinged. "I need to go, captain, if you have no further need of me. Carver wants me in the offices for a debrief."

His captain smiled in understanding. "Be careful out there."

"I will, ma'am." He stood, grimacing at the pain. "I'll be very careful."

The offices of the Star Guardians either smelled freshly bleached, or like the inside of the men's locker room at the Academy; there was no in between. Today the offices smelled of sweaty gym socks, jock straps, and the body odor of too many people packed into a tight space. There were fewer than fifty guardians on the force and they still managed to smell like an unwashed army of thousands.

Titan sat in his office, staring at the lock in his hand and visualizing the tumblers moving one by one into place while he waited for Carver to finish his call with the Jhandarmi.

There was the faintest of clicks, and the lock sprung open.

"You look pretty smug," Hollis said as he walked into Titan's office. "What's that?"

"An experiment." Titan tossed it to Silar. "Selena..." He caught himself. "Captain Caryll mentioned that the entry into the warehouse with the missing supplies was odd. Something about grounders picking locks."

"So you decided to see if you could pick locks?" Hollis guessed as he turned the small, red padlock over in his hand. "Is this the same one we had on the warehouse?"

"It is," Titan said. "Right down to the telekyen. It's a bit fiddly, but it can be done without a physical lock pick." He put his hands behind his head and stretched back in his chair; the muscles in his side pulled uncomfortably.

Hollis studied the lock with a frown. "Can anyone in fleet unlock this with their implant?"

"According to reliable sources? No. Apparently that's the kind of attention to fine, delicate detail that would get your name passed around."

Understanding dawned slowly on Hollis's face. He raised an eyebrow in speculation and then his smile turned to a lust-laden grin of comprehension. "Delicate work?"

"For delicate places." Titan grinned back. "If you ever figure it out, I'm sure your lovers will be impressed."

Hollis chuckled. "I've never had complaints before, but I'm willing to add more weapons to my arsenal." He tossed the lock across the room. "I need your signature."

"For what?"

"Nothing major, just the proposal for a new combatives instructor." Hollis sent a tablet flying at his face. It stopped short of beheading him, but only barely.

"I'm really not in the mood-" Titan cut his argument short when he saw the name of the instructor. "Rowena? Rowena Lee?"

Hollis shrugged. "There's not another Rowena in the fleet. Trust me. I keep track of our beautiful women."

Titan grabbed the tablet and scrolled through the data. "You keep track of everything, pretty, petty, or otherwise. That's why Carver keeps you."

"Speaking of pretty, I hear you spent all day with Selena Caryll and came home intact." Silar eyed the visible cuts on his cheek. "More or less. How was that?"

"Fine." Titan cut him off with a glare. "Why Rowena?"

Hollis sat on the edge of the desk. "If you must know, there's a certain captain in the fleet who was begging me to give her my morning. I couldn't, because of the combatives training, so she recommended several replacements. Lee happened to be the best choice out of the lot."

That made no sense. Titan put the tablet down and gave Silar a look that sent most people running for the exit.

Silar's grinned widened in anticipation of a fight.

"We can't take a recommendation from a Warmonger captain for Rowena's placement," Titan said levelly.

"Wasn't a Warmonger."

"Then it's an attack. How many fleetlings is this captain planning to send to the next training session?"

Silar's eyes sparked with delight. "None. There is no avenue of escape, Commander Sciarra. You've been out-maneuvered. Sign."

"I don't believe for a second that someone recommended Rowena out of the goodness of their heart or appreciation for her skills. Not if the only prize is getting you alone."

Silar's glee made him wish for a shield. Peace or no peace, there was too much bad blood between the Silars and the Lees. Hollis Silar was a tactician known for plotting complex, detailed, and patient strategies.

Leaving Rowena at his mercy was out of the question.

Hollis put his hand to his chest in mock outrage. Then he laughed. "That's almost true. The captain in question didn't want me as much as she didn't want you." He stood, pulled the chair over, and sat down, folding his arms on the desk and resting his chin on top. "Which is why I'm so very curious how your little excursion went today. Come on. You know you want to spill all the juicy details."

Derailment. Another Silar stall tactic. "There's nothing to talk about." And no reason for Selena to promote Rowena. "You know Hoshi Lee won't approve this. He hates Ro."

"Ah! I thought of that!" Hollis said. "Scroll down. We're going to offer him one OIA slot and one position in the next set of Starguard trainees to fill with whoever in his crew he recommends. In return, the Captains' Council gets to request one of his crew for training at the new Academy here in Enclave."

Titan tried to read Hollis's smile and gave up. He'd been outmaneuvered. "An OIA slot? Seriously? You're going to trust a Lee with that?"

"One Hoshi picks? Ancestors, no. But I have full faith anyone he thinks is competent will wash out before the mid-point. When is Rowena going to challenge him for the captain's seat?"

"Probably before you understand Lee politics." Hot pain cut at his side when he breathed in too deeply. Cracking nanites, never there when he needed them. "The only other signature on here is yours. This isn't going to pass without backing. And no one is going to back Rowena." It hurt to say, but it was the truth. The only reason Rowena hadn't been executed for war crimes was because she hadn't reached twenty-three before the war, and hadn't been tried as an adult.

He held the tablet out.

Hollis pushed it back with a mental shove. "You, me, Carver, Caryll, that's our four."

"You're sure Caryll gave this to you before the bombing?"

"She made the recommendation first thing this morning."

"And that didn't raise any red flags? You didn't think to check for head trauma or anything? Because the only thing stranger than Selena Caryll promoting Rowena would be Marshall kissing Mal Baular, ancestors keep him."

Hollis recoiled in horror. "Oh, sky and stars no. Why do you insist on giving me these nightmares? Baular and Hermione would start another war—if he'd survived."

"Or they'd take over the universe together."

Hollis shook his head until Titan was sure he heard a brain rattling around. "Nope. My imagination has limits, and Hermione allying with Baular is well past the event horizon of probability. Ancestors forgive him."

He wasn't so sure Hollis's math checked out. He had a very vivid imagination and many memories of Mal going toe-to-toe with Marshall. The one time he'd speculated that the fiery tempest of their combative relationship was more than pure hatred, Mal had nearly broken his eye socket.

In another world, maybe they would have had a chance. Poor Mal, dead before he had an opportunity to find redemption. "Ancestors forgive him," Titan murmured. He looked over the proposal one more time. "Fine. I'll sign, but if this winds up getting Rowena killed, I'm taking it out of your hide."

"There's only three things that could kill that woman: old age, the heat death of the universe, and me, and I promise to play nice." Hollis winked. "Life gets boring when I don't have a Lee to tangle with."

Titan slammed the tablet down and glared at Silar. "Would you please, for three minutes, turn your libido down and remember that Rowena is my best friend in the world and not one of your conquests? Homicide paperwork sucks atmo. Cleaning blood off the walls is time consuming and annoying. Do not push me."

Hollis hadn't moved. He watched with bedroom eyes and a smirk. "You're predictable, Sciarra, in training and in here. Lee's better to fight with. She takes risks because she's not afraid to fail. Her death threats, I believe." He sat up. "You're bleeding through your shirt, shields down, and breathing shallowly. You're not a threat."

"Right now," Titan said. "But I'll get better."

"Not if you keep playing with Caryll."

Nine percent charge on his implant, no way to teleport out... His hand slid under the desk to the small gun he'd hidden there when he moved in. "Was that a threat?"

"A prediction," Silar said. "Relationships that start with someone trying to break your jaw don't usually end well. You're on day two and she nearly left you for dead."

He pulled his hand away from the gun. "Selena's not at fault here. She saved me."

"That's what I thought," Hollis said as he stood up. "You better wipe that look off your face before one of your crew sees you. Moonstruck. You fell hard, Sciarra."

There was just enough charge on his implant to crack Hollis's shield as he threw the tablet at him. It smacked into his face with a satisfying thunk. "Get out."

Silar laughed and teleported away.

Titan rested his head on his desk for a moment before checking his shirt. The hastily stitched gash in his side had ripped open again. This was not the time to be weak.

Or start a war, he thought guiltily. Throwing things at Silar was a mistake. But...

Selena. She'd walked away from him looking broken. Cut off all contact. She had to know that what Lily Sekoo said didn't reflect what he thought. Selena had been in his thoughts half the day. She knew how he felt.

Which only made her rejection worse. She knew he was falling in love and she'd left him.

He dropped his head on the desk.

:Sciarra?: Carver's mental page cut through his frustration.

:Sir?:

:My office. Now.:

:Coming, sir.:

Was it worth changing uniforms for this?

Yes. If he was going to get kicked out of the Starguard for throwing things at Silar it would be in a clean uniform, with a shiny rank, and all the physical strength he could fake. He changed, washed his face, and headed for whatever chewing out Carver had planned.

He wound his way past desks and down the hall to the dark den that Carver called an office. Papers and tablets were strewn across the desk, along with the remains of several lunches, a thermos with something green growing on the lip, and four computer monitors.

Carver was standing beside the door, scowling at something across the room. He glanced over his shoulder as Titan approached, nodded, and turned his focus back to his office. "Is it straight?"

Titan stopped beside the commander. "Sir?"

"The painting?" Carver nodded at his office.

A painting of roses surrounding a gushing fountain—thank you, Selena, for that imagery—was skittering across the deep-maroon wall under the influence of telekyen and Carver's control

"Um…" He couldn't unsee it. No matter how hard he tried, he couldn't unsee the sexual allusions, or break his mind away from a very personal fantasy of a highly erotic nature. If he'd been fair-skinned, he would have blushed. Instead, his cheeks heated and he was left staring at a dancing vagina on his boss's wall. "Why do you have this, sir?"

Carver grimaced. "Why do humans do anything like this, Sciarra?"

"Lovers. Gen gave this to you? It seems… unlike her." A dark suspicion formed on the edge of his thoughts.

"Selena Caryll gave it to Gen as a gift," Carver said, confirming Titan's suspicions. "She said it was for our new home."

Titan turned to look at his boss. "You have a new home? I didn't know about any new housing on Enclave."

"There's an apartment complex near the university called the Rose Gardens. Selena thinks Gen and I should move there. Together." Carver's frown deepened. "This is supposed to be a painting of the fountain in the main courtyard or something like that. Gen told me there was no room in her quarters and, if I was serious, that I'd find room for it. So, I'm finding room for it. The universe's most banal painting."

"Until you see the penis." The words slipped out before he could stop himself. If asked, he'd have to blame the blood loss and the concussion.

The painting hung in midair. "The what now?"

Titan cleared his throat. "While I was in the company of a certain officer of the fleet, she pointed out the rounded head of the fountain and the almost, ah, yonic shape of the roses on the trellis. If you let your vision blur for a moment you get..."

Carver choked on a laugh. "Oh my, ancestors! Do you think Gen knows?"

"She's a Silar, sir. They're known to have a rough sort of humor." Along with all their other bad traits.

"But... Selena gave it to her." Carver shook her head. "Poor Selena. She probably bought this thinking it was a perfectly innocent picture. Something nice and native for Gen to enjoy. And now I'll never be able to see it without thinking about sex."

The painting slammed into the wall, the self-adhering frame fixing it in place.

"I'm probably going to have this hanging in my living room one day," Carver said. "Every time I walk in, I'll see it and not have to mention what it looks like to my friends." He closed his eyes and shook his head. "You know what the worst part is?"

"No, sir."

"I can't even get revenge, because I know Selena Caryll wouldn't do this as a prank."

Titan smirked. "I wouldn't be so sure of that."

"Selena has many good traits," Carver said, walking into his office, "but a sense of humor isn't one of them." He took his seat with a sigh.

The debris on his desk lifted like a cloud of dandelion fluff, dancing around before landing neatly in the recycler.

Most of the fleet could control more than one object at the same time, but it was Carver's peculiar tech that allowed him to control so much at once. It was what had made his crew a threat so dangerous that his family was killed. It was what many argued had won him the war.

In Titan's opinion, the tech helped, but Carver's true genius lay in understanding people. He always seemed to know who was right for the job.

Titan took an at-ease position and waited for the yelling to begin.

His boss sat glaring at his screen with an intensity that suggested someone other than Carver was going to have a bad day. "Your captain has requested I give you three days leave to recover from this afternoon. How bad off are you?"

"I've had worse, sir."

"That's not an answer, Sciarra. You crashed a fighter into a planet and I still don't know how you survived that, but you did."

He rubbed his left arm over the faded scars and shrugged. "A scratch or two, a couple of bruises, I'm fine. I don't need the leave if you're shorthanded."

"Selena's report said you took the brunt of the impact."

Lies. The one time he didn't file his report immediately and Carver actually read the cracking things. "We were well-shielded. Taking the brunt doesn't mean anything."

Carver looked skeptical. "Hollis says you were bleeding."

Titan made a show of looking down at his uniform. "I don't see it, sir."

"He also said you threw a tablet at him."

"Silar deserved it."

"If Sciarra stubbornness could fuel a ship, I could have this fleet flying again." Carver sighed. "I know Hollis has a mouth on him, and he loves to push buttons for the reaction. But he's one of the best officers we have. Was he really out of line or were you blowing off steam?"

Titan grimaced. "I was… he was…"

"Just tell me what he said about who," Carver said. "Because I know with you the only thing that makes you lash out is insulting someone you're protecting. Was it about Lee again?"

"Sort of. It's stupid, sir. He misunderstood my relationship with someone else and…" He shrugged, regretting the movement as soon as he lifted his battered shoulders.

Carver rolled his eyes. "Ancestors, but you two are predict-table."

"What demands does Silar have?"

"Hollis?" Carver sounded confused. "He thinks it's hilarious he pushed you to the point where you snapped. I already yelled at him and told him not to hassle you when you're bleeding at your desk. He should have taken you to the infirmary."

"If he'd tried to touch me I would have shot him," Titan said honestly.

"That's what he said." Carver frowned. "Your stitches are ripped though."

Titan shook his head. "I'm in prime condition, sir."

"Fine, use that engine if you think it'll run. I'm approving the leave, and you're going to the infirmary. But I want you back here in an hour. The Jhandarmi have identified the dead man you found in the tunnels, and they want to discuss some things. It's not going to be pretty."

Selena. "I can be here, sir."

"I've let your captain and the *Sabiha's* medic know you're coming in. And Rowena Lee."

Titan closed my eyes. "You did not need to tell Ro."

"If you're going to get into a fight with Hollis over a woman, she's important enough that she has a right to know you're being stupid. Bleeding guardians are not good for the fleet. Get yourself cleaned up and get back here."

"Yes, sir." He trudged out of the office, vision blurring, and set his implant to scan for Selena.

14

ROWENA

THREE ALARMS TRIGGERED AT once. Rowena jumped up, shoved her wheel-mounted workbench in front of her wall of remembrance, and dropped every shield in the engineering section.

By the time Captain Hoshi Lee arrived, the place looked as desolate as he probably hoped she felt. And he looked proud of himself. A sure sign that he'd done something monumentally stupid that was going to get the Lee family in trouble. Again.

She focused on polishing the laser scope and wondered how many hours of free labor she'd be doing for another crew to cover this disaster.

The *Danielle Marie* let out a boatswain's shrill whistle. "Captain approaching."

Rowena dropped the scope and cleaning gear and came to attention.

Hoshi swaggered through the room. Before acknowledging her, he made a show of looking around, examining everything, even though they both knew he couldn't tell a wrench from a flinjammer. "At ease," he said as he circled. "Today is a very good day, Yeoman. Do you know why?"

"No, sir." She stared straight at the bulkhead.

He held up a small tablet. "Today, the Lee family will be announcing candidates for the Office of Imperial Affairs and the Star Guardian training program."

The day I breath vacuum. There was no way Hoshi had found someone to sponsor the crew like that.

Hoshi chuckled. "I can see from your expression that you don't believe me. But it's right here. Please. Read."

Cautiously, she took the tablet. There was a lot of formal language but the gist of it was that the Lees were being offered two training slots, one OIA, one for the guard, for candidates of the captain's choosing. In exchange, the fleet training academy in Enclave had the right to take any officer from the crew. It wasn't the worst deal ever. "Congratulations, captain. I know you've looked forward to this day for some time."

"We all have," he said, snatching the tablet from her. "Except for you. Ungrateful wretch of a child. If I hadn't stepped in and begged for leniency, promised the allied crews that I would see you properly punished, they would have executed you!"

"Yes, sir." She'd been locked in the brig of one of the Wariea's ships; she still wasn't sure which one. The Wariea crew hadn't talked to her, but they'd be kind enough. Two ration bars a day, clean water, and privacy.

She'd expected to be executed. *Deserved* to be executed. She'd killed people. It didn't matter what everyone else had done, or what would have happened if she hadn't fought on the front lines.

At the end of the day she owned her choice. She'd chosen to fight. And she'd chosen to come back to the Lees as a yeoman.

Hoshi circled around her. "Aren't you going to ask who I'm nominating?"

"I assumed you'd make a formal announcement to the full crew, sir."

"It won't be you!"

She nodded in agreement. "Understood, sir."

"Hayato will go to the OIA, and Kanon will go to the Starguard." Hoshi beamed. "Do you like my choices?"

"Yes, sir."

Hayato was an obedient young man who'd fought in two battles of the war with her. He'd never keep up with the Elite in the OIA, but he'd be good office staff for someone. Everyone needed a reliable paper filer. Kanon was going to get crushed by the Starguard training, but maybe they'd take pity on her and let her be an assistant.

If they had assistants.

She'd have to ask Titan what in the name of the Emperor he'd been thinking, allowing this mad scheme to happen.

Hoshi scowled at her, probably unhappy with her lack of reaction. "The announcements will be made later this evening. I will be throwing a celebration for Hayato and Kanon."

"I'm sure the crew will enjoy that, sir."

"You will not be welcome."

Behind her back, her fist tightened and her nails cut into her palm. She was Lee too. She belonged with them. "Of course, sir." Blood seeped between her fingers and her implant pushed a new wave of nanites out to heal her, but there was no expression on her face or in her voice. She'd never let Hoshi have the satisfaction of beating her.

"Make whatever excuse you require. Visit Aronia. Find something to repair. Go wander the Enclave. But do not be in the public area of a Lee ship until the third shift tomorrow. I don't want your bad luck polluting the celebration."

Bad luck? She'd followed orders from the same captain he'd obeyed. Her jaw ached from wanting to scream.

"Understood, yeoman?"

"Sir, yes, sir!" Rowena saluted, the blood already drying on her hand.

Hoshi waved a dismissive hand. "Your first stop might be the *Golden Apple*."

That made her frown. "Sir? I'm not familiar with that ship."

"It belongs to the Sekoos," he said the name like they were worms. "One of their techs requested help and named you specifically." The way he said it implied he couldn't imagine why another crew would want her services, even though it was her skill that the Lees traded on for everything they had at this point. "You may take your kit and render assistance."

"Thank you, sir. I'll go as soon as I clean my work station."

He wrinkled his nose at the rack of tools that kept the *Danielle Marie* functioning, and shrugged. "Consider yourself dismissed, yeoman."

Hoshi walked away, humming to himself.

Rowena pinged Titan. She needed the support, but his signal was weak. She pulled out her personal com and contacted the *Sabiha*.

"This is the *Sabiha*, Ensign Mars Sciarra speaking." A younger version of Titan appeared. His face was softer, his eyes gentler, but there was no mistaking the young Sciarra for what he was. "Hello, Rowena. What do you need?"

"Hi, Mars. I'm trying to get in touch with Titan."

Mars made an exaggerated frowny face that was dramatic as it was comical. "There's a tiny problem with that. He's in medical right now. Getting yelled at."

"Why?"

"There was a bomb and his stitches ripped and..." Mars shrugged with both hands in the air. "The captain says it's a bad combination of testosterone and ego. Personally, I think he's just stubborn."

"All Sciarras are stubborn."

"You say the nicest things!" Mars grinned at the screen. "Do you want me to run a message to him? The EMP bomb drained his implant so he can't ping you until he recharges."

She sighed. "No. It's not urgent. I was just-" Hurt, because Hoshi was a mud-sucking parasite and because she felt unwanted.

Mars grimaced in commiseration. "Wanna hang out at Cargo Blue tonight? Some of us were going to take Titan out while he was weak and see if he still scares people."

"I'm not in the mood for Cargo Blue."

"Titan probably won't be either, but the captain says you have an open pass to come visit the *Sabiha* if you want. I can send you the shield code..." It was both a question and a statement.

She nodded. "Yes, that would be nice. Thank you." Titan had given her every code to access the *Sabiha* since her trial had finished, and told her at least twice a week that she could join his crew. But she doubted Titan had told anyone else about his offer, and telling would only get him yelled at more. "I have to go check out something for a tech on the *Golden Apple*, but then I'll come over."

"Great! Bring some of the Giggle Water."

"You know it has no alcohol, right?"

"Who cares? It makes Titan tell jokes," Mars said.

Rowena smiled. "Sure. I'll bring some. See you in a bit." She turned the com off and rolled her eyes.

Titan needed Giggle Water; he needed to relax a bit.

Grabbing her gear, she teleported to the edge of Sekoo territory. She could have gone straight in; their shield was a flimsy network laced with bad code and no real defensive capabilities. They weren't a war crew. Before the wormhole collapsed, they'd been basic scavengers, running errands for the colonists, scooping what resources were available out of the rings of the inner planets, shuttling passengers in and out of the wormhole, or to and from the system's main space station. They were bottom feeders. But they'd supported the Baluars.

That made them allies.

The man who hurried down the ramp was wearing a frayed pilot's jump suit with no insignia. And he had no detectable implant. "Can I help you?"

"One of your techs contacted the *Danielle Marie* and asked for me?"

"Do you know who?"

Rowena shook her head. "All I know is it that was a tech."

"And you are...?"

One of the most infamous people in the fleet, last she'd checked. "Yeoman Rowena Lee."

"Right."

Maybe he'd been one of the people who took head trauma during the war. Some of them hadn't healed quite right.

He wiped a hand across his nose. "Well, you can come in and I'll ask around. Let me unplug the shield real quick."

"You could give me a temporary guest code," Rowena said.

The man stared at her in confusion. "No. We... um... it's not that kind of shield. You can't walk through it."

While he ran back up the ramp, she stuck her hand through the shield. Nothing happened. But she waited, politely, because showing someone else their weak points wasn't her job. Even if it did make her grind her teeth.

The shield dropped with an audible whine and the man waved at her.

Rowena teleported to the ramp. "So, I assume the shield is what you want fixed? If it's making that sound the power source is out of phase. I can tune it, no problem."

"Oh, no, it's always like that."

A brief vision of knocking the inept Sekoo unconscious and fixing the shields without permission flashed through her mind. Probably a bad idea. There'd be a report of some kind, or a reprimand. As if those were having any effect on her career.

"Rowena?"

She turned at the sound of her name, but couldn't identify the woman walking towards her in Sekoo uniform.

"Lily Sekoo. I'm the one who asked for you."

"A pleasure to meet you, Tech Sekoo," Rowena said.

Lily was... off. The uniform she was wearing was too short, and too wide in the shoulders. Her features were an odd blend of genetic features from several major crews, and somehow it gave the appearance of being counterfeit. It sent a shiver up Rowena's spine.

Maybe Titan was right. She'd spent so long locked up with the Lees that she was beginning to think like Hoshi. The war was over and she was done judging people by who they were born to. Except for the Silars. They deserved everything she thought about them.

Forcing a smile, she held out her hand so Lily could check her shields.

Lily ignored it and gestured down the ramp. "Could we talk for a few minutes?"

"Of course." Rowena blinked in confusion. Her implant said the Sekoos used the same physical greetings as the rest of the fleet. She'd have to update that. "What did you need repaired? The man on sentinel duty didn't seem to know."

Lily glanced at the ship. "Who? Taro? He's not on duty."

"Oh." That made no sense.

"The captain gave everyone leave this week to remember the war and all we lost."

Rowena carefully hid her surprise. At least a period of mourning explained the mismatched uniforms and the general feel of malaise hanging around their ships. It was a little extreme, but every crew mourned differently. "If I'd known, I wouldn't have intruded. My captain made the matter sound urgent." But maybe Hoshi was hoping she'd get caught by the bilge crew and die here.

"Oh, it's urgent, but it's not something I need from you," Lily said with what she probably thought was a teasing smile. It made her look like a feral rat. "I have some information I think the Lees will want."

"Your captain will have to take that to Captain Hoshi. I don't speak for the Lees."

Lily shrugged. "Maybe, but in this case you have what I want."

"Which is?"

They stopped where the edge of the Sekoo shield would usually be, under the shade of a derelict battle cruiser being slowly dissected for parts.

"You have Titan Sciarra," Lily said. "And I want him."

Rowena raised her eyebrows. There were always rumors in fleet, and when there weren't rumors there was always amateur entertainment in the forms of books, songs, and videos passed around the back channels. Her name was frequently linked to Titan, but never in such a proprietary way.

"I don't own Titan or have any claim or control over him," Rowena said. "He's not an engine I can trade."

Lily turned, crossing her arms. "Even for medicine?"

"Medicine?"

"We have contacts on the outside that the guardians probably wouldn't approve of." Lily took her arm and tugged Rowena along, forcing her to walk. "You know these things go. Some things are easier to handle without all the legal paperwork."

"Go on."

"I have someone who found part of the warehouse shipment that was stolen."

"You need to tell the guardians."

Lily grimaced. "I would, and I will, but I want it done the right way. Your sister is sick. Don't bother denying it, I know you've reached out to every crew with an infirmary."

"We need medication for the baby because she went into labor early," Rowena said.

"A new Lee." Lily stopped walking. "The person willing to give us the drugs wants a small trinket to sell on the antiques market. It's worthless to us, but see, this is where my genius lies. I can always find the best solution so that everyone walks away happy."

Rowena nodded. "And? What's the solution you see here?"

"Give me time with Titan Sciarra. I'll buy the meds, and give them to you for time with Titan. That's all I want."

"Why?" She stepped back. Titan would do it if she asked, he understood how important her sister was. But she was not going to prostitute out her best friend.

She might offer to sell him and then double-cross the Sekoos; if Lily hadn't thought of that it was a Sekoo problem and not Rowena's.

Lily laughed. "Don't you see? He rescued me today! Saved me when the bomb went off in our storage yard. If he comes back and spends time with me, think of what everyone will say!"

"You do realize he's the Sciarra scion, next in line for the captain's chair? There is no way in this life or any other that Elea would let him marry an enlisted sailor."

"I don't want to marry him!" Lily sounded appalled at the idea. "I don't even need him to like me, or hold my hand, or any of that. I just want to spend time with him. Go for a walk on the beach, maybe. Or sit together on the upper deck. Something small is fine. It'll be enough to show the fleet that the Sekoos are a respected crew. That I'm special enough to have his attention!"

Rowena shook her head. "That's not how it works. If you're trying to boost your ego, this won't do it. Trust me. I'm a bit of an expert on being around the powerful and influential. Hovering in their shadow doesn't make you special."

Lily stomped away.

"I'm sorry," Rowena said, catching up to her. "But wouldn't you rather know now, instead of hoping an hour or two with Titan will make you feel better? I'll trade for the medicine. Name what you want. Your shields? I can make them ten times better. Your implants? I could give you upgraded tech. Engines? Rations? Ships? I have three fighters I own outright, the best machines in this whole cracked fleet. They're yours in exchange for the medicine."

"I don't want ships," Lily shouted. She stomped her foot and a small cloud of dust danced in the waning sunlight. "I want Titan! I want time with him. Why can't you give me that?"

Rowena tried to formulate a logical answer to an illogical request. "Titan's time isn't worth the medicine. It's a bad deal!"

"Not to me." There were tears in Lily's eyes when she turned around. "Don't you see? It's all I want. A few minutes to live my dream. To have what I've always wanted."

Attention. Rowena shut her eyes. "Fine." *Ancestors, forgive me.* "I'll talk to Titan tonight and bring him by first thing in the morning. Can you get the medicine by then?"

Lily nodded with an eager smile. "I'll get it tonight. Oh! Rowena, I can't thank you enough! I've waited so long for this day to come!"

Rowena nodded. "I hope it'll be everything you ever wanted."

"It will be," Lily promised. "It will be."

15

TITAN

THERE WAS NOTHING ABOUT a second trip to the infirmary that made life better. The chief medic from *Julia Cattoni* had been called in and had lit into him. His captain had reamed him.

And then Rowena had sent a blistering, invective-laced tirade first threatening to finish the job if he didn't stop getting nearly killed, and then telling him they needed to talk as soon as he was free.

They all said they yelled out of love, but what he really wanted from them was to let him sleep. But not until he saw Selena and made sure she was all right.

The Jhandarmi had been invited to Enclave and Carver had decided the old museum was a good place to hold the meeting. Now, Titan stood with his back to a wall of pictures from the first landing and resisted the urge to pace.

A simple black Jhandarmi car pulled up with Tyrling and woman Titan didn't recognize. Two more cars followed. All with Jhandarmi agents he didn't know.

He'd expected Selena to be with them. She wasn't in Enclave. She wasn't in Tarrin, as far as he could tell. With her implant low, she couldn't have teleported far and there wasn't a shield strong enough to hide her signal nearby.

"If you stop glaring, this might go better." Her voice came from a shadowed corner of the room.

Titan spun around. "When'd you arrive?"

"A few minutes ago." She looked fine. There were a few tiny scratches on her cheek, and her eyes looked tired, but she was alive and had a minor shield up.

"How are you?"

"Fine. Thank you. Marshall picked me up and did a scan to make sure I was fit for duty. She told me not to stand near any more bombs, but other than that everything checked out."

That explained why he hadn't been able to find her. Marshall could do distance teleports with a passenger.

"How are you?"

"Perfect," Titan lied. "A few bruises, a new scratch or two, but nothing major." He kept a tight shield in place so she couldn't scan him for injuries. "Are you ready to go in?"

She frowned at the gathering assembly. "As ready as I'm likely to be without twelve hours of sleep or some paid vacation."

"Paid vacation? What's that?"

"Nothing but fantasy." She sighed. "Let's go find out what Tyrling is looking so smug about."

Titan had limited experience with war councils outside the strategy sessions Mal had led in the Academy. There, at least, they'd had some precedent for dealing with strangers from other crews. The way Carver and Tyrling were greeting each other, it was clear they hadn't established a working relationship yet.

The Jhandarmi circled like carrion birds, their suits muted grays and browns with spots of color and empty spaces where weapon holsters had hung. The Starguard was uniformly dressed in their all-blacks, crew patches and rank pins flashing under the too-bright overhead lights.

Selena strode across the space, drawing attention. "Director Tyrling, a pleasure to see you again. The conference room is in here."

Everyone stilled, taking time to adjust their understanding of the power dynamics. And then there was an almost synchronized movement. The Jhandarmi split and went to the north end of the hall to wait, the Starguard to the south. Tyrling's lieutenants followed him into the conference room and Titan fell into step behind Carver.

He took a seat next on Carver's left.

Interesting, at least to him, was that Selena seated herself at the far end of the fleet's side of the table. He thought Carver would want her closer. But maybe she was there to cover the door if things hit a flashpoint of tempers and pride.

The door closed with a mental push from someone and Titan felt a shield go up, blocking most communication, though the Starguard channels were still open.

Director Tyrling rested his arms on the table. "Commander Carver, it's a pleasure to finally meet you. I had hoped we would someday, although I pictured happier circumstances." For some reason his gaze went to Selena when he spoke.

Her face remained impassive.

"My associate, Agent Hartley"—Tyrling gestured to a woman with dark hair braided up into a mess of knots that ran like a crest down the center of her head—"is from our home office in Royan. She has been briefed on our agreements with fleet. The rest are senior agents whose files I sent to you earlier."

Carver nodded. "Guardian Sciarra and Captain Caryll you know. The other officers present represent the OIA, and concerned crews within the fleet. You're free to speak openly in front of them."

Again, Tyrling's gaze went to Selena.

Her expression remained neutral but Tyrling nodded anyway.

"In favor of expediting this conversation, I'll be brief," Tyrling said. "We believe that the open threat to the Starguard and the theft at your warehouse were done primarily to gain access to confidential. Jhandarmi documents. A list of our undercover operatives was stolen, and we believe is being auctioned in the coming days. Possibly as soon as tonight."

Carver frowned. "What about the attack at the Sekoo holdings?"

"Either a hate-crime, or an effort to destabilize the Tarrin-Enclave treaty," Tyrling said. "Our techs are still analyzing the debris."

"My techs have finished," Carver said. He held out his tablet and floated it across the table to Tyrling.

The Jhandarmi shifted uncomfortably in their seats.

Selena's voice cut through the tension. "The tablet is meant to do that. It's a standard adaption for low-gravity work. Director Tyrling?"

The director reached out and grabbed the tablet.

"As you can see," Selena said, "the bomb was constructed mostly of local materials, with an antique starter that is fleet tech but can be found in some legal markets. It was also all readily available in the Sekoo yard."

Tyrling nodded. "I see where you're going with this. No one's claimed credit."

"No," Carver said. "Although not all anti-fleet groups would."

"But, if your Captain Caryll is correct, this device could have been put together by a child playing in the yard. Or caused by improperly stored canisters of something."

The expression on Carver's face changed from mildly annoyed to insulted. It was a subtle downturn at the edge of the lip and a tightening around the eyes that the guardians knew meant trouble was coming. "There are very few prodigies in fleet, and fewer idiots," he said in a measured tone.

"But it isn't enough to go to war over," Selena cut in.

There was a pressure against Titan's shield and he realized that he was synching with Selena again, and that Carver was trying to send her a message.

She was purposefully blocking Carver's silent communication.

Agent Hartley shifted her weight, drawing attention to herself. "Caryll is correct. The explosion, while notable, is not our primary concern. Kaffton's behavior breaks from his known psychological profile."

Carver shrugged. "People change. Why are you concerned?" he asked, voicing the question most of the fleet was likely thinking.

"Prior to today, Kaffton has never carried a weapon," Hartley said. "He was wanted in questioning for one murder, but only as a witness. Emery Kaffton has never been caught with a weapon; it's one of his selling points." Her tone grew angrier as she spoke, slowly marching from cold calm to wintery wrath. "Today he killed Kasey Lear of Tatap, Descent. The Lears are a first-wave family and while they are not powerful themselves, they have powerful friends."

190

A quick burst of data from Carver detailed the powerbases of Descent. It was similar to the dynamics of fleet allyship, with a few customs that were uniquely grounder.

Titan raised his hand. "If Lear was well-connected, why was he in a forgotten tunnel under Tarrin going to a dead drop we suspect Kaffton used?"

"Kasey had trouble in his younger years," Tyrling said. "The family was able to sweep it under the rug and have the records sealed, but he was banished from his native city-state. The fleet equivalent would be?" He looked to Selena.

"Banishment and loss of rank," she said.

Like Mal. Ancestors forgive him. It was the fate of a living death. Lear must have done something truly savage to warrant such a brutal punishment.

"But, unlike fleet, his family wouldn't have been punished for keeping in contact. Lear couldn't return to Tatap, but he was welcome other places," Selena said. "In most cases the family would arrange a… tutorship?" She frowned and shook her head.

"A foster situation," Tyrling said. "For the world leaders. For poorer families they might arrange a patronage or an apprenticeship at someone's business. The Lears didn't."

Carver raised an eyebrow. "What did the man do?"

Tyrling looked to Hartley who shook her head.

"It's a matter of speculation with the gossips in Tatap," Hartley said. "The records were sealed and destroyed. There were no acts of extreme violence or criminal disturbance in that time period that were unresolved."

"It's possible the family was responsible for his banishment," Tyrling translated. "His work record his spotty, so is his public imprint. No home of record, no phone, bills in his name only here and there."

Titan frowned. "Can a grounder live outside a city? Without the resources of a government?"

The Jhandarmi had mixed reactions at the word grounder. Several frowned. Hartley sneered. Only Tyrling seemed unfazed by the politest word the fleet used for the descendants of the colonists.

"They can," Selena said, finally making eye contact. "It's rare for the native Maliki to leave the protection of a city-state, but there are small farming crofts in some areas, and there's always the possibility of living off the land."

:What does that mean?: Titan demanded. :Don't they all live on land?:

:It means they hunt and sleep in dirt,: Selena said with a touch of amusement. Out loud Selena said, "The proper term is out of network, meaning they aren't connected to any tech or social network available. It's an option only used by the very antisocial."

"And it doesn't fit Lear's profile," Tyrling said. "He was working, probably getting paid off the books and rooming either in company housing or with friends he made. Lear left home at twenty-three and has spent nearly thirty years staying mostly on the right side of the law."

"Then we need to look at his most recent associates," Carver said, shifting forward.

There was a bump on Titan's shield.

:Tell Caryll to open a channel for me,: Carver ordered. :She's here to observe.:

Titan risked a side glance to catch Selena's expression.

Her smile was placid, her body language calm. She knew something she wasn't sharing.

:Sir, I don't have a priority connection to Captain Caryll,: Titan lied. If Selena thought she needed to keep a secret he'd back her. For now. :She sent me orders to shut up, but that's all that passed between us.:

There was an answering flurry of angry faces mixed with a tone of exasperation. Carver didn't like being challenged.

Hartley took a small, translucent square as long and thick as her finger from her suit pocket and proceeded to unfold it. "This is a, ah, priority tech," she glanced at Tyrling, "belonging to the Jhandarmi. It's a portable screen."

"Very adaptable," Selena said.

Carver's nose wrinkled in annoyance.

The screen Hartley unfolded filled most the table and it lit up with a map of Descent. "The icons show where we can confirm sightings of Lear in the past month."

Tyrling half-stood, looking at it. "That's the weapons depot in Ranten. And another in Quairismoor."

"With several return trips to a Lethe training center," Hartley said. "Lethe Corp controls the majority of our world's transportation," she added.

Guardian shields throughout the room rippled with sudden, silent communication as the fleet bristled at the phrase *our world*, as if the grounders had some special claim the fleet didn't.

Hartley continued on, oblivious to her unintended slight. "Hypertrams all belong to Lethe or one of their subsidiaries. The Lethe family has controlling interest in the two major airlines. They own a major car manufacturer."

"Lethe also has a sizable intelligence arm," Tyrling said with a sigh as he sat back down. "You have a Marshall on your payroll, don't you, Carver?"

"Hermione Marshall," Carver said.

Tyrling chuckled. "There's only three million Hermione Marshalls. Commonest name for a woman next to Hermia. But, yes, a Marshall, from the Marshalls of Descent. I bet you used their intelligence when you arrived."

Caver's face went completely blank. "I'm sure we didn't." It was an obvious lie, but a polite one that was expected.

"My point," Tyrling said, "is that if Lear worked for Lethe, he could have been tracking a theft for them. Kaffton has taken his little stop-and-rob act international before, and Lethe wouldn't like it."

Hartley nodded. "And the information stolen from the Jhandarmi during the incident at your warehouse is something the Lethes would buy. For political leverage, if no other reason."

"Speaking of the theft," Carver said, "how close are we to recovering our medications? I have fourteen individuals in critical need of care."

"It's not a priority," Hartley said.

"We've handed the case to the Tarrin police force," Tyrling said, speaking over Hartley. "We don't believe they left our borders, and we're stepping on their toes as it is."

Under the table Titan squeezed his knee to keep from reacting. The Lees needed their medicine.

"If we don't have a lead by tomorrow evening," Carver said, "I'll send my guardians out to find it. Political toe-stepping or not."

"Or," Selena said, "instead of turning this into a matter of ego, we could provide the police with scanners programmed to detect telekyen. We have some sitting in the OIA building."

A dozen guardians lit up Titan's com with pings objecting. The very idea of tech being shared was going to make Selena the villain of every fleet story written between now and the next war.

"That would need to be discussed with the other captains," Carver said, showing unusual diplomacy.

"Stupidity and pride have gotten us two corpses, an empty warehouse, a burning city lot, and fourteen people with life-threatening health problems," Selena said with a cutting smile. "Under the circumstances, I think both sides can manage to play nice."

Tyrling coughed and Titan was fairly certain the man was hiding a grin.

"What about the address Lear had in his pocket?" Selena asked as more guardians chimed in, some with objections from their captains.

:We're losing the closed and private part of this meeting, sir,: Titan told Carver.

:I noticed.: Carver followed that with a cease and desist order to everyone else.

Hartley tugged at her map and began folding it. "It's possible that the data we want will be auctioned tonight. It's also possible that the medication stolen from you will be available at that auction."

"We'll send guardians," Carver said. "I have a few who can blend well enough."

"No," Tyrling said. He held up a hand to forestall Carver's objection. "No offense to your fine guardians, Carver, but this is a residential district. It's protected with fleet-done shields. Part of the landing treaty. There are very few places to teleport in or out and Caryll, who inspects these things for me, tells me the shield would also mute any communication with your support teams in Enclave. It's not a battlefield you've trained for."

The narrow-eyed look Carver gave the director would have sent even Hollis Silar in the other direction. "Sciarra, is the director's assessment of those shields correct?" he asked in a tone of barely suppressed rage.

"Sir, I haven't inspected the shields myself, but I trust Captain Caryll's assessment."

"Selena?" Carver turned to her. "I need those meds. Tell me I can go get them."

Selena looked down meekly. "I'm sorry, Commander. I don't think that's the best option."

Carver's lips curled in a snarl. "The Jhandarmi have no one, the police are understaffed and already lost one person. Who else do you think can go in?"

"We have someone," Tyrling said. "A Jhandarmi asset who never went to our training house and who has no digital record. I'm her handler, and she is the best choice for this, and would be the best choice even if everyone else was available." He looked over at Selena.

She took a deep breath, then nodded. "I know the person."

Carver's frown deepened.

"Perrin," Selena said, hand reaching down the table. "Please? Listen? You'd like her, if you met her. She's quick, and clever, and very good at lying."

Selena tried to send Carver an emotion without Titan feeling it, but he caught the gist: sincerity mixed with regret.

Carver motioned for Tyrling to continue.

"My operative has an established cover identity in this area. There's a man who owns a party estate. People pay to come to his house, mix, mingle, drink, and there's a number of black market deals done on the back lawn while the music is blaring."

"Is your operative going as a buyer?" Carver guessed.

Tyrling shook his head. "No, but she'll be known and welcomed and introduced to everyone. I won't give any more details with this large an audience." He nodded at the guardians standing behind Carver. "Their expressions all started matching a few minutes ago. I know you lot have telepathy or some such, and they've heard enough. You may trust them, but I don't. I won't endanger my last agent because one of your guardians talked out of school."

Selena's expression changed for a fraction of a moment and Carver nodded slightly in response.

"Agreed," Carver said. "Let's clear the room and you and I can talk. Coms off."

"I'll be staying," Hartley said, lifting her chin.

Tyrling nodded. "Keep one of yours, Carver."

Titan waited for the order to go.

"Sciarra stays. The rest go."

"Sir?" Titan looked at his commander. "Captain Caryll is better versed in grounder culture than I am."

Carver whipped around and scowled at him. "That's an order, Guardian."

"Yes, sir."

"I lived in Tarrin. I think I know it at least as well as Selena Caryll," Carver said with a disdainful tone.

If they'd been alone, or at least back in the Starguard offices, Titan would have taken Carver to the wall for using that tone on Selena.

But she was already standing. Her eyes looked sad, and her body language was closed off, but she was going without a fight.

:I'm sorry,: Titan said to her on a tight beam. :I'm sure he didn't mean to come out like that.:

:You don't need to defend Perrin,: she said. :Just don't let him do anything stupid.:

He sent her back a quick-flash recital of Carver's stupidest stunts and most reckless Academy hijinks before the war. :Are we talking about the same person?:

Selena stood. "Director Tyrling, Agent Hartly, it was a pleasure working with you. Have a good evening. Perrin." She gave Carver a curt nod. "Guardians." She walked out, followed by the others who had been dismissed.

Titan sank back in his seat. :She had good information,: he told Carver. :And you talked down to her. In front of grounders!:

:She'll handle it,: Carver said. :I was doing her a favor. Caryll hates meetings and it's clear Tyrling doesn't like her. Did you see the way he kept looking at her like he expected her to fail? Better to get her out and let him deal with someone who isn't as easy to push around.:

Easy to push around wasn't how Titan would have described Selena, even before he spent time with her.

And the looks Tyrling had given her had seemed more like a request for information to him. He'd shared looks like that with Ro when there'd been things he wanted to say and he couldn't trust even an implant's integrity. It was the kind of thing built over years of knowing someone though, so perhaps he'd misread.

As the door closed Carver rested his elbows on the table. "I don't want to be cut out of this op."

"You won't be," Tyrling promised.

"What are you offering?"

"I trust my operative, but I can have one of my people give running updates on what we have. There are cameras there, a few listening devices. It's not so well covered that we can avoid sending someone in, but if Kaffton or anyone else on our suspect list shows up, we'll know."

Carver shook his head. "Not good enough. What if this op goes nova? Are you going to drop a team in to get your agent out, or are you leaving her alone?"

The word *alone* resonated deep. Memories that weren't Titans flowed through the checklist on his implant. Selena was alone. She'd felt alone. Over half their interactions were tagged with signs of loneliness and isolation. He tried pinging her, but there was nothing but silence in return.

Tyrling was still talking, explaining a Jhandarmi safe house in the area. "And, if things do go – what did you call it? – nova, and my operative sends up a flare, we'll contact you."

"We'll go in," Carver said. "If anything goes wrong, my team will go in."

"Including Sciarra?" Tyrling looked at Titan.

Titan wasn't sure how to read the other man's expression. The mouth was too grim and tight for genuine curiosity, but the way the muscles around his eyes bunched said the frown wasn't from animosity either. On his aunt, he would have said the look was reluctant but mild approval.

Carver glanced his way too. "No. Sciarra is on the walking wounded list. I let him come to this because he's the only guardian who had worked closely with you. I thought a familiar face would help."

"In the future, Selena's enough," Tyrling said. "We all know her and like her."

"Captain Caryll doesn't report to me," Carver said, "and I can't always guarantee she'll be interested in attending meetings. It suited her today. In the future it may not. Sciarra you know. You now know me. In the future, you may meet others."

With a smirk as if he'd won a private bet, Tyrling nodded. "As you say. Hopefully that meeting won't be tonight."

"Agreed."

While they hashed out the final details and exchanged direct communication numbers, Titan scanned for Selena. She wasn't waiting outside the door like he'd hoped. And she wasn't in the limited range he could reach in Enclave. Logic said she was probably hidden behind a friendly crew's shield, but worry still tightened his chest. He wanted a chance to see her again. To make sure she was recovering.

To make sure Carver's thoughtless comment hadn't been taken to heart.

When he was back at full power and not bleeding through his stitches, he and Carver were going to have a word with how his boss talked to women. Several words probably. Punctuated by punches.

Carver stood, nodded, and shook hands with Tyrling. "Ready to leave?" he asked Titan. "Or did you have any other questions?"

"I'm good," Titan said, standing. He held out a hand. "Director, it was good seeing you again. Thank you for your cooperation."

Tyrling shook his hand. "Thank you for taking our field work. I won't forget the favor."

Titan watched him leave and ran another scan for Selena. Still missing.

"What's got your face in knots?" Carver asked. "You looked like you bit a lemon. Was it that bad being near a grounder?"

"It was that hard not punching you for what you said to Captain Caryll." The words ran ahead, beating out good sense. "You don't talk about fleet like that in front of grounders! You don't dismiss a captain like that!"

Carver stared at him for a minute then laughed. "First off, I'm the commander. That means I have to put the needs of the fleet over friendships. Selena knows that, and she knows I dismissed her because if it came to tactics, I needed you, not her. You know how to run an investigation, what protocol to follow, and how people will react. Selena has battle experience, but she doesn't know what to do if she finds information, except to tell me."

The very clear memory of Selena scanning the cooling corpse for fingerprints didn't match Carver's impression, and it left Titan scrambling for an explanation.

"Second," Carver said, "she's tired and injured and hadn't gotten treatment yet. I sent her off to find Marshall, who will make sure she's somewhere safe and quiet tonight."

That sounded reasonable. Titan took a cleansing breathe. "Understood, sir. I apologize. The tone was..." He hunted for the right word. "Not one I would tolerate anyone using on my captain."

"And I understand that. But Selena isn't just another member of the fleet or a random officer. She's a friend. You don't know how shy she is around new people. I do. You don't know how much she hates meetings like this. I do. Trust me to take care of my friend, all right?"

"Yes, sir." Titan bit the inside of his cheek to keep from a terser reply.

Carver thought he knew Selena. Maybe she had been shy before the war. But that wasn't the woman he'd seen walking through Tarrin. It didn't describe the person whose thoughts and memories had comingled with his.

:Selena?: He opened the channel and waited for a response. Nothing but void—absolute emptiness. He'd had better luck getting a response the one time he'd drunkenly tried to ping Mal after he'd died.

Rubbing a hand over the cold scars on his arm, Titan walked out of the building and into the falling night.

16

SELENA

THE ENCLAVE SHIELD WAS a suffocating pressure over her.
Selena fell with her back against the wall and stared in disbelief at
the closed conference room door. She should've said something.

For the first time, the fleet was listening to the Jhandarmi. She
should have confessed her connection, told them why she'd done
it. They might have understood. That had been her opening and
now...

Now it was gone.

She'd betrayed the fleet and kept silent because Tyrling was a
paranoid yaldson who didn't trust the fleet.

That was also her fault. She'd brought too much of the pain
she'd felt with her to the Jhandarmi offices. It colored the way the
grounders viewed the fleet. It twisted their minds, poisoned every
interaction.

Even now the Jhandarmi standing guard at the doors were watching her.

:Selena?: Titan's ping bounced off the tightest shield she had as the doors opened.

Carver and Tyrling walked out, both too busy with their own thoughts to notice her.

Keeping her face impassive, she pushed off the wall and walked away. Grounders on one side. Fleet on the other. All ready to pounce if she let any sign of weakness show.

There was only one place to escape them all.

Stepping into a dark shadow near the portraits of the second wave colonists, she engaged a code she thought she'd never use again.

The world shimmered, losing color until it faded into white nothingness. A chime sounded, and she stepped through the portal into the captain's mess of the *Persephone.*

Alarms rang out all at once and three years' worth of reports flooded her senses. With one brutal, mental swipe, she silenced them all.

The ship lay quiet. There were no engines to hum and make the floor thrum like the slow heartbeat of the universe. There were no crew members left to run, and shout, and scream in pain as the assault from the Baular ships ripped the *Persephone* apart.

Even her own breath seemed like the echo of a ghost, absorbed by the silence.

At her approach, the ancient door to the mess slid open, whining a complaint. An automated program sent her a notification for the estimated time of repair—over three million hours. Hundreds of years.

She dismissed the notification and stepped into the empty hall.

Small skutter bots, shaped like the fabled horseshoe crab, climbed along the walls, making repairs. They scurried away with the quiet scritch-scritch of metal legs against metal bulkheads. It was fine; she knew where everything was.

It didn't take conscious thought to walk to the altar room.

The door remained closed.

:This area has not been cleared of debris. Use not recommended,: the system sent to her implant.

:Acknowledged. Open.:

The door slid wide, revealing the scarred black table the Caryll crew had used for battle maps in the final days of the war, when the battleroom was overflowing with injured sailors. There was a stain of dried blood on the edge of the table.

Quentin had died there as she tried to repair his ribs, mangled by a closing bulkhead door. He'd succumbed to internal bleeding while she'd patched the visible wounds.

She'd left the medkit there.

Now, she rummaged through the old box and pulled out the bright blue nanite patch she needed to repair her own wounds. She slapped it on her neck, over the jugular vein. The gel on the patch melted and the nanites swarmed her bloodstream in a heady rush. It would have been nice to lie down, but her quarters were gone, reduced to galactic dust and memories.

Running her hand along the wall to maintain her balance, she stumbled to the command deck and collapsed on her chair.

Duty stations flickered, striving to become fully operational despite the battle damage. Most of them died, falling back into abyssal darkness before completing the reboot.

Selena rested her head on the back of the chair. Knowing what she had to do wasn't as easy as doing it. Her muscles clenched in anticipation of pain.

She visualized the events of the past few days and started hardcoding them for archive storage. There was no way to erase the physical memories stored in her brain, not safely at any rate, but she could keep her implant from bringing them up again.

In that, Titan had been right; she couldn't drag the emotional trauma of the war forward. Razor-fine reflexes wouldn't serve her where she was going. None of it would.

Titan had fought beside her—fought to protect her—and now she had to break every connection to him. Force herself to give up every hope, because there was none left.

There was no way they could move on from what she'd done. No way to erase the scars burned into his body. And the longer the memories lingered, the more pain she'd endure.

Saving herself meant forgetting what they had shared.

Closing her eyes, she turned her focus inward, cutting inward to destroy every memory. It was a savage psychological attack.

The emotional pain became physical, as if she'd set herself on fire to burn off all traces of the fragile connections she'd held for only a handful of hours. Salty tears stung the cuts on her cheek. "I loved him," she whispered.

There was a whirring sound of a computer turning on nearby. "I do not understand that command."

Selena wiped her face with the back of her hand as the cycle ended. "I fell in love, Persephone. There is no command to obey."

"Love?" The neutral computer voice was replaced by the more feminine tones of the ship's AI.

"Yes."

"Shall I play some sappy music?" There was a grin in *Persephone's* voice. The AI changed with each new captain, learning and changing until it reflected the captain in voice and sensibility.

The pitch and timbre were a little off, but Selena recognized herself in the AI. It was a reflection of her, back when she'd been confident and proud.

"No music, Persephone. We're not celebrating."

In front of her, the main viewing screen lit up with fractured light, cut in facets by cracks from equipment—and bodies— thrown at it during the final attack. A distorted face appeared.

Selena shook her head. "The screen is a lost cause, Persephone, turn it off."

Persephone obeyed. "Would you like me to draft a declaration of courtship?"

"He's not from an allied crew."

"Would you like me to draft plans for a kidnapping?" *Persephone* asked.

Selena sighed. "That method of courtship was outdated before the Malik System was settled."

"But it's still on the books."

Had she really thought like that as a young captain? Probably. The AI was probably quoting from her personal files. "We're not kidnapping anyone."

"Would you like to see the updated repair schedule?"

"No thank you, Persephone."

"Would you like to reschedule regular updates about the repair schedule?"

She clenched her eyes shut. "No. Don't contact me until the repairs near completion."

"Factoring in the average lifespan of an augmented human and your recent history, it seems unlikely you will be alive when repairs are completed," *Persephone* said matter-of-factly. "The recommended course of action is to halt repairs, set a course for the sun, and retire this vessel."

"I know," Selena said. "And we'll make that trip together soon enough. Maybe after this mission. If I survive."

The ship accessed her implant, downloading the data points that made up her life. "Please log the nature of the mission so I may calculate the survival probabilities."

Selena shook her head. "I'm going to go see the man who tried to kill me."

"Which one?"

"Which one?" Her lips cracked as the corner of her mouth lifted in a grin. "There haven't been that many."

"In your last known engagement you were shot at over four thousand times," *Persephone* corrected.

She snorted in amusement. "They weren't aiming at me. That was a general barrage, not a personal grudge match."

"Today you were shot at seventeen times and were near an explosion that resulted in abrasions and a minor concussion."

"I don't think I can be blamed for the explosion. Besides, I have a nanite patch on. I'm fine."

The top left corner of the main screen brightened until the hazy gray-and-white projection showed a generic Caryll face. *Persephone* scowled at her. "I don't believe you are using an accepted definition of the word 'fine', Captain."

"I'll live."

"That does seem likely."

The right side of the screen was less damaged, and *Persephone* opted to show a picture of Titan Sciarra on the largest unbroken piece. His vivid green eyes shone like gems.

"You spent a great deal of time with this individual today," *Persephone* said. "Would you like me to contact the *Sabiha* so you can speak with his captain about a transfer? I have multiple officer postings available at this time."

The memories she'd worked to archive flew across the screen. A hand on her shoulder. A look. A sensation of trust and peace.

"Please stop."

"These recent events were coded with happiness," *Persephone* said. "Your body is exhibiting signs of distress. Reviewing happy events can be calming. Would you prefer to schedule a counseling session? There is no longer a trained therapist on board but I have therapy sub-routines."

An internal signal chimed, letting her know all the nanites from the patch were now in her body affecting repairs. She pulled the patch off her neck and rubbed the lingering itch. "I don't need therapy."

"I find the probability of that being true to be extremely low," *Persephone* said.

"You're starting to sound like my grandmother."

"She was an exemplary captain."

They all had been. Every single Caryll captain had served with honor, until she'd taken the chair. "You can make a note of my failings for posterity."

"The bioscan I just completed does not show any signs of pregnancy and you are not near ovulation. At your current rate of intercourse you are unlikely to have children. Ever. Would you like a list of genetically compatible males?" *Persephone* pulled up a list of words impossible to read on the fractured screen.

"Is that Titan's genetic worksheet?"

"Yes," the ship chirped. "He's a good genetic match and a good officer. He's advanced far ahead of previous projections."

"Yeah, I know, he killed a few people to get there."

"Very efficiently too, from the data available."

"We are not encouraging the murder of senior officers as a route to advancement," Selena said with a scowl.

"Since there are no junior officers or other crew of any kind, it doesn't seem to matter." If ships could pout, the *Persephone* would have.

The AI was programmed to have a very limited self-preservation index—no one wanted a battleship that refused to fight—but every now and then, Selena suspected the *Persephone* had developed beyond what was considered standard for fleet AI. Bereft of crew, the AI should have shown signs of cohesion failure, but *Persephone* continued to be lucid, even improved, every time Selena checked on it.

Her implant reached forty-two percent energy. "I should go."

"Would you like your rank?" *Persephone* asked.

A skutter that had been cut in half at some point crawled up to the foot of the captain's chair with her sunburst insignia clutched between its front pinchers.

"No. I have no reason to wear it."

"Where would you like me to store it?"

She shrugged. "With my dress uniform?" The last she'd seen that thing was the day of her promotion ceremony. It was probably in a degrading orbit around the planet, just like the rest of the debris of war.

"Would you like to take any weapons with you?" *Persephone* asked.

"No."

"Do you have any further instructions?" The AI's voice changed in pitch; *Persephone* was begging her to stay.

Selena looked around the shattered remains of her life. "Continue repairs. If you find a part that you can't replicate or access that isn't on the previous list you sent me, send me an updated list. Who knows, maybe if things go sideways I'll move back up here fulltime."

"That course of action is not recommended. Atmospheric integrity is only at thirty percent."

"Noted." She stood, feeling sturdier, even if she couldn't shake the sense of loss. Fleet officers weren't meant to be hermits, but this had to be done. For the good of the fleet. For the safety of the colonists.

When it was over, she promised herself she'd end her isolation. Come back to *Persephone* and the fate she'd earned.

Selena patted the captain's chair with a forlorn smile before teleporting back to the planet. She landed in a deserted room of an empty house, cut off from everyone and everything. The walls were lined with artwork from over a thousand years of history, the frames bent, scratched, and burnt. The pictures showed Carylls long-dead, worlds whose names history had forgotten, rare flowers that had never bloomed in this star system. It was the art of her family from long before they were even the Caryll crew. From a time when they could have been more than simply fleet.

Before she made the final trip with *Persephone,* she needed to find someone she could trust the artifacts to. But that was a worry for another night.

Now, there were other concerns. She opened her closet and looked at the rows of grounder clothes sorted by season and color. Tonight felt very black. Dangerous. Edgy...

There. The perfect outfit in black, silver, and bright blue. Kaffton wouldn't know what hit him.

17

ROWENA

IN THE EVENING LIGHT, the landing gear of the Sciarra armada stretched like pillars between their shield and the seawall. A forest of shadows and light with loading ramps.

Rowena leaned back in the hastily-constructed chair—a frayed blanket and a metal frame—and watched as Titan paced under the bulk of the *Sabiha*.

Mars settled in beside her. "You watering the drinks, Lee?"

"No." She glared at Mars. She wasn't in the mood for a playful fight.

He was young enough to smile back like it was nothing. Poor kid. "He's not sitting down. Not holding still. If the giggle water you brought won't help, I don't know what will."

"We could knock him unconscious," Rowena said. "Hide him in the cargo bay until this passes."

"Mmm." Mars frowned and still looked like a younger, happier version of Titan. "Do we have options that won't require getting my captain's permission?"

It was Rowena's turn to grimace. "Has he eaten today?"

"Not that I've seen."

"Run down to Cargo Blue, pick up anything that looks edible, and we'll see if a hot meal doesn't work."

Mars nodded. "It'll be better than ship's rations, at any rate."

When he walked away, Titan turned around, startled. "Where's he going?"

"To get food," Rowena said as she stood up, holding another bottle of the drugged water that was supposed to relax nerves and soothe aches. "Here, have another drink," she said as Mars walked out through the Sciarra shield, becoming another ghostly shape in the shadows.

Titan looked away. "I'm fine."

"For someone who took a beating, sure. But the medic said rest and this doesn't look restful to me. You're..." She waved a hand at his jittering leg.

Grumbling under his breath, Titan stilled and sat down. "I'm fine."

"And I'm the princess of the flower festival," she said. "Sit down and stop fidgeting or I'm going to knock you out and lie when Mars comes back."

"There's an op going without me," Titan said as he fell into one of the chairs, making it groan in protest. "My op. It's my case. I should be out there."

"With no weapons, no defenses, and no backup?" Rowena scoffed. "Sure. Sounds very sensible." She sat down beside him. "Should I replay one of your lectures on unity and trust? I have them all saved. From 'Carver Is A Decent Person' to the all-time favorite, complete with laugh track, 'I Can Work With A Silar.' Some of the fleetlings worked out a comedy sketch to that one."

Titan's head lolled to the side; he did not look amused.

She smiled. "We can work with these people. Your words. Not mine." She lifted her bottle up. "Drink! Forget about them! They are mostly competent and have handled situations in Tarrin without you before. So find something else to think about."

Titan took a swig of the giggle water. "Selena—"

"Selena?" Rowena asked in shock. "We're using first names now?"

"Yes."

"No! Pick something else!"

"Carver?" Titan hesitated.

Rowena shook her head. "You are not good at this game. You're supposed to think of something distracting but not enraging."

"Like the Lee's new candidates for the OIA and Starguard?"

"Yes!" After a moment, she punched his arm. "You were supposed to warn me about that. If Hoshi's backed by another crew, it's going to be that much harder to throw a coup without dropping bodies. I hate killing family. Even if it's Hoshi's side."

Moonlight danced in the water as Titan waggled his drink in disagreement. "It's not for Hoshi. It's so we can pick an instructor from your crew for the new training house. Especially since it'll be weeks before they let me take a rotation again. Silar and Carver are decent at hand-to-hand combat, but they're also trying to keep the guard running."

"Lees don't do hand-to-hand combat." Not as a crew, at any rate. She and Aronia had learned because she'd trained with Mal during the war. But... She shook her head. "Hoshi won't recommend anyone worth having."

"The training house gets to take whoever they want," Titan said. "Hoshi can recommend, but we don't have to listen."

A terrible suspicion flared. "Ty, you didn't recommend this, did you? You know the Council will shut it down. Warmonger crews can't recommend promotions for other Warmongers. This is going to blow up in your face."

He shook his head. "I didn't recommend it."

That left... No one that she could think of.

The Sciarras were the only crew she was friendly with, and Hoshi couldn't make friends without bribing them. "Someone is backing the Lees?"

"Not really." Titan looked up at the sky, trying to avoid the conversation.

"Who recommended this?" she demanded.

"Eh." He shook his head. "It doesn't matter."

"It does if it's a trap!" She set her empty bottle down and stood up. "Did you think of what could happen?"

Titan scowled at her. "Who do you think I am? Of course I checked. I went through every angle and threatened someone with a slow and painful death if you got hurt."

"Who recommended this?"

"Selena."

Rowena choked and coughed. All the oxygen had suddenly gone missing.

Titan thumped her on the back. "You okay?"

"Caryll recommended this madness?" Reality asserted itself. "No, that makes no sense. You have brain trauma. That's what happened. Let's go to the med bay." She stood up and grabbed Titan's hand. "You were hit in the head, now you're hallucinating, that makes sense. Come on."

He didn't budge. "I've been cleared. Twice! I'm fit for duty."

"Titan!" She dropped his hand in frustration. "It still won't work." That thought calmed her. "Caryll's recommendation would have to be supported by other allied captains, and you won't get that."

He lifted a shoulder and dropped it. "You'd think, but the Silars backed it."

"Captain Silar? He hasn't left his quarters since landing. How'd Caryll get that signature?"

"She has Hollis's."

The magnetic poles of the planet shifted under her. Up was down. Down was up. It was possible the stars were in the sea now.

She pinched herself. Still awake and alive. "You *must* have a concussion."

"Run a scan!" Titan said.

"Food!" Mars shouted as he teleported in between them, holding three boxes and what looked suspiciously like a nishu book. "Um... Did I miss something?"

"Titan has a concussion."

Mars shook his head. "Not unless you hit him. The medic ran a check while I was there."

"See!" Titan glared victoriously.

Frustrated, and not sure she wanted to finish the argument with Mars around, she nodded at the book bound by thin pieces of metal and filled with the yellow-green paper the fleet made from algae. "What's that?"

"Dinner." Mars floated the boxes to Titan. "I grabbed a couple of sampler platters. Things deep-fried in grease, a salad, and something with cheese and sugar that Fiona Glenndie says is delicious."

"Sugar and cheese?" Titan asked skeptically.

Mars shrugged.

Rowena ignored the boxes and gave the book a mental tug. They were always somewhere in the fleet, illegal, single-copy manuscripts written by bored crew members and filled with ridiculousness. Some of them were entertaining. A few showed real artistic skill. Most were smutty wet dreams that someone decided to share—because having sex on a bunk across the room from your cousin wasn't enough for some people.

With a smile, Mars grabbed the book and held it tight. "You don't want this."

"I do, actually," Rowena said, tugging at the telekyen molecules in the binding. "That's why I'm trying to pull it away."

"Who gave it to you?" Titan asked as he opened one of the boxes and poked a cautious finger at lumps of golden-brown things. "And what is that?"

"Tempura vegetables from the islands," Mars said. He put the book behind his back and raised a light shield. "And I wasn't given the book. The Ravma crew was out celebrating someone's promotion and didn't notice when I picked it up. Not objecting is consent, right?"

Rowena rolled her eyes as Titan said, "No."

"That's theft," Titan mumbled as he bit into the tempura. "And this is... odd. Sweet? Orange. Is it supposed to be these colors?"

"How should I know?" asked Mars. "Do I look like an expert on grounder cuisine? I think it's a root of some kind, if it helps."

"Food grown in dirt." Rowena grimaced, broke Mars's shield, and teleported the nishu book to her hands. "That's worse than sleeping in dirt. Grounders." She shuddered, flipping the book open. "'Taking The Captain Captive.' This looks fun."

Mars teleported over and landed beside her with a grin. "Look at the pictures! That's a decent drawing of Titan."

It was. And a highly sexualized drawing of Caryll.

Rowena wrinkled her nose as she read the opening. "Oh, suns of the homeworlds. This is... This is nasty! Criminally bad. 'She looked up at him with limpid eyes blue as the lakes of Rasare. 'Take me,' she begged. 'Take me away from this crowd to your secret place.'" Rowena raised an eyebrow. "You have a secret place, Ty?"

"Yup, right behind my station on the command deck. I have snacks there for when I'm working at night." He grabbed the book and pushed the box of food at her. "Who did I capture this time?"

"Selena Caryll," Mars said. His grin grew wider as Titan stared down in growing horror.

Rowena laughed. "I told you it was bad!"

"Sciarra grabbed her hair and shoved her against the bulkhead..." Titan read aloud. "Not unless I want my balls cut off." He shuddered for dramatic effect.

"Unless she likes it rough," Mars said.

Rowena and Titan turned. She shook her head. "What? No. You're a youth! You don't get to talk about rough sex!"

The younger Sciarra made a face. "If there was still an Academy I'd be at it. All of you had sex there!"

"No I didn't!" Rowena said.

"No she didn't," Titan agreed. He turned the page on the book. "This is awful. And illegal. Why did you bring it here? No one is allowed to write non-factual stories about living or recently deceased people. The Captains' Council could sanction us if we don't report it."

Mars waved a hand in Titan's direction. "You're a guardian! This is reporting it! Better you than Silar. He's making the rounds in there and if he found one, he'd probably read it."

"One of these days we just need to kill Silar," Rowena said. "It'll make life so much easier. Carver is busy trying to figure out how to have a wife, Marshall is always gone on Descent doing schooling. We'd have run of the place if Hollis wasn't around."

Titan froze then turned to her slowly. "What did you say?" There was an edge of fury in his voice.

She frowned. "Let's kill Hollis? This is not a new idea. Or a bad one."

"About Marshall," Titan said, forgetting about the book. "Where did you say she was?"

"On Descent. At one of the big universities there. Her family insisted she get a grounder education. Don't you listen to gossip? The Allied crews have been talking about it for days. She had some big test today, defending a theorum or thesis or who knows what. A challenge of some kind." Rowena shrugged indifferently. "She left yesterday and is out of coms range until tomorrow. Unless the challenge kills her. Which would be nice."

Titan's smile had turned into a mask of pure rage. "Marshall wasn't in Enclave today."

"Not once, as far as I know." Rowena looked to Mars for explanation. He seemed as confused as she was about Titan's sudden mood shift. "Why does it matter?"

"Carver said Marshall was seeing to Selena's wounds."

Mars frowned. "That seems unlikely."

"But it doesn't mean someone else didn't," Rowena said quickly, trying to keep control of the situation.

Titan pivoted, fists clenching at his side.

"I'm sure she's somewhere safe," Mars said. "She's a captain. She'll have found somewhere to hunker down."

Silence descended as Titan stopped moving.

Rowena held her breath.

218

Bowing his head, Titan swore. "I'm an idiot."

"No argument there," Rowena agreed. "But, for clarification, what were you thinking you were being an idiot about?"

"The Jhandarmi director cut the guardians out of the op they're running tonight. He said that they have a safe house nearby with a shield provided by the fleet during Landing." He shook his head with a bitter smile. "The Baulars were out. Carver and Marshall were busy handling the negotiations. That left who?"

"Caryll," Rowena said. The name left a bitter taste in her mouth.

Mars wrinkled his nose. "It wouldn't have been her choice. Back then Carver held full control, she was one of his top lieutenants. All he had to do was give her the order, and tell her to classify it. She couldn't tell you if she wanted."

That was debatable. Technically, Titan was high enough in the Starguard that he should have had access to that kind of priority data. It was the kind of tiny, insulting oversight that could start another war. Stifling her own angry thoughts, she said, "It's a logical place for a wounded captain to go. She can keep an eye on the Jhandarmi and rest. If she set up the shield, she can probably slip into the safe house without even noticing."

Titan nodded.

She smiled at him. "Nothing to worry about then."

"I have to go stop her," Titan said.

"What?" Rowena stared at him in disbelief. "Why?"

"Carver told the Jhandarmi we'd stay out of it. If Caryll steps in, even if she means well, it could damage our treaty. We're dependent on their good will to get the rest of the medicines back." He held out his hand. "I have a two percent charge. Come on, Ro. You promised to back me. Even for the stupid stuff."

She closed her eyes and went through a litany of her grandmother's best curses in her head. "You're an idiot, Sciarra." Teeth clenched, she reached out and touched the back of her hand to his, initiating the energy transfer. Her hand warmed, the pulsing of her heart creating small sparks as she gave Titan the strength he needed. She wasn't below sixty percent when he pulled his hand away. "Is that enough?"

"It's just a teleport and a shield unlock. I know her codes. I'll be fine."

Rowena crossed her arms. "Fine. Thirty minutes, and then I'm coming for you. Enclave shield and orders can get wrecked."

"Thirty minutes is all I need," Titan said. He smiled as he teleported out.

"All Sciarras are idiots," she muttered under her breath.

Mars jabbed her with his elbow. "Hey now. Look at me. I'm adorable."

"Like my little brother who outgrew me six years ago," Rowena said, letting the cadet jolly her back into a smile. "Come on. Let's try this sweet cheese thing you found while we wait."

"Do you think Titan will be okay out there?" Mars asked as he took a seat and set up the rapidly congealing meal.

Cold grease had an unpleasant odor that made her push the box away. "He'll be fine. Boil down Ty's personality and what you get is loyalty. Once he's given his loyalty, it's there forever, whether you deserve it or not. That's why we make a good battle team."

"Because you're loyal?" Mars asked as he held out the second carton and a wedge of something that didn't look like cheese or sugar.

Rowena poked the creamy lump with the fork Mars offered her. "Because I'm stubborn. Ty knows I'll come rescue him. If I promise to do something, it gets done." She cut into the food and sequestered a piece.

"Titan says you have integrity. You always do what you promise."

"I try," she mumbled before biting into the grounder food. It was tart with a following sweetness. Not bad considering it had the consistency of caulking putty.

Mars claimed the rest. "How much longer until we go rescue Ty?"

"Twenty-three minutes," Rowena said as she sat back and stared up at the sky. "Twenty-three long minutes."

18

TITAN

IT WAS QUIET DOWNTOWN. There were no generators running to keep ship air pure; no family arguments spilling out of cargo holds to become fistfights on the rocks. On the horizon there was no wall, and no OIA building standing sentinel.

A light breeze ruffled luminescent leaves, pale and green, on the thin branches of the terraformed trees lining the road. Their soft light was enough frame the row of elegant homes, subdued visions of grounder wealth.

Caryll's signature was here, but cycling, like she was walking in and out of a shield.

Titan raised an eyebrow and slipped on the Guardian Veil. A faint shimmer gave away a hidden shield over a large house in the middle of the block. There was a wide, inviting porch held up by white columns, and three stories of windows.

There were smaller ships in Enclave.

He approached cautiously, testing the limits of the shield. The first layer was a scatter field meant to make people look away. It would discourage random intrusions but not much else. The next layer in—Titan jumped back, mentally stung. He'd wager a week's pay that the next layer was set to kill anyone who touched the house.

It was not the kind of shield someone put over a Jhandarmi safe house during peacetime. It was a war shield meant to repel everything up to and including an orbital bombardment. Someone had been making a point.

The Carylls had a few shields like that, most of them tuned to attack only things or people with telekyen in their system. A groundsider was probably safe knocking on the door.

He wasn't.

Rocking back on his heels, he grimaced. Teleporting home was probably the best option. Selena was safe enough behind that.

As long as she stayed there.

Her signal appeared again, inside the house next door to the heavily shielded one. When the Jhandarmi director had said there was a safe house in the area, he hadn't expected the two addresses to share a fence line. But the address was the one Kafftan's victim had dropped.

Pulling his shields in close so that Selena wouldn't sense him, he weighed his options. If she'd gone in, it was to make contact with the Jhandarmi operative. It could mean nothing. Or it could mean trouble.

Titan hesitated, watching the movement of shadows in the windows of the house.

The door to the house opened, spilling light outside. "Hey!" a figure in the doorway shouted. "You coming in, man?"

Titan tilted his head to the side.

"Party's going raw!" The figured gestured wildly.

Telling himself it was due diligence, Titan approached, grateful he'd changed out of his uniform before going to meet Rowena. The long-sleeved shirt meant to be worn under a pilot's jacket and black cargo pants didn't scream Fleet, although it probably wasn't the height of grounder fashion either.

As Titan drew closer, he could see the man, tall and muscled with blond hair pulled back in a bun. He was wearing only shorts.

Apparently, cargo pants made him over-dressed for this event.

The blond tipped his head. "You new in town?"

"I'm from Descent," Titan said, a plausible lie. Hard for a Tarrin to check, and he knew the accent. All he had to do was think back to Marshall's first year at the Academy.

"Right!" The man held out his hand. "Arwel, Arwel Art and Design. Come on in. Did you bring swim gear?"

"Um... no," Titan said as he stepped into the domed entryway. Life-size photographs of women lined the walls, all strikingly beautiful, all painted with elaborate body art.

"Stunning, aren't they?" Arwel asked. "All mine."

Titan raised his eyebrows. "The women?"

"Oh!" Arwel's eyes went wide in shock. "No, no, no. All the art. I painted them. I'm painting tonight too. Was that... Wasn't that what you were expecting?"

An honest answer wasn't going to work, so he found another lie. "I met a woman downtown in an art gallery. She mentioned she might be here. I found myself at loose ends this evening so..." Titan let him fill in the gaps.

"Brunette, blonde, or red head?" Arwel asked.

"Blonde." Titan's searched the gallery for Selena's face, but she wasn't on display.

Arwel's face brightened into a wide smile. "Willowy blonde with fair skin and ocean-blue eyes?"

Titan nodded.

"Selena!" Arwel said. "She brings in the best international clients. She's out back by the pool. I just finished her shoulder. Unless you're an artist, you probably won't notice how flawless her skin is, but trust me, she's the perfect canvas."

"I've noticed she's flawless." In so many ways.

Arwel chuckled. "Yeah, good luck with that." He patted Titan on the back. "That woman is married to her work. I have watched many a man and woman fly to that sun and be burned."

"Moon."

"What?"

"Selena means moon," Titan corrected. "And I'm not Icarus. I won't get burned."

"That's the right attitude." Arwel clapped him on the back again. "Come on through the kitchen. There's a guest bathroom with outfits over there if you feel like taking a dip. Have you been to an event like this before?"

Flight team parties probably didn't count. "No."

"It's more a Tarrin thing, I think. This is a networking event. Jorjes Kerl of Kerl Investments is looking to hire new talent, so he scheduled with me. Anyone interested can come. I provide the venue, the food, the models, and everyone else gets to shine. You will notice the models are exceptionally good at getting your logo seen. Feel free to ask any of them about the advertisements painted on them. Everyone I hire is tested for memory and trained for sales. This is the least intrusive way to get your brand noticed by investors." Arwel's sales pitch rambled on.

Titan tuned him out, nodding where needed, as he assessed the situation.

The kitchen had been laid out with trays of food and drinks ready to be taken outside. Tidy packets of swim wear and towels were available for guests. He didn't reach for one, though Arwel made a point of offering the packet to him. Titan had never learned to swim and didn't see a reason to start now.

The gray-tiled kitchen flowed out to a seating area, then to a wide deck and a garden beyond. People in a variety of swim accessories moved between tables and lounging areas. Painted men and women worked the crowd, standing and posing in the lights before moving away again.

At the center of the garden was a waterfall, rushing over artfully arranged rocks into a jewel-blue pool lit from within. A plaster gem in an artificial paradise.

Arwel stepped up beside him, beaming at the stage he'd set. "Lovely, isn't it? All the exotic colors of the islands without pesky things like traveling or insects."

"It's... something," Titan agreed.

"Give it an hour," Arwel said. "It's early and no one's relaxed yet. Once they're done sorting out dominance and using up their best pick-up lines on my models, they'll start having fun. That's when the real networking begins. Get two people chatting by the pool about macroeconomics and a year later we have a new company in the commerce district. It's magical!"

Titan didn't even feign interest. Grounder commerce and capitalism were—thankfully—above his pay grade. All he was interested in was spotting Selena, and the Jhandarmi operative, before they spotted him.

A man in the crowd noticed Arwel on the patio and waved him over.

"Excuse me," Arwel said. "I've got to go play host. If you need introductions, come find me."

"I will. Thank you." Titan nodded as Arwel walked away. A sweeper pass brushed against Titan's shield like a cold breeze. In it, he caught Selena's now-familiar touch and an echo of concern. She was on guard, but not aware he was there. Yet.

It took all of his focus to keep his shield from adjusting and melding with hers.

Behind him, someone opened the patio door and then shut it with a slide and a snick. "Are you from Descent?"

"Yes," Titan said as he turned.

Kafftan stood beside him. A little shorter than he'd seemed in the tunnels, bonier than most grounders, with a sandy stubble on his chin and red-rimmed eyes. He looked more like a destitute dock worker than a thief and a killer. But it took all kinds.

"Didn't I say I'd handle it?" Kafftan demanded, lips curling in a snarl. "Tell your lady I don't need a bodyguard or a babysitter."

Titan kept his face emotionless as a thousand possibilities flew through his mind. "I'm not here to do either," he said carefully. "At the moment, I'm a casual observer."

"Ha!" Kafftan stalked over to the ledge and gripped the railing like he meant to strangle it. "So you're the cleaning crew."

"Only if you need one."

Kafftan's right hand jerked to the front pocket of his pants, then darted away. "You can leave. Sonya and I had an agreement; she got what she wanted and I got what I wanted. Almost didn't because of that fish-brained gizzard-eater who put a hit on the spacer." He sneered. "It was me that made this work. Not you lot. Without me, you'd still be sitting around panting after those parts. I made good on delivery. Any by-product is my profit, not your catch."

"I'm not arguing with that," Titan said calmly. "Still, this is a sale."

"Yeah." Kafftan shrugged. "What of it?"

Titan looked around. "Sales have buyers. Auctions have bidders."

Again, Kafftan's hand dropped to his pants pocket.

"I have money," Titan said.

"Your own?"

"My employer has a far healthier account." Carver was going to kill him. The guardian's slush fund of grounder cash wasn't enough to buy new office chairs, let alone the information Kafftan was auctioning.

But Kafftan was already shaking his head. "Not happening. Rules is rules. Can't do business with the same person twice in a row. It's bad luck. Starts a pattern. Gets a man noticed."

"There are different kinds of notice," Titan said. "My employer is influential, powerful, wealthy."

The thief's eyes narrowed in pecuniary speculation.

"The authorities are only a problem if they can find you," Titan said, dropping to a conspiratorial whisper. "With the right *friends*... you won't need back-alley dodges and side hustles. You wouldn't need to be a guest at pay-as-you-go parties."

Kafftan took a deep breath in, inhaling the possibilities. Then he stopped and shook his head. "No. No! Rules is rules. Besides, I have other things to do tonight." He nodded to something in the distance.

Titan turned to look just as Selena stepped into view.

Creamy white skin and hair pale as moonlight... She was an alabaster goddess in a single piece of black fabric that Titan hoped wasn't actually paint. Or maybe he hoped it was. Either way, she was all he could see.

His mouth went dry as Selena tied a sheer, black skirt around her waist and posed in one of the spotlights.

Her left shoulder was painted with a nebula and three shooting stars. When she turned, she was everything: night and stars, fire and magic, promise and hope.

Selena moved, breaking away to pose by the edge the pool. She took off her skirt, tossed it aside, and dove in.

Suddenly, Titan saw the merits in learning to swim.

Kafftan tapped the balustrade, oblivious to the exchange. "Lovely girl. Arwel says she's here nearly every night. Pity, really, but she was in the parking garage earlier."

Now that Titan looked at the shield running along Arwel's eastern perimeter, he recognized the familiar whorls of coding that were unique to Selena.

A house next door. A job as a model.

All those looks between her and Tyrling hadn't stemmed from the Jhandarmi director's frustration—they'd been coded orders.

"It won't be a problem for long," Kafftan said, misinterpreting Titan's furious frown.

"Good," Titan muttered.

Kafftan watched her. "It's going to be a fun night."

"Taking your victims home is messy," Titan said. "Unprofessional. Your DNA will be all over her."

"Don't worry," Kafftan said. "I'm good at making these things look like accidents." He smoothed his hand over his pants. "If you'll excuse me, I need to go circulate. Can't get a good auction if you don't have buyers frothing at the mouth."

"Kafftan?" Titan said, stalling.

The man turned. "What? What I says goes. Done is done."

"This is a side matter, something personal."

Kafftan slowed and pivoted back to him. "I'm listening."

"During this operation, my employer hired some local talent. Sent orders outside our usual chain of command. Me and my fellows had a bet about whose name was to be rubbed out. Care to give me a hint? I can make it worth your trouble."

"Shame I'm a thief, not a liar, I'd love to take your money. But I don't know. The supplier said it would be easier for them if a certain officer of the law was scrubbed out. Would have put the city on high alert if any more of them dropped. It was bad for business. If the supplier wants to do something now, that's their business." Kafftan shrugged as he walked off.

Titan stared after him in horror. Employers and suppliers did not add up to a small operation. He turned just in time to see Arwel sweep through a group of giggling women who were enjoying an anecdote from a dark-haired model.

"Sir! I apologize, I didn't catch your name."

"Ty is what my friends call me." He watched as Selena moved out of view, following one of the illuminated paths into the artificial jungle. "Was there something you needed?"

"Need? No. I want to introduce you to someone, if you feel inclined to socialize."

More like Arwel wanted to steer his unvetted visitors away from the black market traders, but at this point any information would help. His host gestured for him to follow along a flagstone path. "Are you enjoying the garden?"

"It's... interesting," Titan said.

"Different than the formal gardens in Descent, I imagine. I've been to Kytan, of course—it's practically a requirement if you love horticulture—but it was the wind forests in Essan that really captured my imagination. The little rock pools and hidden forests tucked away in the rills and valleys were quite breath-taking."

Titan nodded as he made a note to look up the places Arwel was naming.

"That couldn't be done here, naturally," the man continued on as the path snaked across a decorative creek and behind the crashing sound of the waterfall, "but I think my designer did a good job of catching the creative spirit of the original. There are hidden vistas around every corner. And hidden beauty." He stopped and smiled.

It took Titan a moment to realize that Selena was standing in the shadows of the artificial rocks, watching the party. Their approach hadn't triggered a response.

His approach hadn't trigged a response. He'd expected their shields to synch again, but they weren't. She'd reconfigured hers in the brief time they'd been apart.

Arwel winked at him and mouthed, "Good luck," before slipping away down the path.

Time stood still, captured in the still of the night. Selena Caryll, alone in the moonlight and shadows, waiting for a chance to step into the spotlight. She was beautiful.

And tired.

There was the first dark shadow of fatigue under her eyes, a hint of strain around her eyes, a pinch to her lips that spoke of anger, weariness, and control. He wanted to take away her worry, rush her away from here, or fight the battle, or do whatever needed to be done to wash the darkness from her eyes.

Stepping loudly, he walked up behind her.

Selena pivoted, a wide-eyed expression of startlement and fear on her face. For a drawn out moment, she stared at him uncomprehending. "Titan?"

"Yes?"

She shook her head in disbelief, shields and data tight as the night she'd punched him. "You're not supposed to be here! You need to leave. Now."

"I will, in a moment." If she gave him no other choice. "But I behaved badly earlier and I wanted to apologize."

He expected her to draw up her shoulders and nod knowingly, the way most people did when he acknowledged he treated them poorly. Selena only looked at him in confusion.

"This afternoon," he said, slowly trying to feel his way across the sudden gap between them. "I left. With Lily Sekoo. Because she was injured, and I didn't check on you. As your partner I should have followed up."

"You were concussed, bleeding, and your implant was exhausted. You didn't need to do anything but get to the *Sabiha's* medical bay without collapsing. Which it seems you did. Well done. Go home."

"I came to make sure you were okay."

Selena shrugged. "I received the medical treatment I needed. Does that satisfy you?"

"Not really," he admitted. Again, there was a key piece to the puzzle missing. None of her reactions made any sense. Immediate forgiveness had been unlikely, but being locked out hurt.

She raised her eyebrows. "What?"

"I thought we'd developed a bit more of a dialog and I'd get more information than an ensign their first day on the bridge."

Glancing back through the trees at the party, Selena sighed impatiently. "Would you believe me if I said it wasn't personal?"

"If it didn't feel personal, yes."

She glared at him, blue eyes cold as the black between stars. "I did what you suggested and archived my war memories so I could focus on the task at hand."

Titan expanded his shield so it brushed against Selena's. It was like trying to catch mist in his hand. "Did I hurt you so much that you had to erase me too?"

"It was a calculated decision." Her voice was chilly and distant. "Painful. Torturous. I can't go through that again. I can't take another loss like I did with the *Persephone* and my crew."

"And you think I'd leave you?"

"Wouldn't you?" Her forehead crinkled as she let her fear bubble to the surface. "When this is over and you have no reason to keep company with me? When your crew, and captain, and allies started questioning why you spend time with that worthless Selena Caryll, what did you plan on doing?"

"I planned on asking permission to court you."

She closed her eyes. "Oh, Titan."

"Did you not want that?" He sorted through every moment they'd spent together, trying to find the cues he'd missed.

"As a woman, yes, I'd be delighted to be courted by you. As a senior officer? No, I can't let you, for the same reason your captain will reject the suggestion: I have nothing to offer."

Titan took a step closer. "What do you mean?"

"There is no advantage to your crew if you court me. I can't offer ships, officers, training berths, or even a social boost. I'm worthless."

Force teleporting a captain somewhere so he could yell at her gave him an estimated survival rate of zero-point-nine percent, his implant informed him. Besides, he didn't have a suitable venue picked out. Clearly an oversight.

Selena crossed her arms, signaling an end to the discussion.

"What about your intelligence?" Titan asked.

She shrugged. "What about it?"

"Isn't that something you can offer? Your years of experience? Your contacts with the locals, which are obviously much more developed than you led anyone to believe. My captain doesn't need ships, she needs to build a future. I need a future."

233

"I doubt your crew would accept that argument."

"Then I find another crew."

The nearby waterfall seemed to grow louder as the silence stretched between them.

Finally Selena said, "You don't mean that."

"I do." He tried to force a smile. "It was bound to happen anyway, wasn't it? If you wanted to change crews, you would have done it by now. That means you want to keep the Caryll name, and any spouse will have to join your crew."

"I don't want to ask for that kind of sacrifice."

"You don't need to." He risked taking another step closer.

Her crossed arms became a closed-shoulder self-hug. She shook her head. "You think you know how this ends. You think you'll spend more time with me, learn my secrets, and still love me. You won't. Whatever fantasy you've built in your head, I'm not that woman."

"I don't have any fantasies. Not about who you are, at least," Titan said. "I've seen you work, and fight, and lead. I'm not promising you every day will be perfect, but the good days together will be worth fighting for. I know that. Because when I'm around you I'm happy. I have hope."

"Don't do that," she said, her voice breaking. "Don't make me your source of happiness. I can't give you that."

Titan stepped close enough to reach her if he dared. "I'm not asking you for anything but a chance to be beside you every day. The good days and the bad. I promise you, I'll always be there."

She shook her head again. "No. No you won't. There's things I've done—"

"We've all done things!" He inhaled sharply to keep from yelling. "We've all done things," he said again, quieter this time. "We aren't children. We're survivors of a war and there isn't anyone here who can't tell you who they killed, or who they wanted dead, or who killed someone they loved. That happened. There's nothing you did that would make me think less of you."

"You don't know that."

"Then tell me," Titan challenged. "Tell me what you did that you think I'll never forgive. If you're right, I'll leave. If you're wrong…" He spread his hands. "We're all wrong sometimes."

Selena turned away, shields tightening around her.

"If you're going to banish me from your life, shouldn't it be like you're imagining? Let me storm out."

"Can't you just accept that you'd hate me?"

He took a deep breath and resisted the urge to start the next civil war at some grounder's garden party. Luckily, his ancestors had blessed him with a wealth of stubborn women in his life, so he knew the right answer here. Very calmly he said, "You do not get to dictate my feelings or my reactions. You can give me facts, but that's all you can do. I get to choose whether I am angry or not. I'm not an infant who needs protection. Let me take my hits like an adult."

An angry silence shimmered in the air between them.

Titan smiled. "That's what I thought."

Selena frowned over her shoulder at him, half question, half condemnation.

"You're not worried about what I think at all. It's not my forgiveness you're doubting."

"That's ridiculous."

"If your goal was driving me away, and you had a weapon to use, you're smart enough that you would have used it by now."

She turned slowly, unfolding with a quiet fury until she looked every inch a fleet captain. "Did it ever occur to you that I was trying to spare you?"

"I don't need to be spared."

Silver-blue lightning flickered in her eyes. "I shot you down. That night Baular led the strafing run? It wasn't Hollis Silar with Perrin and Hermione, he didn't have the fighters. I did. I took the shot that should have killed you."

The memory was still raw, the smoke in the cockpit burning his lungs, the alarms and sound, the rushing sensation as true gravity grabbed him and pulled him down. His throat tightened around a remembered scream.

"I shot you down, and you weren't there when Baular needed you. You missed the war. You let people die."

He shook his head, forcing his thoughts to the present. "No. That's not me. That's survivor's guilt. You may have heard the echoes in my mind, and I'm sorry for that, but that's not me. I know if I'd been there for Mal, I would have either died in war or been executed after. The Sciarra crew wouldn't have survived. My Aunt Elea never would have taken control of the crew. Mars. Rowena. All of them would have died if I hadn't been there after the war. I was the only Warmonger the Starguard would take. Carver trusts my loyalty and common sense, and me being free of the war is the only bridge we had to rebuild on."

"That doesn't make it forgivable."

"Maybe it makes it inevitable," Titan said. "Maybe our ancestors knew and changed your shot."

She curled back in on herself. "Or maybe I'm a worthless shot. If you'd died, we may not have ever gone to war."

Stepping forward, he held out his hand, silently willing her to reach for him. "Our other option was starvation. Maybe not for your crew, but most of the Warmongers were low on rations. We'd been limiting births, cutting back training... We were dying. Landing at least gave us a chance to live, even if it meant changing how we do things. I'm not ever going to be angry that you shot me down. It was the right choice." He gave her shield a gentle nudge as tears filled her eyes. "Selena, I'm here."

With a tiny grumble of forfeit, she stepped forward into his waiting arms.

Titan wrapped his arms around her, lowering his shields so there was a place for her and her wet cheek rested on his chest.

"If you say I'm beautiful when I'm angry or something stupid I'm going to drop-kick you into vacuum," she muttered as she hugged him back.

"Not a word," he promised, though she was always beautiful. He traced the painting on her arm, the stars and comets with silver tails that were three thick, wide grooves in her arm. They started just above her elbow at almost the same place his scars ended.

Selena shivered and pulled herself together as her shield melded with his. Gently, she pushed him away. "I..." There was a tsunami of emotions flooding his senses. She wanted to apologize, wanted to yell, wanted to run away from all of this, but the core of Selena had always been duty. Loving a captain was like that; it meant loving not only them, but their work.

He leaned forward and kissed her forehead. "I know. The mission comes first."

"I need to go keep an eye on Kafftan."

"He knows you were there today," Titan said. "He saw you."

She tossed her wet hair. "I was counting on it." The words dripped fleet arrogance. With a smile, she ran a hand down his shirt. "You really should go, though. You're exhausted and you're injured."

"I'd rather stay nearby, even if I'm not involved in the op. Kafftan said something that makes me think we don't have a

handle on this yet, and I don't want you walking into this alone."
He shot her the conversation as he felt her gathering her objecttions. "I promise to stay out of the way and only jump to the rescue if you actually need it."

"Hmm, Captain Sciarra trained you how to be a second in command very well."

He chuckled. "Don't I get credit for doing anything myself?"

"Mmmm..." She wrinkled her nose. "No. Not when you're wounded. Maybe when you can fight back..."

The thought of hitting the wrestling mats with Selena made his heartrate jump.

Soft fingers caressed his jaw. "It's been a while since I had a training partner."

"I'll tell Silar he needs to find someone else's ribs to break." He kissed her fingertips before she pulled away.

Her smile was pure bliss.

"Couldn't we leave Kafftan for the night? There are so many better things I can think to do."

"Tempting, but if the Lees need the medicine, we need information now, not later. If we catch Kafftan selling the information, we can probably get him to hand over the details of the heist."

Titan closed his eyes and sighed. When he'd pictured declaring his undying love to someone, he hadn't factored in the possibility she'd be in the middle of a mission. Although, considering the kind of women he was attracted to, that was a dramatic oversight. He made a mental note to warn his future children that chasing aggressively intelligent lovers would mean chasing them into the field sometimes.

Selena leaned in. "I can hear your brain overheating."

"I'm making notes."

"For children we don't have yet."

"It's still something I need to remember." She'd said 'yet'. He was giddy with hope. "I should let Ro know I'm staying here for a bit before she raises a fuss."

Nodding, Selena stepped away. "And I need to find Kafftan and convince him I'm enamored with his self-absorption and money." She winked at him. "How do I look?"

"More beautiful than the moon and stars."

She sent him a burst of affection and then hurried away through the shadows back to Arwel's party.

:Ro?: He kept the message on a tight beam so he didn't trigger any of the grounder's safety precautions.

:Where in the name of my ancestors are you?: Rowena demanded. :Mars is pacing and I almost bit my nails.:

:Don't lie. You never do that.:

She sent him an image of a thread she'd unwound from her socks. :We're worried. And bored. Mostly bored. Are you done chasing shadows?:

:I'm staying here tonight.:

Rowena responded with a memory of her banging her head on the hull of the engine room.

:It's not what you think. Selena is helping the Jhandarmi and I'm being a perfect gentleman.:

:I know what that means,: Rowena said caustically. :And I can't imagine you have the energy to make their whole team that happy in one night.:

He smiled. :I'm a talented man.:

:You're going to be a dead one if you—: Rowena cut short.

Titan waited, then pinged her. :Ro? Are you okay?:

There was the faintest trace of contact, a simple message on a distress frequency.

He pinged Selena and felt the message break apart as soon as it left his shield. Someone was jamming fleet communications. They were under attack.

19

SELENA

SELENA STEPPED INTO ARWEL'S climate-controlled house and slid the door shut behind her. All the party guests were outside, mingling and giggling as the first effects of the free-flowing alcohol took over their good judgment. Titan being here changed plans considerably. Titan knowing she was working with the Jhandarmi changed her long-term plans more than she wanted to calculate at the moment.

Leaving the lights off, she pulled the gauzy curtains shut with a twitch. She wouldn't be invisible to anyone outside, but they wouldn't be able to see her easily either. It was enough. Walking across the kitchen, she found the electronic juicer Arwel had purchased on a whim years before and never locked against tech invasion. On one of her earliest forays into his house, she'd programmed it to suit her purposes. Suspicious people would find her purse and check her phone, but they wouldn't find anything compromising there.

She turned the juicer on and typed in the code.

Tyrling's face appeared next to a logo with oranges circled by stars. "What's going on? You were out of visual contact for a quarter hour."

"Sciarra showed up."

The Jhandarmi director rubbed his face as he swore. With a grumbling sigh he asked, "How much trouble are you in?"

"None, I think. Sciarra…" She wasn't sure what to say exactly.

"He likes you," Tyrling said. "Enough to be protective, at any rate."

Selena smiled. "Enough that you need to factor him in as a long term variable. We can read him into my operations later."

Tyrling's image split and broke for a second.

With a frown she checked the juicer's energy supply. "Is something happening on your end?"

"Not a thing. The city's quiet," Tyrling said. He paused, and then his eyes narrowed. "When's the last time nothing happened in Tarrin?"

"My implant says never." She started to smile and then realized what the silence implied. "None of the corps or gangs are near war. Everything's been quiet."

Tyrling arched a shaggy eyebrow. "Except the theft."

"Fleet has no plans for retaliation."

"All the same…"

She nodded in understanding. "I'll get the information from Kafftan tonight."

"Are you sure you can without blowing your cover?"

"The Baulars weren't the only ones who learned torture techniques," she said. "Trust me. I can make him talk. And I won't leave a mark." She turned off the juicer and looked down at her hands. Over the years she'd had a lot of blood on them, and it was rarely hers. But she'd worked hard to make sure the blood on her hands hadn't been spilled by her either. With a little luck, and a lot of booze, she'd be able to resolve all this without anyone being the wiser.

Outside, the music had been turned up, people were finally dipping their feet in the pool, and Arwel was drying the paint on a man who'd decided he had to try a free sample before the night was over.

Selena looked over the garden and her implant tallied the recording devices. Kafftan was standing conveniently close to one on the eastern edge of the yard. She put on her best smile, swung her hips, and sashayed over to the thief.

He looked up with hungry eyes. Not, she couldn't help notice, filled with the adoration and love she saw in Titan's eyes. Kafftan's look was predatory. To him she was a victim.

The poor fool.

"Hello," he said, reaching for her as she walked up. "Have you been avoiding me all evening?"

"Of course not," Selena lied. "I was waiting until I could catch you alone." Her hand warmed as she sent a very specific code to her implant. Casually, she ran her hand across Kafftan's back and watched him relax, the soporific effect of heat combined with slow sound waves below the range of human hearing.

Kafftan's pupils dilated in pleasure as she pressed her body against his side. "Well."

"You looked so busy earlier," Selena murmured in a softly modulated tone meant to set him at ease. "You must be very important." Her hand stretched down his side, reaching for his pocket.

He grabbed her wrist and pulled her hand to his torso with a laugh. "Important enough, but I'll be more important later. Rich. So rich." His eyes shut.

Too much stimuli. Selena cut the dosage in half, her hand cooling. She squeezed his shoulder and pulled away. "Too important to get a drink with a body paint model?"

His eyes stuttered open and he looked her over lazily. "What else do you do?"

"Advertising work. Modeling. Sometimes I work at a bar up by the High Street Market. It's paying the bills for now." With a flirty smile, she took his hand, pulling him towards a table near the lights and the next recording device. "I love meeting new people, but there's not really a degree for that at the university. I suppose I could try politics, but not here. I have too much of a reputation here." She winked at her willing victim.

There was a static-y ping against her shields.

She sent a query to Titan and returned her focus to Kafftan. "What do you do?"

"This and that," he evaded.

Selena turned the relaxant up. "Someone said you were in shipping. That sounds important. Getting this and that here and there."

"I do that," Kafftan agreed as she slid him into a chair. "I do a lot of that."

"Anything recent?" She kept her hand on his arm as she reached across the table for a wine bottle.

The liquid sloshed into his glass with a hypnotic sound. "Rearranged some inventory on the docks. Brought in cash for a buy. The seller did the exchange. Then I moved the goods out."

"You must know the docks so well," Selena cooed. "Where did you—"

An explosion of light and sound knocked her from her chair. The soft grass cushioned her knees.

Kafftan jumped to his feet as he reached for a gun.

In the confusion, someone screamed.

Kafftan pushed away from the table and took off running.

She tried to teleport but her implant couldn't find a path. :Titan?: There was nothing on the other end.

It was possible to modulate energy waves to disrupt communication, like a white noise machine balancing out sound, but she'd never seen one on this scale.

"Selena?" Titan ran up to her, Arwel trailing behind him. "We need to get out."

Arwel grabbed her arm. "What is happening?"

"I don't know. I think Kafftan's sale just went nova though."

The sound of gunfire ripped through the air; turf exploded.

There were too many options. Keeping civilians safe took top priority, but she needed to finish the mission.

Titan squeezed her shoulder. "Go," he said as if he could read her thoughts. "I've got the civilians."

"Civilians?" Arwel echoed.

"Another time," Selena said. "Go with Titan." The words 'I love you' hung on her lips, not willing to fall. All she could manage was a tight smile. "Be safe."

"Always." His smile was enough.

Selena turned and ran into the debris cloud after Kafftan. Cycling her shields kept them up against the assault of the destabilizer, but keeping them at full strength was impossible. A concussion grenade exploded near her feet and the shrapnel pummeled her bare legs.

Underfoot there was sharp rock and glass from a broken cup, all hidden by a smoky blue haze that burned her eyes and throat.

Whoever had interrupted the party wasn't worried about wasting resources. This was overkill.

"Minus ten points for style," she muttered as she brought up a battle code. Let the grounders see her eyes glow; she was done pretending to be a civilian.

In the blink of an eye, the battlefield changed from a field filled with chemical fog to a muted gray background where bodies appeared as bright red targets and the furniture became a soft green.

Kafftan was ahead of her, crawling on all fours towards the dubious safety of the house.

Rolling a clearing shield in front of her, Selena brushed the debris away from her feet and ran after him.

Hot air turned to sticky condensation on her skin as Selena stalked forward. Her implant was filtering out sounds now, but she knew what she was missing: the screaming, the crying, the shouts of angry denial.

Ahead of her, Kafftan managed to take down a guard with a quick stun shot. It wasn't a bad idea: leave the soldier naked and unconscious, and escape in his uniform. Kafftan was confident enough in his plan that he was stripping the guard down before the invaders opened fire.

Kafftan scrambled backward.

Selena blocked his path. "Oww!" Stupid yaldson was wearing boots.

The thief turned to her in surprise. "You again?"

She nodded.

"Sorry about this. Business gets messy sometimes," he said as he raised his gun.

She pushed him so he was pointing at the attackers. "Did you bring them?"

"No!" He struggled to turn but she held him in place with telekyen and muscle.

"Who are they?"

"Someone who didn't like the buy-in price for my auction, Arwel's old clients, who knows. Let me go. What are you doing to me?"

She reached for his pocket where the datcube was. "Nothing personal. Just business. I know someone who will pay very well for the data you have." Her fingers touched a hole in the lining of his jacket. Frantically she patted down the other side. "Where is it?"

Kafftan's hand dropped, clenching and unclenching around the empty fabric. "I had it. It was... I fell." He broke away from her, desperately searching the littered ground.

Everything looked the same to her. The datcube looked no different from a shard of glass and there was no way to do a search with her implant or by satellite. Panic closed her throat. She switched to normal vision and searched the grass for any sign of the datcube.

In the fog, Kafftan squeaked joyfully.

She leaped, tackling him as another round of bullets ripped through the air.

"Trying to save me?" he panted.

"Not likely." She punched him.

Kafftan rolled, pushing her away. He kicked her bruised ribs.

The burst of pain made her see stars. Her muscles froze in agony. It was only for a few seconds, but it was enough.

Kafftan and the datcube were already out of reach.

But it was the little hairs on her arm standing on end that made her raise her full shield. A sense born of war and loss. When the blast hit, she was thrown several meters, but she was alive.

She looked up, searching for Titan, and saw his broad shield ripple and fall. He lay on the ground by a quivering Arwel.

Between her and safety, the enemy was lining up another battery, like they were trying to herd everyone away from the exits. No, not herd. *Corral.* Like forcing a squad of fighters into close formation so they could go down with one hit.

Without Titan's shield, everyone would die. She watched Kafftan bolt for the house, then turned and ran for Titan. Falling to her knees, she checked his pulse. Alive, but bleeding, and his eyes were glazed. "You were supposed to stay safe."

"I tried."

Arwel grabbed her arm with a bruising grasp. "What is happening? Why? Who?" He shook his head in confusion. "Your eyes are glowing."

"I don't know, but we can't escape."

"Can't get a signal out," Titan said weakly. "No rescue imminent." He sighed and his eyes fluttered shut.

She brushed her hands across his face, assessing the damage and trying to attract his attention. He needed a full medbay, but even a nanite gel pack would be better than this. There was a box left on the *Persephone.*

Time slowed as she looked up beyond the haze and shields. "I can signal for backup."

Titan managed to move his head. "Can't reach Carver or Silar. Can't reach *Sabiha.*"

"I don't need *Sabiha.*" *I need Persephone.* She opened the link to her ship.

:Yes, captain?:

:Prepare a ground strike for these coordinates.:

There was a pause punctuated by another round of bullets spraying in front of the partygoers.

:Captain,: Persephone said, :those coordinates are very close to your current location. This action is not advised.:

:Story of my life.:

:Would you like to belay your order?:

The battery was nearly charged.

:Fire, Persephone. Make it a very precise hit.:

There was a muted grumble of protest from the AI.

Selena pushed Arwel down. "Close your eyes." She held a hand over Titan's face and looked up, watching the spear of deadly light fall.

It only took a moment. A ring of energy hit the ground with enough force to drive the attackers to their knees, and the following breaths let them inhale the heavy gases and fall unconscious.

A heartbeat later, the entire district was red with alarms. The disrupters that had silenced communication were gone, the shield over the district burned with warning, and police sirens screamed in the distance.

Selena slumped down. "The cavalry is coming."

As the dust cleared, she saw Kafftan, now in a white business suit, walking toward a waiting car. Looked like he was going to get his sale after all.

20

TITAN

AT FOUR IN THE morning, Titan gave up and lay down on the small couch in the back room where he'd been quarantined. The front rooms of Selena's house had been turned into a Jhandarmi control center to handle the mess outside.

So, that was battle on grounder turf. Not nearly as neat and tidy as war viewed from a fighter's cockpit.

Things had... splashed. Shattered.

He ran a hand down his leg, over the healing burns of a broken oil lamp.

The nanite gel patch Selena had given him was speeding things up nicely. He'd have to figure out where she'd found one. It'd be a good segue to the conversation they were about to have about how she'd just bombed the planet from orbit.

Ancestors above, that had not been expected.

The Carylls were supposed to be out of the game. Defanged and harmless. The *Persephone* was listed as a floating wreck, no engines or weapons left, no repair possible. Selena wasn't supposed to be able to produce a targeted strike like that. He wasn't sure he could coax the *Sabiha* into half that precision, and she was the best ship in the Sciarra armada.

That was another thing to put on the to-do list. He sighed, and stared at a painting of blue flower alien to him. The pearlescent white frame hid the scorch marks on the canvas well, but not well enough.

"Do you like it?" Selena's voice startled him.

Titan stood up. "The flower? Yes, although I don't know the name of it."

"The blue dianthus is native to the Caryll home world. It's been extinct since before the settlement of the Malik system. One of my ancestors painted the flowers in her garden before our family was called into the Emperor's service. I had them removed from the *Persephone* before her final battle."

She walked over to another painting and tapped the glass flame. "See this? The painting was burnt over three hundred years ago during a candlelit dinner between lovers."

"How did that relationship end?"

"Poorly." She sounded angrier than she looked.

Titan moved toward her, tugging gently with telekyen until she stepped into his embrace. "This is an impressive defensive position you built yourself." Her skin was chilled and there was a lingering scent of floral soap. At least she'd taken the time to wash away the blood of the day.

"Oh?" She lifted her chin so she could maintain eye contact. "Do you like my shield?"

"I do. Almost as much as I like the woman it's guarding."

Selena's hands slid around his neck, caressing him, holding him… Her head fell to his chest.

Titan's hands wandered from her waist, massaging the muscles in her back. It was a stolen moment that wouldn't last, but all happiness was built in stolen moments.

She groaned with pleasure, lifting her head.

He leaned down and trailed hungry kisses down her neck.

Her eyes fluttered open. "You're making me forget why I came in here." She touched his chest, starting to push him away, and then her fingers curled, pulling him closer. "I came to check on you."

"That wasn't a bad idea. It saves me from having to come find you." His found her lips, brushed across them in silent question.

Selena's tongue ran across his mouth, begging for entry, and he let her in.

Their shields intertwined, melting together until every emotion circled back. He could feel her pleasure as he lifted her up; the hunger wasn't in her kiss alone, but in her thoughts and pressure of her fingertips digging into his shoulders and pushing for more.

He stepped back until he fell onto the couch with Selena on top, her long, blonde hair falling around them. Her whole body grew warm. It was like holding the warmth of a flame. The tension in his muscles eased, and he was lost in her touch. Lost in the pleasure of finally holding her, kissing her. He'd risk death to stay beside her. Kill to keep her happy.

It took all his strength to open his eyes and focus on reality. The stunning, amazing, reality of Selena Caryll in his arms. "You're beautiful."

The look in her deep blue eyes was soft, glazed with pleasure as she stole another kiss he willingly gave.

If he could control time, they'd stay here forever. Forget about the smoking ruins next door, and the mob of Jhandarmi and police on the other side the wall. All he wanted was to hold this moment forever.

Selena pulled away, leaving him cold.

Reluctantly, he let his eyes drift open. The look of despair on her face stabbed at his heart. Words failed him. His blood pounded in his ears as he realized she was getting up. "Selena?"

She held up a hand covered in blood.

Titan stared at it, light headed. "I…"

"You're bleeding!"

Relief that she was angry over his health, not over his kiss, made him slump back into the cushions. "It's bleeding less than it was. I'm fine." He reached for her again.

Selena's glare was fierce, not nearly as playful as he wanted.

"I will live through this."

"Sick leave, Sciarra. Ever heard of it?" She spun around and marched off down a dark hall.

:Romance, Caryll, ever heard of it? If I have to chase you down, I might rip my stitches again.:

She teleported back to the room holding a square patch of a swollen, blue cloth. "You think I wouldn't have noticed your stitches had ripped again? What was your plan here?"

"I'm not sure I had plans. Fantasies, yes, but not plans."

The look she gave him was only a few degrees warmer than zero Kelvin. "You must not have gotten very far in your fantasies if you kept your shirt on." A first-aid kit floated out of the cupboard. "Or were you planning on blindfolding me?"

"Tempting idea." Titan pulled her back between his legs as she unwrapped the bandage. "But I doubt you want any more surprises after the day we've had."

"Yet here you are," she said as she lifted his shirt off, "surprising me in the worst ways." Tender fingers ran along his side. "Why didn't you say something? I could've had a medic in here."

He glanced at his scars long enough for Selena to notice them.

"Oh." She ran her hand along the grooves in his arm, then kissed him.

Titan drank her in, moonlight and power, the stars and the sky here with him.

"Who knew you had a poetic side?" she said with a smile. "I'll put the nanite patch on, then find you another shirt. Tyrling has almost finished out there and he'll want to debrief you soon." She peeled the backing off the blue patch and stuck the cool gel against his side. "All-purpose patch," she said by way of explanation. "It'll boost your all-purpose nanites for twelve hours and help you recover faster." Her smile was sorrowful.

"What's wrong?"

"I have to let you go, don't I?"

"Possibly, for a little bit. Elea will expect me to tell her face to face that I'm transferring to your crew." Saying the words out loud felt strange, but there was pleasure in them. "And I ought to pack my gear. I won't be gone long, promise." He lifted her hand and kissed the palm.

She twined her fingers with his. "What am I going to do with you?"

Through their shared link, he suggested multiple ideas.

Her cheeks blushed a bright pink as she smiled. "I think the zero-g one is probably out of the question in the near future. And at least two of those would require me to have my old Academy uniform. Is this a kink I should know about?"

"It's an old fantasy," Titan said, wrapping his arms around her. He let his gaze drop, running along her body like a caress.

"Gi pants and a silver shirt dropping off your shoulder? Barefoot and soft-eyed on my lap?"

There was a twinkle and a hunger in her eyes.

"I think you underestimate how attractive you have always been. Said with all due respect, Captain."

Selena laughed before kissing him again.

"Caryll!" Tyrling's bellow echoed through the room as a door slammed open behind them.

:Not a part of my fantasy,: Titan grumbled.

:Reality rarely is.: Selena stood up and teleported in a shirt that she tossed at him. "Sir? I'm over here."

Tyrling walked around the couch and nodded to him. "You look more alive than you did."

"Thank you," Titan said. "I hope you'll forgive the lack of proper reception."

"Kafftan's dead," Tyrling said without preamble. "Shot in the head at point-blank range and dropped behind the hypertram station. A couple of patrollers found him ten minutes ago already going cold. The datcube was missing."

Selena crossed her arms. "That's it then? We don't have any other leads?"

"I might have one," Titan said. "The Sekoos reached out to Rowena and said they had some of the medicine Aronia needs."

The look Selena gave him could have peeled paint off a hull.

"It was something I wanted to talk about in private, but then we were getting shot at." He shrugged apologetically. His side ached in protest.

"Convenient," Tyrling muttered.

"Very," Selena agreed. "How did they get the medicine?"

Titan tipped his head in acknowledgment. "How do they get anything? They're a C-class crew, non-combatants, but they adapted to Landing quick enough. They sell scrap metal for the most part, and I'm sure some of their contacts would have black market contacts." He grimaced as he realized how bad that sounded. "Maybe just back channel. Not illegal, but unofficial?"

He reached out to Selena, floundering. :What's the grounder word for this?:

:Black market is probably accurate.: She crossed her arms. "What do the Sekoos want from Lee in return?"

"Me," Titan said.

Selena's eyes went wide and the memory of a burning precision strike hit his shield with full force. :No.:

"Lily wants an hour of my time," he said out loud for the director's benefit. "Not for anything physical, she wants to talk," Titan said. He reached for Selena. :I love you. It won't be anything but a talk.:

"Do you object to going?" Tyrling asked.

"Not unless Selena objects." What he wouldn't give to have a few hours truly alone with her. To talk. To hold her. Giving time to Lily Sekoo seemed like a crime, but he was a fleet officer and someone needed his help.

Selena smiled softly. :We'll have time together.:

:Never enough.:

"I don't mind Sciarra going," she said in a formal tone. "It's business. Part of the job is sometimes spending time with people we wouldn't pick to socialize with in our free time."

"Too true," Tyrling said but his eyes were narrowed in thought.

Titan gave Selena's arm a mental tug until she took a step closer and he could touch her hand. He needed her touch right now, the memory of moon and starlight, of safety and serenity.

:Poet.: Her gentle laugh was a balm.

Tyrling cleared his throat. "Did I miss something here? I thought you didn't know him well," he said, pointing from Selena to Titan.

"We're, um…" Selena frowned and Titan saw the tumble of words her implant was sorting through. "I don't know what the grounder equivalent is. Not dating, because that's how you get to know someone, but not officially a spousal couple? Engaged sounds a bit too militant."

"We're courting," Titan said. "It'll be official once my captain gives her seal of approval and permits me to move to another crew. Which will probably be later today unless someone starts another war." He squeezed Selena's hand.

Tyrling blinked. "That's… fine? Does this mean I'm losing you, Caryll?"

"Titan will be my second. We'll negotiate a new contract, read him in, and you'll get my full crew backing Jhandarmi operations. It'll open avenues of inquiry for us. We've talked about investing more in my business-person persona. It'll be easier to sell that with Titan beside me."

"Fine. We're going to be renegotiating with Enclave anyway. Might as well rearrange everything in my life. Maybe I can go home and move my furniture around tonight. That way I can know everything's changed."

The word 'move' triggered a cascade of memories from the previous night. Titan raised a finger. "I forgot something."

Selena and Tyrling both turned to him.

"Last night Kafftan said the suppliers ordered the hit to clear a guardian out of the way. If he stole the medicine to sell, he wouldn't have called them suppliers"

Tyrling rolled his neck, glared at the ceiling, and cursed. "I knew we were missing something! That's why Kafftan was on the tram. He wasn't coming to town, he was working on the tram. Switching goods in the boxes. The medicine never made it to Tarrin."

"Then, what, someone took what he smuggled in out of the warehouse?" Selena asked.

The director nodded. "It's a classic move. Change out the already cleared cargo, leave money or goods, take the boxes from the warehouse after they're unloaded."

"Why leave the disaster then?" Selena asked. "If Kafftan could get in and out without leaving a trace, why would he need to blow the warehouse doors in?"

"Amateurs," Titan said thinking back on his conversation with Rowena. "Kafftan knew what he was doing, but whoever he was working with didn't. They were amateurs, inexperienced, so they didn't know how to cover their tracks. They probably thought the threat of an assassination attempt would be enough to keep the guardians cowed."

Selena shook her head in disagreement. "No one would think that. No one in fleet."

"It makes sense," Tyrling said. "Basic crime theory says the first crimes a person commits are the most personal, and the most likely to reveal how they work. Look at what they left: explosive markings, a mess, and signs of fear, not of the Jhandarmi but of fleet. Which makes me wonder what they were giving Kafftan."

That seemed obvious. "Tech," Titan said. "The weapons last night, the disruptor that silenced communications, I bet they were all old fleet tech. Obsolete for the most part, but every crew has a junk ship piled up with bits and pieces they hope they can one day re-purpose. You don't destroy anything because there's no way to replace it once it's gone. We don't have the resources to be wasteful."

"And the antiques market is the biggest source of income for the crews," Selena said. "Selling off old scrap computers can be profitable. Crack the hull! A crew wouldn't even need to sell weapons. Some of those could have been sitting in grounder vaults since before isolation. All they needed for half of them was an upgraded power source."

Titan stood up. "I know how we can find out. Want to bet me dinner I can sweet talk Lily Sekoo into letting the name of her contact drop?" He winked at Selena.

She rolled her eyes. "Ridiculous man. Fine, yes, go be charming. But be back by lunch. I don't want you gone that long." She reached up and brushed debris from his shoulder. "Stay off the training mats, okay? You're supposed to be healing."

Titan leaned down and gently kissed her. "I'll be back in time for lunch. Promise." He smiled to Tyrling as he headed for the door.

"What, no kiss for me?" the director demanded.

With a grin, Titan leaned over and kissed Tyrling's cheek. "Love you too. Promise. Just not as much as her." He teleported to Enclave, catching the full strength of his aunt's wrath as he passed through the Enclave shield. The orders were clear: Report to the captain. Immediately.

It was time to let Captain Sciarra know where he'd been all night, and with who.

Elea Sciarra was, at least in Titan's opinion, the best captain the crew ever had. She was also his nearest surviving blood relative.

Her perfection was tempered by humanity and a forgiving heart.

In the old day, she would never have been promoted past junior gunner.

But these weren't the old days, and now Titan stood across from her gaping, black desk and watched her warily. Black uniform against black skin and against the oh-so-typical black walls of a Sciarra captain's office. The whites of her eyes stood out like twin moons.

She moved, and the lights changed, projecting the image of a baby blue nebula against the wall. The black desk lit up with files, images, and status icons. "Well. Titan. How are you?"

"I'm well, thank you, captain."

The captain leaned back in her chair. "I understand there are rumors running around the fleet that someone left a hole in the middle of the expensive end of Tarrin. I'd normally ignore these rumors, except someone swears it was the Caryll's Persephone that launched the attack and, curiously enough, you've been chasing Captain Caryll for the past few days and weren't in your quarters last night. During lock down. When you were on medical leave." Her tone cooled noticeably. "Which begs a very interesting question: Where were you last night? And, don't lie."

"I was in Tarrin last night. With Captain Caryll. But there isn't a hole in Tarrin."

"That's the engine you want to run on?"

"Yes, ma'am. I'll share a recording of the event from my implant with time stamps and everything, if that's what you need." It'd be an unusual request, invasive by most standards;

captains weren't supposed to have a second in command they couldn't trust. But these were unusual times.

She narrowed her eyes. "Am I going to like what I see?"

"No, ma'am. I was in combat when I should have been resting."

"Ancestors above, protect this stupid boy!" His aunt turned her face to the ceiling and shook her head. "What would your mother say if she were alive, ancestors keep her?"

"In my defense, ma'am, I did not plan to be in combat, and if I hadn't been there, civilians would have died. I was doing my job, not because I went looking for trouble, but because it found me."

She didn't look convinced.

Well, all in all it had been a good life. Short, but memorable. Hopefully Selena wouldn't start a war if his aunt killed him in a fit of over-protective rage.

Elea rocked her chair back and forth with a meditative creak like a clock counting down to doomsday. "Captain Caryll?"

"Yes, ma'am."

"As outrageous as that sounds, I can only assume it's the truth. It doesn't have the logic of a lie."

He kept his mouth shut.

"Was it fleet business?"

"In a manner of speaking, captain."

The creaking stopped.

"Explain."

He took a deep breath, closed his eyes, prayed to his departed ancestors, and threw himself at his aunt's mercy. "After meeting with the Jhandarmi director this evening, I tried to find Captain Caryll to ensure she'd received proper medical treatment after this afternoon's events. Carver assured me she was being treated by Captain Marshall, but Rowena said Marshall was out of coms range. The Jhandarmi had let slip the address of the operation they were going to run tonight"—only a small lie—"and I found Captain Caryll's implant signature in the area and concluded she was probably observing the operation. I felt that I was healthy enough to check on her wellbeing and return to Enclave without risking further injury."

"It looks like you failed," his aunt said dryly.

"The Jhandarmi considered the operation to be low-risk."

"They weren't trying to go in the field after being hit by an EMP blast and having their abdomens sliced open."

"My implant was recharged to a safe level." If thirty percent counted as safe.

The captain's chair began creaking again. "What did you find?"

Selena was going to kill him if this went nova. No, scratch that, everyone was going to kill him if he couldn't convince his captain the plan had been sound. "Captain Caryll was near a safe house established in the first days after landing. It has a heavy shield, one of the Caryll specials, and while it wasn't on my personal database, I don't believe it's illegal in any way. She has an established grounder identity that the Jhandarmi were using to infiltrate the auction of the stolen data and apprehend the thief."

"Why did she have a grounder identity?"

Titan shook his head. "I'm unclear on how it came to be, but it was part of the Landing protocol and signed off on by the Captains' Council."

"Was the data recovered?"

"No, ma'am."

"The thief?"

"Found dead after the incident."

Elea leaned on her desk. "Caryll is trouble."

"People have said that about me, too," Titan said. "They've probably said it about you."

His captain smirked. "Eventually, but by then it was far too late." She sighed and her eyes glowed a silvery sage green. After a moment of stillness, she shook her head. "Is there any way I can persuade you that further contact with Captain Caryll and the Jhandarmi is too disruptive to the health of the crew?"

"Only if you can prove that this crew doesn't need a little disruption. We're on a collision course with extinction, Captain. If something doesn't change in the next decade, we're dead. Our way of life, our culture, our crew cannot live ground-bound and entombed alive in this ship. Someone has to change the course we're on. Why not me?"

"Injury, inexperience, head trauma," the captain said, ticking the items off on her fingers. "I can think of a dozen reasons I ought to lock you in the brig for your own safety."

Titan smiled. She was his favorite relative for a reason. "But you won't."

"But I won't," she agreed. "What do you need from me?"

"Immediately? Permission to go spend time with Lily Sekoo off the *Golden Apple*."

His captain watched him in damning silence. "Titan, please tell me you are not so brutally stupid that you think you can string a fleet captain along with promises of romance while keeping a low-class scavenger on the side."

"No! The Sekoos told Rowena they have access to the medication Aronia Lee needs. Selena is aware of this and supports this action."

"You're talking about Captain Caryll as if she were your spouse."

"She will be."

The declaration hung between them.

Elea tapped a slow tattoo on the table as she thought. Finally, she asked, "Is Captain Caryll aware of your intentions?"

"Yes."

"Is it even legal?"

"With a declaration of courtship, yes. Unprecedented, a bit extraordinary, but so is everything in life."

His captain shook her head in disbelief. "I never thought I'd see the Sciarras allied with the Carylls. But I never thought I'd make captain either." She waved her hand. "Fine. Yes. I'll draft a declaration for you. And you—" She paused to look him over and shake her head. "Shower before going to meet the Sekoos, eh? You're filthy."

"I've looked worse."

"Yes, you have. Dismissed."

Titan saluted.

"Come home alive, Titan," his aunt said.

"I will."

21

ROWENA

ROWENA WAS QUIZZING MARS on the historical battles he needed to know for the officer candidacy test when Titan walked up grinning like a lunatic. She raised an eyebrow. "You look cheerful for someone who had a bomb dropped on his head."

"Was it an orbital bombardment?" Mars asked, a little too excited by the idea. "Rowena said it was, but the official story was that some grounders had a battery cannon that blew up."

Battery cannons didn't sear streaks of light over the night sky.

"It was a precision orbital strike," Titan said in the infuriatingly calm voice he used when he wanted to understate the amount of danger he'd been in. "No one was killed."

She rolled her eyes and she stood and stretched. "Only the Carylls would design a weapon that has that much precision and doesn't actually kill anyone."

"It would kill an intraorbital craft," Titan said. "A precision strike like that would swat down fighters like flies. It would have been devastating if they'd ever used it."

"I suppose it's good she can't break shields with it," Rowena said. "Caryll's had enough fights over the past few years, she could have rattled some cages with that."

Titan pressed his lips together.

She shook her head. "There're no shields down there, Ty. We all know that."

Mars held his breath.

"Titan." Rowena gave him a warning look.

He shrugged. "There's a shield. A Baular shield. Mal offered it up for trade after Landing."

"To get banishment?" Idiot. Mal always expected as much from other people as he was willing to give, the good and the bad.

"To keep you alive," Titan said with an apologetic look.

She closed her eyes. *Poor Mal.* Ancestors keep him.

Mars made a cooing sound. "That's romantic."

She glared at him as Titan shook his head.

"It wasn't like that with me and Mal," Rowena said. "We were life partners. Old Baular wanted a Lee as Mal's spouse, but it was never a romantic relationship. We were friends." She looked at Titan. "Tell me he didn't leave a note coded in the shield or something pointless like that."

"Selena told me," Titan said. "I don't know if I would have guessed it was Mal's shield otherwise. It was much more elegant than the ones he made at the Academy. Beautiful work, while it lasted." He sighed, then frowned. "That doesn't go past us." He pointed a warning finger at Mars. "The grounders think the shield was a warning system only. If they knew the *Persephone* could crack a shield on the surface, we'd all be in trouble."

Mars crossed his heart with two fingers. "Deleted from my implant already. I didn't hear a thing."

Rowena nodded. "Not that a grounder would talk to me, but same. I know nothing about any shields or Caryll death rays." What a weird thought. Caryll really wasn't the kind of person who would do something huge and showy. Rowena wrinkled her nose in thought. "I hate myself for asking… but was Caryll hurt?"

Titan frowned in confusion. "No. Why?"

"I was trying to figure out what pushed her over the edge."

Mars clicked his tongue and looked pointedly at Titan.

"Were you hurt?" Rowena asked.

"Not significantly," Titan lied badly. He didn't look worse than he had before, but she'd known him too long to ignore that tone of voice.

"Should I be taking you near the Sekoos?"

He rolled his shoulders in a shrug. "Honestly? I want to go. They might be the only ones with answers right now."

"I'll come too," Mars said, hopping down from his perch on the *Sabiha's* landing gear.

"No," Titan and Rowena said in unison.

Mars' face crumpled in hurt shock. "What?"

"They're not a crew for you to spend time around," Titan said.

"What happened to equality and all fleet's the same, respect every crew?" Mars argued. "You can't say the Sekoos aren't 'our kind of people' when you're spending time kicking your heels with them."

Titan looked over at her for support. "This is different. The Sekoos aren't expecting you."

"They're scavengers," Rowena said, cutting across Titan's delicacy. "Users. What's the heart of every crew?"

"Kids and research," Mars said automatically, looking baffled.

Rowena nodded. "The Sekoos have neither. They take in disaffected people from other crews, the ones who can't learn to keep their hands to themselves or never know when to shut their mouths. The strays bring old tech."

"There's a place for them," Titan said in his tight, calm voice that sent most people running for cover. "The Sekoos have skills the fleet needs, but that doesn't mean you have a place near them right now."

"They're in trouble," Rowena translated because she doubted Captain Sciarra had sat her fleetlings down for lectures about the importance of the right allies the way she and Titan had been lectured before going to the Academy. "Lily Sekoo has medicine that was stolen from the fleet. If she went looking for it so she had an excuse to spend time with Titan, that's one thing. Dubious, but forgivable. If she knew about the theft in advance?"

Rowena shook her head. "The Jhandarmi are the closest thing the grounders have to marines. They're the major law enforcement entity for the planet. And someone attacked their agents. That's a declaration of war. The Sekoos are opportunistic idiots. One of them traded short-term benefits for lifelong consequences by working with Kafftan. We all know how that engine runs." She gestured to the graveyard of ships filling Enclave and the great, domed shield overhead. "Our ancestors, may they freeze in the black for eternity, decided their petty wars were better than keeping enough orun to breathe. Now look at us."

Titan cleared his throat.

She grimaced in apology. "We would have still run out of fuel. But, the fact remains, if you don't think of the future consequences, you aren't likely to have a future."

"Do the Jhandarmi want to question the Sekoos?" Mars asked. "Would the Captains' Council allow it?"

"I'm allowed," Titan said. "I'm a guardian and Selena is the OIA liaison with the Jhandarmi and she approves."

"Selena?" Mars' lips curled into a frown.

"Get used to it," Titan advised. "She'll be one of your in-laws soon enough."

Rowena's implant chimed. "We got to go, Ty. The Sekoos are waiting for us." She nodded to Mars. "Keep out of trouble."

"I won't get caught," he said with an impish grin.

"Mars." Titan's voice held a note of warning. "What you heard stays between us. You, me, Ro, and the captain. That's it."

:And your other captain?: Rowena asked, nudging him.

"And Selena," Titan said out loud. "She's aware of the full scope of this investigation. If anyone else asks, you know nothing. If you hear something relevant, you get the info to one of the four of us. Light speed. Got it?"

"Got it," Mars said. "I'll be the model of discretion."

Titan nodded. "Good. Get back to the ship. I know you have studying to do." He waited until Mars teleported out before turning. "He's a good kid."

"If he doesn't make captain one day, I'll eat my rank," Rowena said as they walked through the forest of landing gear.

"Sounds yummy. What's yeoman rank taste like?"

"Stale bread and moldy ration bars." One day she'd burn her rank. Toss it up in the sky and hit it with a plasma beam until there was nothing but slag.

Titan must have caught her expression because he bumped her shoulder. "We're trying not to scare the Sekoos."

She gave him a bored look. "Hate to break it to you, but anyone with three working brain cells knows enough of our histories to shake in their boots when they see us coming. Everyone knows what we can do if we want to."

He nodded in agreement. "Still rules out the Silars."

Rowena covered her mouth as she giggled. "Oh, ancestors, Ty! What are you going to do if you actually court Selena Caryll? I mean..." She shook her head in disbelief. "The logistics of it are insane. You realize that, don't you? Captain Sciarra has to either invite Caryll to the *Sabiha* or meet her on neutral ground. They have to sign a non-aggression pact at the very least. There have to be introductions, and there are protocols. These things can take years."

"Elea has until I finish packing my quarters," Titan said.

"So, what? You'll go live in Caryll's hovel of an apartment? Or are you going to knock a wall out in the BOQ so you can push two of those tiny beds together?"

He smirked. "We'll make it work."

"You're crazy."

"I'm in love." His smile was kind. "You'll see. One day when your head is spinning because all you can think about is a person who lights up the night, and makes you feel whole, and loves you even though you know you don't deserve it, you'll understand."

Rowena sighed and rolled her eyes. "Yes, I see that happening. Me? In love? Probably not before the heat death of the universe, but stranger things have happened. Even if I felt something, which we all know is as likely as the Emperor returning, we'd have to convince them to love me back. There are not enough mind-altering drugs in the universe."

"I love you," Titan said.

"Not the way you love Caryll."

"No, not in that way," Titan admitted as he put an arm around her shoulder. "But then again, I was never the brightest star in the fleet. Someone will come along and realize what Mal and I knew all along. You're amazing, Ro. You're loveable." He gave her a tight, sideways hug that made tears sting at her eyes.

"You're an idiot, Sciarra."

He let her go with a smile. "So you've told me."

"Does Caryll know that we come as a package deal?"

"I told her," Titan said as the bulk of the *Golden Apple* came into view. "You two will get along." His steps faltered as he got distracted by his thoughts. "Eventually."

Rowena let it go. It wasn't that she couldn't get along with other people. It was that she hadn't, and there was no reason to expect anyone to forgive her for that. Apologizing wasn't going to bring back the dead. Guilt and self-loathing wouldn't erase the war. She'd tried it. What was left was survival.

She fell in step with Titan and pushed away a nagging sense of doom. Her instinct for trouble was well-honed, but it was useless to worry about now. Her best friend was in love, and in time he'd drift away from her, but that didn't mean she was going to abandon him now.

A Sekoo guard with a too-loose uniform motioned for them to stop as they approached the outer perimeter.

Titan took an at-ease stance and Rowena followed suit.

"You Sciarra?" the Sekoo asked.

"Yes," Titan said. :Do I look that different from usual?: he asked.

:I'm not in charge of explaining Sekoo behavior,: Rowena said, pushing a memory of utter confusion at him.

The Sekoo walked behind the *Golden Apple's* shield and contacted someone with a box device.

:Are none of them augmented?: Rowena asked.

:Most of them aren't,: Titan said.

271

:You'd think they would have traded for that by now.:

:No medics, maybe? Or implant allergies? I've heard it can happen.:

Lily Sekoo hurried down the ramp, dark hair neatly braided and pulled back. She looked almost professional.

Almost.

Rowena's teeth ground together as she fought the sense of wrongness in the scene. The two Sekoos lurking by the ram weren't a problem, probably just chaperons trying to make sure that Titan didn't woo one of their better techs for the Sciarra crew. She didn't like Lily's smile, but that wasn't new, the Sekoos all made her angry. All that tech and they still never managed to do more than scrape by. They kept waiting for a hand out, waiting for help, waiting for the Emperor or whatever else. If she had all that tech, she'd build a whole new ship.

:Think friendly thoughts,: Titan advised. :Your shield's slipping to battle mode.:

:All that pretty tech hoarded by people who want to melt it for scrap,: she complained. :Makes my heart break.:

:And here you keep saying you don't have one.:

She sent gave Titan a mental kick in the leg. He only grinned.

"Commander Sciarra," Lily said as she approached. "And, Yeoman."

Rowen was definitely an afterthought.

"It's good to see you again, Technician," Titan said. "How are you recovering?"

Lily's laughed coyly and dropped her eyes.

:Flirting?: Rowena said. :She's flirting?:

:Some people like flirting.:

:Just get me the meds so I can get out of here.:

Titan smiled. "Do you have the medication the Lees need?"

"Of course!" Lily looked over her shoulder and waved to one of her crew members. "Three boxes, as promised. Enough for the current crisis, and a little extra to set aside for even future misfortunes."

Rowena watched the box with a knot in her shoulders. Ancestors, but she really was the worst friend ever. Eighteen pills for her best friend.

:It's fine,: Titan reminded her. :Even if I didn't need to interrogate the Sekoos, I'd do this.:

She took the offered boxes and checked the seal. "Looks good. Thank your supplier for me," she told Lily. :Do you want me to stay?: she asked Titan.

:I'll scream if I need help.:

:Scream loudly,: Rowena said. :You're isolated out here.:

Lily's eyes narrowed as her smile turned sharp. "Is there anything else, Yeoman?"

"Nothing," Rowena said. "Good trade. Enjoy your, ah, hour." She stepped away, still trying to shake the feeling of dread. Taking a deep breath, she walked faster. There was time for Aronia and the baby. The meds would buy them more time. "It's going to be okay, Lee. Believe it." *I want to believe.*

Deep in the heart of the *Danielle Nicole*, the halls outside the medical bay were silent. Hooks overhead and clefts in the wall showed the age of the ship, built before artificial gravity. Welding marks ran along the bulkhead, ripples and patterns that Rowena knew by heart. When she'd been young, the old zero-grav hooks had held flowers. She could still remember being carried to the medical bay by her father and trailing her hand through the multi-colored blooms. The plants had been taken down the following year by the new captain. Not military enough.

One day… One day she'd bring the flowers back.

The medbay door slid open as she approached and the chief medic looked up. "Yeoman."

"Doc." Rowena held up the medications.

Doc's perpetually worried face melted into softer lines. "Wonderful. I should never have doubted you."

Rowena handed over the medicine. "How is Aronia?"

"Awake," Doc said. "I gave her the patch the Sciarras sent over and she seems a little more lively now. Good tech. We'll have to see if we can get a bit more for emergencies?"

Rowena perked up at the idea of new tech. "No one mentioned anything to me."

"Maybe they thought you wouldn't be interested." Doc gave her a pointed look.

The old woman had never quite forgiven Rowena for not pursuing medical research. Her explanation that she was not a People Person hadn't gone over well. "I pay attention to tech," Rowena said, side-stepping Doc and hurrying to the small corner room where Aronia was waiting. Someone, probably Aronia's husband, had brought in a tiny tree with twisting branches and bright red chokeberries to sit on the table by her bedside. It was the only decoration in the otherwise sterile room.

Aronia smiled, eyes brighter and more alert than Rowena had seen all week. "Hello, Ro, how's the engine?"

"Still working," Rowena said, taking a seat so they could be at eye level. "How are you two?"

Her sister ran a hand around her swollen belly. "His heartbeat has stopped dipping. Doc says the nanite gel Sciarra sent over is helping stop the internal bleeding. My nanites were trying, but I just can't produce enough to keep the placenta from tearing." She took a deep breath and grimaced as she pushed on her belly. "His foot is in my ribs."

"At least he's head down," Rowena said. "And, I'll talk to Ty about getting some more of the... the whatever."

Aronia lifted the corner of her shirt to show Rowena a square patch of blue cloth on her side. "It has a gel filled with undefined nanites. They pass the skin barrier, scan for major injury, and gather for repairs. It tickles a little, like being attacked by rogue bubbles. Doc says they're limited life and non-replicating."

"I've never seen one." Rowena reached out and scanned the material. It wasn't coded with any Sciarra signifiers and the nanite structure was one she hadn't seen. Didn't mean it wasn't Sciarra tech, but it was something she would have expected them to use during the war. "Odd time to bring it out."

"Limited supplies maybe?" Aronia sighed. "Don't worry about it."

"I'm not!"

"Liar." Her sister reached for her face. "Are you okay? You look like you haven't slept all week. I heard the formation running past in battle gear and Doc keeps pacing by the door. Want to tell me what's happening?"

"Not really."

Aronia dropped her hand.

"You don't need the stress. And it isn't..." She was about to say a threat, but that was a lie. "It isn't a direct threat. Just a little SNAFU downtown. Someone triggered the security shields in Tarrin and suddenly everyone's jumpy."

"Do you know what triggered it?" Aronia asked.

Doc cleared her throat loudly as she walked in. "A malfunctioning piece of tech," the old woman said in a firm tone that meant she would accept nothing else. "Yeoman, your sister needs her rest. Come here, please. Now."

Rowena looked apologetically at her sister. "I'll be back tonight once I'm off-duty. Rest up." She squeezed her sister's hand and trundled out after Doc. As soon as Aronia's door was shut she said, "I'm sorry. I wasn't trying to stress her out."

"No one is," Doc said in a kinder tone. "But I need you to look at something all the same." She led Rowena into her small office space where a bulging pipe had warped the ceiling and wall, and motioned to two piles of pills on her desk. "The white ones are the bio accelerant we need for Aronia and the baby. The pink ones came from the other, sealed packs. They're meant to treat bacterial imbalance in the intestines. Is that what you traded for?"

Her heart stopped in fear. "No." The word sounded so small in helpless. "No... I... This is a misunderstanding." It had to be. "I'll contact the supplier immediately."

Doc nodded. "Thank you. We have enough for five days, and that might be enough to get Aronia to a point where she can deliver the child safely, especially with the Sciarra patches, but..." She shrugged.

Doc was old fleet. She'd survived two civil wars and at least four hostile command changes that Rowena knew of. Who knew what in-fighting the old woman had survived to get to be the chief medical officer of the Lee flagship. Her generation expected things to be done a certain way. Giving them bad medicine made Rowena look bad and it made the Lees look bad; there were captains who would interpret it as a declaration of war.

"Can you avoid telling Captain Lee until this evening?" Rowena asked. "Give me time to sort this out? It's an allied crew, but I used back channels to expedite things." Hoshi would drag his heels until Aronia died. *I'm not ready for another war.*

"If it was the Sciarras, I will contact them directly," Doc said. "They owe me."

Rowena shook her head. "Titan helped with the payment, but it was a C-class crew."

Doc wrinkled her nose in distaste. "Unfortunate."

The rebuke was well-earned. "I was desperate."

"It made you stupid."

"I'll fix it," Rowena promised. "Give me an hour. I'll fix it." She teleported to the safety of her engine room. Double-checking her perimeter, she pinged Titan. No response.

She tried putting a quick trace on him. It would have gone better with the right tech, since she was essentially hacking the Enclave security system to scan for his image, but nothing turned up. And the Lees didn't have access to a satellite.

Hands gripping the console of her communication station with white-knuckles, she stared blankly ahead as she assessed the options. None of them looked for appealing.

"Crack my hull." She punched in the code for the *Golden Apple.*

After a moment the screen showed the face of an older veteran with a long scar running past his ear. "Golden Apple, who are you?"

"Rowena Lee for Lily Sekoo, please." Polite wasn't easy, but sometimes it worked with the older generation.

The man snarled and stepped away from the com screen. A few minutes later he returned. "Lily's not in coms range." The screen went dark before she could ask for anything more.

Frustrated, she dialed the official code for the *Sabiha*.

Jata Sciarra came on screen looking grim as he ever did. "This is Lieutenant Sciarra of the *Sabiha*." He blinked. "Yeoman Lee?"

"Is Titan on board?"

Jata shook his head. "He left this morning and hasn't checked back in or crossed our shield."

"Is Mars available?"

Jata didn't need to check, he shook his head. "He's in training for the rest of the morning, then goes to do his crew rotation at fifteen-hundred. Would another officer be acceptable?"

Rowena sighed. "Captain Sciarra, please."

The com officer gave her a look of derision. "Yeoman?"

"It's an urgent matter. Patch me through or I'll come over in person." She might have been demoted after the war, but she'd be trained for command. A little ice in her voice and a stern look was all it took to make Jata look away.

"It's your career," the com officer muttered. "Patching you through to Captain Elea Sciarra now."

The image on her screen waivered and the com officer was replaced by the sharp angles and black eyes of Elea Sciarra.

Rowena bowed her head out of habit. "Captain Sciarra, thank you for taking time for me."

"The com officer said it was urgent. Talk."

"I need to know where Guardian Sciarra is," Rowena said. "He was helping recover the medicine my crew needed."

"I'm aware of that." Captain Sciarra's voice was cold as vacuum.

Rowena met her eyes with unfeigned rage. "Titan secured three packages of medicine my sister desperately needed, but they were tampered with. I need to let him know so no one is injured. Where is he?"

The captain raised her eyebrows and crossed her arms. "Last I saw him he was leaving in your company to contact the Sekoos. We haven't heard from him since and I know he hasn't left Enclave. The Jhandarmi director reached out to us about ten minutes ago asking for Titan's presence."

"Has he ever gone off coms before?"

"Since Landing?" Captain Sciarra's face wrinkled in thought. "A few times when he was in the lower levels of the Starguard complex. There are thick walls meant to prevent communication. It's possible he's there. I could find send a runner."

Rowena quickly shook her head. "I'll go. There's no point in having a Sciarra run over when I'm the one with the information."

The captain nodded. "Yeoman?"

"Ma'am?"

"The *Sabiha* has an opening in our engineering section. With all the changes that are imminent I feel you should know you will have allies here, should you ever need them."

"Thank you, captain. I'm quite comfortable with my current assignment."

Captain Sciarra tilted her head, accepting the rejection. "Let me know if the situation changes. And, when you find my nephew, tell him to check in. Our medic says it's bad for my health to worry about him this much."

"I'll have him signal you first thing," Rowena promised.

The Starguard...

The com deck went dark and she took a deep breath. Thus far she'd avoided the Starguard's vault of paperwork and Allied fighters.

Off the top of her head, Rowena could only think of three things worse than having to go deal with the guardians. Letting

Aronia die and letting Titan die were the top two of the list and the third was such a wild nightmare that the chances of it happening were too low to worry about.

Even if it did involve a Silar.

Rowena shrugged off her coverall and looked down at what was left: a plain black combat tee, her six-pocket pants, and her combat boots. She patted herself down for contraband weapons. Picking up misplaced wrenches and knives wasn't a bad habit, but there weren't any Warmongers besides Titan in the Starguard.

Going unarmed and looking helpless was her best bet for getting cooperation.

Once she was sure she couldn't kill anyone with anything other than her bare hands, her bootlaces, or her implant, she took a moment to wash her face. With the water, she slicked her hair back and tied it into a tight knot out of the way.

There. She looked suitably defanged and helpless.

Teleporting to the OIA building, she took a deep breath, and then pushed the door open and stalked down to the dungeon-like offices. Titan said they reminded him of deep space, but she couldn't shake the feeling that it needed engines. If there weren't engines, it wasn't meant for living in. And no amount of citrus-scented cleaner was ever going to erase the unpleasant organic scent of dead leaves and dirt.

She pushed open the doors to the main bullpen and scanned the room, desperately hoping Titan was somewhere in the maze of desks, cubicles, and glass-walled offices.

"Yeeeeeooooomannnnn Leeeeee." Hollis Silar stepped into view, stretching her name out and accenting all four syllables. He sized her up with a predatory smile. "From the battle shield you have up I'm guessing you aren't here to flirt. How disappointing."

"Guardian Silar." Her jaw clenched as she bit off his name.

The redhead held up a hand. "Wait!" His eyes glowed a deep gold as he accessed his implant. Quiet seconds ticked by.

Rowena raised an eyebrow.

Silar snapped his fingers "Seventy-three!"

"What?"

"This is now our longest civil conversation on record. The last civil interaction we had lasted seventy-two seconds."

She remembered easily. If there hadn't been a drill instructor nearby, and if her place on the Academy flight team hadn't been at risk, she would have broken his jaw. "You're an idiot," she muttered, hoping it was low enough Silar would miss it.

"Ninety-eight seconds. A new record."

She rolled her eyes.

"Should we push for two minutes? You're looking remarkably non-combative now."

"Can you be serious? I'm not here for your sadistic entertainment." Rowena resisted the urge to strangle Silar with his obnoxious, too-long hair. It hung above his collar, and even tied back it made her eye twitch. Pressing her lips together, she kept herself from starting another civil war. Barely. "Where's Titan?"

Hollis shook his head. "No idea. He's on medical leave." He shrugged. "Did you check the *Sabiha*?"

Rowena narrowed her eyes. "For the love of... Of course I checked the *Sabiha*! There's protocols." Taking a deep breath, she counted to five and changed track. She tried smiling. "Guardian, let me rephrase this; I know you have ways of tracking everyone traveling in or out of the Enclave shield and you can find anyone from the fleet anywhere they are. Right?"

Silar walked in front of his desk, casting an intimidating shadow, and then sat down so he was nearly eye level. He was a big bastard. Somehow she always managed to forget how small he made her feel.

Habit made her take a fighting stance, feet slightly apart, muscles tensed.

If Silar noticed, he didn't say anything. "Now, Lee, you know I couldn't confirm or deny that sort of thing. The tech the Starguarduses is classified and can't be shared with individuals who do not have the appropriate clearance." He was going to bury her in red tape, is what he meant.

"I don't need you to confirm," Rowena said slowly enough for his one functioning brain cell to process. "I need you to do. Find Titan for me. He's not responding, his crew has no clue where he is, and neither do you. Under some law I'm sure this qualifies as an emergency and reasonable use of your tracking skills."

Silar raised an eyebrow. "Guardian Sciarra left a message saying he was going to meet with Lily Sekoo off *The Golden Apple* last night. I'm not one to judge—"

"You better not!" Rowena snapped.

"But shouldn't you check to see if he's there first? He isn't scheduled to work this morning. Maybe he decided to go... relax." Silar's smile managed to be suggestive, pitying, and dangerous all at once.

She took a second to look around the room. There were four other guardians in view, all carefully pretending not to watch. Violence was out of the question. "Titan is not looking to court Lily."

Silar rolled his eyes to the ceiling. "Not to tell tales, but most the women in fleet don't mind spending time with a man like Sciarra without a promise of commitment."

"But he wouldn't," Rowena insisted.

Silar's brown eyes locked onto her with interest.

Internal alarms flared. If she wasn't careful, she'd give away more than the Lees could afford to lose.

Taking an at-ease stance she tried waiting him out, but he wasn't looking away and no one was filling the silence. Finally, she said, "Titan has drafted a declaration of courtship."

"Congratulations!"

Rowena's fist collided with Silar's shoulder before she could stop herself. "Not for me! You crack-brained Silar!" She glanced around to see if anyone else had noticed her breach of conduct.

Silar rubbed his shoulder and chuckled. "How faithful—"

She glared up at him, furious beyond words at the suggestion.

"Right. Forget I asked." He sighed in resignation. "So Sciarra wouldn't have a reason to go off-coms around Lily so he could have some privacy. Did he go see this other individual?"

She hadn't thought of that. "Possibly, but he wouldn't have turned off his com if he were. Not after everything last night."

"You mean the malfunctioning battery cannon?" Silar asked, radiating innocence.

Rowena sucked her cheeks in. "For one minute, Silar, remember who you are talking to. I'm not some numble-brained fleetling that can't tell an orbital bombardment from ground ordinance. Titan was at ground zero for that, and medical leave or no, he'll be going back today."

For a second Silar's eyes sparked gold as he accessed his implant. His growing smile was hard to read, but she knew she'd made a misstep. He looked far too pleased for her comfort. "One final question. Why do you need him?"

She crossed her arms.

Silar held up his hands in mock surrender. "He's off duty, Lee. If this is a matter another guardian can resolve, we should try that."

Rowena weighed her options, shut her eyes, and went all in. "The Sekoos said they'd found some of the missing shipment. The price of the medicine Aronia needs was one hour of Titan's time with Lily Sekoo. He agreed because he knows I love Aronia, and because the Jhandarmi have no other leads on the case."

"Why do you have better information for this case than I do?"

"Because I'm better than you," Rowena said flatly. "Titan left with Lily eighty-six minutes ago. He should be back, and in coms range" She looked at Silar to see if he understood.

He nodded.

"The first box had the appropriate medicine but the other two didn't."

"And Sciarra could help you how?"

She took a deep breath. "I... He..." She hadn't thought past forcing the Sekoos to give her the rest of the medicine. "I had to tell him. In case someone else didn't recognize them, or if the other boxes were packed with something dangerous. It's his case, and this might mean something. Now... can you check for him? Pl—"

"Please!" Silar's eyes went wide. "Rowena! Control yourself!" he said too loud for her comfort.

She snapped her mouth shut and glared.

Silar leaned so he was close enough to slap. "There are other people here. If they see you being polite to me, they'll know there's something between us."

"There is," Rowena said quietly. "Animosity and atmosphere. Same as always."

He laughed and walked around back to his monitor. "See? That's what life's been missing. I don't suppose the Lees would consider letting you become a guardian?"

"Are you not getting punched enough?"

"Combatives training isn't the same when there isn't a tiny woman trying to knock your lungs out through your back. You'd be so disappointed," he said as he typed something into the computer. "Some of them have started pulling their punches."

"Marshall isn't training anymore?" That was good gossip. Made sense with how much she'd been away.

Silar shrugged. "Nah, she's around, but I like my eyeballs in my head. Thanks. And Carver leaves me with bruised ribs. Sciarra is good, but he's been too friendly this past week. I think Selena rattled his brain when she punched him. Poor guy. That is not a woman you want on your bad side."

"Caryll? He's on her good side."

Silar shot her a quizzical look. It quickly became another enigmatic smile. He clicked his tongue. "Caryll and Sciarra?" He shook his head. "Who would have guessed? I had the likelihood of that pairing below twenty percent."

"Why'd you run the probability at all?"

He shrugged. "I do it for everyone. Want to know who you're a good match for?"

"No." That was a trap she didn't need to walk into. Silar would probably give her some random name, and then tell her it was the name of his charge pistol.

"Ah, well another time." He twirled in his chair. "Titan is probably in the Tarrin city center at the Jhandarmi offices."

She frowned. "What? Why? And what do you mean probably?"

Silar spun the monitor around so she could see. "We can track shielding and tech signatures. This is a ninety-nine percent match for Sciarra's last scan two days ago. He likes to tweak his shields, so it's a safe bet it's him. Unless you know of someone else with the exact same tech signature. You know him better than me, but

I don't see Sciarra handing out his shield parameters to anyone, courtship or no."

"But that can't be. Captain Sciarra said he hadn't crossed the Enclave shield. They track that. Why isn't he responding to coms? I sent him an emergency code." They were best friends. No matter what, Titan was the one person who had never abandoned her. Never hated her for what had happened. Fear rubbed across her raw nerves. She stepped away, shaking her head. "He... he wouldn't ignore me."

Not unless things had changed.

Silar watched her without a readable expression. "There's no distress signal, no reason for me to send a guardian. But, if you want to go down to Tarrin, you can."

"No. I can't." She looked him the eye, wishing she had an ally.

He shook his head, not understanding. "Why not? Grounders aren't that scary. They don't bite unless you ask nicely."

"I'm a yeoman. And a Lee. I don't have travel access without authorization."

"Oh! Right." Silar stood up. "You need permission from the Captains' Council or the senior guardian on duty."

Rowena nodded, and then looked around for Carver. "Right..." They hadn't always been friends, but they'd been on flight team together. Maybe he'd let her go for nostalgia's sake.

"Which is me."

She looked up at Silar in horror. There went that faint hope.

"There is a form you can use to file a request." He held out a stack of papers. "Usually you need a senior officer from your crew to vouch for your self-sufficiency but that can be waived under certain circumstances."

With a scowl she looked at the form. "That's a declaration of hostile command change."

"Is it?" His brown eyes widened in surprise. "Well, dear ancestors, how did that get there?" He stubbornly held the form out.

"I'm loyal to my captain." And not stupid enough to start an internal war with no backing and her sister vulnerable. Clever of Silar though. If she went charging after Hoshi, the Silars wouldn't have to worry about the Lees—or her—ever again.

With an eye roll, Silar withdrew the form and picked up a small, green envelope off his desk. "Rowena Lee," he said, taking out a thick, clear rectangle, "put your thumb on the right side and transfer the requested data."

"What is this?"

"Take it." He wiggled the card at her.

Rowena took it and pressed her thumb into the clear gel. Her crew information and face appeared. The rectangle split, forming two thin cards.

"One for you, one for me. This is an official travel card for fleet officers under the aegis of the Starguard. All the travel details are there. You have a code to leave and return to Enclave. Please use it."

She clung to the card with both hands. That was too easy. "Thank you? I'll go now."

"Ah-ah!" Silar reached for her arm as she started to walk away. "I'm not done yet." His hand hovered at the edge of her shield. "Safety rules. No fleet weapons outside Enclave. Do not use your implant in front of grounders, it scares them. If you run into trouble, send a distress code to the guardians, not your crew. If you can't communicate for some reason, break the card."

She frowned down at the travel card. "Break it?"

"Snap it. Smash it. Step on it. Throw it in a fire. Break it. It'll send out a distress beacon and I will be there in seconds to come get you."

"You?" She didn't mean for it to sound rude, but dismay crept into her voice.

"Me, or whoever is the senior field guardian on duty. It's always someone combat trained. Usually me or Carver."

Rowena tried that thought on for size. "My own evil genie." She put a shield around the card to protect it and slipped it into her pocket. "Anything else?"

"One more thing." Silar held up his hand and something flew across the room and smacked into his palm.

Most people were careful when they made something levitate, but not Hollis. He'd always been aggressive. It made most people flinch.

She held her ground.

Silar held out a cloth-covered object slightly longer than his hand and fingers.

Gingerly, she picked it up and flipped the cloth cover over. "A stone knife?"

"Most shields aren't programmed to stop one of that size, and grounders can't detect it. Keep it out of sight. Only use it if you need to. If you do use it, contact me directly, not the Starguard or your crew."

She wrapped the black knife up again. "Seriously? If I'm in trouble I'm supposed to ask you for help?"

"It's worked so far." Something in his voice made her look him in the eye. There was an undertone of sincerity and concern she'd never heard from a Silar before.

Rowena shook her head and offered him the knife. "No."

"Yes." Silar pushed it back with a telekyen shove and a smile. "Can't have my favorite Lee going out there unarmed. Be safe." He turned away, acting completely disinterested. "Let us know if you find Titan."

288

The knife was heavy in her hand, but a quick scan came back clean. "I will." She tucked it into her pants pocket and teleported out. For the first time, she was free of Enclave.

The coordinates landed Rowena on a grassy hill, under the shade of a pagoda covered in vining plants. It was out of sight of the city cameras, windows, and pedestrians. She patted the knife in her pocket for comfort. After this was over she'd have to find a way to get it back to Silar. It had a good weight to it. She could throw it at his head.

In Cargo Blue while he was drinking would be the best time.

If she could get it to smack into the wall right by his head, that'd be perfect.

Grinning, she headed down to the Jhandarmi offices. She'd never studied architecture, but the white column against the mirrored glass and silver dome was pretty, if not functional. There was undoubtedly some long and storied history that the mudders—she caught herself—that the *grounders* liked.

"Grounders. Ground-siders," she whispered under her breath. "They are people. I will treat them like people. Even if they are people who don't like engines." Highly suspicious that. Who didn't like the comforting sound of an engine to fall asleep to?

The broad double-doors slid open as she approached and the fresh air smelling of grass clippings was replaced by a rush of chilled office air. The Jhandarmi needed a new filter for their air cycler. And, possibly, soap.

A young woman with brown hair pinned in rosettes at her nape smiled from behind a desk as Rowena walked in. "Good morning, ma'am. May I help you?"

Rowena bit back the need to correct her. Yeoman was an enlisted rank, she wasn't Ma'am any more. But, according to her implant, the ground-siders sometimes used it as a respectful title for someone they didn't know. "I'm looking for Guardian Sciarra from Enclave. I've reason to believe he's here working with the Jhandarmi on a case."

The woman smiled brightly. "Of course, ma'am. If you'll sign in here." She held up a tablet. "And I'll get you a badge. The joint offices are on the fifth floor."

Rowena took the round badge and pinned it to her shirt. "Do you have stairs?"

"The lift is around the corner on the left," the woman said. "If you have any trouble, come back and I can take you through the worker's entrance. The lift is supposed to be fixed though."

She nodded. The building felt strange, overgrown almost. The ceilings were too high and the halls too wide. Unless they planned on running a regiment through here, they were wasting space.

Around the corner was a bank of silver doors.

Rowena stepped in front of one and tried to trigger it with her implant. There was no data receiver and no telekyn in the doors. "Fifth floor," she said.

The doors remained inert.

"It's a push button one," said a voice behind her.

She looked over her shoulder at a bullish, bald man who her implant hadn't been able to find because of his lack of telekyen. Her first real grounder. She blinked.

"Tyrling," he said reaching out and hitting a small, rectangular button. "From Marjori, originally."

"Rowena Lee off the *Danielle Nicole*," she said. "Are you going up?"

"I am indeed." He placed his hand over the open door as she stepped inside, then followed.

"Fifth floor, please."

Tyrling nodded and pressed a button on a panel. "Danielle Nicole, famous scientist from the start of the space age, right?"

"Yes."

He nodded as the lift ascended quietly. "You here on business?"

"Trying to contact someone from Enclave who is working on the theft of fleet property."

His head bobbed. "I know that case. Are they expecting you?"

"No, but I needed to get the information I came across promptly." That seemed like a safe answer. It justified her presence without giving too much away.

The bullish man smiled. "Excellent to hear. The Jhandarmi appreciate fleet support. I'm Tyrling, by the way. Director Tyrling." The lift chimed and the doors slid open. He motioned for her to proceed. "One of my best field agents is on that. I'll send her your way. Can I persuade you to take a seat in our conference room?"

"That would be agreeable."

Tyrling led her to a small room with frosted glass walls and a thick sliding glass door. "Just here, if you don't mind. It won't be but a moment."

Rowena glanced around as she walked in and took a seat. At the far end of the hall, there was a small gallery that looked like a break room. And on the table, a white cup with Titan's name scrawled across it. She relaxed.

He was here.

The director shut the door with a smile, leaving her to watch the spectral figures who passed. They spoke in hushed voices and moved with urgent purpose.

Rowena closed her eyes, trying not to remember the brig she'd sat in for months at the end of the war. The first days had been like this, no news, no contact, only voices of people out of sight.

It made her want to scream.

The door opened and Selena Caryll walked in wearing grounder business clothes. Her shield was muted, offering no information and hidden from all but a direct search.

She stared at Rowena for an uncomfortably long moment then quietly closed the door. "When Tyrling said someone from fleet had come looking for Titan, I wasn't expecting you."

"I wasn't expecting you either." Rowena refused to take a defensive posture or be goaded into a fight, but every hair on the back of her neck stood on end. "I know Titan's here. The guardians tracked his shield here and there's a cup with his name on it." Her belligerence wavered under Caryll's quiet stare. "He's here. If the Jhandarmi are holding him—"

Caryll shook her head and sat down. "No, we aren't holding him."

The *we* rocked Rowena to the core. Selena Caryll was a lot of things she hated, but she wasn't a traitor. "We? You've left fleet?"

"I'm the OIA liaison. Over the course of my work I took the Jhandarmi training." She took a seat across from Rowena. "I hold rank in both places. It's not all or nothing any more. It has to be if we want to survive."

Rowena sucked in a breath, trying to hold back her growing unease. "Where's Titan?"

"I wish I knew. The cup in the break room was from breakfast. I ordered for him because he didn't come directly here after his meeting with Lily Sekoo. He didn't answer when I pinged, but I thought he might have had crew business." Caryll's expression was hollow, guarded and worried. She was watching Rowena like she held the secrets of the universe.

"He left with Lily." Rowena shook her head. "That's... that's the last anyone's seen of him. But the Sekoos say he isn't there. I went to the Starguard and they tracked Titan's shield here."

"Most likely tracked my shield," Caryll said. "I helped Titan modify his shields when I realized he'd be around grounders. I imagine they'd look very similar. It'll keep him safe from any local weapons though. Including the obsidian knife in your pocket."

Rowena started, looking up in surprise. "That wasn't supposed to be detectable."

"It's not... to most people. Carver had five of them; one each for Gen and Hollis, Marshall, me, and one for himself. I added it to my security scans. It makes it easier to track them all down in hurry. Except most of us have quit wearing them since the war ended, and I doubt you bought yours on planet."

"Silar gave it to me," she admitted, touching her pocket. "So I wouldn't be outside Enclave unarmed."

Caryll seemed to consider this and then nodded slowly. "That's a very Hollis thing to do. Especially if he thought I was down here in trouble."

"I'm not your backup."

Caryll's eyes flashed a white-blue as she smirked. "I don't need backup, Lee. I need answers. Where do you think Titan is?"

"I don't know. I don't know how to find him."

"Did you need to find him right now?"

Rowena weighed her options. At the end of the day, Aronia's life was worth what little pride she had left. "I traded the Sekoos for medicine for my sister. Three boxes, and they got an hour with Titan. We scheduled the trade last night and I sent them an alignment coil for a stabilizer since they put the word out they needed one."

"Good trade tactics," Caryll said with a nod. "What went wrong?"

"The medicine wasn't what we needed. Some of it was, but some had been switched."

Caryll frowned. "Could it have been accidental?"

"No." Rowena shook her head. "It was repackaged and resealed. Either the manufacturer made a mistake, or someone tampered with it after shipping. I haven't heard of any recalls on the grounder communiques."

"Neither have I." Caryll sighed and sat back in her seat. With a sigh, she closed her eyes. "I have a really bad idea."

"Sounds like you."

Caryll shot her a glare. "I know how to find Titan, but I need Sciarra resources to do it."

"Good luck with that."

"You're going to help," Caryll declared as she stood up. Her sudden smile was not reassuring.

Rowena crossed her arms. "How are you going to convince me to do that?"

The room shifted abruptly, the grounder offices being replaced with a scene of broken chairs and the smell of a burning ship.

"Welcome aboard the *Persephone*," an AI voice said as the captain's whistle rang around Rowena.

Selena Caryll walked across the bridge of her warship. "You should know better, Lee. Captains never ask, they order."

22

SELENA

PERSEPHONE'S FACE FILLED THE cracked screen. "Captain, it's good to see you alive again."

"Likewise," Selena said.

A skitter bot brushed past her like a cat.

"Commander Lee," Persephone said, using Rowena's rank from the war, "it has been five hundred years, twenty-three days, and thirteen hours since a member of your crew was welcomed on board."

"Persephone, where's my rank?" said Selena.

"Your rank?" Rowena asked, finally breaking her stunned silence and peering around. "Where in the name of the nine stars are we, Caryll?"

Selena looked around the burnt bridge. "This is the Caryll flagship *Persephone*. In orbit around Malik IV."

Rowena sputtered in protest. "You can't just force a teleport from ground to orbit!"

"I can though."

"She can," Persephone agreed. "Captain, the rank you threw is under the logistics station. There's a crack in the computer casing. You threw it with some energy."

Selena knelt in front of the logistics station and blindly groped in the crack until she felt the cold metal of her captain's stars. A golden circle around a field of golden dots and a single shooting star in the center. She stared at it in her hand until Rowena walked over.

"Why did we come here?"

Selena closed her fist around the rank. "I need to meet Captain Sciarra, and it can't be informal. You'll need to do the introductions."

"You aren't my ally," Rowena scoffed.

"Persephone?"

"Yes, captain?"

"Draft a declaration of allyship, effective immediately for one Captain Caryll and Commander Rowena Lee of the *Danielle Nicole*."

Rowena balled her hands in anger. "It's yeoman."

"No." Selena stood up. "According to the *Persephone's* records, you were never officially demoted. And only senior officers can sign treaties." The data stream from Persephone flashed across her inner eye. "Here." She shot the declaration to Rowena. "Acknowledge and sign while I go change into my uniform."

Her uniform has where she'd left it before disembarking after the war. She'd thrown her rank, because no captain would leave their ship and because she'd been too much of a coward to die

296

like she ought to have. Selena ran her thumb over the stars. It had seemed like the easier choice back then, walking away from the wreckage and letting herself get caught in the flow of rebuilding.

Carver had given orders. She had obeyed. Tyrling had given orders. She had obeyed.

For years she'd been drifting. Cut off from family and crew, and what was the difference?

A little more oxygen. It was a slower death, but a death all the same.

And then there was Titan.

The memory of his smile, his kiss, strong hands holding her and the promise of so much more. Titan was offering her life after death. And she couldn't find him.

The wall beside her buckled and Selena jumped in surprise.

"Captain?" Persephone's face appeared on a corridor screen. "Is everything well?"

She stared at the damage she'd caused. Lashing out was something she'd learned to control when she'd put on her first gauntlet. The Caryll implants were too sensitive to allow someone who couldn't control their emotions to be augmented. "I need to locate Titan Sciarra and I can't."

Persephone's face split in static lines then reformed. "I have targeting computers online, Captain, but my sensor array is still non-functional. Would you like me to put those repairs at the top of the priority list?"

Selena was about to say no, then nodded. "Yes. Top priority. If this doesn't work I'll need them."

"Estimated time to repair is one hundred fifteen hours."

"Understood." In the quiet of the *Persephone's* war room, she changed into the navy blue flight uniform with the silvery-gold piping and the Caryll's twelve-star insignia on her shoulder. She walked out to see Rowena waiting in the center of the bridge. "Are you ready?"

"To rescue Titan? Yes. To get between two feuding crews? Never. But I'll do it anyway."

"That's the spirit, Lee." Selena grabbed Rowena in a modified shield and transported them down to Enclave on the outside of the Sciarra shields.

Rowena landed beside her, scowl in place. "I'll go talk to them."

"They see us," Selena said as a sailor waiting at the ramp moved toward them. "Give it a minute."

The sailor approached. He grimaced at Rowena, and his frown deepened when he saw Selena. "Yes?"

"Captain Caryll for Captain Sciarra."

The sailor squared his shoulders. "The captain isn't expecting you and isn't taking social calls at this time."

Selena glanced at Rowena and nodded.

"I'm here at the behest of Captain Sciarra," Rowena said. "She asked me to report back on an urgent matter."

"Fine. What about you?" He nodded to Selena.

"I'm the urgent matter that Commander Lee is reporting on. If you hurry, there won't be a war."

His eyes widened in fear as shuffled backward. "I'll... contact the captain immediately. Please wait here."

"Thank you." Selena took a breath and scanned for Titan again.

Nothing.

If he was hurt... She couldn't let her mind go down that path. She couldn't give room for the fear that he'd been taken from her after they'd only just found each other.

"Incoming," Rowena muttered.

The sailor was running their way.

Selena allowed herself a tight smile of victory. "I thought they'd see things my way."

"Watch it, you're starting to sound like Marshall."

"Ma'am, yeoman." The sailor sounded slightly panicked. "Captain Elea Sciarra welcomes you the *Sabiha* and requests you teleport directly to her office. If you'll hold out your hands I'll transfer the necessary codes."

"That won't be necessary," Selena said. She entrapped Rowena, shield and all, and transferred them to Elea's office. It was very satisfying to see the look of indignant shock on Rowena's face. But there wasn't time to indulge. "Captain Sciarra, thank you for welcoming us."

Elea Sciarra stood. She looked older than she had across the room at the Captains' Council. More stretched. More stressed.

"Captain Caryll, Yeoman Lee. I presume you bring news about Titan?"

"We have a theory," Selena said. "After conferring with Commander Lee, it seems likely that Titan is being held by the Sekoos. Since they won't communicate with the commander or myself, we'll need your help."

Elea looked at Rowena. "I believe her rank is Yeoman."

Rowena nodded.

Selena shrugged. "The Caryll crew never recognized her demotion, and we will continue not to recognize her demotion. I may not love everything about the commander, but I won't have a fleet officer insulted."

There was a ping against her personal shield; Rowena trying to get clarification.

Selena pinged her, sending a flurry of memories of Titan praising her and the understanding that Titan and Rowena would always be close. Rowena was important to Titan, so Rowena was falling under Caryll protection whether she wanted it or not.

Captain Sciarra raised her eyebrows. "Now that you mention it, I can't find any record of the Sciarra crew accepting the demotion in our records."

Selena nodded to Rowena.

With a heavy sigh, Rowena nodded back. Her eyes lit up, a glowing black with silver streamers of light. "Now this moment shall be recorded for posterity."

The formal words sent a shiver of fear up Selena's spine. Generations had passed since the Carylls had made an alliance like this. *Ancestors forgive me. I fell in love. Accept him. Welcome me.* The prayer was as long as a heartbeat, and just as important.

"Captain Elea Sciarra, born aboard the glorious ship *Hazel Ying Lee*, you are an ally of Lee crew, laud and honor to you. I am Yeo-ommander," Rowena tripped over her title. "I am Commander Rowena Lee, born aboard the glorious *Danielle Nicole*, flagship of the Lee armada. Captain, I wish to formally introduce you to Captain Selena Caryll, born of—"

:The *Diana*,: Selena said.

"Born of the glorious *Diana*." Rowena took a deep breath and gave her a side-eye glare. :I can't believe I am going to say this on official fleet record.:

:Do it for Titan,: Selena said, keeping her eyes on Captain Sciarra.

"Captain Caryll is known to me. She is a fierce fighter with combat skills." Rowena rolled her eyes. "She is praised, and honorable. A good captain."

Selena could hear Rowena grinding her teeth.

"Before her, enemies flee," Rowena said. "Or they are destroyed. In the defense of Malik IV she destroyed *Bassi*, *Aryton*,

Theoano." All Lee ships. "She defeated the Baular flagship *Sárkány*. I recommend her to you as an ally."

Captain Sciarra raised an eyebrow. "Why does that sound like a threat?"

"Because Commander Lee values military might," Selena said calmly. "What she does not mention is that I have powerful allies who will becomes your allies. I have contacts in the city-states of Tarrin and Royan. Allying with me will open trade for your crew, entry to training programs on Malik IV, and access to the Tarrin universities. I also have lands and holdings should you wish to house your crew in shielded places outside Enclave. Furthermore, I come with a gift of priority Caryll tech." She held up a datdisk she'd brought from the *Persephone.*

Captain Sciarra nodded. "Is it the targeting program you used last night in defense of the Jhandarmi?"

"It's an invasive code that can decrypt an enemy's code in a matter of minutes, giving you full access to their computers."

Rowena sucked in her breath in surprise.

"You have something like that?" Captain Sciarra's eyes narrowed. "If you did, why didn't you use it?"

"The Caryll senior officers considered it too dangerous," Selena said, still holding the datdisk out. "I haven't written a counter program to it. Yet."

"Commander Lee, the Sciarras offer you our thanks. Captain Caryll, your offer of allyship is accepted."

The light in Rowena's eyes died. She shook her head to clear it and wrinkled her nose.

Elea Sciarra took the datdisk. "What is your plan?"

Selena took a deep breath. "I think Titan is with the Sekoos. They're one of the few crews with access to the grounders, they had rights to the warehouse, have grounder contacts—"

"None of which adds up to them taking Titan," Rowena argued. "Being a Warmonger doesn't automatically mean they contributed."

"No, it's not about them being Warmongers. It's about the explosion." The thought had been nagging her all night. "It was out of place. Unless someone was targeting Titan. The Jhandarmi knew there was an assassination ordered, but the assassin didn't survive. Kafftan blamed his suppliers."

Captain Sciarra frowned in thought. "Why my nephew?"

"The shields," Selena and Rowena answered in union.

With a glance at Rowena, Selena nodded. "The Enclave shield tracks anyone who moves through it, and everyone knows Titan wrote the code. Earlier they might have just wanted a window to move goods, but now they've lost Kafftan and their contacts, their plan is crumbling, they need to get out. Titan makes a good hostage."

"How does this work?" Elea asked.

Contact the Sekoos and talk to them. Anything that will keep them connected for at least a minute. The program here will hijack the com link and search for Titan."

"How?"

"It'll identify anyone with two implants," Selena said. "Titan still has parts of the original implant fused to his bones."

Captain Sciarra inhaled sharply. "That was classified information."

"There's only one way Titan got those scars on his arm and no medic in the fleet would have authorized a full removal," Selena said with an apologetic shrug. "Don't waste secrets on something anyone with half a brain could figure out."

"It's a good way to find Titan," Rowena said.

She hadn't expected backup, but it was nice.

Elea nodded. "If I can verify that they have Titan?"

"Tell me which ship they're in and I'll handle the rest," Selena said.

"Shouldn't we call the Starguard?" Rowena protested. "We don't want another civil war."

"Don't worry." Selena smiled. "I have every intention of making sure they understand this is a personal matter."

With a nod, Elea walked back to her desk. A blue shield shimmered into place as she made the call.

Selena looked over at Rowena. "You'll want to stay back until you see my signal."

"And what's that likely to be?"

"When people start screaming, you can come running. If I'm dead..." She smiled. "I'm sure you've kept up your combatives practice. Feel free to kill them all."

"You were weird to begin with. I don't think I like this creepy side of you."

"I'm not creepy. I'm angry. And no one in fleet has ever seen me angry." She chuckled to herself. "Actually, I'm kind of looking forward to this. I've never had a chance to let loose."

Rowena looked skeptical. "You're going to lecture them to death?"

"Killing people isn't what wins wars. If you want to truly defeat someone, you crush their hopes and dreams. Let them sit by as everything they love dies. You break them without ever shedding a drop of blood." She took a deep breath, inhaling the cool, clean scent of ship's air. "It's what the fleet did to me."

23

TITAN

THE ENGINES WERE COUGHING.

It was a stupid thing to think when he felt like he'd been hammered to the ground, and his implant wasn't responding, but that was his first thought. The engines needed a tune up. Maybe he could convince the Lees to loan him Rowena for a week.

Titan opened his eyes, blinking not at darkness, but the half-lit gloom of a damaged ship that wasn't the *Sabiha*.

A support beam leaned against the wall, cracked. The flooring had been ripped up to repair the wires. Ancestors, if his chief engineer saw this mess, the man would weep. The wires weren't meant to be tangled.

He shook his head, tried to turn on his implant, and screamed as his arm burned.

"Finally!" Lily Sekoo stepped in front of him wearing cast-off Baular battle gear with a Sekoo patch inexpertly stitched on. "I was beginning to think you'd never wake up."

"Not to be cliché, but where am I?" Titan asked. His brain felt like it was swimming through oatmeal. "Why..." He looked down at his arm. Tubes with red and blue liquid ran from needles in his skin and a poorly constructed wrist cuff with more wires strapped him to an interrogation chair. "Ah."

Lily paced in front of him. "This should have been finished hours ago, but your encryption is good. We'll crack it in time. Don't worry. But it is causing us an inconvenience."

He rolled his eyes. Those exact lines had been in a very popular holovid when he was a teen. What was it called? Eden's Fall? Something like that. The Baulars had been the villains in that one. Kidnapping a guardian and forcing him to reveal where the Eden was hidden. As if the guardians knew where the old space station was. He rolled his eyes. "Whatever it is you want, this isn't the way to get it."

"You may not feel it yet," Lily said, "but your implant is draining. The nanites are being destroyed by the serum. You may not want to give up the code for the shield, but I don't need it. As soon as your implant loses its charge, the shield will drop."

Only if he were an incompetent idiot who kept the largest shield in fleet hooked to his personal energy source. He didn't even have his implant on. It was the one major change he'd made after the crash; if his implant misfired, it turned off. Being unconnected from his crew and mechanical memory was annoying, but infinitely better than burning alive again.

He looked around at the broken ship, slumping in frustration.

Hopefully someone would notice he was missing before suppertime, because he could spend the rest of his life waiting for the Sekoo's plan to come to fruition. Even Rowena couldn't get this ship in the air again.

The sound of running boots on metal flooring made him twist to look over his shoulders.

Sadly, it wasn't the guardians come to get him out of this ridiculous situation. Or his crew. He sighed and turned back, wondering if he was clear-headed enough to break everything and escape on his own. His focus was drifting, but in an hour or so when the knock-out drugs had cleared...

"Lily!" Another Sekoo stepped in, panting. "Captain Sciarra contacted *The Golden Apple*."

Lily crossed her arms. "And someone answered? I gave orders!"

"She's—" The man sucked in air like he'd run a marathon. "She's talking about a Declaration of Courtship."

"What?" Lily looked at Titan speculatively.

He could see her tallying up the advantages. Titan let her do the math. If Elea was offering anything, it was because she was already hunting for him. A little bit of patience was all he needed.

The man coughed. "Said something about wanting you to transfer to the *Sabiha* so this one could spend time with you."

"Oh, Titan..." Lily laughed. "That's pathetic. Did you think I actually liked you? Did you think anyone forgave you after you betrayed the cause?"

"The cause?" Titan raised an eyebrow. "There's a cause now?"

She lifted her chin haughtily, ignoring the belief in his voice. "You betrayed the Baulars."

"I never even fought. How could I betray anyone?" Even without his implant the memories were too raw. Lingering guilt over deaths he couldn't prevent.

And then he remembered the look on Selena's face when she stood in the shadows and showed him the scars on her shoulder. If he was guilty, so was she, and he'd never hurt her like that.

"You were there when they banished the Baular heir. You could have saved Mal. You should have! You were his sworn second!"

"In school!" Titan argued. "And once I knew what would have happened when the Baulars won, I didn't support their goals. Neither did Mal. He knew the war was stupid. That's why he wasn't executed."

Lily sneered at him. "The Baulars promised us land. Power. Positions. They owe us. Win or lose."

"Then go collect from the Baulars. They're dead and you will be too if you try to start another war."

"There's no need for a war." Her eyes lit with fervor. "When the shield is down, the *Aconitum* will rise, like a phoenix from the ash of despair, and destroy the enemies of the cause."

"On these engines?" For the first time he felt genuinely worried. "Can I get off, please? Before you try to fly?"

Lily stamped her foot. "The engines are fine!"

"They really, really aren't though. Can't you hear them? Those aren't engines you can fly on!"

"All they have to do is make us move."

"And combat gravity!"

Selena was going to kill him. He wasn't just going to die. He was going to die stupidly. "This is embarrassing."

Lily chuckled. "You thought you were so special. A guardian. A Sciarra. The Baulars' best fighter. How does it feel to be taken down by someone you wouldn't give the time of day to?"

Titan looked up at the ceiling. "I was supposed to have breakfast somewhere outside the mess hall this morning. I am

307

missing breakfast with a beautiful woman to listen to your bad ideas. Would you just—"

The ship tilted and Lily laughed with mad delight.

"Engines working, captain," a voice reported from somewhere out of sight.

Titan shook his head vehemently. "No, they're not. You hear that whine? Those are your stabilizers about to hit max capacity and overload. You have, what, seven of them running? Maybe eight? You'll get a few meters off the ground at most."

"We have three," Lily said.

The *Aconitum* was a war ship one size smaller than the *Sabiha*. It ran with a bank of thirty stabilizing energy relays and common Sciarra wisdom was to shut down any ship that didn't have ten fully functioning. Anything less was courting death.

Titan stared fatalistically at the wall. After all this. *I almost had everything.* He closed his eyes and pictured Selena standing in front of him. Hopefully she was with the Jhandarmi today.

The Enclave shield wasn't going to go down, the *Aconitum* was. Between the shield, the Enclave wall, and the active weapons on other vessels, they'd never get far. Selena didn't need to see his body pulled from the wreckage.

"We've reached an altitude of ten meters," a man reported.

"Ten more," Lily said. "We need to clear the wall."

Titan shook his head.

"The shield's not down!"

Lily turned to him. "Drop it, Sciarra. I know you're barely able to hold it."

"Put the ship down," Titan said.

Lily took a deep breath and turned. "Activate energy cannons."

"But—" someone smarter than her started to protest.

"Do it!" The order cracked against the hull.

"The energy will splash back on you," Titan said. "On us. Your stabilizers won't be able to absorb the overload."

Lily crossed her arms. "They will. This once, they will."

"Cannons two minutes to full charge."

Two minutes? How had these yaldson castoffs survived the war? Two minutes was an eternity.

Something metal-sounding crunched, echoing in the dark ship.

Cold terror ran up his spine. "What was that?" It sounded like a hull decompressing. It was a sound that gave him nightmares. He'd been trained since he could walk to run from that sound.

"It's nothing," Lily said.

There was another spine-chilling crunch.

Titan's eye twitched.

"It's not decompression," Lily said. She sounded brave but the pulse at the base of her throat was jumping. "We're not in orbit. A ship can't decompress on ground."

Somewhere in the depths of the ship, someone screamed.

Titan focused on the needles in his skin. Teleporting with drugs in the system was always rough. Thankfully, the Sekoos hadn't had the foresight to use grounder materials. The needles slid out, scraping against his arm, and leaving him to bleed freely.

"Lily!" Two more Sekoo crew came running in. "The engine room is collapsing."

"Collapsing? How?"

"It's... it's crinkling in. Being squeezed."

She shook her head. "That's impossible."

Titan squirmed a little. He'd need to turn on his implant to get the wrist cuff off and it was going to hurt.

Lily kicked him. "Why are you shaking your head?"

"The Sciarras... we've done that before. During the first war we had a few people who could destroy a ship by crushing it. We took out a few of the Carylls that way. My captain? She could do it." Elea's call to the *Golden Apple* hadn't been a signal he was safe, it was a warning to get out.

"Bring on the stabilizers," Lily ordered. "Whoever is doing this has to have a close focus. We'll move out of their range."

The ship tilted under them as the engines whined in protest. There was another sickening crunch of metal and the ship lifted.

Tossing her hair, Lily smiled. "We're out."

"Captain?" The man at the com turned, face ashen. "Our... our engines are gone."

"Then how are be airborne?" Lily asked.

He shook his head. "Someone's... holding us up? Maybe?"

"Impossible!"

Not for an elite. Not for someone like Carver or Marshall. The only thing holding them back was the political fallout of an attack. *Selena.* He licked his lips, remembering her crumpling a heavy metal door as it were cobwebs.

"We're getting a transmission!" The comtech yelled.

"From who?" Lily walked over to the console. "I don't know that code."

The man shook his head. "There's high level encryption behind it. The message says, 'Teleport out now' with a count-down." His voice was filled with panic. "Ma'am, I can't teleport. I'm not augmented. What... what are we going to do?"

"It's a bluff," Lily said. "We ignore it."

Another section of the hull fractured and buckled under the weight of someone's rage.

"It's not a bluff," Titan said. The smell of fear and desperation filled the bridge. "There are officers who could destroy this ship."

"They won't," Lily said. "We're allies of the Baulars. Of the Sciarras! Of the Warmonger crews. No one would dare go to war with us again." Her face turned dark with rage. "I have other allies. Other weapons. I'll take them all out." She whipped around. "Put that out," she ordered the comtech. "Tell the Allied crews to back away or I'll fire on their home ships. I'll kill their children if I have to."

"No!" Titan strained against his shackles. "Belay order!"

The comtech hesitated, torn between duty to crew and fleet.

Titan sucked in the hot, stale air. "You can't. Lily, it's not the Allied crews. Carver would never do this. The Captains' Council would never allow an attack. They would never get together that fast. This is one person. One Elite."

She narrowed her eyes. "I can destroy one person."

"You can't." He shook his head, ready to beg. "If it's who I think it is, she has a ship in orbit that will take us all down." If it was Selena, she was probably expecting him to rescue himself. "Give me an open line. Let me talk to whoever is out there. I'll negotiate. For you. Whatever it is you want, I'll find a way to get it for you if you'll let me stop this."

The comtech jerked his chin in an eager nod. The rest of the crew had fallen silent. The *Acontinum* floated there, wrapped in a deadly cage of telekyen and power.

"Please?" His voice shattered with fear.

Lily drew in a deep breath and her rage returned. "You had your chance. You had thousands of chances to give us what we were owed! You're a traitor, and I'll see you die as one." She nodded. "We don't need to teleport out. Bring the secondary engines online."

"The old garbage burners?" The comtech asked in confusion. "Do those work?"

"We used them a few times during the war. They're slow, but they'll get us over the wall."

"But... the shield?"

Lily lifted her chin. "It'll be down."

The techs scurried, rushing to secure themselves as the old tub rumbled.

It was a fight they couldn't win. Maybe with a good crew, an officer or two with elite ranking, and some backup they'd have some hope, but like this? "It's suicide," Titan said. "Surrender so your crew doesn't suffer. Lily, you need to surrender. It's the only choice."

"Incoming message from the *Golden Apple*," the comtech reported, sounding happier than he should. "They have a sniper trained on the person below. There's obscuring shield, but they won't be expecting a grounder weapon."

Lily smiled down at him. "Surrender is for cowards and traitors. I'm neither. Mister Esmer, tell the gunnery crews to go to their stations. Let's see what the Allies think when we show them how we've spent the last few years."

"Aye, ma'am," a deep voice said behind him.

The bridge blurred as war memories threatened to engulf him. The feeling of utter helplessness that he'd felt when he was trapped in the medbay watching Mal and Rowena fight ran like ice through his veins. They'd had each other in the end, but Selena had no one.

He couldn't let the Sekoos hurt her.

Titan braced himself for discomfort and turned his implant on, it was the only way. Fire and crippling pain crawled up his arm. He focused on the wires connecting him to the torture device, blocking everything. Still, in the background he felt an echoing scream of anguish.

Selena had connected to him and was sharing his agony.

Shaking, he fused the wires, melting them so they fell away from the cuff.

The hull buckled rapidly, sending screams of the terrified gunnery crew into the confusion. Running boots echoed ahead of the stale air rushed inward as the ship was devoured.

Aching, Titan stood as the light flashed out, cut with the power. *Out.* All he needed was to get out. But he couldn't draw on teleport coordinates. He couldn't focus. He closed his eyes, trying to find the one thing that would get him out.

And then the ship was gone.

He was standing outside, in the sunshine, staring at the rapidly constricting hull of the *Aconitum* crumpling into a ball, eclipsing the sun. The air hummed with a fury and a power.

Staggering, he looked at the fallen Sekoos lying in the dust where there ship had been. They were all alive, although at least one of the men wearing a gunner's uniform had a broken leg. He watched them, waiting for a response, but the stayed down.

It was the first smart thing they'd done.

Taking a deep breath of air chocked with dust he turned.

Selena stood alone, hand outstretched, glaring at the Sekoo's ship.

The rest of Enclave was unusually silent, accenting the sound of screeching, tearing metal.

Titan limped toward Selena. Something was wrong. There was something catastrophically off and he was too muzzy headed to recognize it. "Selena?"

She didn't acknowledge him.

"Caryll? Captain?" He reached for her hand and the air sparked bright green and gold. "Selena!" He shouted to get her attention. His words reached his ears muffled by unmoving air.

Titan looked up.

Nothing was moving in Enclave.

The dust he'd kicked up trying to reach her hung in the air.

Crews who had run outside to find out what the noise was were in a ring around them, silent and unmoving. Soundless. Not breathing...

He took a deep breath and tasted the same stale air. The kind found on dead ships and in very dangerous shields.

Selena hadn't just put a battle shield up, she'd locked one down. This was a containment field. Isolating everyone. Limiting their movement.

He was the only one able to move through the mess.

:Do something!: It was Rowena on a tight beam.

He looked up, saw her trapped on the edge of the field standing next to his aunt. Their faces were a rictus of fear.

The sound of tortured metal stopped and the sun grew bright again. A ball smaller than his fist - all that remained of the Sekoo's warship - dropped to the ground like a bomb.

"Selena," Titan tried again. "I'm here."

"They hurt you." Her voice was distant, her eyes unfocused. The pain had drawn her back into the war memories. Whatever she was seeing was a ghost of the past.

The closer he drew to her the thicker the air became. It was like walking through thick mud. Every breath was a struggle. "Selena, you have to let them go. You have to let everyone go or you'll kill them."

"They deserve to die."

"Maybe." He pushed as far as he could on trembling legs. It wasn't close enough. "Maybe they deserve this. Maybe the whole fleet deserves this for what we did. But not you. You don't deserve to take this pain."

Her eyebrows drew together in frustration.

"You're not a killer," Titan said. "That's the one thing you have that no else can claim. We're all battle-scarred. We're all broken. But you're bloodless. You don't ever need to fall asleep remember the face of people you killed. You can't. I know you, Selena. I know your thoughts, your heart, you'll never forgive yourself for this if you let them die."

The air shivered between them as a sea breeze snuck through her defenses.

He took a step forward. "Please. Not for them. Not for me. Please let them go because I can't lose you, and I will. This will destroy you, and then I'll be alone." The air was getting easier to breath.

Selena reached out along their shared link, gently assessing the damage. Then the containment field snapped back in place. "They hurt you."

He fought his way through the shield. "Not that badly.

Titan wrapped his arms around her. The sleeve of her blouse slipped up above her elbow revealing four deep, silver scars that merged into three.

"I don't want to have another war. I don't want to hurt like this." A tear shimmered at the corner of her he.

He smiled, then bent to kiss her neck. "Love, I'm fine."

Her hand dropped as she shook. The terror and rage were seeping out of her mind like a poison. "They made you bleed."

"I did that by pulling an IV out."

"They're monsters." The *Golden Apple,* the Sekoo's family ship filled with their remaining crew, trembled. An engine collapsed on itself.

Titan held Selena tighter, trying to make her turn away from the remaining Sekoo ships. "Yes, love, but so are we all. Made of flesh and machine, cut off from the stars of our homeworlds. We are not the children our ancestors bled for, but we're here. Making the most of every day we have. Making good choices and bad, because we're human, and we're only human if we choose. Right now, I need you to choose to forgive. To let them go. Please, Selena? Come back to me." He turned her around so she could see his face.

The blue of her eyes burned brighter than burning copper chloride. "They hurt you."

"Not badly. I'm a guardian, a Sciarra, I can take a beating." He felt rather than saw her rage. "No. That's not how this ends. You can't destroy all their ships."

"I could." Her voice was calmer now, not threatening simply stating a fact.

He believed that. "It's not the right thing to do."

Selena took a breath, hesitating, uncertain…

"Drop the shield. Let the guardians take it from here. There's more here than me being a little bruised. This is an attack on Enclave. On the fleet. And, right now, you're the biggest threat. No one can breathe."

She closed her eyes. For a moment it was like holding a statue; he couldn't even see her inhale. The shield fell as she opened her eyes.

Air rushed back into Enclave with a clap of thunder.

Noise returned, a babble of voices and chaos.

People pinged him for information. The guardian's channel was in an uproar. Every Sciarra demanded to know where he was.

Selena stood still, cold and beautiful as moonlight in the darkest night.

"Titan!" Elea pushed through the crowd with Rowena on her heels. "What happened to you?"

He opened his mouth to lie when a scream interrupted him. Turning, he saw Lily Sekoo stumbling forward.

Lily staggered to her feet, her face a rictus of pain and wrath. "How dare you?"

The crowd widened, leaving room for what everyone likely saw as a personal matter.

:Carver,: Titan pinged his commander. :Now would be an excellent time to stop the next war.: It was all he could do to stay standing and keep Selena from going nova.

Perrin Carver and Hollis Silar teleported in front of Lily.

She screamed wordlessly.

"Technician Lily Sekoo, you are under arrest," Carver said, voice low and calm.

"You have no rights! No right! I'm a pureblooded daughter of the Empire. I was born to better things than licking grounder feet and bowing to weak fools." Lily glared past the guardians to Selena.

Selena started. "Weak?" Her voice cut through the morning air like a knife. "You think I'm weak?"

"You let me live," Lily said.

For a moment Titan thought Selena might change her mind about that.

Then she nodded. "Yes. I did. You will live. You will remember every choice you made. You will remember every single thing you did. It will replay in your mind until you lose your sanity. And even then, it will flay your soul so when your broken, withered body finally falls silent, there will be nothing for your ancestors to find. I let you live. Welcome to hell."

24

ROWENA

ENCLAVE WAS QUIET IN the pre-dawn hours. The only sound was Hoshi's angry stride crunching gravel, and the warble of early morning birds greeting the rising sun.

Rowena kept pace, staying a little behind and to the side of her captain as they approached the OIA offices.

Hoshi led the way through the doors and under the dome to the deliberation chamber that had been sealed after the last war trial. It had been reopened after all the week's events.

Jhandarmi and Tarrin police milled by the OIA exit, giving the dark blue crew uniforms of the fleet curious looks.

"Interlopers," Hoshi muttered under his breath, halting by the chamber doors. "Lazy—" He bit off the insult as Hollis Silar stepped into the hall, wearing his Starguard all-blacks, and glared.

"Captain Lee, yeoman." Silar nodded. "We've been waiting for you."

Hoshi sneered at him. "Then let us in."

"Yeoman Lee only," Silar said.

"Why is she allowed in and I'm not?" Hoshi demanded. "I'm her captain! I won't be locked out of this."

"Apologies, captain. My orders are to escort Yeoman Lee in and no one else. She's here to be a witness."

Hoshi rolled his shoulders back, squaring off for a fight he could never win. "The Captains' Council will hear about this."

"The Captains' Council is equal to the Star Guard," Silar said. "If you want to make a complaint you'll need to file a report with the fleet marshal. Yeoman, if you'll come inside, please."

"There's no fleet marshal left!" Hoshi complained as Rowena walked inside.

Silar shrugged. "The Captains' Council can elect one in times of duress," Silar said. "The Starguard would be able to ratify the decision. Good day, captain. The Starguard will see Yeoman Lee is safely returned to her vessel when this matter is concluded."

The door shut in Hoshi's face with a nudge of telekyen. A heavy shield formed, silencing Hoshi's shouted protests of unfairness.

Silence being a better tactic than braggadocio, Rowena kept her mouth shut.

Silar led her down a narrow back hall, past the courtrooms, and to a small room with a large conference table and an eclectic assortment of people.

At the head of the table on the right, Hermione Marshall sat flanked by two empty chairs. She was wearing her dark gray uniform, shot with gold flecks and her family's crest pinned where her ship emblem should have been. Captain Carver sat across the table from the door, wearing his all-black uniform and facing Titan and Caryll.

At the left end of the table a woman with a pale pink suit sat, a grounder tablet in front of her, two men and woman who might have been a bodyguard behind her.

Tyrling paced in front of the false windows on the far wall.

"Good," Marshall said as Silar held out a seat for Rowena. "Now that everyone is here, we can move on."

There was a murmur from the assembled fleet personnel.

The woman in pink appraised Rowena. "Very well. We shall proceed. From this moment on, all conversation will be recorded." She touched her tablet and pushed it to the center of the table to record. "For the record, will all parties please state their name and reason for attendance. In the case of sub-ordinates, the senior member of the party may speak. I will go first."

"I am Felila Conn, speaker for the continent of Icedell, Council Member in Full, born of the city-state Omul, descendant of the ship *Quiet Way*. With me are my advisors and trouble-shooter. I speak on behalf the Assembly of Malik." She nodded.

"Director Nate Tyrling, regional director of the Jhandarmi of Malik."

"Captain Perrin Matteo Carver, commander of the Star Guard, speaking on behalf of the Starguardand the fleet."

"Captain Hermione Marshall, member of the Captains' Council, Council Member in Full, born of the city-state Ryun, junior delegate to the assembly of Mithila, speaking on behalf of the Marshall clan of Descent, the Captains' Council of the fleet, and advisory chair for the Imperial Officer's Academy."

"Captain Selena Caryll, captain of the *Persephone*, member of the Captains' Council, fleet-Jhandarmi liaison, lead investigator for the case number 18038-9R."

"Commander Titan Sciarra, second-in-command of the *Sabiha*, senior officer of the Star Guard, speaking on behalf of my crew and as lead investigator—fleet—for case number 18038-9R."

"Commander Hollis Silar, senior officer of the Star Guard, speaking on behalf of myself." He looked at Rowena.

"Yeoman Rowena Lee of the *Danielle Nicole*." She looked to Titan questioningly.

"Rowena is here as a witness," Marshall said, "and as an Academy representative. She's taking over as a drill instructor when classes resume next month and has a vested interest in the future of the fleet."

Nice of someone to tell her that in advance. Considering the Academy had been shut in the early days of the war, she wasn't even sure how they'd train, but if it made everyone feel better about her presence, then so be it.

Felila Conn nodded. "Now for the matter of the trial."

"Shouldn't the Sekoos be here?" Rowena asked.

Conn shook her head. "The Sekoo matter was resolved, according to all reports."

"Sentenced and transported to one of the coastal prisons," Tyrling said as he continued pacing. "They'll rot in the damp."

Conn nodded. "That matter being resolved, we will begin with the trial of the Enclave Treaty." She reached out and touched her tablet again. The tension in the room dropped by a factor of 12. "Enough formalities. Let's hash this out. I'm in the wrong time zone and I want dinner."

"We are taking war off the table," Marshall said. "Aggression, submission, and withdrawal of treaty are all off the table."

"Agreed," Conn said in a quick way that made it seem as if she'd done negotiations like this a dozen times.

"Upheld," Tyrling said.

Behind Conn one of her minions made a note.

Carver raised a finger. "Can the current level of peace be maintained?"

"Arguably," Tyrling said as Conn and Marshall both shook their heads.

"Make a note that both fleet counsel and Assembly reject the option of status quo. Changes must be made."

"Agreed," Marshall said as quickly as Conn had.

Tyrling grimaced. "Upheld with reservation."

"Isolation and the idea of separate-but-equal was unpalatable three years ago and has proven unfruitful at best. Recommendation is full integration." Marshall's eyes narrowed, making her recommendation a threat.

Carver held a hand up to object but Conn's raised hand silenced him.

"Define," Conn said.

"Full access to lands held by the people under the governance of the Assembly of Malik for the fleet," Marshall said. "Open enrollment to the Academy and pilot training programs for everyone in the system."

Rowena tried to tally up what it would take to rebuild the Academy, once a space station for aspiring fleet officers, as something on the ground. None of the buildings were well-suited to the task. Even if they gave up the BOQ there was no place for zero-g training.

Conn shook her head. "No."

No need to worry about finding gauntlets for grounder applicants than.

"Counter," Selena Caryll's voice was a surprise to everyone in the room. "A seat on the Assembly for Enclave, incorporation and recognition of Fleet as a House on the public rolls of the Malik System."

One of Conn's assistants leaned forward to whisper something in her ear.

She nodded pensively and turned back to Caryll. "To allow this someone in the fleet would need to own lands untied to another house. If you use the lands of Captain Marshall you will become a vassal of the Marshalls."

Caryll looked over at Titan as they shared some silent conversation. He nodded, and Caryll turned. "I hold land and companies in two city-states on Icedell, purchased at Landing as housing for my crew." Her smile was bitter. "We were larger at the time. The holdings have served as rental properties since the time of purchase."

"What of the company?" Conn asked.

"Kore Information Systems, which specializes in researching historical documents and authenticating antiquities."

:How did I not know this?: Rowena asked Titan.

:She kept the records very well hidden. It would have been public, but her crew pre-empted the announcement with their decision to leave for other ships.: He sounded smug.

Rowena sent him the memory of an eyeroll.

:Don't hate me because I didn't underestimate my enemy,: Titan said. :Selena was front and center in the war, anyone could have courted her.: There was a moment's pause and then he said. :It's good she's on our side.:

Rowena kept her face emotionless. There weren't sides anymore. There was only chaos.

Conn's assistant passed her a data tablet and conferred quietly before Conn nodded. "Icedell welcomes Enclave into the Assembly. You are permitted the standard twenty-three member team as other city-states. You will have five years to establish trade agreements with your neighbors."

"Agreed," Marshall said.

Shock rippled around the room. Her implant tagged over a dozen different messages pinging around the room. The fleet had always been separate. They had a different history, different reasons for being in-system.

Rowena took a deep breath as she re-coded her decision-making algorithms. The fleet had never had a voice in the government before. Being welcomed in, given equal status and citizenship. She pinched the bridge of her nose. :Half the fleet is going to move out tomorrow,: she told Titan.

:No, they won't.: He sounded amused. :There's a housing crisis in the city-states. And even if they move out, they can teleport back for work in the morning. It did just open up the dating pool though.:

She considered this, and shook her head. :All I can picture is the Silars expanding exponentially.:

:A redhead in every house?: Titan sent the memory of a laugh.

She snuck a look at Hollis to see how happy he was. She'd expected a smile, but his face was blank, there was no sign he was taking pride in Marshall's leadership skills or joy at the prospect of flirting freely with the grounders. If anything, he looked a little concerned. There was a tightness around his eyes that didn't make sense to her.

Silar looked up, catching her gaze with his chocolate brown eyes. His eyebrows lifted a fraction in silent question.

Rowena looked away, feigning disinterest.

"I'd like to make an addition," Tyrling said, interrupting the silent conversations around the room. "The Jhandarmi request a skills exchange and a Jhandarmi presence in Enclave."

There was a murmur of disapproval from the fleet and grounders alike. Tech expertise was the only thing the Starsiders had to trade.

"You get Caryll and Sciarra," Carver said. "They'll be Jhandarmi and Starguard."

:There goes my free time,: Titan grumbled on a tight beam.

Tyrling nodded. "The skill exchange?"

Carver looked over at Caryll. "Your call."

"The Jhandarmi training isn't anything strenuous. It's adapted for the unaugmented, so we wouldn't need to restrict it to higher ranks, and it would be good for the fleet to learn techniques adapted to living in a gravity well." She looked at the other fleet officers before nodding. "Skills exchange is approved. We'll train Jhandarmi on how to handle weapons that may have leaked because of this incident, as well as provide consulting experts for unique problems. Weapons specialists will be made available to help review the Sekoo's records and identify what might be in the general population now."

"Do you have a weapons expert with that breadth of knowledge?" Conn asked.

Marshall and Carver looked at each other and then to Silar. There was a conversation going on a tight beam. Marshall nodded and Silar turned.

There was a light tap on her outer shield, someone knocking for attention.

Rowena raised an eyebrow and made a place in her shield for the non-priority message.

:Would you be willing to be the fleet weapons expert?: Silar asked.

She let her confusion at his asking her instead of Titan slip through.

:Would you?: Silar ignored the question she couldn't form.

With a tight nod, she accepted.

"Rowena Lee," Marshall said, it was more question than statement.

"She's the fleet's most qualified engineer," Silar said, smoothly taking control of the conversation. "The Starguard already consult with her on other matters, and she works for the OIA already, so there's no clearance issue."

The Jhandarmi director gave her a dubious look. "Do you have much experience with groundside operations?"

"No," Rowena admitted, "but I'd be happy to take the Jhandarmi training courses you're offering. In exchange, my expertise is at your disposal. I promise you no one alive knows as much about weapons and engines as I do."

Tyrling nodded and smiled. "Accepted with amendments. The matter is resolved."

:Hoshi is going to love this,: Titan said with a chuckle.

:Hoshi can breathe vacuum. And so can Silar. Why was he the one reaching out to me? You're my Starguard liaison.:

Across the table Titan gave her an apologetic look. :When we were planning the hypothetical Academy here on the ground, Carver put Silar in charge.:

:What?: She looked over at Silar again.

He was waiting for her this time, watching, probably wondering when she'd realize that she now reported to him. :What's that look for?: he asked.

:I'm wondering how many of your bones I can *accidentally* break in training.: She sent the Academy color code for a fight.

Silar sent back a memory of that last time they'd had a real fight, on the desk of the Silar's crippled warship *Aquila*. It hadn't ended well for her. :Looking for a rematch?:

:Name the day.:

Titan rapped at her shield with a stinging shock. :Be good and stop looking at Silar. You're making me nervous:

:He's the one who's going to go home bloody.:

"Would anyone like to present further business before we adjourn?" Conn asked.

Titan held up a hand. "Were the Jhandarmi able to track the information Kafftan stole?"

The grounders exchanged grimaces.

"We were able to identify one of the injured men as a contract mercenary for the Lethe Combine. Their lawyers contacted the Jhandarmi the next day," Tyrling said. "The Lethes control a majority of the transportation on all three continents. They're wealthy, powerful, and very, very careful. There's no way to prove they did anything wrong."

Titan looked surprised. "With a smoking hole in Arwel's backyard and witnesses?"

The Jhandarmi director's expression transformed from calm professionalism to a bitter scowl. "Two months ago Sonya Lethe's security detail reported her missing. They found her within a few hours with the help of the local police and the Jhandarmi, but she'd been drugged and beaten. The Lethe family told us today they believed family secrets had been taken during the time she was missing and that the Lethes acted within their rights to retrieve their secrets."

"But there were witnesses," Titan protested. "Selena and I weren't the only ones who were there."

"Arwel withdrew his claim earlier this morning," Tyrling said. "The explosion was blamed on an unfortunate sink hole. They do happen occasionally in Tarrin, and someone generously volunteered to pay for repairs as part of their civic charities."

"Lethe," Marshall said. "Everyone at the party will get a generous donation to their bank accounts and a note telling them they saw nothing out of the ordinary. If they speak out," she looked pointedly at Caryll and Titan, "they'll be silenced. She wants to see who she can push, and who she can control."

Caryll snarled audibly. "So, she's made herself untouchable?"

"Patience is power," Conn said. "Powerful families like the Lethes will spend years setting the stage for a power play. Decades. Centuries. It doesn't matter to them."

"Why do the Lethes want the information?" Carver asked.

Marshall sat back in her chair with a chuckle. "Power. It's always about power. Sonya and I went to school together. I remember her, an unremarkable child convinced she was destined to rule the world. She's descended from the first governor of Malik, a title that's been in abeyance since the wormhole collapsed. When we were both eight, she signed her papers Governess Sonya Lethe of Malik IV. For all that, she has only a passing understanding of how power is used. She probably hopes to either curry favor with the Jhandarmi or blackmail them. The Lethes rarely go to battle. They look for chinks in your armor, exploit your weaknesses." Her words drifted off into a nostalgic smile.

"Power." Conn shook her head.

"Patience first," Tyrling advised. "We know where the information is. Now we watch and wait. We attend to the weak spots and let the enemy show their hand."

Marshall grimaced. "Still, if Sonya has shown her hand like this it means she plans to expand her little empire. Much like the Sekoos, she believes she's entitled to control of the population. Kafftan wasn't a stupid man, he would have encrypted the data and kept the key safe until he was away with his money."

"What are the chances he gave her the key before dying?" Conn asked, looking between Marshall and Tyrling.

Tyrling tilted his head back and forth in thought. "Time of death compared to when he left, very low. He was dead within an hour of leaving. Either the Lethes didn't anticipate an encryption or they had someone already lined up to crack it. We'll keep our ears to the ground. Rumors about these things always turn up, you just have to turn over enough rocks."

"The Jhandarmi will have fleet backing if Lethe moves against you," Carver said.

Tyrling nodded in thanks.

The meeting closed rapidly. Papers and tablets were passed around the table for signatures and witness statements. Conn spoke with Carver and Marshall, then with Silar. Tyrling had a few quiet words with everyone but Rowena on his way out. History was made with a quick exchange and no fuss. One word—agreed—and everything was different.

Rowena drifted out of the conference room, not quite ready to return to the *Danielle Nicole*, but at a loss as to where else she could go. A ping from Titan told her to wait, so she stopped at the intersection of a back hall and a service corridor.

At the far end of the hall she heard Titan say, "I love you, I'll catch up soon." He kissed Caryll before she teleported away, and then walked to Rowena. "How does it feel to be in the room where history happens?"

"Surreal," she admitted. "It was all... easy. Like a play. Everyone seemed to know their lines except me."

"Selena spent most the night filling me in on the political history," Titan admitted.

Rowena smirked. "What a waste of a first night as a courting couple."

He laughed and looked up at the ceiling to avoid her gaze.

"Are you here to gloat or did you actually need something?"

"I want to get Selena a proper courting gift."

"Isn't it a bit late for that? The entire fleet saw you two yesterday. Courtship declared and accepted."

Titan rolled his eyes. "I know, but we won't have the celebration for a few months. Or at least not until Carver and Silar have theirs."

Rowena looked up in surprise. "Carver finally acted on that?"

"Genevieve told him she was tired of him trying to get killed before their wedding. They were either signing the spousal contract or she was going to find someone else who wanted to be with her. Selena offered them a house in Tarrin since the news about her land holdings was going to be public anyway. They'll have a celebration in a few weeks. Then Selena and I will have ours."

"What do you want to get her?"

Titan's smile lit up the room. "You'll back me on this?"

"For every crazy plan," Rowena said. "That's what friends are for."

25

SELENA

THE WATER FALLING FROM the three-tiered fountain in the center of the plaza shone with an ethereal blue light. Climbing roses framed every arch and window, and someone had come through to brush them with a luminescent nanite gel so they glowed a pale pink. Strings lights overhead mimicked distant stars, and already people were congregating around tables of food. Officially, the reception for Perrin and Genevieve didn't start for another thirty minutes, but no one wanted to be late for a party.

Selena hung in the shadows, watching people arrive on the transport pad and via grounder cars. The warm summer air was encouraging everyone to come out.

Already, the happy couple was surrounded by well-wishers. Perrin's adopted grounder family was there, although the youngest daughter had wandered off to flirt with Mars Sciarra. Captain Sciarra and her new second-in-command were there. The Lees, the Silars, most of the fleet, but Titan was nowhere to be found.

She pinged him again, trying to get a location, but he'd gone dark after breakfast this morning, promising only that he'd be back in time for the party. Looking over the crowd, she found a promising lead: Rowena Lee hiding in a small alcove. Selena made her way through the growing crowd. "Hello."

Rowena put her hands behind her back, taking an at-ease stance. "Captain Caryll."

"Do you know where my husband is?"

"I do. And I'm not allowed to tell you anything more than it is a surprise and he is safe." She paused, then shrugged. "I've checked on him twice and he wasn't bleeding, dehydrated, or in danger of losing oxygen either time, so he's probably okay."

Selena crossed her arms. "I thought he was planning to be here tonight."

"Everyone is planning on being here tonight," Rowena said, dropping her guard. "The invitations almost started a civil war and did trigger three mini-mutinies in crews who are stir-crazy. You opened up new housing outside Enclave, are throwing a party, and didn't think anyone would come?" Rowena scoffed at her. "Hoshi's favorite cousin almost killed him when the captain threatened to boycott the celebration."

Wrinkling her nose, Selena considered the outcome. "Would it really have hurt...?"

Rowena gave her a glare she'd learned to accept over the past few weeks. "I'm not ready for a war."

"When you are, Titan and I will be there for you. We owe you that. Meanwhile, Gen deserves a party after as long as she waited. So does Perrin."

"We all deserve a party after this past month." Rowena took a deep breath.

Selena nodded and waited for Rowena to leave, but the woman stayed stubbornly present. And silent. They watched more fleet and grounders arrive, more tables teleport in, more presents appear on the reception table. Finally Selena said, "Was there anything else you needed, or are we faking this buddy thing until Titan gets here?"

Rowena wrinkled her nose and raised a light sound shield. Nothing that would draw attention, but enough to keep anyone else form overhearing, or recording, their conversation. "I wanted to say thank you for the nanite gel you sent Aronia. The medicine helped, but we aren't sure they would have both pulled through without it. The internal bleeding was extensive."

"You're welcome. Although that was meant to be a secret. I know Hoshi's opinion of me; I didn't want to start any trouble."

Rowena lifted one shoulder in a shrug. "No one knows, officially, but I knew the Sciarras didn't have anything like it, and that Titan had used something similar. It wasn't very hard to draw the right conclusion. I haven't told anyone."

"Thank you. How are Aronia and the baby doing?"

"Nia is up and moving. She's feeling a lot better. The baby is good. They named him Ki, after a great-grandfather of ours."

"Good. I'm glad that worked out then." She stared off into the distance, not quite certain how she felt about the idea of sisters, babies, and bonding with Rowena Lee. It wasn't as awkward as she'd imagined.

"You had a sister, didn't you?"

Selena nodded. "Losna. She was eight years older than me and in crew training when I was born. We weren't close like you and Aronia."

"I'm sorry she won't be here for your reception."

She shook her head. "I don't really remember her. She bunked with her age mates by the time I was old enough to remember anything, and then she went to the Academy. I was only home three weeks before she led a charge in battle and died."

"Do you know who killed her?"

"No. I could. I have access to the files as captain. But I don't want to carry that around."

Rowena tipped her head in acknowledgment but not agreement. "I don't know if I could be that restrained."

"It's easier when you know they didn't love you." The words seemed heavier than they were. She'd named the beast that had haunted her all these years. No one loved her. No one could love her.

But now, that was changing. She was making a new family and crew with Titan. And—she glanced sideways—apparently with Rowena. Every family needed uncomfortable sibling rivalries, didn't it?

Rowena straightened up and looked around. "Titan says he's incoming."

"Why didn't he tell me?"

"Because you're shielding to the point of being invisible again," Rowena said as she stood on her tiptoes. "Uh oh." She dropped to her feet and spun around to inspect a rose.

Selena turned with her. "What's uh-oh?"

"Silar is here."

"Be more specific!" Half the crowd had red hair and freckles. Gen was well loved.

"Hollis!" Rowena sneered. "I promised Ty I wouldn't get into a fight tonight and…" She curled her lips in a dramatic look of disgust.

Selena rolled her eyes. "It's his baby sister's reception. He'll be on his best behavior."

"How do you find that reassuring?" Rowena asked. "His best behavior is flirting until your clothes spontaneously combust."

"Never worked on me," Selena said, amused. It wasn't a bad description, but she'd never expected Rowena of all people to notice. Hollis had never flirted with anyone from the Lee crew that Selena knew about.

Rowena gave her a pained look.

"If I see you starting to smolder, I'll dump the punch on you."

"There are two of my three favorite ladies!" Titan's voice made them turn.

Selena reached up and wrapped her arms around his neck in a hug, greeting him with a kiss. "Two of three?" She smiled at him. :Who am I forgetting?:

"Can't forget my auntie," Titan said before he gave her another quick kiss. "I'm glad to see you two getting along. What were you discussing?"

"Hollis Silar," Selena said as she rested her head against Titan's chest.

Titan raised his eyebrows. "Ways to kill him?"

"No!" Selena hit his chest. "We've talked about this. You can't joke about killing my friends."

"I'm confused," Titan said. "Rowena talked about Hollis and murder didn't come up as an option? Are you feeling all right, Ro?"

Rowena rolled her eyes. "I was up all night with the new baby on family duty. Call it a lapse of judgment. Or my present to Genevieve and Carver. I'm sure I'll get over it soon enough." She smiled viciously. "Where's the present you've been teasing Caryll with for weeks?"

"Yes," Selena held him tighter. "Where's this present that kept you away from me all day while I was party planning? I was in desperate need of help," she said dramatically.

"I saw you and Marshall out here. You didn't need help, you wanted willing slaves. That's what fleetlings are for." Titan's grin lit up the night.

"Excuse me?" Rowena held up a hand. "I'm leaving before you two have your first fight as a married couple. Caryll, try not to shoot the planet. Again."

Selena pinged Rowena's shield with the thought of someone sticking out their tongue as Lee retreated. Then she turned back to Titan. "Well? What's this secret present you've been hiding from me for weeks?"

"I was getting this." He teleported a small stick with a bundle of roots and four large, green leaves and let it hover in front of her.

Selena frowned at the twig. "Okay. It's… a plant." She looked from the stick to her husband. "Right?" There was nothing in her implant about Sciarra courting rituals. Was it a special plant? Was she supposed to eat it? Grow it? "Am I supposed to give you a plant?"

"No!" Titan laughed happily. "This is one of the plants that was sketched by your ancestors, or a descendent of the original at any rate. I spent the week tracking down a crew that had the seeds in stasis. I was thinking we could put it in our hydroponics section."

"Greenhouse," she corrected. The house didn't have any-where for a contained garden, but she'd make one for this, and for him. "Down here they have greenhouses, or conservatories. This is beautiful, thank you, Titan." She kissed his cheek and took the plant.

He smiled and whispered in her ear. "I meant hydroponics."

A shield she hadn't noticed all day vanished and *Persephone* hit her with a dozen updates. It was a whirlwind of information that took her a minute to sort through.

"Estimated time to repair completion... two days?" Selena stepped away from Titan as she processed everything. "Two? Titan? What did you do?"

"You know the fighters that were mine as dowry?"

She nodded.

"I traded them for a convoy ship that lost its environmental controls but which had engines that matched *Persephone's*. And then I twisted Rowena's arm to help me fix it. My captain deserves a ship."

Her jaw dropped. "Really?"

Titan nodded.

"We have a ship? A working ship? It's perfect!" She fell into him again, teleporting them away from the party and to the bridge of the *Persephone*.

Everything was gleaming. The broken screen was repaired, the duty stations were waiting for a crew... Titan had even taken the time to install a chair for her second in command and her chief medic on either side of the captain's seat. It was perfection, the one thing she'd wanted but never dared dream of having.

"Permission to come aboard?" Titan asked.

"Permission granted," she whispered, unable to bring herself to say anything more. Selena walked around the bridge, touching the chairs and looking at the waiting consoles.

Persephone's face appeared on the screen. "Welcome aboard, Captain."

Titan wrapped his arms around her waist. "What are you thinking?"

"There's no place to land her in Enclave. We're still out of fuel." There were so many things she'd overlooked.

"So we make new fuel. We land her somewhere else. We—"

"We have no crew." A tear ran down her cheek.

"Love, what's wrong?"

"You said we." Selena looked up at him. "We. Every time I stood here as a captain, I stood alone. No future. No hope. No one there for me." She'd bled and fought for her crew. She'd been ready to lay her life down for them. But, in the end when she needed them the most, they had left her. They'd fled to the life pods when she stood against Old Baular. They'd run to other crews when she arrived in Enclave, broken and heart-sick. "It's always just been me on the *Persephone*."

Titan held her close. "That won't happen again. Whatever fight comes next, I'll be here. With you."

She smiled as she claimed his lips in a kiss. "You'd better be."

:Is that an order?: His hands slid down her back to squeeze her buttocks. One hand kept going, slipping down to the hem of her short dress to caress her leg.

Selena laughed as Titan brushed feather-light kisses down her jawline and slid the strap of her sundress down. "Persephone, dismissed."

"Yes, ma'am." The computers on the bridge shut down, leaving them truly alone.

Titan held still, watching her, waiting for her.

She blushed. "I don't think our every moment together has to be recorded for posterity." Sex on the bridge. There was a teenage fantasy she'd never envisioned coming true. "How long do you think we have before anyone notices we're missing?"

Titan's smile widened. "I enlisted help from the Sciarra troops to accomplish my mission."

"Your mission?" She couldn't help but laugh.

"I have to see to the morale and happiness of the crew." He stole a lingering kiss that melted away her fears. "Relax," he whispered as he massaged her back. "The Sciarras are on the ground handling that. If anyone asks, they just saw us go past or we just turned the corner. They'll even cheerfully help people go search for us. Elea is going to answer our pings, and Rowena promised to make sure they don't run out of food. We have hours before the festivities are over."

She walked her fingers up his chest to reach the top button of his shirt and looked up at his gorgeous green eyes. "Have I ever mentioned how wonderful you are?"

"Several times." A smile tugged at his lips as his eyes sparkled with joy. "Permission to proceed with my mission, Captain?"

"Proceed, Commander."

PERSONS OF INTEREST

CPT Selena Caryll: the only person in the fleet to both fight in the war and have zero confirmed kills, Selena is known for her skills as a pilot and a shielder. After she destroyed her last ship, the *Persephone*, in the final battle, the remnants of her crew left her. She's isolated and ostracized within the fleet, but still believes they can rebuild without losing their way of life. She's worked for three years as the go-between between the grounder police force and the fleet government.

Commander Titan Sciarra: his family name comes from the knives they use to assassinate their way up the chain of command. In the final days of the war, Titan backed his aunt (now captain) Elea in a mutiny, killing three Sciarra officers. Even before the war, he had a reputation as skilled killer and dangerous man. He was Mal Baular's sworn second until a fighter crash put him into rehab for over a year. He's scarred, but working hard to rebuild the good name of his crew and the fleet. He currently works for the fleet Starguard. He hasn't killed anyone recently, but that doesn't mean he won't.

Yeoman Rowena Lee: once a commander, she survived the infighting and feuding of her family to go to the officer's Academy. Promised to Mal Baular from a young age, she stuck close to him and Titan Sciarra throughout her education. Despite being a fighter pilot during the war, Rowena is best known for her hand-to-hand combat and engineering skills. Deadly with a knife, impatient, and quick to judge, Rowena isn't someone you want on your bad side. After the war she was punished for her crimes, reduced to the rank of Yeoman, and kept under house arrest on the *Danielle Nicole* for several years.

CPT Perrin Carver: orphaned in a shuttle crash at age 6, Perrin is a walking genetics experiment conducted by his family. His tech is beyond what anyone else has, his reflexes are faster, he hits harder and he's near impossible to kill. No one wants to replicate it, but after being raised by a grounder family, the fleet invited him back to the officer academy when he was 17. He made friends, but he made enemies faster. When Old Baular declared war on the planet where Perrin grew up, he rallied the defense and led the fight. Once the best fighter pilot, he's now in charge of the Star Guard. He's keeping the peace, but wants more for the fleet than to die of old age and irrelevance.

Commander Hollis Silar: Hollis is known for two things in the fleet: being the best tactician and the biggest flirt. He'll chase anyone with a pretty smile, and most people forget that behind his easy smile is a very dangerous mind. Passionate and combative, Hollis favors brute force when he can, sneakiness when he can't, and blind luck when all else fails. He was a fighter pilot during the war and twice took command of the Silar armada when his superior officers were injured.

CPT Hermione Marshall: born to a grounder family with claims to Imperial lineage, Hermione was raised to be competitive, confident, and aggressive. When the fleet allowed a single grounder to join the Academy, she fought for it tooth and nail—then fought even harder to overcome fleet prejudices and understand a culture isolated from her own for over 600 years. During the war, she was a fighter pilot who led boarding parties. She was captured and tortured, but survived, escaped, and now heads the Office of Imperial Affairs, liaising between the fleet and the various governments on the planet's surface.

Lt Commander Genevieve Silar: the younger sister of the fleet's hottest flirt isn't so bad at emotional manipulation herself, but she's a better shot. Two years younger than her brother, Gen started as a gunner before taking over for a dead pilot in the final weeks of the war. She's been with Perrin since the beginning, his best support, adviser, and a sounding board, but the housing situation means their relationship is in a permanent holding pattern. When not teasing her big brother, seducing her boyfriend, or keeping the under-18s in the Silar armada busy, she builds racers and competes against the locals for fun and money. She's wild, loud, and most people forget that behind that pretty face is a woman with a very high kill count and a very focused temper.

SHIP NAMING CONVENTIONS

If you read through *Bodies In Motion* and found yourself saying that some of the ship names sounded familiar, it's because they probably are. Each crew picks names picked on a theme.

The Caryll ships are all named for goddesses or other women who were known for their strength, wisdom, and leadership.

The Sciarra ships are all named for female aviators.

The Lee ships are all named for female scientists. The *Danielle Nicole* is named for my friend Dr. Danielle N. Lee who studies African giant pouched rats and does science outreach through The Urban Scientist, Scientific American Blog Network, and National Science & Technology News Services (of which she is a co-founder). You can find her on Twitter as @DNLee5. The real D. N. Lee is much nicer than a warship is, I promise.

The Sekoo ships are all named for dangerous plants. The *Golden Apple* is, of course, a reference to the golden apple of Discord that started the Trojan War. Sekoo is a derivation of the word Sego, as in Sego Lily. *Acontinum* is a genus of poisonous plants that include wolfsbane and queen-of-poisons among other plants.

AFTERWORD

Dear Reader,

Thank you for coming on this journey with me. I hope the story was worth the time you spent with the fleet. Future adventures with the fleet are coming soon. If you just can't wait, feel free to visit www.lianabrooks.com and check out my other books.

Love always,
Liana <3

ABOUT THE AUTHOR

LIANA BROOKS WRITES SCIENCE fiction and sci-fi romance for people who like fast ships, big guns, witty one-liners, and happy endings. She lives in the Pacific Northwest with her husband, four kids, and giant mastiff puppy. When she isn't writing she enjoys hiking in the redwoods, playing at the beach, and watching whales.

You can find Liana on the web at www.lianabrooks.com or on Twitter as @LianaBrooks.

ACKNOWLEDGEMENTS

AS ALWAYS, IT TAKES a village to write a book, or at least a small hive mind. Novels are beastly things and often it takes more than one brain to keep track of everything that's going on. I'd like to thank my husband and children for their infinite patience as I tried to finish this project while dragging them through Canada. I'd also like to thank Amy Laurens, Jason Nelson, Derek Hawkins, and Kerryn Frampton, who were all instrumental in getting this book out on time (despite my many failures with deadlines). Special thanks also to Skyla Dawn for the beautiful cover art, Misa Buckley, Pippa Jay, and Stephanie McGee for their endless enthusiasm, and to all my readers who followed along with the first draft on my blog. Readers make the long nights all worthwhile. <3

LAWS OF ATTRACTION
Newton's Laws #2

CHAPTER 1

THE HYPERTRAM FROM RYUN to Kytan was running three minutes late. It was one of the little inefficiencies that made Malcolm Long hate ground travel. That and the other passengers, of course.

He settled into a single seat on port side of the tram and bullishly stared out the window as they rushed across the barren rock between the city-states. High overhead a Koenig-1-11 caught the sunlight as it turned for a landing in Dreyun to the north.

Long's lips twitched into a frown as he pulled out his note pad. The one-elevens were supposed to be phased out by now. Blue Sky Air Transport had been sold off six weeks ago to Lethe and Lethe was replacing the one-elevens with the Koenig-360, a plane with a fabulous interior and fuel consumption that made him wince. He assumed that was why Lethe had contacted his offices two days ago to request this meeting.

They were paying for his travel, and had offered a consulting fee that was generous without being obscene.

And still the whole set up made the hair on the back of his neck stand up.

Senior engineers at small research firms did not generally get attention like this. Especially since he hadn't published anything in over a year. His team had been busy, an he'd been juggling too many projects finish anything of substance.

He checked his watch as the rocks gave way to the cultivated terraces of Kytan. Red rock formations ringed what was laughably called terraformed plateaus filled first with grain crops, and then pools of water lilies, and finally the interior a sea of blue-green iridescent irises that sparkled like a dragonfly's wing.

Kytan was famous for the blossoms that appeared for six weeks during the height of the Descent wedding season. Right now, the city-state was overflowing with tourists who wanted to wander the parks and young couples taking engagement photos for next summer.

It was just as well that the tram went straight to the hanging gardens at the heart of the city. The air was cooler there under the shade of the vines and the crowd hurried past him to catch the city transports while he walked, briefcase in hand, along a stream-lined road. The fake waterway was filled with silvery-blue fish that swam through the sun-dappled water against the current that flowed from the step pyramids at the city center.

Pausing in the shadow of a flowering tree Long took a moment to appreciate the mad grandeur and arrogance of the city-states design. The original home of the Imperial Governor of Malik IV, designed to match the legendary summer palace of

Emperor Insei Qui the Third, the pyramid covered in waterfalls and greenery was an architectural wonder.

And somehow his first thought was the cost of maintaining the ostentatious monolith t bad genetic understanding.

"A thousand years of freedom and still we bow," Long murmured to himself. He couldn't remember the rest of the poem now, but he remembered when he'd first heard it, in the halls at school spoken by a girl who'd captivated and challenged him.

She would have appreciated the architecture of Kytan. Probably had, considering her family and wealth. Or perhaps not. With the powerful families on the first continent it all depended on who you knew and who you were allied with.

The Longs were a small family with no allies, unless his mother's book club friends counted, which he personally didn't feel they needed to be. A family name, the right genes, a pittance of an inheritance, and an acre of land somewhere out in the wilds between city-states. It had been enough to gets his family off the islands along the edge of the second continent, and earn him a scholarship to the most prestigious university, but it wouldn't keep him alive if the Lethes ordered him dead. Especially not here in the their capital city.

"I suppose I should have asked for a bodyguard." One of the lab interns had the height and reach to be a good shield, but also the personality of a frightened rabbit, which made have made the graceless man more a liability than an asset.

Long followed the streams to the pyramid, and walked up the first flight of steps until he reached the main entrance. The arched glass doors opened into an atrium where the light passing through the waterfalls outside rippled and splashed.

Jewel-colored hummingbirds zipped past, chasing each other to the background music of a drowsy orchestral melody.

He felt he should applaud the theatrics, but restrained himself to a small half-smile. The Lethes didn't sound like the kind of people who would enjoy his sense of humor.

A man in the Lethe colors of deep purple and slate gray approached him. "May I help you, sir?"

"Doctor Malcolm Long. I have an appointment."

"Of course, sir. If you'll please follow me." He gestured to a bank of lifts behind a discreet reception desk. The greeter stepped around and peered at a screen that Long had the good manners not to peek at.

Or at least the good manners not to get caught peeking at. He knew there was a difference.

"You're a few minutes early, sir."

"My apologies. I have the day free if you would like me to wait." He must have rushed.

And now I look too eager, he berated himself. On time is on time. Eager looks weak. Late is disrespectful. It was these little social mores that kept the culture of Descent afloat.

The greeter shook his head. "No, I apologize, sir. The computer recalculated the time based on the tram delay. You have arrived on schedule, but a few minutes later would have been acceptable as well. If you'll take lift number seven, sir, it will take you to your meeting room."

That wasn't much information to go on. The invitation had come from Lethe Corp, but without a signature. It was one of the annoying habits of the business people on the first continent that they used to keep their rivals guessing.

Not knowing who he was meeting with meant he couldn't study or prepare for the meeting, not unless he wanted to study the several hundred middle managers, division leads, and board members at Lethe.

He stepped into the mirrored elevator and tried to avoid glancing at his reflection, he was afraid he'd catch himself glaring at himself and remember what a bad idea it was to get caught up in the machinations of political fanatics.

The mirror image of himself glared back anyway.

For good reason too, he should have worn a touch of Lethe purple somewhere to show a willingness to work together. The dark gray suit with white shirt was a little too neutral.

The door to the lift opened to a long, wide room with a row of slit windows overlooking the city. The only furniture was a stone desk carved to look like it had come out of the stone floor. The walls were lined with silent pools of water and small reeds that had either been genetically engineered for the poor lighting or were fake, he couldn't tell at this distance.

At the desk a woman was silhouetted in the light, her hair swept up into a coiling, sleek up do held in place by a pin with a dripping chain of amethysts.

Long waited for her to acknowledge him.

Several minutes crept by before the woman finished her work, turned off her screen and stood. Recessed lights in the ceiling turned on as she moved, spotlighting Sonya Lethe, the sole heir of the Lethe fortune.

This is what a fish feels like when it sees a shark. I always wondered.

"Doctor Long, please, come in. I'm delighted you could make time in your schedule to come to Kytan today."

"The delight is mine," he said, repeating the proper polite phrasing. "I've been looking for an excuse to come to Kytan."

"Wedding season," Sonya said with a slink of a smile. "Is there someone you were hoping to show the flowers to?"

"Much to my mother's dismay, there is not."

Sonya walked around her desk and perched on the front edge. "Yes, she Nettie Amherst of the [XCity] Amherst's, isn't she?"

"The last of that line to bear the Amherst name, yes." Sonya had done her homework. It was a threat and a show of strength. Or maybe she thought it put them on equal footing. After all, any schoolchild raised on Descent could name the Lethe heirs back to the first ship.

"Perhaps your future spouse will see fit to revive the name. Long is...." She pursed her lips as she looked him up and down in an appraising way. "... perhaps a little generic?"

"My father days it's a dialect word meaning Dragon from the Grizhjan System. I make it a rule never to argue translations with a linguist."

Sonya laughed. It was a calculated move, the arch of her neck, the degree of her smile, the uplift of her breasts, all mathematically designed to hide the fact that the muscles around her eyes never moved. She wasn't amused, she was manipulating him.

There were few things in the world that felt worse.

Long waited her out. Social graces did not require him to laugh along with her, so he didn't.

"Doctor Long, you look so grim. I do not like grim faces at business."

"Forgive me, Miss Lethe, I wasn't sure what response you anticipated. My name is not often a topic of conversation."

She smiled with an apologetic head tilt. "Engineers, you're always so delightfully focused, aren't you?"

"It's been mentioned before."

"Excellent. Focus, I believe, is something this project needs. Please, take a seat." She brushed her hand along a control set in the stone desk and a chair materialized to one side, perfectly set to give the occupant a view of the city and Sonya at their best angles.

He regarded the chair with quiet suspicion. It was a trap, that much was obvious, but he wasn't sure exactly what kind.

Days like this he thought about throwing it all away and moving back to the islands. But then he'd never be able to fly again. And flight was the one thing he could never give up.

"It's quite safe," Sonya assured him as she took a seat. "The matter transporter is something new our research and development team is working on. It could replace all travel one day."

All the more reason to hate it.

Aloud he said, "I'd heard of research along those lines, but I thought we were decades away from a breakthrough." Unless someone was getting tech from the space fleet that had landed on the third continent. He, like most people, wasn't privy to the fine details of the treaty the planetary representative had signed with them, but he felt certain the tech they'd brought was off limits.

"This can only move objects a few feet. But it is fun to bring a chair in from the closet at the touch of a button. There's an awe factor I appreciate."

"I can imagine." He took a seat and dutifully surveyed the view of the city.

Sonya sat in the chair across from him, blonde hair framed by the distant red terraces and shimmering flowers. The effect was stunning, albeit contrived. "Tell me, Doctor Long, do you have your father's gift for languages?"

The question blindsided him. He let a frown slip. "No. Some, I suppose. I speak all the regional cants of the first and second continent and can read the Journals Of Discovery in the original Imperial Script, but that's a talent any well-educated person on Descent can boast of." Especially since the dialects only changed a handful of slang terms between all of them. Calling them languages was a bit of an insult to the idea of diversity, really.

"You claim to have no gift for languages but you broke the hardest cipher we know while at university."

"Ah, cryptography is a ghost from my misguided youth." And he hadn't broken the cipher alone. The key to the whole thing had been in an obscure text his classmate found. Technically, he should have credited her, but that would have required finding her after the move to Descent, and he hadn't had the resources. "I work exclusively in aeronautical science now. That was why I thought you'd called me in, to solve the fuel efficiency problems with the Koenig-360?" He let the opening dangle.

Sonya waved the comment aside. "Planes are relics. We can burn all the fuel we want. In a few years the new matter transporters will be the foundation of Lethe's transportation division. Let the Koenig's burn fuel. This project is much more time sensitive." She held up a datcube.

Long raised an eyebrow in question.

"This belonged to one of my employees," she said. "At the time of his death he had no heir so the data became company property."

How convenient for Lethe.

"My techs have been able to decrypt a portion of the data on here, but the rest is unworkable. We've applied to other experts Lethe already has a working relationship with, but neither were able to decrypt it. Both experts mentioned you." She held the dat cube out to him.

It was a small black cube, maybe twice the size of his thumb tip, and heavier than the size would suggest. Someone had coated it the anti-theft paint that had been popular for the past two years—which meant it wasn't too old to be recoverable—but on one side he felt an indentation as if someone had pierced the cover with a fingernail.

It was all too easy to picture the previous owner holding this in a death grip in their final moments.

"Have you considered the possibility that the information is corrupted?" Long asked. "I can guess which experts you would speak to, and who would recommend me, and there's very little I could do that they wouldn't have. There's no point in wasting your time if the data isn't salvageable."

Sonya shrugged. "I give it a twelve percent chance of being corrupted. It might be a keyed cypher, but the balance of possibility says it is most likely an encryption."

"And, the data?"

"Time sensitive only because of the employee's death."

"I realize it's tactless to ask, but is this datcube part of an ongoing investigation into that death? My clearance for several of my projects requires me to steer clear of the Jhandarmi and all local constabulary."

Sonya gave him another calculated smile, this one undoubtedly meant to make her look innocent and charming. "The employee died because of a burst heart. The coroner ruled it death of natural causes."

The coroners of Descent would rule a stab wound death by natural causes if the right people asked. But he didn't dare follow that line of thought. "The best I can offer is to look at the encryption. Without seeing it I can't tell you anything more."

"Can you have a status report to me by the end of the week?"

Three days to unlock the datcube and analyze the contents was a tight timeline if he wanted to focus on his other work, but it was doable. He nodded. "A status report, but nothing more. Do you have a copy of the cube that I can take with me."

Her lips slipped into an uncharacteristic grimace. "That is our only copy."

"Ah." He set it down on the desk between them. "That makes security problematic."

"Your lab is secure?" she asked.

"The research lab is, the outer office is designed with client comfort in mind."

Sonya nodded in understanding. "The datcube will be sent by armed courier this evening. Lethe can offer the standard security fee for priority technology as well as a consultant fee." Numbers appeared on her screen. Standard fees, nothing that raised any red flags, although the whole affair seemed suspect. "If you are able to decode the data there will be a sizable bonus. Have you ever worked with Lethe before?"

"I've never had the pleasure."

She pulled a paper contract from her desk drawer. "This is our consulting contract. While working on this project you are not considered a Lethe employee and will not receive shares, benefits, or protections from Lethe. You will be paid commiserate to your skill level, and at the rate agreed. The contract terminates automatically after six weeks unless both parties agree to extend the contract. Before, during, and after this project you are forbidden from disclosing the focus of the project with anyone other than your Lethe contact. Do you have any questions?"

Long looked over the paperwork. "Do you have the work of the previous groups that tried to decrypt this cube?"

"Would it be useful?"

"Knowing what they tried and what failed will save me time. "

Another small frown. "The other experts said they didn't want to be influenced by other people's processes."

"We all approach work differently," he said. "I will probably look at it before reviewing their notes, but I don't feel the need to reinvent the wheel. Appearing like a genius to the world usually involves standing on the backs of geniuses who came before. It's how I did the decryption that I published in university."

"In that case, I'll make their work available to you. The records, the datcube, and a machine to process it on will arrive tomorrow. It goes without saying that everything stored on the computer becomes the property of Lethe after the contract is over."

"Of course." He made a mental note to scrub the machine for spyware and keep it away from his work lab and notes when it arrived. Lethe had made their empire by playing fair.

Sonya stood up. "Then all is in order."

Following her lead, he stood up.

"I look forward to working with you, Doctor Long."

"And I look forward to working with you."

ALSO BY LIANA BROOKS:

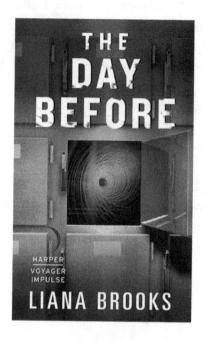

THE DAY BEFORE
Time & Shadows Book #1

A dead body is found in the Alabama wilderness. Is it a human corpse… or just a piece of discarded property?

Available from all major ebook retailers.

NOW AVAILABLE IN PAPERBACK!

ALSO BY LIANA BROOKS:

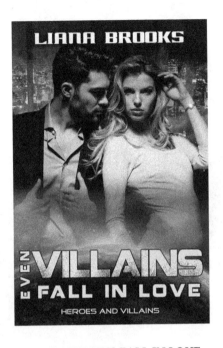

EVEN VILLAINS FALL IN LOVE
Heroes & Villains Book #1

Can a super villain at the top of his game drop everything to save the woman he loves?

Available from all major ebook retailers.

NOW AVAILABLE IN PAPERBACK!

CPSIA information can be obtained
at www.ICGtesting.com
Printed in the USA
FSHW010511201020
75035FS